I0671075

OH, SO CLOSE

First edition July 2014 Copyright @ Marie Cullen
Second edition March 2025
cullenohsoclose@gmail.com

Cover Design and Art by Hanna Vogul. ginkgocore@gmail.com

I dedicate this book to my enthusiastic readers and supporters who celebrated the 10th anniversary of the original publishing and encouraged me to pursue more writing.

A special thanks to Shelley Flood, whose inspiration brought this story to life.

There is no such thing as perpetual tranquility of mind while we live here; because life itself is but motion, and can never be without desire, nor without fear, no more than without sense.

Thomas Hobbes

OH, SO CLOSE

CHAPTER 1

Jack McDermott was the life of the party from the moment they met at Queen's University. Newcomers to Kingston, Jack and Michael immediately formed a unique bond reserved for the young. They were eighteen, athletic, smart, good-looking, and living away from home for the first time. They planned to enjoy every minute of it.

It was a warm September afternoon in 1991 when they arrived. The air still held the warmth of summer, only hinting at the cooler seasons to follow. Michael's mother was busy stacking the small fridge in his dorm room with homemade frozen perogies and cabbage rolls while he and his dad started moving in his meagre belongings.

"Hey, need a hand?" came the call from below on the stairwell.

Years of hard labor had taken a toll on Michael's father's back, and it was impossible to score one of the elevators with the constant stream of new arrivals. Michael worried about his father struggling to get his desk around the corner.

"That would be great!" shouted Michael over the top of the desk, gratefully accepting the offer.

Jack took over and they climbed the final two flights. Since Jack's father was overseas for work and his mother had his little sisters to worry about, his parents hired a moving company to get Jack settled. With little to do, he didn't mind helping.

At eighteen, Jack displayed all the fine features of a privileged young man. Standing six feet two inches, he had a strong, well-defined build developed from the many sports he played. Tennis was his first love, followed by soccer, and his winter months were occupied with weekend ski trips and hockey games. His naturally blond hair was bleached by the summer sun, enhancing his intense blue eyes. His face radiated the healthy exuberance of a summer spent at his cottage which was a couple hours north of Toronto.

Unlike some of his city friends, he was fortunate in not having to work at summer jobs given his parents' mindset that their son would have plenty of work in the years ahead, and they could easily afford to pay for his education. Jack saw how his father's hard work as the head of a software company had provided their family's comfortable lifestyle, and he believed he was destined for a great future.

Jack's young summers were carefree and filled with outdoor adventures. Besides the usual cottage pastimes, like swimming and games with his family, he enjoyed the freedom to roam through the woods. He'd set out for hikes, imagining he was in training for the army or on a secret spy mission. His parents thought exploring was natural for a boy and it was good for him; teaching him how to fend for himself and help him become a man.

The cottage was a special place where Jack's family came together when he and his sisters were young, the opposite of their fractured city lives.

Jack's father lost interest in coming north by the time Jack was a teenager, but by then, Jack's interests had shifted to friends, fast boats, parties and girls, so he didn't mind.

His mother increasingly checked out over Jack's teen years. She had put her career in medical research on hold after having children. She loved being home when the children were small but once Jack's younger sisters were in primary school, she lost her focus, her sense of purpose. Sadness enveloped her like a fog. The bottle helped hide her anxiety about the passage of time.

Michael's background was starkly different. His parents emigrated from Yugoslavia when he was three years old. After participating in the student protests of the Croatian Spring in the early seventies and feeling the harsh crackdown of the Tito communist government, they were anxious to find a more peaceful country to start their young family. They arrived in Canada with very little and were thrilled when Michael's father quickly found work at a huge mining company in Sudbury, four hours north of Toronto. The union fought for good wages and his family was able to move out of their apartment into their first home by the time Michael was ten.

Being the only boy, Michael was lavished with love and praise. The large Croatian community was a warm extended family providing a refuge within their new country.

Michael was smart and athletic. His dark, handsome features didn't hurt in getting him noticed. After an awkward adolescence he grew comfortable with his chiseled jaw line and dark, brooding eyes. He kept his thick black hair slicked back, looking very European to the giggly girls at his high school. He had plenty of admirers. He didn't mind working hard, especially in the summers. He landed a great paying job with the forestry department planting trees. After a grueling day of physical work, he and his buddies drove to the lake and spent hours goofing around, swimming, and drinking beer. They were all working hard to save money to get on with their lives. Some had their sights on university or college, others on an apprenticeship or union job. Michael had no doubt about his path; he wanted to make his parents proud by going to university and getting a white-collar job. He wanted to be able to provide for them later in life and to be able to enjoy the finer things that were out of his family's reach. With his top grades, he had his pick of universities. His parents couldn't have been prouder loading up the truck to make the drive to one of Canada's premier universities.

Left adrift in their new world, away from home for the first time, Michael and Jack headed to the campus pub for an inaugural beer, hoping their fake IDs would pass. The energy of new beginnings and open possibilities permeated the air. Thousands of bright, ambitious eighteen-year-olds were descending in droves. Their youth and vigor were in sharp contrast to the historic stone buildings and ivy-covered archways. Each new annual crop of young men and women felt like they were the chosen ones who would set out after a few years and reshape the world. The promise of all to come was exhilarating. Michael and Jack were quick to pick up on the many pretty heads following them as they walked by. The combination of the tanned golden boy and the dark European made an attractive duo and put a little more strut and swagger in their step.

They hadn't gone more than a couple of blocks when they heard Queen's 'Bohemian Rhapsody' blasting out of a huge red brick frat house. A massive porch was overflowing with people chugging drinks and dancing. A couple of flirty girls called out to them from the second-floor balcony to join the party. They waded inside, snaking their way through the crush of people.

As they climbed the stairs to the balcony Jack didn't waste any time sizing up Blondie with gorgeous, tanned legs hugged by short denim shorts. He thought her brassy blond hair was a good clue she enjoyed a good time. The gaudy neon toenail polish, loud barking laugh, and large vodka laced slurpy beverage completed the picture. They were throwing back shots and grinding to the heavy bass without exchanging more than a couple of lines.

Michael soaked up the charged scene. He caught bits and pieces of people's lives between the pulsing music, but unlike Jack, he didn't want to feel tethered to one person. He thoroughly enjoyed bouncing around, getting buzzed, and taking in different stories. One sweet girl in a pink and yellow sundress kept surfacing, trying to keep him engaged. Jack caught sight of what he deemed an opportunity and gave Michael a go-for-it look. It wasn't Michael's style to take up with someone so quickly and obviously intoxicated. Any thought of getting to know her was squelched when she staggered to the edge of the balcony and vomited on the revelers below. Michael took pity on her and helped her get steady, then found a friend of hers to take her home.

When he turned around to look for Jack, he caught a glimpse of him slipping away with his hand steering the girl's lower back. The girl was giggling as they rushed to find a more private place to continue their party. Michael left the party alone and walked for a long time to clear his head and take in his new city. If today was any indication, they were in for one hell of a time.

CHAPTER 2

The four years of university flew by. Jack and Michael grew to be best friends while making their way through economics, girlfriends, football games, house parties, and all-night exam jams. Although they went separate ways for their summers, they always picked up again in September without missing a beat. After their first year, Michael and Jack and a couple of friends shared a house Jack's father purchased as an investment.

Michael realized their friendship was partially based on the theory that opposites attract. Michael liked Jack's natural ease with the world. He supposed it came from living a life where things came easily, where Jack's family was always treated with respect whether it was at the best restaurants, resorts, or at their sailing club on the lake. The private boys' school Jack attended from grades one through twelve also played a big part in instilling a sense of entitlement. Michael thought it was so strange, almost primitive, the ritualistic chants Jack told him about that the boys would do at the beginning of each day at United Stanford College. They were told they were special, they would be the leaders of tomorrow, the brilliant new minds. Life was theirs for the taking, they just had to choose a path and the waters would part.

In grade three, Jack became a boarder at USC even though his family lived in the same city. At first Jack fought against it, not understanding how his parents could be so cruel. His father traveled a good part of the year with the demands of his business, and his mother had her hands full with the girls. Jack told Michael she had never seemed very strong and was prone to *spells* as his parents called them. As Jack got older, he knew this was code for depression, a term considered negative in his parents' generation.

From a very young age, Jack always felt a great deal of pressure to succeed. USC was an established, traditional private boys' school known for the rewarding connections one could make to enhance one's career path. Jack came to understand it was the price to pay for future success. Even though about a third of the boys were in the same situation as boarders, Jack still thought it unfair at first. Coming home for Christmas and March break was bittersweet since leaving again was so debilitating.

After a couple of years Jack no longer yearned for home, having no choice but to accept his arrangement. His new control and maturity were like shiny scar tissue over a nasty wound. Jack swore he would never do this to his children. He believed his own family was going to be a happy, cohesive unit; his beautiful wife, and children, and extravagant lifestyle, would be the envy of all his friends and associates.

During the third year of university, Jack dated another student a couple of times. Late one evening, Michael heard yelling and scuffles coming from Jack's room down the hall. Michael heard the girl crying, then leaving during the middle of the night. Jack and his various girlfriends often ended up in messy fights after a night out drinking. Jack seemed drawn to strong and volatile women, so Michael hadn't thought that much of it. An hour later, two police officers arrived and took Jack away, charging him with sexual assault. He was back at their apartment the next day after some interviews and meetings when all charges were dropped, so Jack was free to leave. There were rumors about a pay-off and the girl soon left the city, but nothing was ever confirmed.

~~~

Toronto, as the business capital of Canada, was a natural place to land after university. North America was coming off a long recession and optimism was ripe. While MBAs were becoming a more common requirement for entry-level jobs, it was still feasible with the right connections for undergrads to get a foothold in the banks and consulting firms.

The sexy jobs and big money were in investment banking. It didn't take long to get offers from Boston Consulting Group and Goldman Sachs. The hours were brutal and the work-hard/play-hard ethic reigned supreme. Being only in their early twenties, they found it easy to do twelve-hour days and still have the energy to hit the clubs to flirt, dance, and drink until well after midnight. It was a heady time when there was big money to be made and splashed around.

They shared an apartment in a low-rise older building. It was spacious but the cockroaches were brutal. They were common enough in the densely populated downtown areas of Toronto, given the many restaurants that occupied the main levels of buildings, but never in good homes like Jack's family home in the affluent Rosedale neighborhood.

9

Michael saw them more as a nuisance; lurking in dark corners, hiding in shoes, scattering with the flick of a light in the night. But Jack connected them to poverty and filth and killed them with a vengeance. He couldn't wait to move up to a better place.

Jack missed his spacious home his parents sold when his sisters went to university. His parents said they didn't need the 4,000 square feet, the pool, and the spread of property. The penthouse condo in the heart of the theatre and museum district better suited their childless lifestyle. They had two spare bedrooms decorated as an office and guest room, all taupe and beige, stripped of any personality by the interior designer that staged every inch. Jack thought it had about as much warmth as his mother. Without any genuine invitations, he didn't see his parents often even though they lived in the same city, not so different than his boarding school years.

The new friends Jack and Michael made were from the firms, and like them, they were all smart and ambitious.

Brett started around the same time, graduating from Western University in London, another exceptional school for business in southern Ontario. Brett who had been on the football team at school and was still the lead guitarist in a rock band, was the quintessential party guy. He grew up on a farm in southern Ontario and was naturally big and strong. He hadn't thought much about life after high school, but his girlfriend was heading to Western and encouraged him to apply. High school was a breeze for Brett, and good grades came easily, so when he got accepted at Western, he saw it as a new adventure. In Toronto he often joined Jack and Michael on the weekends hitting the clubs. He wasn't much of a dancer, but he was one hell of a drinker.

Larry was more of the bookish type, but he also liked to escape the intensity of the office environment and soak up city life. He loved analyzing the social scene, and because he saw himself beyond the delayed adolescent debasement that made up most of their weekend nights out, he was a handy designated driver. Larry was partnered with Jack on many of his assignments at Boston Consulting and they made a great team. With Jack's charisma and Larry's keen intellect, they were very successful and quickly moved up the corporate ladder.

CHAPTER 3

Jack knew it was a stretch to bid as high as he did on his and Rachel's first house, but he didn't want to get shut out again. Bidding wars were common making securing property a challenge. He was twenty-seven years old, making solid money, and knew downtown Toronto was a good place to invest. His father had always done well with real estate and Jack wanted to do the same. The house was modest, but it was all theirs, and he saw it as just a starter home. He had no doubt in a few short years they would sell it and buy a bigger, better home.

Rachel's approval helped him make the jump. Rachel had been his girlfriend for almost a year—a big departure from his noncommittal dating years during university and his first few years in Toronto. Rachel was a stunning, driven, sexy woman working on mergers and acquisitions. She did her BA at University of Toronto and followed it up with an ambitious twelve-month MBA at the acclaimed Rotman School of Management. She was smart and ambitious, things he admired beyond her striking good looks.

Rachel was diligent with her early morning training sessions, getting up by 5:30 am so she could hit the gym with her personal trainer. Some people saw it as an over-the-top luxury, but Rachel loved being pushed and challenged. She craved the endorphin release she experienced with the drills; like a drug to ramp her up for her battles in the boardroom. While she never admitted to knowingly using her body to her advantage, Jack thought her confidence and aggressive posturing she recreated in telling him of her latest coup made her hot as hell. Her impeccably tailored dark suits accentuated her figure. Her pencil skirts hugged her well-toned thighs and firm backside. Her jackets darted at her trim waist while the lapels suggestively flared at her full breasts. How she never teetered on her four-inch heels was a mystery to Jack. She wore her dark sleek hair simply parted falling to her shoulders. Her green eyes flashed when she was angry or victorious, two common states for Rachel. It was lust at first sight for Jack; the love followed later.

Rachel wasn't into playing house, but she liked the idea of building equity with home ownership. It was a three-bedroom bungalow on a decent lot in mid-town Toronto that rarely saw home values sag. She couldn't deny that sometimes she enjoyed playing at being married, especially when they curled up on the couch on Sunday mornings with the *New York Times* and their take- out lattes. After sixty-plus hour work weeks, they would often join friends on Saturday nights at the latest trendy restaurants.

While Jack had many friends, Larry and Brett became his closest along with his best friend, Michael. Brett was still footloose and fancy free, often arriving with a new girl to keep things interesting. Larry had moved in with Alison, an aspiring writer, freelancing for different political magazines. Larry was lucky to orchestrate a one-year assignment in Russia with an oil client he worked with at Goldman's so he could follow Alison, who was writing an in-depth review on the Putin regime. They were now experts in vodka, caviar, and corrupt politics, adding an element of sophistication to their evenings. Brett was plugged into the live music circuit, so they'd often move on to a club scene for more drinks after dinner and let the loud music and the frenetic dancing drain the dregs of work out of their systems.

Sarah and Michael rounded out the gang. They met at a seminar she was orchestrating as a special events coordinator. She moved around the room with ease, seemingly unfazed by the hundreds of hyped-up executives ironically pouring in to absorb a time management talk. Sarah had gently taken Michael's arm to direct him to a bank of seats reserved for thirty of Boston's top staff. Sarah's smallest gestures captivated him, like tucking her wavy blond hair behind her small ears and her singsong laugh. Michael was entranced by the kindness in her gold-flecked blue eyes. She blushed when he asked her for her card on the pretense of using her services in the future.

On their first date, they connected effortlessly over pasta and red wine in an authentic Sicilian restaurant in Little Italy, eating home-style with many extended families. Sarah was shy at first but became more animated with the wine.

Nobody was surprised when Sarah and Michael married. They were the couple everyone said seemed so perfect together. They were only together for a couple of years when they got engaged, but they never doubted that they'd spend the rest of their lives together. Their wedding was a beautiful traditional ceremony followed by a raucous party with family and friends from high school, university, and work. It was a wonderful day filled with an outpouring of love and the promise of a blessed future.

Jack and Rachel balked at traditional pomp and ceremony and chose to marry six months later on a whirlwind trip through Italy. They had been living together for three years, and Jack was anxious to start a family. Rachel said she wanted children but wasn't in any hurry to derail her successful career, and her phenomenal figure, with 'a screaming baby' as she often referred to the plan when Jack brought it up.

Jack wasn't worried. He had his way of making things happen and was sure Rachel would be all for it soon enough. He was ready for the next big chapter. He lived his life planning for the next major event and always succeeded in attaining it. The initial thrill of being a big shot in a highly successful consulting firm had abated. He still loved the money and the thrill of the win, but the daily grind was dimming the glamour. Rachel, on the other hand, was full speed ahead on the career front. She thrived on her travel schedule that kept her on the road half of the time.

Jack and Rachel's impressive double income financially catapulted them ahead of their friends into their second home; a large 3,000-square-foot modern build in a leafy part of posh North Toronto. Their sizeable incomes supported their mortgage application, and they managed the hefty monthly payments. The big lots and quiet cul-de-sacs were ideal for raising families. Jack was excited at the possibilities. He daydreamed about the beautiful babies they would make and what a great-looking family they would have in a couple of years. It perfectly rounded out his idea of success.

Jack felt smug at their rapid climb in society. Larry and Alison seemed content still renting in the Annex area near the university and living a bohemian lifestyle. They didn't mind the futon and thrifted furniture which now seemed depressing to Jack. He couldn't fathom why Larry hadn't seized the opportunities handed to him by Goldman Sachs. Instead, Larry chose to move to a non-profit firm that helped immigrants with legal matters. Houses and children were not even on the radar. Jack and Rachel still hung out with them, but it was becoming harder to keep a middle ground on which to connect.

Brett continued embracing his bachelor lifestyle. Rachel had liked Brett in the early days, when they were all into serious partying. Now, she felt some annoyance with Brett and his goofy, immature antics, and his bragging about his latest conquests, so Jack saw him mostly over golf and the occasional boy's weekend.

Jack would have loved to take his buddies up to his family cottage if his parents hadn't sold it once his sisters were in university. He begged his parents to hold off as he wanted to buy them out, but they wanted to sell while they felt like they could get top dollar. Jack was already stretched with hisToronto mortgage, so he couldn't meet their asking price. Although years had passed since then, he still got angry at their disregard for his wishes to keep the cottage in the family; the place holding his few happy family memories sold to the highest bidder.

The next best thing for a boys' weekend was Jack's fathers' hunting cabin in the woods about twenty kilometers from the main cottage. Jack, Brett, Michael (Larry declined the invitation, being a strict vegetarian and opposed to any kind of violence), and a couple other buddies went up for the odd weekend sharing the cabin and camping on the pretense of hunting deer. They mostly enjoyed being together, sharing stories of the past and their dreams for the future, and knocking back beer like the good old days.

CHAPTER 4

Michael was hopeful they would conceive quickly, within the first year of going off birth control. He came home on Friday after a boring, all-day meeting, and flopped on the couch after cracking a cold beer. The house seemed quieter than usual. After calling for Sarah and not getting a response, he hauled himself up to have a quick shower. He took the shallow stairs two at a time to avoid the creaky spots that served to remind him of all the work he should be doing on the house. These houses were built in the thirties and in need of constant renovation. Although it was small, it was central which was a big priority for them. Their neighborhood had a fantastic strip of shops and restaurants only a five-minute walk down their leafy street. A weekend ritual often included grabbing a coffee at The Daily Grind, an independent coffee shop with a fair-trade policy, followed with a stop for French patisseries and fresh fruit from the market. Relaxing back home on their deck in their backyard was heaven. After the demands of the week, it was lovely to sink into this tranquil routine.

Michael was in a happy haze thinking about their domestic weekend when he popped into the spare bedroom to drop his gym bag full of sweaty gear from his lunchtime workout. The room was cluttered with sports gear, books, winter coats, random poster art, and an old desk. He paused when he realized something was different. The desk normally covered with bills and books had been cleared and scrubbed clean. In the center sat a blazing white bassinet, about two feet long, its hood up with wicker handles. His heart skipped a beat, and he felt goose bumps.

"Sarah – Sarah?" he shouted. The emotion he felt choked him up and strangled any repeat attempts to call for his wife.

He haltingly approached the foreign-looking basket and peeked inside. His excitement built with each step. Perched on top of a yellow crocheted baby blanket nestled inside was a simple card outlined in silver:

Congratulations Daddy!

He was totally unprepared for the news after only three months of trying. As he slowly lifted the card, he felt her arms encircle his chest from behind. She had been hiding in the closet to capture his first reaction. Turning to return her embrace he gazed at her radiant face. Sarah's eyes sparkled through the tears.

"Yes," Sarah said, "you're going to be a father."

~~~

Jack was truly happy for Michael and Sarah. Being highly competitive and anxious for his own family, he started pressing Rachel more emphatically to try for a baby.

At just thirty, Rachel felt she had plenty of time and her career was flying high. She now had a team of six reporting to her and was taking on a higher-level strategic role. Jack continued to do well but felt somewhat upset that Rachel was recently promoted and now raking in more money than him.

The four couples went for a celebratory dinner at one of their favorite Italian restaurants to congratulate Sarah and Rachel on their different achievements. Michael and Sarah were beaming. Sarah was ravenous as she was just beyond her third month. The morning sickness had abated, and her appetite roared back.

Jack felt pangs of jealousy as he coveted their status as a real family unit, creating something strong and secure.

They enjoyed celebratory cocktails, Sarah content with her mineral water, and then paired each delicious course with a different bottle or two of wine. Rachel may have been showing off a little since she had recently completed a wine-tasting course to help her look more sophisticated when entertaining clients. They began with a light Sauvignon Blanc and mussels, a more robust Chianti with the main pasta, and then a Pinot Noir with their meat dishes and sides. They were nearly at a bottle each, not counting the cocktails. Jack had a hard time not staring at Sarah's new belly, full breasts, and her happy serene expression. Michael's pride filled the room whenever baby plans came up or when he looked at Sarah. Jack's anxiety ratcheted up along with the drinks.

After arriving at home Jack was particularly insistent, desperately pleading with Rachel about trying for a baby. He shifted closer to her on the couch and nuzzled her neck. He planted feverish kisses across her collarbone and down her breasts. His strong hand stroked the inside of her thigh, and she groaned as she willingly parted her legs to let him explore. Her thong was soaked and his body responded immediately. Using the same hand, he teasingly pulled down her lower lip, letting her taste herself as she playfully sucked his fingers. Rachel purred and surrendered to the moment. The wine helped transport her to a dreamy sexual state. She sank into the couch, kicked off her heels, and swung her legs up on the cushions. Her skirt rode up around her waist. Jack's hard body climbed on top of Rachel after quickly dropping his jeans to the floor. Rachel thought he looked as sexy as ever with his toned abs and strong thighs from running.

As their bodies were poised to become one, he whispered in her ear, "How about that baby now?"

Caught up in her desire and feeling positively delirious she panted, "Yes, yes, yes," while pulling him deep inside.

Their sex was frenzied and done with complete abandon. Jack pinned her arms tightly over her head as he thrust himself wildly. She squirmed and panted for him to slow down. With great effort he focused and took in her rhythm and made sure she was ready to come with him. They climaxed together with loud shouts and Jack collapsed in a heap. It was a great show for anyone walking by since the lights were still on in the living room.

Rachel awoke at noon the next day to an aching head and sore body. She dragged herself to the living room and curled up on sofa with a glass of ice water. Jack had already done his morning weight class and came bounding in the door with fresh breakfast sandwiches and mango juice.

He was charged with excitement about the baby plans and was talking a mile a minute about how great it would all be. "We can convert the spare bedroom beside ours to a nursery. I really don't care if we have a boy or girl first – do you care? Our baby and Michael's and Sarah's baby will be like cousins so close in age."

Rachel retreated into her own headspace. What the hell did I say last night? Her mind raced through the previous evening. A baby already? No way!

She was about to speak when she saw the empty pill packages on the table.

Jack gleefully held up the cellophane packages with the empty pill casings; prior to his workout he popped each pill and flushed them down the toilet.

"How great is this right? I can't think of a better way to celebrate the next phase of our relationship, of becoming parents."

"But I don't think I'm ready," Rachel protested. "I'm only thirty and really want to focus on my career for a few more years. I thought I—"

"I thought, I thought," he mimicked in a high-pitched voice, cutting her off mid-sentence, flipping from his happy ramblings to a verbal assault in a heartbeat. "You agreed to this last night," he stated, taking a few quick strides towards the couch. He slid the greasy wrappers across the coffee table and slammed down the drinks. "It's all about you, isn't it. Well, what about me? I've been wanting this for years!"

His eyes were glassy, and razor focused. She had never seen him like this. It was unnerving and a bit frightening.

After a few seconds she found her balance and shot back, "Wait a minute! I was drunk when I said yes. You can't seriously hold me to something I said after two bottles of wine?"

Her head throbbed at the pressure of getting to her feet too quickly and she dropped back down and held her head in both hands.

He hesitated for a moment, quickly calculating his approach. He didn't want to sabotage the idea completely. He took a deep breath and looked down while apologizing.

"I...I was just so excited. I thought you wanted this too?"

Through frustrated tears Rachel blurted out, "I do, but just not yet."

After a few beats Jack responded calmly, "Nobody is ever really ready. We'll be great parents. We have lots of money, and we can hire help, a nanny. We can still have plenty of trips. Our babies will be so beautiful! Our parents can help. Our kids will be great friends with Michael and Sarah's kids! I'll be fully involved, I promise."

By the end of his speech, he was addressing an empty space. Rachel mentally drifted out of the conversation midway and was now heading down the hall.

CHAPTER 5

Jack and Rachel's sex life had always been great. The frequency and intensity in their first year or two together had eased into a more settled but still exciting and fulfilling part of their marriage. Their schedules and punishing work demands made it challenging to find time but they never had trouble reigniting their desire. Whatever tension or stress they carried from their day-to-day lives, or petty differences they built up, sloughed off like a second skin with their intimacy.

Rachel loved Jack's dominance and let herself be swept away and completely seduced. The trust and love she felt freed her to try playfully dangerous sex games. Nothing too crazy, the usual soft S&M stuff, like using the handcuffs Jack received at his bachelor party. They still had spontaneous sex too, like when Jack crept up on her in the kitchen in the middle of her making dinner and slowly won her over with his passionate caresses and wandering hands. If they felt reckless, they pulled the car over onto a quiet street or parking lot, and she straddled him in the front seat while he gripped the steering wheel. After sex they felt a deep sense of connectedness, like it was just the two of them, the rest of the world revolving around their private universe.

All this shifted after their intense fight a couple months back. Rachel saw how happy Sarah and Michael were and felt she was losing Jack, who became remote and reserved after their terrible post-Italian dinner fight. They were using condoms since Jack had flushed her pills away and that wasn't working. Rachel relented to try for a baby.

The first few months after agreeing to try, Rachel enjoyed Jack's renewed ardent insistence on lovemaking. They had intercourse virtually every night. For a man who enjoyed oral as much as traditional sex, this was a big change. Rachel even felt herself warm to the idea of starting their new family. She caught herself peeking into strollers they passed on the street and noticing maternity stores she had never seen on her route to work. Date night conversation moved from real estate values, work drama, and marathon goals, to baby names and nursery designs. They were both high achievers and saw themselves as an attractive new threesome. They agreed on a personal trainer for Rachel so she could stay fit post-baby, and a live-in nanny so they could both stay focused on their careers.

~~~

With only a few more weeks of pre-baby freedom, Michael and Sarah threw a casual BBQ at their house. Sarah's belly was huge, and she lumbered when she walked. She maintained a balanced exercise routine and a good diet, so from behind, she still had most of her shape. Even in her advanced stage of pregnancy Jack found her very beautiful and was strangely attracted to her physically. He noticed how healthy her hair looked, a few stray strands resting loosely across her ample breasts. She seemed vulnerable and open, surrendered to her role, and excited about the upcoming birth.

"Hey buddy," Michael said, intruding on Jack's reverie. "So glad you and Rachel could make it. You're such highflyers now we hardly ever see you."

They clinked Coronas and easily sucked back half a bottle each.

After a slight pause Jack loudly proclaimed, "Here's to Michael Junior," and quickly finished off his beer.

A few moments of strained silence followed. "You know, Rachel and I are going to have a baby too," Jack stated, cracking the lid off his fourth beer of the afternoon.

Michael was quick to respond, "That's fantastic! Congratulations."

"Hold up my friend. We're just in the *making* stage." Jack clarified.

"Oh," Michael fumbled, "Well, still, that's great news."

"I'm sure it will happen any time now," said Sarah who had wandered up beside them. She placed a gentle hand on Jack's arm.

"I have no doubt," said Jack. "Our kids will have a blast together! They'll be like cousins. Maybe when they get a bit older, we can rent a cottage—the two families together—or a ski chalet." Jack was looking slightly manic as he rambled on about their plans.

Michael felt sorry for Jack. "That will be awesome, we'll make quite the pack."

Sarah excused herself from Jack's monologue, feeling uncomfortable at his intensity. He was gesticulating wildly with his hands, bobbing on his feet, and his eyes danced as he described the possibilities.

It had been six months since they started trying. Jack suggested Rachel put on some weight since she was very lean, but she didn't think that mattered and she certainly wasn't planning on 'getting fat' before being pregnant.

There were several friends with babies at the party. Jack paused to chat with Larry and Alison. The Annex couple had their baby strapped in a hemp papoose that seemed permanently fixed across Alison's chest. They proudly informed those willing to listen that attachment parenting was the only way to go. A crop of dark soft hair and a tiny profile was all anyone could make out of the content tiny newborn safely tucked into his mother's body. Jack gently stroked the baby's head.

Party boy Brett joined the group. "I'm happy to stay in the non-baby camp. We've got the right idea, don't we Jack!" Brett exclaimed, clamping a meaty paw on Jack's shoulder then staggering away.

"To Jack Junior," slurred Jack as he searched for a willing participant to hoist a beer. Michael had moved off to tend to the BBQ and Jack found himself awkwardly alone. Addressing no one in particular, Jack continued, "He will have every opportunity, just like me. Swimming, golfing, skiing, sailing, hockey lessons, whatever he wants."

"Or she," Rachel interjected as she stepped up beside him. She was worried as she saw him staggering and muttering to himself. Jack paused as he finished another beer. "Yeah—sure—maybe she," he said, trailing off and moving away.

Michael and Sarah exchanged a quick glance, catching the tension between Jack and Rachel. They were happy about their good friends' plans to start a family but also concerned about the disconnect they noticed. Jack barely noticed Rachel as he went on about their plans, scanning the partiers like a salesman looking for a buyer. The more animated Jack got the quieter Rachel became. Although they hadn't been trying for very long, Rachel was beginning to question their ability to conceive.

CHAPTER 6

In the first months of trying to conceive, Rachel purposely arranged her calendar to avoid travelling in the middle of her cycle. After a few months her management noticed and started questioning her commitment to the firm.

"Rachel, please take a seat," Len suggested. "We've noticed you seem less interested in your demanding travel schedule over the past while and thought Sampson could be promoted to pick up the slack. He can take on some of your more junior clients."

The suggestion was like a hard slap across her face. I've busted my ass to climb to the position of managing director. No way will I let this happen. I've given up so much and always placed my work commitments before my own over the past five years.

She visibly straightened her back, pulled up her chin, and levelled her gaze while shifting in her chair. She purposely recrossed her bare smooth legs, digging her spiked heel into the plush carpet. With her hands flat on the heavy mahogany table, she leaned in.

"Thank you for the offer, Len, but there is no need to promote Sampson to lighten my responsibilities. I am as determined as ever to contribute to the success of the firm and making senior partner within the next five years."

Len chuckled with a sign of relief, adding he was thrilled to hear it. "I've never seriously doubted your drive, just looking out for your best interests. I've seen enough people burn out in this business and don't want you to join the ranks."

The tension eased and Len declared drinks were needed to review the next strategic plan for their new fast-food client.

Rachel felt elated as she excused herself for a moment to gather her thoughts. All the plans and frantic attempts at conceiving had taken on a life of its own. The process and decision to have a baby had become a thing, a monstrous thing, controlling and sucking the life out of her.

Shaking her head Rachel reprimanded herself in the bathroom mirror, "How the hell did I let myself get so lost?"

With a new sense of control and determination she happily steered a successful night of brainstorming. Once the key concepts were agreed upon, the whiskey flowed easily. Rachel happily matched shot for shot celebrating her renewed sense of liberation.

~~~

Jack spent the evening alone and his anger slowly built as the hours passed. He didn't wait long to launch into Rachel after she came home, tipsy and happy.

"Where the hell have you been? You know its mid-month on your cycle."

"Getting my life back," Rachel spewed. "I can't believe I almost blew it. All my dreams and hard work nearly tossed aside. All for this ridiculous phantom baby you want."

"I want?" he shouted. "What about what we want. What we've talked about for the past six months?"

"More like what you've been talking about. This is nothing more than another win, a prize for you. A big conquest for big Jack. Something you can brag about, to show what a real man you are," she hurled at him, losing her balance slightly as she steadied herself on the dining room table.

Jack's shock and hurt at her accusations quickly morphed into anger. He felt the heat radiating off his forehead, his heartbeat quickened, and a vein pulsed along his neck.

"What the fuck? How dare you," he growled crossing the room to tower over her only inches from her face.

She snickered and snorted. She was sick and tired of him dictating her life. "Oh, come off it. You know as well as I do that—"

In that instant he grabbed her by the shoulders. His strong hands dug into her upper arms. "That's not true," he shouted. "You're drunk and you're talking bullshit!"

"Am I, Jack?" she threw back. "Why so urgent? Why can't you be happy with what we have? What are you trying to prove?"

She yanked free of his grasp and fell backwards, striking her thigh on the edge of the table and falling to the floor. Her dress hitched up. She was too drunk to notice or care.

His fury mingled with desire. He needed to gain the upper hand, show her who was in charge. He needed to blow off steam. He dropped down beside her and grabbed the back of her hair, forcing her face up to his. He lunged on top of her and kissed her aggressively, forcing his tongue deep into her mouth. Rachel tried to push back, caught off guard, but was completely ineffective. His hold was too strong, and she felt dizzy from the drinks. His free hand yanked up her dress exposing her black bikini bottoms.

"Get off of me," she said, struggling to find her footing to no avail.

Her vain attempts only served to increase his want. He strained with desire. As she tried to wrestle free, he effortlessly caught both wrists in one hand and painfully pinned them above her head. He muffled her protests by forcefully kissing her, rendering her efforts to twist away futile. His free hand reached down and ripped her panties off and he forced himself between her legs. He found her pathetic struggles arousing.

With clenched teeth and his mouth close to her ear he hissed, "Don't ever talk to me like that again." He drove into her without mercy over and over.

When he was finally spent, he rolled off, breathed heavily on his back, and stared at the ceiling. Rachel staggered to her feet. Her head was spinning as she ran sobbing to the bathroom. She threw herself to the floor, grabbing the toilet seat, and was violently sick. Her body heaved as she emptied herself. After she finished, she stumbled down the hall holding the wall for support. She slammed and locked the bedroom door and crashed into bed, immediately passing out.

Jack awoke early to a grey dawn seeping through the blinds. He was thankful for the light drizzle to accompany his dark mood. He slept on the couch and now surveyed the disheveled room. The previous night played back. Oh my God, what have I done? He swung his heavy legs to the floor and slumped forward, running his hands through his hair. After a few minutes, with a deep sigh, he got up and quietly went upstairs. He tried the bedroom door but found it locked.

"Rachel? Please Rachel. Can we talk?" he called but received no reply. He went back down into the kitchen and numbly put on coffee.

Replaying the night, he vacillated between feeling sorry and angry. This fight was all her fault, saying those hurtful things about me, as if I want the baby as some sort of achievement. Why can't she just see that I want us to be a real family? I'll be such a good father and not a selfish prick like mine was to me. I'm not going to abandon my kid to some cold-hearted boarding school. It will be so different, so great.

As he refocused on the night, his anger pushed his daydreaming back underwater. Her bloody career, what a selfish bitch! Drinking with the good old boys thinking that will help her advance. I can just see her flashing her eyes, her megawatt smile, using her quick wit. She loves to put on a good show. She shouldn't be drinking anyways. It's bad for fertility and maybe that's one reason we haven't conceived yet. I'll have a talk with her about that and other lifestyle changes she needs to make.

His mood brightened as he thought about these changes. This will definitely help us get pregnant. She just needs want it more and be willing to make a few sacrifices.

His thoughts of pregnancy led him to think of Sarah and he let his thoughts drift. She positively glows with good health pre-and post-pregnancy. She exercises and does yoga. She was a good weight before her pregnancy, nice and round in her hips and breasts. Rachel is so lean from her long-distance running that she doesn't have an ounce of fat. Her stomach is flat as a board. Her narrow hips look more like a girl's than a woman's from behind. It's been proven it's less likely for a woman to conceive if she's too thin. Jack smiled as he felt he was regaining control of the process. He was so deep in his thoughts Rachel's presence startled him. She clutched her robe tightly. Her hair was disheveled in a rat's nest clumped at her neck, her eyes rimmed red, and her skin pale. Her messy appearance and smeared make-up halted his thoughts and brought back the previous night's sexual episode he had almost blocked out. He was about to offer an apology he didn't really feel, thinking perhaps he'd been a bit rough. Rachel wasn't a prude about sex, and she had provoked him, but he realized an apology was worth it to smooth things over, to get back on the baby track. He was excited to talk about her lifestyle changes he felt so surely would make things click.

"Listen, Rachel," he started quietly.

"No, wait," she said with her hand pressed against the side of her forehead. "I feel horrible and don't remembering much about last night."

Shaking a few Extra-Strength Tylenol into her hand, and filling a glass with cold water, she added, "I remember a cab ride home but not much else. I have a vague recollection of a fight. I hope I wasn't out of line."

She threw back the pills and slid onto a breakfast stool. "Was I dreaming or did we have sex on the floor?" She looked bemused and winced as her head began to throb again.

Jack's body relaxed. He let out a big breath and flashed a sly smile which pulled his mouth to one side. He gently kissed her forehead.

"Ouch," she giggled, "that hurts," she cooed while gently massaging her temples.

"You were some crazy chic last night," Jack laughed, "dragging me down on the floor, writhing and groaning, begging for me to give it to you like some trampy porn star."

Rachel peeked out from behind her hands covering her eyes and then moaned with the pain that shot across her forehead. "Oh, how lovely. I must have been some sight. I hope I wasn't too brutal."

She tore off a hunk of bagel hoping to soak up some of her hangover.

"Nothing too terrible, nothing I can't handle."

He turned on his heel so Rachel wouldn't see his smirk opening to a full self-congratulatory grin as he popped his bagel into the toaster.

CHAPTER 7

Paige came fairly easily into the world, but you'd never know it by the sounds of her first screams. She was as perfect as they hoped. After Paige spent some time resting on her mother's body, the nurses cleaned her up and the thrilled parents got their first proper look; light peach fuzz covered her round head, her eyes were still tightly closed, her legs were bunched up like she was still waiting to enter the world. A pretty little red mouth and fair skin, just like the princess they dreamt about.

Sarah was lucky to have her mother come and stay for a couple of weeks, to help with the house, and with the care of her granddaughter. Michael charged through the door after work each day with a big 'Daddy's Home' declaration making Sarah smile. She was also in a state of bliss at this bundle of love they were so blessed to receive. Their nights and weekends moved from movies, dinners, and friends to walks, home-cooked dinners, and the odd drop-ins by well-wishers. Perfect as far as they were concerned.

Jack and Rachel came by one Saturday, a few weeks after Paige was born with a lovely gift basket full of pink dresses and a massive pink teddy bear, something Rachel's assistant ordered out of a catalogue. While Rachel was sweet enough, remarking how lucky they were, and how lovely Paige was, Jack couldn't help but hear a note of sarcasm; like it was great for them but not really what she had in mind. He was trying not to be overly sensitive, but he was pretty sure he knew what he was picking up on. On the drive home he couldn't help himself.

"Don't you think it will be fantastic to have our own baby?" Jack enthused.

"Sure, when the time is right," Rachel replied absentmindedly checking her email.

"Listen, hon, I was thinking you should really make a few changes. You know, put on a few pounds, ease up on the hard work, your drinking, shorten your running routes. That kind of thing."

"I see," Rachel said. "It's all my fault. Why don't you just say it? Oh wait, you just did, you asshole. You just can't accept this, can you?

You can't control this part of our lives so you're trying to control mine."

After a minute or two of strained silence Rachel gently eased back into the conversation.

"Look, I'm sorry, Jack, for calling you an asshole. Maybe it's not in the cards for us right now. Why don't we focus on all the good stuff we have going on, like we can travel wherever and whenever we want, we have money, a beautiful home."

Jack stared straight ahead, refusing to respond. The cool breeze flowing through the car was like a physical barrier between them. The space between them vast. Rachel gripped her phone and continued her scrolling.

"I've booked us an appointment at Best Start fertility clinic at Bay and Wellesley, next Tuesday at 1:45 pm," Jack stated.

Rachel felt like someone had kicked her in the stomach. She couldn't believe what she was hearing.

"A fertility clinic? Next week? Without even a discussion, Jack? Don't you think I deserve a point of view on this?"

"I've tried talking to you, Rachel. I've tried to get you to change your lifestyle, and you simply refuse to listen. Perhaps you'll be more motivated to engage in the process if you talk to a professional. Get a third party involved that has the knowledge and training to give us some good advice. I feel like this dream I—we—have of starting our own family is slipping away. I can't believe we aren't meant to have children. Rachel, I love you. If you love me, please, just come to the appointment and see what Dr. Jordan has to say."

Darkness descended and the trees were bare silhouettes. The lights in the houses only served to make Rachel feel lonelier. Jack's drive for a baby was becoming an obsession.

CHAPTER 8

Work had been a killer that day with frustrated clients. Jack's boss was on his case about a major presentation they were pitching to an important new client the following week. Business had slowed down over the past year. While they were still one of the top players in the business, consulting wasn't the cash cow it used to be. The scent of seemingly easy money had drawn new competition, so they had to work harder to keep existing clients and dazzle new ones.

Jack drove his BMW fast, aggressively changing gears as he turned sharply into their expansive driveway. Even though it was a cool October day, he liked the feel of the sunroof open, and rock music blaring to crowd out his work thoughts. But it wasn't working tonight. Taking the porch steps two at a time, he threw open the front door and tossed his leather satchel and trench coat on the bench in the foyer. He flopped on the living room couch, the cool leather feeling good against his neck. He let out a few deep breaths while raking his messy hair. He was surprised to see Rachel coming down the stairs, towel drying her hair and looking comfy and relaxed in her robe.

"Looks like somebody had a rough day," she said, padding over and dropping down beside him. It was rare they were home together right after work.

"Yeah," Jack let out with a heavy sigh. "Jeffrey is insane with his deadlines on this Royal Oil pitch. I mean, I've been putting in twelve-hour days, six days a week for the past two months and it still isn't enough for that greedy bastard." Jack pushed off the couch and headed to the kitchen. "Do you want anything?" he offered while peering into the fridge and pulling out a Corona.

"No, I'm good," Rachel replied. "Why don't you get out for a long run tonight? It would be good for you after being cooped up all day."

Jack paused and thought about it. He hadn't done much exercise lately and was starting to feel the effects. Never had he thought he would become one of those sad, paunchy, middle-aged executives. Not that he thought he looked like that, but just the idea of the possibility, and thinking about his physical lethargy lately, was enough to make him reconsider.

"Come with me?" he ventured.

"I'm good, thanks. I cut out a bit early today to take advantage of the fading daylight to run. Now that I'm getting used to only running ten kilometers, the thought of getting out there again isn't overly appealing. You go ahead and I'll get some dinner started."

"In the old days, you would think nothing of clocking another five to ten."

"Well, now that you have me on the new regime, that's just the way it is," she said, flipping back her long damp hair and tossing the wet towel on the back of the stool.

After their terrible fights around the fertility issue, she agreed to scale back on her exercise. In reality, she had done nothing of the sort. She didn't think for a second that it would make any difference, and she loved the high she got from the endorphin release. She figured there was no harm in not letting him in on her little secret of running fifteen kilometers a few times a week.

~~~

Jack went into the bedroom and quickly pulled on his running gear and laced up his shoes. He set off to the west taking his usual route, but got distracted with his presentation ideas, and didn't realize he ended up near Michael and Sarah's house. Although they lived only four kilometers apart, there was a marked difference in their neighborhoods. Jack and Rachel's was quite affluent with mostly new stucco and stone builds and the modern glass box styles that were all the rage. Not much was left of the solid brick two-story houses, small by today's standards. There was the odd one wedged between half a dozen new houses that towered ten feet higher with their third-floor master bedroom suites, hotel-styled marble bathrooms, and Jacuzzi tubs. Most of the owners were like Jack and Rachel in their thirties and forties; upwardly mobile with young families and two European vehicles, one almost always the requisite SUV or minivan for hauling sports gear and expensive toys like kayaks and high-end bikes. The retired couples tending their gardens, still living in the red-brick rarities, with a modest Corolla in the driveway, seemed like a sweet reminder of the past. But not something Jack ever wanted for himself. He loved their house and was excited about their move to a bigger lot with a pool. He knew this would be after the cottage they'd purchase in the next couple of years, once they had saved up enough after getting their house mortgage under control. He thought the timing would be perfect for when they had their kids.

He slowed down as he recognized Michael's street and maintained a slow pace as he cruised by their house. Jack knew Michael was out of town servicing a client in England; he was gone almost half the time.

After passing Michael's house, Jack stopped to catch his breath. He stretched his calf muscles while leaning straight legged into a pole and glancing back. The air was crisp with the scent of autumn; damp grass and decaying leaves gave the evening a settled feel. Lights glowed softly from kitchens with earnest kids hunched over homework. It always amazed Jack the way the streets cleared out after Labor Day; one week people were out enjoying restaurant dinners on patios, lining up for ice cream, walking hand in hand languidly pushing strollers. A few weeks later, bikes lay abandoned on their sides against the house, flowerpots with decaying mums sat mutely on porches, and houses waited blankly to be adorned with holiday decorations.

The lights were on in the front room and the upstairs bedrooms at 266 Eastborne Street. Jack crossed the road in the shadows of old oak trees; one on the front of each property that created a lovely green tunnel down the modest starter home street. The expensive stroller Michael's work bought them was parked along the side of the house, sensibly covered. The front door was closed tight and likely locked. As he absentmindedly looked across the road thinking about breaking into his running stride for the journey home, he caught sight of Sarah in the front window leaning down to scoop baby Paige from her basinet. The sheers didn't provide much privacy for the deep bay window.

Sarah lifted Paige up to eye level. Sarah was already in her nightgown and gently hugged Paige close to her chest, slowly lowering herself into the rocking chair he knew sat in the corner of the living room. He could just see the top of her head bent over, apparently looking down to watch her baby. Jack was mesmerized by this loving and intimate scene. He dared to cross back over to their side of the street to get a closer look. One house away, he saw through a break in the sheers, Sarah rocking and nursing Paige. Her nightgown was open, and the top of her full breasts exposed. The baby was turned inwards, nestled against the warmth and sustenance of her mother. It looked so natural and peaceful to Jack, a scene played out through the history of time.

Jack fumed. Is it too much to have this basic need of producing a child fulfilled? I can't help it if it's programmed into my DNA to reproduce and carry on my own gene pool.

He didn't know why, but felt it was of utmost importance to produce a new generation of McDermotts. He ached at the idea of having his own child.

Deep in thought, he crept closer to the bay window, making his way up along the mutual driveway. What is it that Rachel doesn't get? Does she not want me to be happy and fulfilled? As he was thinking she should be making this her top priority, he felt his anger rising, and his breathing becoming more rapid.

He watched intently as Sarah smiled sweetly, lost in the happy trance of a tired but contented new mother. A few moments passed when a bark from inside the house next door startled both Jack and Sarah. The high-alert, deep-throated bark snapped Jack back to reality and he instinctively ducked low. A split second later, he bolted down the street away from the house. He didn't look back. By the time Sarah stood up to look out into the darkness, Jack was a good block away. His heart pounded well beyond what it should be doing given the excursion of the run.

A cold sweat broke across his forehead, and he shivered. He didn't let up on his pace and got home with his heart ready to burst. He leaned against the side of his house and struggled to control his breathing. I've got to get a grip and focus on my life. The visit to the fertility clinic can't come fast enough.

CHAPTER 9

Rachel wasn't ready to commit to seeing a fertility doctor like Jack wanted but offered an olive branch by suggesting they start with her family doctor. It was a year since they'd been off birth control.

Dr. Shriver had been Rachel's GP since Rachel was eighteen.

"Your blood work is excellent," Dr. Shriver reported while glancing at Rachel's chart. "You seem to be in excellent health, taking good care of yourself, eating well, and exercising. A few extra pounds wouldn't hurt but that really shouldn't have any effect on your attempt to get pregnant."

Jack maintained a blank expression.

Dr. Shriver was in her late forties with a couple of pre-teen kids. "My goodness, what's the rush! Take it from someone who's in the throes of soccer and hockey and school plays," she chuckled. "You're only thirty-one and haven't been trying that long. Give yourself time to enjoy each other and a carefree life of adult luxuries before you go down the baby path."

"I think that is great advice," Rachel replied as she bounced out of the patient seat. She grabbed her purse and playfully tugged on Jack's arm adding, "And that is what we are going to do tonight!"

Steering Jack into the elevator, Rachel pressed in close as the doors closed and suggestively whispered she had a special night planned, starting with one of their favorite French restaurants, Amour Toujour.

It was a chilly walk ten blocks to their destination. The restaurants and independent shops, and the hustle of the after-work crowd gave the air a sense of purpose, but Jack felt coldly detached from the scene. They huddled inside the restaurant quickly while shivering and settled into the booth.

"You heard her yourself, Jack," Rachel said over the menu after ordering a bottle of white wine.

"I'm really thrilled she has a personal opinion, but I thought we had gone for some professional advice," Jack shot back.

"Oh, come on, sweetie," Rachel said. She was decked out in black; her eyes shone and the gold jewelry he bought for her thirtieth birthday looked rich. She reached across the table and took his hand in hers. "I'm sure it will happen when it's supposed to happen."

He took a large gulp of his cocktail to take the edge off his nerves. He wanted to believe it was true. He didn't want to turn their lovemaking into a major science project. Rachel went ballistic when he brought home the ovulating prediction kit a couple months back. After that, she happened to have an out-of-town work trip mid-month for the next two months. He was convinced she purposely scheduled it that way as a means of getting back at him.

Everyone else made it seem so easy. The worst was Jim from the fifth floor, who loved to boast, 'I just look at my wife and she gets pregnant,' before announcing yet another baby on the way. Everyone would respond with fake forced laughter.

"I just want us to move on with our lives," Jack said. "I feel like we are stuck in neutral. All my life I've been anxious to tackle the next big life event, and I really thought having a baby was meant to come sooner rather than later."

"But we are moving on with our lives. I was recently made Junior Partner and couldn't be more excited! I thought you'd be thrilled for me too," she pouted.

"Of course I am, honey. I just don't know why we can't have both."

~~~

Rachel knew why. She hesitated for a split second and then regained her composure and smiled reassuringly at her husband. This was something she didn't share with even her closest friends. She knew how old-fashioned her management was at the firm. They talked-the-talk about no glass ceiling and equal opportunities, but Rachel knew how they operated and rewarded their staff. They expected one hundred and fifty percent and generously rewarded those who excelled. She saw the men with young families in the office and knew they weren't leaving early to pick up Johnny from daycare, let alone do the shopping and get dinner on the table. She knew firsthand from other good friends it was never a fifty/fifty split on the home front. Someone's career had to take a back seat. With Jack's macho image and inferiority complex firmly entrenched, thanks to his dysfunctional family, she knew it wasn't going to be him.

They'd had a hypothetical conversation in their dating years about who would be the more domestic partner. Jack had snorted and cocked one eyebrow before answering, "You've got to be kidding right? As the mother it's your natural job to be the primary caregiver. My mother did it and it worked out fine."

CHAPTER 10

The bleak overcast day, and the exhaustion from work, provided the perfect conditions for a Sunday afternoon nap. The shrill ringing jarred Jack out of his sleep. He grabbed it on the fourth try.

"Hullo," he answered, rubbing his eyes.

"Oh, sorry, Jack. You're sleeping. I shouldn't have called," Sarah quickly apologized.

"Hey, no problem," Jack said, managing to sound alert. "What's up—are you looking for Rachel?" he asked as he looked around the house not seeing any sign of her.

"No... actually, I was hoping if it wasn't too much trouble, you could help me out."

Jack could hear the hesitation in Sarah's voice.

"It's just that the heat has gone off and the utility company said they are backed up on calls and only promised service within the next twenty-four hours. I'm worried about the baby. Michael is away, so I hoped, if you know how to check the pilot light and could check it for me, I'd really appreciate it."

"The high winds from the morning storm near the termination cap may have snuffed out the pilot light," Jack offered authoritatively. He wasn't surprised they'd be backed up on calls. "No problem. I was looking for motivation to get out for a run anyways. After a lazy day, I'm happy to help."

"Are you sure?" Sarah asked.

"I'm already on my way," Jack said as he ended the call.

He didn't mind having a reason to get out of the house to get some much-needed exercise to clear his head. The storm had died down and there was just a light drizzle now which he liked for running. He easily made his way over to their house and was about to knock when Sarah swung open the large wooden door.

"Hey, Jack, I really appreciate this. You know how worried new mothers can be," she said absent-mindedly while glancing at little Paige nestled in the crook of her arm.

"Glad to help. Where is Michael this time?"

"Back to Brazil to continue the negotiations with Phillips Mining. I think he's gone down there every month since Paige was born."

"So how are you managing with the new baby?" Jack asked as they made their way downstairs into the rec room.

Sarah walked ahead and he inhaled her fresh scent. She wore tight stretch pants and a snug button-up flannel shirt, open at the neck. The shirt skimmed her hips. Jack thought she looked amazing, having had the baby only six months ago. She carried a bit of extra weight, but it only made her sexier. She was lovely and curvy, a nice contrast to Rachel's sharp edges. She moved with a relaxed, easy sway. He trailed close behind as they passed through the laundry room and into the rough side of the basement.

"Wow, there is so much room down here!" Jack noticed as his eyes swept the room and acclimatized to the dim light.

"Michael keeps talking about finishing some of it, to turn it into another bedroom, but he barely has time to help take care of the rest of the place let alone start a major project," Sarah said.

Jack saw the work bench cluttered with tools and hardware. The sports corner was jammed with skis, racquets, golf clubs, skates; a testament to the fun and active lives they led. Some discarded chairs, an old side table, lamps, etc., took up another area. The furnace was tucked away in a far recess of the room. Behind a rail of clothing and coats stood the hot water tank. The overhead light was weak with only two bare bulbs illuminating the basement. The windows were covered in a layer of garden dirt and didn't let any light through. Jack couldn't help but feel very alone with her in the confines of the cramped damp space.

"Do you mind holding her for a second?" Sarah asked. Without waiting for a response, she slid the baby over to Jack, who instinctively accepted her into his arms. "I just want to flip the laundry. I'll take any chance I get." She sauntered back into the laundry room and bent over the washer to scoop up a load of wet baby clothes.

He fought his desire unexpectedly building as he watched her from behind while she leaned down to toss the things into the dryer.

The baby gurgled, which brought him back into the present. He looked down into the little face and was entranced by this beautiful creature, all perfectly formed with her tiny parts. Her hands spastically opened and closed, grasping at nothing in particular. At six months, she mutely accepted this stranger holding her. Her large blue eyes stared boldly into his and he saw Sarah all over her.

"Just beautiful," Jack said weakly as he gently stroked her soft cheek. At this gesture the baby started to root and turn her head towards his chest. In a bird-like movement, her mouth craned to one side and she let out a guttural cry.

"Uh-oh—now look what you've done," Sarah said playfully. She came in close to accept Paige back into her arms.

Jack was nervous about dropping her since he didn't have any experience with babies. Sarah got close and brushed his forearm with her chest without registering the effect, as she expertly took the baby back.

"You've got her thinking about food which is her favorite pastime," Sarah said smiling sweetly. "That stroking of her cheek triggers her rooting reflex. Do you mind if I leave you to try and get the furnace working? This little lady knows how to get what she wants and you're going to have to hear about it if I don't oblige."

"Of course," Jack said while forcing his eyes away from the intoxicating scene in front of him and back to the task at hand.

As he heard her slide a basket of clean bedding to the side as she passed through the laundry room, he glanced back and hungrily followed her figure as she retreated. He was surprised at his erection and turned toward the hot water tank in case she came back. He was confused and ashamed at his physical reaction. Her fullness and fecundity had a strong and powerful effect. How I'd love to see Rachel like this, ripe with the effects of giving and providing life. It's all about control with that woman. Controlling her figure, her job, her colleagues, the situation. She is effectively controlling me too.

"How is it coming?" Sarah called down, snapping him out of his brooding.

"It shouldn't be long now," he said getting down on his knees to assess the problem.

CHAPTER 11

"Okay, okay, make the bloody appointment if that makes you happy," Rachel relented. She was ready to go along with it to get him to stop nagging her. "I think it's premature, but I can tell you won't relax until we go."

Best Start boasted a high success rate. Their slick marketing vaulted them to the top of Google when Jack was searching for options. They needed to wait until early January for their first appointment, after Jack was forced to cancel their initial visit booked in September due to Rachel's travel commitments. Although Jack was frustrated by the delays, he was happy to have a plan.

The few months during the fall were hectic with work. Rachel had taken on a new client and her team worked late more nights than not. She was happy and loved the challenge of determining the strategy for a major acquisition. Her year-end bonus at a surprising 25 percent of her salary was another reason to love it and a good reason to celebrate. Sarah planned a special night to surprise Jack with the good news.

She booked into one of Toronto's nicest restaurants, La Bodega, overlooking the lake with the restaurant perched on top of the TD Bank, forty-two floors high. The city was dazzling with downtown lit up for the holiday season. The CN Tower at 1,400 feet, perched at the edge of the lake, pulsed with vibrant red lights. Colorful lights lined the major streets contributing to the festive air. The city hall ice rink, so far down, looked like something you would see in a snow globe, with dozens of tiny figures circling below.

The restaurant was filled with beautiful people. The commotion of end of year parties amped things up, with bursts of laughter and loud chatter washing across the room. Couples sat close with heads bent together, hands entwined, across white linen tablecloths. Rachel wore a stunning black silk dress that skimmed her taut figure, and five-inch heels accentuated her shapely legs. Even in the dead of winter, she still managed to move effortlessly in heels. The candles caught the warmth of her gold cuff and tear-drop matching earrings.

"You look absolutely stunning, Rachel. A toast to my beautiful, successful wife," Jack said as they raised their champagne cocktails and clinked to the night ahead.

The effects of the alcohol felt great for Rachel. She took another long drink before setting down her flute. She was glad to see Jack was relaxed tonight and not on her case about drinking. After ordering their courses Rachel settled back in her chair.

"Guess what Goldman decided to pay me for a bonus this year," Rachel said coyly.

"I thought we could stay off the work topic tonight, honey," Jack deflected, not wanting to focus on Rachel's career, or more specifically, her success.

"You must be just a little bit curious?" she teased, leaning forward and lifting her glass to her red lips.

It had been a hard year for Jack. His firm hired some young guns with their MBAs from the London School of Economics. They were five to seven years younger with little real-world experience, but they were touted as the firm's crack critical thinkers coming out of the TRIUM program. Clients were suitably impressed, and the new team showed positive results on their initial major assignments. Rachel looked slightly perturbed, leaning back with her arms crossed and glanced about the restaurant as she waited for him to get back into their conversation.

"I'm sorry, Rach, work fog swamped me." He drained his glass, trying to flush any lingering work thoughts.

She couldn't stay too mad; he looked very handsome in his navy-blue suit with his dark blond hair slicked back. His boyish good looks had sharpened now that he was in his thirties, it was a good change. His cheekbones and jawline were more defined. His hairline had receded a little, but it made him look more serious and showed off his light blue eyes. His body was sculpted by his workouts.

Setting down her glass Rachel reached across the table and tugged on his lapel to bring him close and mouthed, "Two-five." She paused for dramatic effect. "Twenty-five percent. I'm talking seventy-five thousand dollars!"

Looking like the winner that she was, she beamed radiantly, waiting for his praise. Jack simply stared in disbelief.

"Jack, did you hear me? I just told you we are seventy-five thousand dollars richer." She went to pull the champagne bottle from the bucket to refill their glasses when he caught her wrist.

"A lady doesn't pour her own champagne," he said, topping up their glasses.

Rachel waited patiently as the bubbles rose.

Snapping to, he stammered, "Holy shit. That's huge, Rachel. Fantastic!"

"You heard it, baby. Isn't it amazing?"

"Yeah, you can say that again."

Jack drifted again, thinking how he had never made that kind of money. *She's been working hard but so have I. The past year may not have been my best, but still, I've done great work, and my established clients still want me.*

Rachel cut into his thoughts bursting with enthusiasm. "We should do something crazy—like go on a wild trip to Tahiti! Or maybe Kenya on safari and sleep in those luxury tents. We could take a balloon ride over the Serengeti and see the migration. Clark was telling me about a trip he did like that, and said it was incredible!"

"Or" Jack dragged out. "We could take a good chunk out of our mortgage. The sooner the mortgage is paid down, the sooner we can seriously look at moving up or buying a cottage."

A few of Jack's friends had bought land in the county, hoping to build down the road, once they had more cash.

"Oh my God, Jack, don't be so pedestrian. Do you think I bust my ass to be like all those dull bourgeoisie types that pile into their minivans to clean up mice shit and mindlessly watch their kids doing the same stupid jumps off the dock all day while swatting away mosquitoes?" Rachel sneered.

"Watch it, Rachel," Jack snapped. "Those dull bourgeoisie types you just slammed happen to be my family and my summers growing up."

"And look how well that turned out," she baited, looking around for a waiter to order some wine.

"Well, aren't you just the little bitch tonight," Jack fired back. "Little *miss bonus* lets it go right to her head, and she thinks she's better

41

than the rest of us."

"You're just jealous." Rachel smiled as the waiter approached.

After a beat, Jack replied, "What did it really take to make that bonus?"

Rachel's smile dropped like a lead balloon. The well-trained waiter backed off, knowing when to discreetly turn away and tend to another table.

Rachel stood up, smoothed down her dress, and grabbed her purse from the corner of the table. Stepping around to Jack's side, leaning her left hand on the table, she picked up his full glass of champagne and threw it at his face. She knew it would sting. A few patrons looked aghast.

"Don't even think about coming home tonight," she spat at him before turning on her heel and strutting out of the room.

CHAPTER 12

The cold air felt good as Jack made his way back uptown, heading towards home. Taxis were scarce during the holiday season, and he knew he needed to clear his head. A light snow was falling, creating a soft blanket of white over everything. It all looked so lovely. It could have been a beautiful backdrop to a great night.

Why was I such an idiot? He lambasted himself over and over as he played back the night. She was so excited. Good for her. She deserved the bonus given the money she's raking in for the firm. She was just so smug and full of herself. It was that control thing again—makes me crazy. Did she really need to cut up my family? But then again, I did shoot down her travel dreams.

His head was spinning. It shouldn't be this hard. We've only been married a few years and life is good.

He trudged along, the revelers thinning out as he made his way up Yonge St. He'd been walking for over an hour and found himself at the beginning of Eastborne Street. He turned right and headed towards Sarah and Michael's house, killing time to let Rachel cool off. It was only ten o'clock since their night was cut short, so he wandered familiar streets along his running route. He glanced up at the bay windows as he passed, catching glimpses of family scenes unfolding. He saw a father standing behind his teenage daughter at the dining room table. She was holding up a textbook and her father was engrossed. They shared a quick laugh, probably at his lack of understanding grade ten algebra. Simple exchanges of love and support. His hand on her shoulder. So normal. So foreign.

Jack thought about Stanford College and their study support classes. Only the geeks would go. Brown-nosing with the teachers. It was far better to struggle through on your own than admitting you needed help. The boys learned early on not to show weakness within the tribe.

266 Eastborne. He saw a figure pass by an upstairs window. Sarah most likely. A couple of seconds later he recalled Michael was away for one last trip before Christmas. They had the large old-fashioned primary-colored lights strung around the porch railing and along the bushes. A good size Christmas tree filled the window hampering his view. It was all

very simple and unaffected, giving off a look of happiness and contentment. Grounded people living authentic lives, building families with love and support.

He started to shiver in the frigid air. Maybe I could pop in for a visit? She would probably like some company.

He went up the front walk and as he came to the top of the steps, he saw through the front door window Sarah standing at the kitchen sink at the back of the house. She was wearing a white terry cloth robe cinched at the waist. Her hair was twisted and clamped at the back of her head with a few loose strands of damp hair clinging to her neck and curling around her shoulders.

Jack backed down the steps and walked up the driveway extending alongside their house to the backyard. It was a dark night with snow clouds obscuring the moon. The lack of wind and the sprinkling of snow made for a muffled step. He quietly unhooked the backyard gate and stood beside the garage looking into the family room. They had large floor to ceiling glass walls, a nice modern touch they added after buying. They hadn't gotten around to getting blinds since their yard backed onto another yard and the tall spruce trees provided a natural barrier to the houses behind.

Jack was in a trance with no plan but was excited by his clandestine activity. A slight smile played on his lips.

Sarah was moving about picking up dishes, straightening books, and opening mail. She flopped into a large chair and swung her feet up on the ottoman. Her robe parted as she lifted her feet, and he saw her bare legs and was surprised to see she had painted her toes. Deep red. Her figure was back, and her legs looked gorgeous. He moved a few steps closer. Her cleavage was easily visible at the opening of her robe. She rubbed the back of her neck and stretched her head from side to side. He imagined him rubbing her neck. She had a beautiful pink glow on her cheeks. Michael was always raving about her being a good cook.

Jack felt like time was suspended and he could watch her all night. She took a brief phone call. After ten to fifteen minutes, she stood up and gathered a couple of garbage bags from the kitchen. She was heading to the back door. With no time to leave, he ducked down behind the cedar hedge lining the garage. After stepping into her boots and clutching the top of her robe with one hand and holding two garbage bags in the other, she strode across the yard from the house to the garage and activated the code to open the door. The door creaked and swung high. She passed within five feet of him. He clamped his mouth after noticing his breath hanging in the cold air. Being down low he didn't risk looking up. All remained quiet except for the thump of the bags landing in the bin and the reverse creak of the door. She was walking briskly back to the house when she suddenly slowed and looked at the ground near the gate. She was puzzled seeing footprints near the gate but was interrupted by Paige's demanding cry. She resumed her pace to get back inside and slammed the door behind her, flipping the lock before disappearing down the hall.

Jack sprinted back through the gate and out to the front sidewalk fully intending to go home, but paused, and held back. He wasn't wanted at home. Rachel wasn't quick to soften if she felt she was in the right. It was too soon to look for forgiveness. Michael is a good friend who would totally support him and let him spend the night. Sarah would want to support her husband's wishes, like all good wives should.

Emboldened by his escapade, he went up the porch steps and rang the buzzer. After no answer he buzzed a second time. He saw the curtains part upstairs. Hopping from one foot to the other he stepped back and gave Sarah a big wave along with his megawatt smile. A minute later Sarah opened the front door.

"Jack, what's up?" Sarah asked, looking at Jack but also behind him and out to the street. "Is everything okay? Is Rachel with you?"

"Not really and no," he replied. "Rachel and I had a big fight, and she booted me out for the night. I just hoofed it here from downtown and I thought I'd drop by and shoot the breeze with Michael, if I'm not interrupting anything."

"Oh, I'm sorry Jack, but Michael is still away," Sarah said while a shiver shook her body.

"Still? What's it been? Two weeks? Well, that's too bad."

Jack blew into his bare hands cupped to his mouth.

"Oh, my goodness, my manners. Come in Jack, you must be freezing."

Sarah pulled the door open wide to make room for him in the small foyer. The warmth of the hall radiator felt good. She smelled like lavender.

"I know I'm not what you had in mind," Sarah chuckled, "but you're welcome to stay and have a cup of tea or hot chocolate if you'd like to warm up."

"That would be great," Jack said as he kicked off his wet shoes. "As long as I'm not bothering you,"

"Not at all. Some company would be nice for a change," Sarah said as she made her way into the kitchen and clicked on the kettle.

"How's Paige doing?" Jack asked as he leaned back on the kitchen counter.

"Growing like crazy! You know, she's already twenty-five pounds and just over a year!" Sarah beamed when she spoke. "It's not always easy but I can't possibly imagine my life without her now, you know. New mother speak I'm afraid," Sarah blushed.

She pulled down a tin of cocoa powder and a box of Earl Gray tea.

"Pick your fancy," she said, holding up the options.

"The tea sounds perfect," Jack replied. He reached up high in the cupboard and pulled down two matching mugs. He felt the warmth of domesticity all around him and was totally at ease; almost at home with it. Sarah poured the steaming water into the mugs with the teabags and added milk and sugar. He followed close behind her into the family room. Jack took one end of the couch and Sarah the other. She innocently tucked her legs sideways underneath her and looked cozy and comfortable as she blew on her tea.

"So how bad was it? If you don't mind me asking?" Sarah ventured.

Jack thought since her life revolved around feedings and laundry, she might find a little juicy adult gossip quite refreshing.

"Pretty bad. We were supposed to be celebrating Rachel's big bonus but somehow it got ugly," Jack said. "Probably both our faults. Rachel and I have different opinions on where our lives are heading. She wants to keep on spending and partying and rising the corporate ladder, wasting our hard-earned money. I want to put down roots by buying a cottage and starting a family."

"You sure sound reasonable to me," Sarah offered. "You guys are both in your early thirties so it's not too soon to try for a baby. Does Rachel still enjoy the corporate scene that much?"

"She thrives on it," Jack said, dropping his voice down into a low, flat tone. "She works the room like a gladiator using her full arsenal. She knows just how to play it to get them riveted and then wows them with her intellect. I'm not saying she isn't good at what she does. She is brilliant. But it seems like an unfair advantage when you're stacked with all the female advantages, pardon the pun, plus have the brains to take on anyone."

"Not to be judgmental, Jack, but you do sound a tad jealous," Sarah said as she leaned over the coffee table to set down her mug.

"You've got a point," Jack said. "But I don't understand how she can't see how much I want to move on and start a family? And then I think, what's worse is that she can see and doesn't care. That's what I'm really afraid of."

Jack could see Sarah looking concerned, so he layered on, "What if she's never ready?" He stared into his mug. "What then?"

"Oh, Jack," Sarah sighed and slid across the couch. She put her arms around his shoulders and gave him a quick squeeze. His heart was in his mouth. He didn't breathe or move. The urge to seize her was overwhelming. He managed to stay calm as she gave him a friendly pat on the back and sprung back to her spot. "Give it some time. I'm sure she'll come around." She grabbed her mug again and took a deep drink.

Paige started to fuss from her room upstairs, and he could see that Sarah needed to go.

"I'd better head out. Thanks for the talk and the tea."

"Will Rachel let you in?" Sarah asked as she got to her feet.

"Ha! That's a good one! Jack laughed. "Have you seen her mad? I wouldn't even try to get within twenty feet of our property tonight." He made his way through the kitchen towards the front door. "I'll just walk some more, maybe hit a hotel if something is available if I get too tired before sunrise."

Paige grew more insistent.

"Listen. If you want, I don't mind if you crash downstairs. We have a small guest room Michael's mom uses when she comes down. If you can handle homemade crocheted polyester quilts, it's all yours." Sarah offered with a lovely smile.

"Really? Only if you're sure it's no trouble. The thought of spending the next six to eight hours out there isn't too appealing. I'd sleep at the office, but they started this new lockout policy to keep everyone away for at least twenty- four hours over the weekend. Their attempt to keep us balanced with a home life."

"Of course, no big deal. I'm sure Michael would insist. There should be enough covers. If you need the bathroom, you'll need to come upstairs since we only have the one, on the second floor. Grab anything you want from the fridge and feel free to let yourself out in the morning as I may not see you. Sleep well and good luck patching things up with Rachel."

She sprinted up the stairs at a fast pace as Paige's hunger cries reached their crescendo.

"Do you need anything?" Jack asked, looking up at her as she reached the top of the stairs.

Sarah paused for a moment and shouted down, "Nope, I've got everything I need right here," while placing an open palm just above her chest.

The baby's cries quieted down within a couple of minutes. He heard the slow creak of a rocking chair just above the foyer. He knew that was where the nursery was; he had seen the buttery yellow drapes from the street. He thought they looked sweet with the animal motif that circled the upper wall.

He paused at the fridge and pulled open the door. Peering inside, he realized he was famished since they hadn't got around to eating at the restaurant before the fight began. He made himself a salami sandwich and popped open a can of Coors. Dropping down to the couch again he imagined Sarah upstairs. So close. If only Rachel could slow down and see how great this could be. She'd see she could be fulfilled with him and their baby, she wouldn't need the rush of the boardroom wins.

He didn't want to dwell on the subject again and felt a wave of fatigue wash over him. All was quiet upstairs. He checked his phone to see if Rachel had called. Nothing.

He descended to the rec room and found the spare bedroom. It had a grandma feel; a single bed with an orange, yellow, and black square patterned quilt, a basic dresser with a discolored lamp, and a wooden chair needing a fresh coat of paint. A black enamel crucifix hung over the bed.

Jack thought of his high-maintenance mother. How she would scoff at such a set-up. This woman's needs were Spartan! Where were the 500-plus thread count sheets? The hotel styled duvet? The Evian bottle of water on the dresser? She'd never sleep in a room like this. I'd be lucky to have her show up at all to spend time with my new baby. She never enjoyed parenting the first time around, why would the next round be any different.

He pulled his loosened tie over his head, dropped his pants in a heap on the cold thin carpet, and climbed into bed in his boxers and dress shirt. As he struggled to get warm tossing and turning, he realized he needed to use the washroom. He took the stairs two at a time and was quickly at the top of the second-floor hallway. All was quiet. He lightly made his way down the hall, not daring to peek into the baby's room for fear of waking her. Finding the bathroom on the left, he went in and relieved himself. Leaving, he caught sight of Sarah and Michael's room another few steps down the hall. The door was open, he figured Sarah was asleep. He took a couple steps down the hall and paused at the doorway. As his eyes adjusted to the light, he made out the womanly shape. Sarah was on her side, facing away from the doorway. Her light breathing caused her shoulders to rise and fall ever so slightly. Her hair splayed across the white pillowcase, and her bare shoulder was tinged blue in the dark room. He waited and watched. Ten minutes must have passed. She was so sweet and caring. Giving up everything for her baby. So considerate and warm. Another step brought him into the doorframe. Michael had done well marrying Sarah; easygoing, compromising, thoughtful. Why couldn't Rachel be a little softer? This draw to Sarah just seems so right. Maybe she feels it too? Maybe that's why she asked me to stay over?

Another step and he was right inside her room. It was just the two of them in the middle of the night. He imagined sliding her nightgown further off her shoulders. Feeling her soft skin. He shifted his weight to take another step closer, only thinking about getting closer, to be with her. The floor creaked and he froze. He looked down as if the hardwood floor was the guilty party.

He had barely looked back up when he saw Sarah turn over and call out, "Is everything okay? Is it Paige?" she said through bleary eyes as she tossed off the covers on autopilot, clearly on a mission swinging her legs to the floor.

"No, no, sorry. I was just looking for the bathroom. I'll find it. Go back to sleep," he said as he backed up, bumping into the wall as he stumbled back down the hall.

Sarah was so tired. The sleep deprivation took a toll. She happily flopped back on her pillows and said, "Just on your right," waving her arm and then let it drop like a stone. All was quiet again, except for the sound of Jack's heart beating wildly in his chest.

He went through the charade of using the washroom, being sure to flush and run the sink water before returning to his bed in the basement. He dozed off and on for a couple of hours but was fully awake before dawn unable to get back to sleep. His phone said 5:15 am and he thought he'd wait for a hint of sunrise before heading home. After finding sleep impossible, he sat up and wrapped the quilt around his shoulders and went into the hall. The tile floor was cold underfoot. The laundry room was just ahead, and an accordion door led to another room. He walked on the outside of his feet to avoid the cold contact and pulled the door open, more bored than curious.

He looked around with the help of the dim lighting overhead. Although most things looked completely disheveled, he noticed the photo albums were neatly stacked on a bookshelf with the dates on the side. 1995 - their graduation year. He pulled out the album and quietly slid down to the cement floor and leaned back against the sweaty cold walls. Flipping the cellophane pages he nostalgically went over the pictures. Four per page, slid into place without captions. He remembered the scenes vividly like it was only last year. The ski trip to Mont-Tremblant over the reading week. There were ten of them, including Michael and himself sharing a small two-bedroom hotel suite with a bunch of guys and girls.

Going on no sleep and lots of booze, hitting those icy slopes like madmen! He couldn't decide what was better; skiing or the après-skiing. A few shots of Michael and his family at Easter, the spring half marathon.

Then came the graduation pictures. Wow, we looked so young. And handsome! He remembered thinking at the time he looked so much like the Wall Street traders you saw in the movies with his dark suit and slicked-back hair. Now seeing these pictures, he thought he looked like a kid trying to play at being a grown-up. He remembered trying to tame his thick wavy hair to look sleek and serious while Michael had that hungry serious look, without even trying.

Michael in his tux beamed on graduation day. He protested when his father passed it over to him as he thought it was overkill. Michael tried to refuse, and when that didn't work, he tried telling his father he would just try it on. On seeing his son, Michael's father's eyes welled up with tears and he told him how proud he was. Michael was the first Babic to have graduated from university. Michael wanted to make his father proud, and do the right thing for the family, including the relatives in the old country, so he wore the tux that must have cost his father a small fortune.

They all looked so radiant, so full of promise and possibilities. It was a heady time with nothing but the future to go out and grab. Jack ran his hands through his hair. He tipped his head back and closed his eyes, drifting further back down memory lane.

Jack's father had a lot of well-placed friends at Queens and Western. He talked about all the great connections one made at university that would set one's path for the future. This pep talk happened at a rare family dinner at a high end established steak house; the requisite talk about university choices done expressly to ensure he didn't actually choose for himself. Jack had very little agency to influence which university he would attend, since his parents were paying his full fare.

In the basement Jack lost track of time and didn't know it was close to 7 am when he heard footsteps overhead. Looking at the album wasn't that bad, but he felt sheepish nonetheless, and didn't want to get caught snooping. He stayed calm and quiet calculating his options as he listened to the sounds of the fridge opening and closing and the coffee maker coming to life. The mundane banality of daily life, so comforting here. He stiffened when he heard Sarah moving towards the back of the house and heading downstairs.

She stepped into the laundry room and tossed a load of baby blankets into the washer. Jack hadn't completely closed the door behind him, so he could see her through the crack in the door. Her hair was beautifully tousled, and she was barefoot. Her dark blue nightgown, flounced just above her knees and had a button-down front. Her breasts looked full and moved freely. It was a simple cotton shift but accentuated her figure. He felt his erection and shifted uncomfortably. He swallowed hard, his mouth dry. She looked around the small room absentmindedly, like she had just remembered something, and then took two steps back towards the guest room. Thankfully he recalled he had closed the bedroom door behind him out of habit. She gently pushed the door open to see the abandoned bed. Going back into the laundry room, she scooped a load of dry towels into the hamper. As she hoisted the basket onto her hip she paused and frowned when she noticed the door leading into the rough side of the basement ajar with the light shining on the other side. She slid the basket back onto the counter and pulled open the door. She felt for the switch, about four feet off the ground on the right, placing only one foot into the rough side. Jack sat flush against the wall. He was in plain view if she took one more step inside. He waited with his eyes closed to appear to be sleeping in case she came in and found him. She felt around, careful not to knock the tools that hung on the pegboard. Her familiarity with the switch saved him. She flipped it off and backed down into the laundry room. Pivoting, she retrieved the basket to make her way up to the fresh coffee.

He let out a deep sigh as he quietly closed the album and carefully returned it to its place. A few breaths later he calmed down. He looked at the grimy windows and momentarily thought about making an exit through the window but remembered his shoes and coat in the foyer closet. While he waited, hoping for some bright idea on getting out of the situation, the water started to run through the pipes. He could hear Paige laughing and water splashing. They were in the bathroom. Sarah was singing to her over the sound of the running water. Rising slowly, he crept out of the furnace room, back to the bedroom, and slid on his discarded pants that were lying in a heap on the side of the bed away from the door. Tiptoeing upstairs, he paused to continue listening, before he paused to look out the back window. He was thankful for the new snowfall last night that covered his footsteps. No movement on the main floor and the water still ran. Stealthily crossing through the family room down the galley kitchen, he silently opened the hall closet, retrieved his shoes and slung his coat over his arm. He slipped out and gently closed the door.

Back upstairs, humming contentedly, Sarah smiled at Paige sitting excitedly in her bath chair suction cupped to the bathtub floor. She dropped to her knees and leaned over to bathe her baby girl. A sudden chill made her shiver as cold air crept into the room. She leaned over, assuming it was just her drafty old house, and shoved the door completely closed and went back to giving Paige her full attention. Sarah dumped a few Colorful fish and rings in the water. She had started reading the Dr. Seuss series to Paige a few months ago, since it had been her favorite as a child. She was surprised at how interested Paige was, even though she knew it was too early for any real understanding. Sarah figured the cadence of the rhyming words must be a part of the appeal.

By heart Sarah recited, "Red fish... Blue fish... Old fish... New fish..."

CHAPTER 13

The round of Christmas parties was tough on Jack. Everywhere he looked there seemed to be some smiling new family. Rachel's company party included lots of wives and kids Rachel never talked about, and likely never saw. Feeling generous after such a good year, Goldman threw a big bash, renting out a party place with laser tag, mini putt, bumper cars etc., all under one roof. Kids of all ages loved it. The new parents patiently held little hands while guiding their young ones through the activities. Bigger kids howled while revving full speed into their dads' bumper cars. Wives mostly sipped white wine and chatted in the dining area where the noise was more muted but loud enough to allow them to gossip about their husbands. They were experts at holding a baby in one arm while sipping wine with the other and keeping a keen eye on their toddlers ready to escape into the forbidden laser tag area.

"I told Frank, just tell them you're worth it! I'm not giving up my husband every Saturday and taking on the extra work for the good of my health, you know!" chirped Mandy. "Get that raise you deserve".

Without missing a beat, she bellowed, "Stop right there, young lady!" to a pudgy three-year-old making a run for it. Little Gracie froze in her tracks.

"If I have to tell you again, there will be no visit to Santa today," Mandy threatened which promptly brought a floodgate of tears and snot. Sighing loudly, Mandy droned, "Okay, okay, enough with the drama already, go play with those dolls." She swept her now empty glass towards the dollhouse in the corner of the room. "Where the hell are those baby-sitters, they promised us?" she hollered to anyone willing to listen.

Rachel mostly commiserated with her team at the bar laughing at their insider jokes. She tried to pull Jack in, but it was too much effort on both their parts to bother, and she gladly let him wander off.

"To the victors go the spoils," they toasted, knocking back scotch and champagne. "And here's to all our supportive wives, and husbands," snorted Mitchell just loud enough for Jack to hear.

The party circuit with their friends and family wasn't much better.

Larry and Alison hosted an afternoon open house mid-December. They had Sky a year earlier and the secure triangular base of their new family status was obnoxious as far as Jack was concerned. Although Sky was a healthy twenty pounds, Alison wore him like a third appendage in a sling strapped across her chest nestled on her hip.

The din of topics like parenting philosophies and feeding schedules replaced the now passé subject of the newest health club trend or the latest restaurant opening. Toddlers belonging to other young parents were left to run amuck, bashing into furniture and Christmas decorations, much to the amusement of their parents. Michael and Sarah were happily engaged with a few other couples and discussing the merits of all-inclusive family vacations. Once derided as the antithesis of adventure travel, these young families were now extolling the virtues of the babysitting clubs, the casual twenty-four-hour buffets, and the cleanliness and security of the resorts.

"Please, just shoot me now," Rachel chided, sidling up to Jack with fresh drinks in hand. "They are so full of themselves. You'd think they were the first generation ever to have procreated."

She took a long drink of her vodka and cranberry cocktail. Jack agreed and tightened his grip on Rachel's lovely slim waist. After a couple of cool weeks between them after the debacle of their failed dinner celebration, they made up in time to enjoy the holiday season.

"We'll never be like that, sweetie," Jack said tenderly. "We won't cave to conventionality. I don't see why we can't keep up our lifestyle and do interesting things just because we have kids."

Rachel gave Jack a sweet smile which he found a little hard to read. They held each other's gaze for a few seconds before being interrupted by a shout from a messy-looking blond across the room, "Hey, Rachel! Is that Rachel Madison?"

"Oh my God!" shouted Rachel, pulling away from Jack. "Melanie Meyers—I don't believe it," she gushed crossing the floor. The two women quickly embraced and then pulled back to take each other in.

"What the hell are you doing in town?" asked Rachel. "And at this party?" she added more incredulously. They wandered off to the back of the house where Jack saw Melanie pulling out a pack of cigarettes as they disappeared laughing out the back door to the patio. He knew Rachel only smoked occasionally at parties, but he still didn't like it.

Feeling adrift, Jack looked around and thankfully found Brett with a few band buddies. He sauntered over and Brett gave him a big bear hug greeting,

"Hey, man, what's shaking? How many of these rug rats are yours?"

"None that I'm owning up to," laughed Jack, raising his beer for a toast. "How's life been? I haven't heard much from you lately."

"Oh, you know, I've been busy with The Dunes playing the bar circuit across the province. We're not exactly getting discovered, but it pays the bills, and Christy doesn't mind the lifestyle, at least she doesn't yet," he added with a smile.

Christy and Brett were an item for almost two years now. Christy was a booking agent Brett was lucky enough to have been set up with by another guitarist. Christy was well known in the entertainment industry, and she was indifferent to the trappings of the upper-middle-class lifestyle desired by many of her university-educated friends. She had a degree in classical music but preferred pop and rock, and the nightlife scene that came with it. With a natural talent for business, she was an entrepreneur at heart and had established a thriving booking business. Doc Martens and Lee jeans were enough of a signature brand for Christy.

"There's my little buttercup now," Brett hoarsely called out towards Christy as she gathered a plate of goodies and a glass of eggnog. As she turned towards them it was her stomach that greeted them first.

"Holy shit! When the hell did that happen?" Jack asked while combing his hands through his hair.

Brett let out a good laugh, "You'd better ask her. I have yet to get a straight answer."

"Hi Jack. How have you been?" Christy asked while leaning in to give Jack a kiss on his cheek, careful not to press her swollen body against him.

"Great, just great!" he said a little too loudly. "Rachel and I are living the high life, footloose and fancy free!"

"So, no kids yet I guess?" Christy asked while caressing her belly with slow circular passes.

"No, why rush it? Rachel is doing amazingly well with Goldman Sachs and is set to make senior partner within a couple of years. And my gig with Boston Consulting is terrific. Never a dull moment in the M&A business." He beamed, rocking back and forth confidently on his feet.

"Good for you guys," Christy said. "We hadn't really planned this family thing," she smiled sheepishly at Brett. "He never was a very thorough packer. All it took was one crazy night of messing around without a condom after a long night of playing to a packed house and voilà! This little bun is almost done cooking. Should be popping out in February."

Christy still managed to look cool dressed all in black sporting her signature boots and sassy short hair.

"That's great, Christy, I'm really happy for both of you," Jack said and clamped a strong hand on Brett's shoulder.

Jack felt a wave of jealousy roll over him. They didn't even plan on having a kid! How is that fair? The cacophony of partyers seemed particularly loud, and he felt the room begin to swim when Brett broke through, "Hey buddy, are you feeling all right? Do you want to step outside for some air?"

Jack regained his composure. "I'm fine, thanks. Just a few too many of these pops," he grinned. "I'm going to check on Rachel. Maybe we'll see you over New Year's?" he lied as he turned away not waiting for an answer.

He had to drag away Rachel, who was having a great time getting re-acquainted with party girl Melanie. They said a few hasty good-byes and moved quickly to escape the biting cold. After covering a couple of blocks they hailed a cab, leaving their car at the party. Rachel slid across the seat and her sheer hose caught on the rough upholstery.

"Damn it, these are expensive," she said, fingering the damage with her gloved hand. She clutched her short leather jacket across her chest, shivering to shake off the cold.

Jack piled in beside her, "Sixty-three Brentcliff Drive."

"Wow, Melanie looks amazing, doesn't she? Did you know—" Jack cut her off with a deep kiss while holding her head in his hands. She barely had time to come up for air when he went at her again, this time more insistently pulling her body into his.

"Jack, you're crazy!" Rachel teased, enjoying the attention. She placed her gloved hand midway up Jack's thigh while sneaking a look out of the corner of her eye at the driver's rearview mirror. She caught the driver discreetly glancing back then slowly shifting his gaze out the back window. Rachel slid her hand higher. Jack leaned back, grabbed Rachel's waist, and easily hoisted her over his lap with her legs straddling him.

"Jack—are you nuts?" Rachel laughed while trying to push off of him, but he held her fast. Her knees pushed into the back seat. After a few futile attempts, she exhaled, giving in to her pleasure and deeply kissed him while letting his hands roam up the back of her legs. He playfully found the tear in her hose exposing her smooth bare skin. He worked his hands up and down her upper thighs and then forcefully cupped her backside. His erection pressed insistently against his pants. Her hair fell across his face. The drinks at the party loosened any inhibitions they may have typically harbored. Pushing her back upright, he slowly unbuttoned her blouse to take in the erotic sight of her breasts, barely contained in her demi-cup black lace bra. With one pull he released them from their flimsy hold and her hard nipples spilled over the top. He greedily took them in his mouth and tugged on them to heighten her desire. His hands groped under her skirt and through her torn hose to reach the top of her bare buttocks. The lacy thong left her cheeks exposed and barely covered her privates. She moaned as he continued to roam over her body. He cupped one side of her bottom with one hand while working his fingers to her crotch, stroking the silky stand of underwear now soaking wet. He easily pulled it aside.

Lost in her ecstasy, she arched her back and totally forgot about the driver-spectator. She was bare from the waist down and open to her husband. He enjoyed playing with her and making her squirm. His fingers plunged deeply into her, only to pull out again, leaving her begging for more as he massaged her engorged clitoris. Finally, unable to hold out any longer, he unzipped his pants and entered her easily. She gasped and groaned with pleasure. They immediately were at the edge. With a few final gyrations Rachel threw her head back and called out as she came. Her spent body collapsed into his. He was right behind her shuddering as he released.

They both laughed and moved to cover up as much as possible as Rachel bounced back to her seat. The cab driver, who had been circling the block for the past ten minutes, pulled to a stop in front of their house. Rachel grabbed her purse and bolted to the front door covering her mouth to suppress her laughter. Jack didn't look the driver in the eye as he pressed two twenties into his hand for a twenty-five-dollar fare, snatched up Rachel's heels, and made a hasty getaway.

The next morning Rachel woke up feeling happy. The party was good fun, especially seeing some old friends. The holidays were almost here, which would be a nice break, even if it was only for a couple of days. A new pitch was lined up for early January. And of course, there was the X-rated scenario in the cab last night. She smiled, replaying their rendezvous, as she poured fresh water into the coffee maker.

Humming, *You better watch out, You better not shout*, she passed their calendar on the side of the kitchen pantry as she reached for the coffee grounds. Even though they both lived through their phones, they still marked important dates on a paper calendar that was full of December festivities and obligations. Jack, with his fixation on getting pregnant, had marked the beginning of each of her cycles in red so they would know her optimum ovulation time. She stopped short when she realized last night was day thirteen of the month. Oh my God. Did he orchestrate last night based on my cycle?

She finished with the coffee, pressing the button to start the process of fresh brewing. She walked down the hall lightly and peeked in to be sure Jack was still asleep. Upon confirming he was, she slipped into the bathroom and closed the door. Opening the lowest drawer, she reached in the back and pulled out an old, quilted make-up bag. She opened the rusty zipper and rummaged around the expired foundation bottles and out-of-date eye shadows until she found an unmarked bottle of pills. She twisted the top and shook out a loose white tablet. The Plan B pill went down easily. She was lucky that she didn't experience any of the side effects that some women got such as nausea or vomiting with these types of morning-after pills. She had only popped a couple of these over the past year when their timing had been especially close to the mid-point in her cycle. Luckily, they were available over the counter so Jack wouldn't be able to trace them through their drug plan. She knew Jack would be furious if he found out. He refused to accept her point of view of wanting to wait a while to start a family. She determined this was better than fighting over it and rationalized it by telling herself she wasn't planning on delaying things much longer. As soon as her senior partnership was secure, she would be ready.

CHAPTER 14

Rachel pushed off the fertility visit one last time before finally promising to go to the appointment in April. Best Start was in a gleaming office tower in the heart of downtown. From the parking garage, the sterile elevator whisked them up to the thirty-second floor. The foyer was tiled in a gray-blue marble and a sleek silver desk with Best Start in bright green lettering greeting them twenty feet away.

"How are you today, sir?" sung a sunny twenty-something-year-old receptionist with *Cindy* etched in silver across her name plate pinned to her blazer.

"We're here to see Dr. Jordan. Jack McDermott and Rachel Madison for ten o'clock," Jack said with a tight smile.

Cindy looked at her screen and confirmed the appointment, "Of course, Mr. McDermott." She pulled two clipboards from her tray and passed them over. "Please fill out these forms and the doctor will see you shortly."

Rachel had taken a seat and was checking her phone.

"Rachel, could you put that damn phone down for a change and concentrate on why we are here?"

"Yeah, yeah, sure, Jack," Rachel said in slow motion as she quickly checked a couple more messages before tucking it into her purse.

In the space for the number of pregnancies Jack put a zero. Another zero for the next box asking for number of live births. "Ouch, that's got to hurt," Rachel said casually.

After a few minutes they both finished and slid the clipboards back to Cindy. Low soft rock played over the speakers. The waiting room was beautifully furnished with sleek white leather chairs and modern green and blue carpeting. An oversized glass urn with calla lilies stood in a corner. A panel of crushed glass ran ceiling to floor with water trickling down in a continuous cycle. A single dispenser brewing machine provided different types of herbal tea. Rachel sauntered over to help herself to pass the time. Nearby was a bulletin board covered in baby pictures with notes from ecstatic couples holding tiny new parcels with scrunched-up faces peeking out from blue and pink blankets.

Thank-you, Dr. Jordan, you've made our lives complete.

Dr. Jordan, you're a miracle worker—God bless you. You're a lifesaver! Lots of love, Dave, Marsha and baby Sasha.

Rachel still thought they were jumping the gun. It had only been two years, and she thwarted a couple of attempts that may have worked out, so they really hadn't been at it all that long.

A young couple looked almost giddy and held hands tightly as they waited and shared intimate whispering. So hopeful and happy.

An older man flipped through a magazine while a younger wife stared off into space looking tired and disappointed. They were seated in a different area where a sign said Ultrasound Screening. There were several women waiting in the same area. One sat wringing her hands quietly crying. Another stared straight ahead seemingly in a trance.

New couples emerged in various states of expectation or stress from the dinging elevator.

"Mr. McDermott and Ms. Madison, you may go in now, the first door on your right," Cindy said with her blazing white smile while motioning them down the hall.

Jack let Rachel lead. An enthusiastic Dr. Jordan rose from behind his desk, pulling off his reading glasses and loudly introducing himself with a firm handshake and ready grin. "Very pleased to meet you both. May I call you Jack and Rachel?"

"Of course," Jack replied.

Dr. Jordan was in his mid-fifties with a full head of wavy dark hair and a healthy tan for early April. Rachel immediately registered, fake and fake. A beautiful photograph of a golf course hung on the wall. He was sporting a crisp white shirt, an expensive-looking tie, and a lab coat. His hands were perfectly manicured.

"So pleased to meet you both, Jack and Rachel. Please, have a seat."

Dr. Jordan's office had the feel of a sleek advertising agency instead of a medical office. His desk was a distressed dark wood supported by iron legs. The chairs were molded plastic. The only giveaway of the real business being transacted were the reproductive posters on the walls.

Dr. Jordan took a cursory glance at the medical reports they completed. He glanced up over his glasses, "So you're here to make a baby! You've come to the right place. It looks like you've been trying for almost two years. No birth control at all during this period?"

"No," replied Jack.

Rachel stared mutely at Dr. Jordan.

"And I assume you brought your ovulation tracking and temperature charts?" he asked evenly, reading them for a well-educated couple that would have tried the basic steps to help with conception before coming to a clinic.

Jack burned at the thought of the unopened kit Rachel had claimed she would get into eventually. "I'm sorry, Doctor, but we haven't been very proactive," Jack said while directing a stern glance at Rachel.

"No problem," he said, jotting some notes in their new file folder. "We'll be conducting our own ovarian function tests and hormone tests."

Rachel looked pleased.

"Do you find your menstrual cycles to be regular?" he asked, finally engaging Rachel.

"Yes, every twenty-eight days and they last about five days."

"Okay, good. And when was your last period?"

Rachel thought for a moment. "About a week ago."

"All right. This will be good timing for you to start tracking your ovulation. You'll need to chart your temperature every morning before rising from bed and check your mucus level. You'll be watching for changes in its consistency. At the time of ovulation your mucus becomes more abundant, clear, and stretchy. Like an egg yolk. You simply swipe yourself with your bare middle finger and stretch the mucus between your thumb and middle finger— like this," he said as he pumped his appendages like he was keeping a beat.

"Oh goody, I can't wait," Rachel said with an eye roll.

"I can help," Jack added playfully. Rachel ignored him.

Dr. Jordan passed over a trifold temperature chart. He continued asking questions about their medical history, which was uneventful. He asked about their lifestyle. Rachel told him about her heavy workload, boasted about her personal fitness, and said she ate quite well.

"How about drinking? How may drinks would you have in a week?"

"It depends. A couple of times a week I may have a few glasses of wine, maybe some scotch," Rachel replied in a matter-of-fact tone.

"Please define a few. More than five drinks a week?" Dr. Jordan pressed, clicking his pen at the ready.

When Rachel paused, he pushed, "More than ten?"

"Not ten," she replied firmly. "Only if I'm having a particularly tough week," she laughed. He didn't join her.

"Smoking?"

"Not really. Maybe the odd one at a party," she said, shifting in her seat. She looked at Jack with a *can you believe this* look only to be met with a harsh return.

"Can you explain your current and past sexual practices?" he asked.

"I'd say we have a good and active sex life with intercourse a couple of time a week," Jack answered with authority. "Sometimes Rachel's work has her travelling which obviously doesn't help with the process."

Oh great, now it's a process, thought Rachel. How romantic.

Dr. Jordan, apparently feeling the tension, took control, "All right, first we'll do some physical and medical tests to rule out any complications. We'll need to take your blood samples, get a semen sample, and we'll also perform a pelvic exam on Rachel. Once we have the results of these initial tests we can talk about the next steps."

"Sounds good to me," Jack answered with enthusiasm, rubbing his hands together. "I'm so glad we're finally taking some action."

"Can you give us a rundown on the costs of the various treatments?" Rachel asked, surprising Jack. He hadn't thought about the expense yet.

"There are so many options it's difficult to be specific until we know what we're dealing with," Dr. Jordon replied with a serious look meant to shut down this line of questioning. "Have you had an internal ultrasound before?"

"I'm afraid I've not had the pleasure," Rachel replied with a deadpan expression.

"I'll admit, this part of things does seem a bit unfair." Dr. Jordan sympathized. He handed Jack a specimen bottle after writing Jack's name, date of birth, and the date. "If you'll both come with me, we'll escort Jack to the specimen gathering room. Jack, there is an assortment of magazines to help if need be. We also have movies; the remote is beside the TV."

"Hey, you've got to love this," Jack joked a little too playfully, holding up a Playboy magazine. "I haven't seen one of these since high school days!"

Dr. Jordan played along neutrally to be sensitive to Rachel. He knew this first bubble of excitement most couples felt. The elation that came from finally doing something to make what they wanted so desperately a reality. Most people came in optimistically assuming they'd be in the successful thirty percent group. It was a bit unusual to feel it more from the man than the woman, as was the case between Rachel and Jack.

"Take your time," he said and pulled the door closed.

"Rachel, please come this way," Dr. Jordan said quietly as he led her into an examining room. "Please get undressed from the waist down and put on this gown and I'll be back in a few minutes."

Rachel glanced at the heavy machine near the table; all so clinical right from the get-go. She supposed it was to be expected. Dr. Jordan came back after a few minutes, entering with a polite tap on the door. Snapping on white rubbers gloves he helped place Rachel's bare feet in the stirrups, supporting her ankles.

"Scoot your bottom down a little lower," he requested. After she slid down a bit he added, "A little more if you don't mind."

She did mind. Big time. What had she gotten herself into? Some slick, rich, smarmy doctor, giving her orders to strip down and scoot. It was all so debasing.

"All right, Rachel." he said in his professional voice, "Let's have a feel."

He inserted a couple of fingers deep into her vagina while pressing down with his other hand on her lower abdomen. He shifted his pressure from one side to the other, explaining he was checking her ovaries.

"Does this hurt at all?"

"What do you think?" Rachel snapped.

"I'm sorry, and I know this is difficult, but try to remember it's all towards a greater goal."

Rachel turned her head to one side and stared at the blank wall.

Extracting his hand he said, "Okay, Rachel, stay put and I'll take a swab for the Pap test." He ran the steel speculum under warm water. "We need to take a sample of cells from your cervix."

Rachel felt the speculum expand with the whirling sound of the screw. "I've had a Pap test before you know."

"Of course," Dr. Jordan responded.

Approaching with a long Q-tip he explained, "This may hurt a little," and she felt a brusque jab deep within her body. She inhaled sharply.

"Well done," he said as he unscrewed the clamp and slid it out of her vagina.

Snapping off the gloves he proceeded to perform a breast exam with small circular pressure around each nipple, then did more probing inside her arm pits. Gentle pressure on her neck was done to check her thyroid.

"I think you've had enough for one day," Dr. Jordan said. "We'll save that ultrasound for your next visit."

"Oh goody," Rachel replied.

"I'll leave you to get dressed."

Rachel was thankful he didn't need to do an internal ultrasound. She was raw and worked over and this was only the initial visit. Keep them wanting more, she thought sarcastically as she pulled on her dress pants. After touching up her make-up and combing her hair, she emerged and found her way back to Dr. Jordan waiting for them in his office.

Jack looked relaxed and pleased with himself.

Rachel sat down. Her body language with her arms and legs crossed didn't do much to hide her feelings.

"Almost done. Last thing we need to do today is take a couple vials of blood," the doctor concluded.

After depositing them in the lab area, he warmly shook both their hands and told them he looked forward to sharing the results at their next meeting that Cindy would schedule on their way out. Rachel was not won over with his phony double-palmed handshake and deep eye contact. She knew a good salesman when she saw one.

"Thank you so much," Jack gushed like a schoolgirl. "We'll be looking forward to it."

Five vials apiece later, they stood in front of Cindy, who blinded them again with her perfect orthodontic smile.

"How does Wednesday, May fifteenth sound? That's three weeks from now."

"Great," replied Jack. "Rachel, is that fine with you?"

"Sure," she answered after checking her calendar.

"Super! So that will be three hundred fifty dollars for the consultation and four hundred fifty for the testing for a total of eight hundred dollars. Debit or credit?"

CHAPTER 15

The spring weather brought out the best in everyone. Patio chairs appeared outside of cafés and restaurants. Hearty patrons, oblivious to the chilly temperatures, enjoyed taking coffee and lunches outdoors again. For the first time in six months, bare legs and arms were visible on the streets. Strangers smiled and said hello. The last dirty dregs of snow clung only to north-facing gardens. Dogs and bikes proliferated. The early buds on shrubs, and the beauty and timelessness of spring bulbs; daffodils, tulips, and hyacinth popping up across the city contributed to the general air of optimism.

"We're so glad you guys could make it!" Michael said as he greeted Jack and Rachel at their front door.

"Are you kidding? We never see enough of you, with all your travels and Paige in the mix," Jack responded.

They made their way through the house and out to the deck in the back. Michael invited them, with a few other friends, for a casual BBQ. Draft and Chardonnay were on ice in the shiny red drinks bucket, and the grill smoked, waiting for the steak stacked on the platter. The table was set with a yellow Provence tablecloth and fresh spring flowers in a sky-blue glass vase.

"Wow—everything looks amazing!" Rachel said. "It's so great to be outside again."

Sarah trailed behind them with fresh salads and a plate of cheese and crackers. "Tell me about it! To be able to plop Paige in her stroller and head out for errands without having to struggle with snow suits and blankets is a real treat."

She poured a glass of wine that she passed to Rachel and the boys helped themselves to beer. Sarah poured herself a glass of sparkling water.

"Where is the little princess?" asked Rachel.

"Nap time," said Sarah and they all clinked glasses.

"So how's work been, Jack?" asked Michael.

"We've been super busy working with a telecommunications giant hell bent on eliminating the competition by buying them all. The usual 'I needed that yesterday' climate prevails," Jack said with a shrug. After working in the field for almost eight years, Jack was hardened to the demands and didn't buckle and bend like he used to do to satisfy his clients' needs.

Michael wondered if that was one reason Jack hadn't climbed as high and fast as some of their friends in the same type of business. It was one thing to stand up for yourself, and another to come across as arrogant, and above complying with client requests.

Michael was glad he left the cut-throat business of consulting a few years ago to join a start-up specializing in wireless networking. At first the money was bad and the hours ruthless. But knowing he owned a real piece of the business, along with the other three partners, infused the company with amazing energy. Everyone was under thirty-five, brilliant, and excited about the technology. The fact that they could all end up very rich didn't hurt. The government grants and venture capitalists kept them afloat for the first two years. Selling their first product to Sony catapulted them into the tech world spotlight, and they were now being courted by the tech giants that dominated the sector. It was tempting to sell given the lucrative deals they were presented with by Samsung, then Microsoft. But they were confident by holding out, and moving the development to the next level, they would be that much more desirable. The Apple meeting couldn't be far off.

"How about that crazy start-up you've disappeared into for the past little while? Anything actually getting sold?" Jack joked.

"We're doing our best," Michael said. "Things look really good and we're moving into phase two on the development this fall."

Jack raised his bottle with fake enthusiasm, barely masking his jealousy, "Here's to phase two."

"Speaking of phase two..." Michael paused for dramatic effect.

Sarah rolled her eyes and smiled sweetly at her husband, "It could have waited until dessert, you know."

"You have something to share with the class?" teased Rachel, affectionately draping an arm around Sarah.

"We're expecting—again!" bubbled Sarah. "Wild, eh?"

"That's fantastic, Sarah!" Rachel enthused, as she gave her a full embrace. "So soon after Paige. Isn't she just two? Are you sure you know what you're doing?" Rachel added while looking for signs of a belly.

"No," laughed Sarah. "We honestly didn't think it would happen as soon as it did. So much for the theory that you can't get pregnant while you're breastfeeding."

"Even with your travel schedule, you still managed to get her knocked up?" Jack said. "Way to go, my friend." He gave Michael a hearty handshake.

He moved over to Sarah and pulled her in close for a hug.

"I'm really happy for you, Sarah," he said with his mouth almost touching her ear. Sarah tried to pull away, but Jack held her a few seconds beyond her comfort zone. She shot him an inquisitive look after he released his grip, but he kept turning away to snatch up a couple of cold beers along with the bottle of wine.

"This definitely calls for another round of drinks to celebrate!" shouted Jack.

Michael smiled as he slapped the steaks on the grill. "Enjoy your freedom, my friend," he joked. "I'm sure you're not too far behind."

Jack didn't respond. He and Rachel agreed to keep their fertility doctoring a secret, as a way of not turning their efforts into a sideshow, and to avoid the inevitable well-meaning but hurtful queries as to how it was proceeding. After lunch they got up to clear the table and stretch their legs.

"If you don't have any plans for the long weekend, we were wondering if you'd like to head up north with us?" Michael asked Jack. "We're planning on doing some poking around cottage country. Do some research if we can hopefully buy in a couple of years. Thought we'd book into Algonquin Lodge and line up a day with an agent on Saturday, stay over until Sunday."

"I think we're free," said Jack. "Need to check with the boss, of course." He motioned towards the family room where the two women fawned over Paige, just getting up from her nap.

"Our family cottage was in that general area, you know," mused Jack. "We were on Bruce Lake. Spent a lot of happy summers up there. Gorgeous. Things are quite pricey now though."

"No kidding," Michael agreed. "But no harm in dreaming. I remember you telling me about your folks selling your cottage a few years ago. Too bad you couldn't keep it in the family."

"Too bad is right," said Jack clenching his jaw.

CHAPTER 16

They were back in the sanitized environment of the clinic to receive feedback on their initial tests. It was freezing in the over-air-conditioned office, especially since it was only May.

"Good news," Dr. Jordan said. "Jack's semen volume from his first sample was four milliliters, strongly in the healthy range, recognized as between two to five milliliters."

Jack's chest expanded like a proud peacock.

"We found a concentration of eighty-five million spermatozoa with seventy-five percent alive."

Hearing seventy-five percent alive, Jack appeared a little deflated. Rachel remained neutral. Dr. Jordan noticed they weren't holding hands or sitting close like most couples at these early stages.

Dr. Jordan quickly reassured them, "Seventy-five is the normal number of alive spermatozoa. You've got good swimmers too, Jack; fifty percent were found swimming forward. So, it all looks promising on your side of things, although we will require a total of three samples to ensure consistency and accuracy. Measuring sperm count is a very technical business and results can be affected by many factors, including the length of time between ejaculation and semen sample analysis. A single sample is inadequate to assess semen quality."

Rachel was skeptical. She thought this was all part of the money grab she read about with some clinics.

Dr. Jordan addressed Rachel, "Good news for you as well. Overall, your health is excellent. Your blood work is all normal, Pap was normal, hormones seem to be in good shape."

With no encouragement from Rachel Dr. Jordan pushed on, "How did the tracking go?"

Rachel produced her homework, and he was pleased with the results. "See here how your temperature rose around the twenty-fifth last month? This indicates ovulation. And your mucus?"

"As expected," Rachel replied.

"All right then, we are off to a good start," Dr. Jordan said while rubbing his hands together. She noticed he was sporting a very expensive designer watch.

"We'd like to have Jack provide a second semen sample today and then book you both to come back for a post-coital test. The PCT allows for evaluation of the sperm in the cervical mucus. Jack's sperm must swim through the cervical mucus from the vagina, through the cervix, and into the uterus. If numerous dead or non-motile sperm are seen in the mucus, it can indicate the presence of antibodies leading to male infertility. Basically, it means that some vaginal environments are hostile to the presence of sperm and kill them off. The good news in these types of circumstances is that it isn't a major hindrance to getting pregnant, we can use a method like artificial insemination or IVF to circumnavigate the traditional pathway. We perform the PCT with Jack providing a semen sample, then, insert it into your vagina with a syringe, not unlike a turkey baster, to simulate ejaculation. You are also welcome to have intercourse in one of the clinic's private rooms if you prefer."

Rachel wondered if they would be offered the visual aids for this too or if that was reserved for the men's club.

"After thirty minutes, we'll take a swab of your vaginal mucus and have a look at it in a microscope, to see the activity level of the semen. Since you are close to mid-cycle, next week would be perfect."

"No can do," Rachel said. Looking at Jack she said, "I've got my annual bankers conference in England next week."

"Can't Brian and Tim from your team cover for you? Let some of the younger team step up."

"And leave the most important clients we have in the hands of schoolboys?"

"How does June work with your schedule, Rachel?" Dr. Jordan intercepted. "You're early along in the assessment so waiting another month is no problem at all."

"I guess that will be fine," Rachel replied.

"Perfect. Right this way, Jack, we'll get that sample from you."

"Of course, Doctor, whatever I need to do to help," Jack added a little more loudly than necessary.

CHAPTER 17

Jack was happy testing his BMW handling on the country roads and Rachel was glad to escape the city and their recent doctoring. They all agreed to meet for lunch at the Algonquin Lodge at one o'clock. After grabbing their café lattes, Jack and Rachel hit the highway and within an hour were cruising on back roads.

Rachel enjoyed feeling the wind in her hair and listening to pop country music. The trees were iridescent light green, bursting with new life. Traffic was sparse and they shared the road with GM trucks and minivans. They drove through small towns with candle shops and general stores. Glistening lakes sparkled as they passed, dotted with small fishing boats.

Rachel had never been a big lover of the country, but she did see the appeal of a waterfront vacation property — not a traditional cottage, more like a summer home. She thought she could enjoy it as long as she had a cleaning lady and some nearby restaurants.

The trip north brought back strong memories for Jack with very conflicting feelings. He remembered happily piling into the family's Ford Sierra at the end of June each year escaping the shackles of private school conformity. His father came with them for the initial long weekend of the summer and then went back to the city, returning for most weekends through the rest of the summers during Jack's younger years. His father's visits trailed off during his teen years as his mother checked out mentally more and more. The excitement of packing up always triggered some fighting about what to bring and how to possibly pack it into one vehicle. Miraculously, they managed to cram everything in: clean bedding, gourmet foods, favorite games, golf clubs, bikes on the back rack, etc. The coolers were shoved under their feet, which always brought a chorus of 'It's not my turn. I had the cooler last time!'

There was connectivity, a special bond, that surrounded them like a silent halo. The bickering would die down after an hour or so, and the chatter turned more to what they were going to do over the summer while his parents discussed which projects they might tackle this year. The talk of what needed to get done was as much a ritual as the cottage time itself. The promise of the new projects, long summer days and star-filled nights, languid swims, and fresh fish and burgers on the BBQ put everyone in a good mood. It was partly the anticipation that made it so magical.

Jack couldn't remember a summer without the cottage as a kid. They bought it when he was a baby. When he was young it was a real cottage, a rare find these days. Rough pine floors withstanding fifty years of wear and tear. Three small bedrooms off the main hall, a big open kitchen with a wood-burning stove, a basic living room, and a large screened-in porch. Not only was this where they shared their meals and stories from the day, it also had an oversized couch that was perfect for napping or sleeping. Books were piled up on the floor nearby giving one an excuse to flop down and read, or sleep, or just listen to the stillness of the outdoors. A rough wooden shelf was jammed with cards and classic board games like Monopoly, Scrabble, Trouble, and Cribbage.
The front yard sloped gently down to the water and was a dumping ground for badminton racquets, frisbees, water volleyballs, and towels.

His parents had their designated Muskoka chairs, navy blue for Dad and Coca-Cola red for Mom, with an old-fashioned wooden milk carton serving as a table. They'd contently sip on cocktails late in the afternoon, enjoying adult stories that the kids weren't allowed to hear. They'd absent-mindedly praise the kids for their athletic efforts in the water while flipping through the weekend newspaper that was delivered Saturday mornings by boat. Things were good at the cottage during those early years; for a couple of glorious months the stresses of everyday life were set aside along with their school uniforms and busy extracurricular and social schedules.

But having three kids took a toll on Jack's mother's mental health. She was irritable, anxious, and tired most of the time. Some days she cried inconsolably before slipping into despondency. The bottle was never far away. On particularly bad days she suffered from headaches, numbness, and hyperventilation. Her attitude towards her children was mainly one of ambivalence or disinterest. The doctors diagnosed her with depression and prescribed antidepressants, but she was inconsistent in taking them. Although depression was a known and accepted condition, it wasn't something many people admitted to having or were open to discussing. The marital strain on Jack's parents was more evident every year. Or maybe Jack simply saw more as he matured and understood more about the problems between his parents.

There were a few early teen years when he tried refusing to go to the cottage, to no avail. He was given the option to stay behind to attend Stanford summer school. Some choice that was. More of the same torture I endured the other ten months of the year.

His father only came up now and then and would leave with no warning. His parents came in separate vehicles. Jack had drifted from his sisters, whom he found terribly annoying and obnoxious. They were almost like one person the way they finished each other's sentences, dressed alike, sounded alike, and irritated alike. They were a unit, and whenever Jack tried to get in on their games, they treated him like an outsider. 'Everyone knows three's a crowd,' they'd crow.

"Jack!" yelled Rachel. He looked at her from a faraway place. "Helloooo, I said, you just missed the turn onto Birch Lane."

"Shit. I was thinking about the old days," he mumbled as he pulled a sharp U-turn to get back to the cut-off.

"Well, get your head into today, will you?"

The day was clear and warm as they pulled into the parking lot. They easily hoisted their overnight bags over their shoulders and entered the lobby. Soaring cathedral ceilings with massive beams gave the place a stately rustic feel. Moose and deer heads with impressive antler spans adored the walls. Jack counted the points on one head and found twenty-six tips.

"Wow, now that would be a kill to brag about," Jack said.

Rachel simply shuddered and asked if they could upgrade their room to a suite.

After dumping their bags, they sauntered down to meet up with Michael and Sarah. The restaurant was cozy but almost deserted since it was still early in the season. After warm greetings they enjoyed a delicious lunch of grilled salmon and greens with crisp white wine. Michael declined the waitress's offer of coffee since they were meeting an agent in the lobby at 2:30 pm.

"You guys are welcome to come too, of course," offered Michael.

"We'll pass," Rachel said. "I read they have an amazing hot rocks treatment here. I'm booked for 3 pm. Not to mention the private hot tub," she added, squeezing Jack's leg under the table.

"Sounds like more fun that what we'll be having," laughed Sarah. "Come on, Michael, let's not hold up these two love birds."

Sarah was secretly glad they'd have the afternoon to themselves. Sarah's parents had taken Paige for the weekend, and she was looking forward to spending some time with just Michael. She'd found Jack a little unsettling at their last get-together and didn't want to be too chummy with him. She hadn't ever told Michael about Jack sleeping over and after a while it seemed weird to bring it up. She assumed Jack would tell Michael, but Michael never mentioned it.

After Rachel made her way to the spa, Jack pulled on his hiking boots and asked at the desk about nearby trails.

"There's quite a few to choose from," said a burly man, pointing at a topography map. "You can do some easy trails anywhere from two to four kilometers, or if you feel like a challenge, there's a great ten-kilometer loop. It's hilly in places and it gets quite remote going deep into the woods. You'll get a real taste of God's country."

"God's country it is then!"

The air felt crisp and clean as he trudged along the path. Sunlight dappled through the canopy overhead. Maples, birch, oak, and pine trees towered overhead, each one craning for the opening to reap the benefit of the sun. The ground was damp with the odd patch of snow clinging to the earth. Jack was content taking in the fresh air, the scent of the forest, and unencumbered by the noise and pace of the city.

He stopped just short of a massive spider web glistening with dew and paused to appreciate the beauty of its fascinating design. A few flies and a bug awaited the spider's appetite to finish them off for good. A small yellow beetle wrestled madly to extricate itself from the sticky trap. The ugly spider paid no attention as it single-mindedly worked on expanding its lair. Its dark hairy legs worked furiously fast and seemed oblivious to its own threat with the presence of a human. Jack was mesmerized at the beetle's basic struggle for life and felt a little sorry for it. But he was more impressed at the determination and survival skills of the spider and admired its handiwork. Gingerly stepping around the web to not disturb nature's work, he hiked further along the path.

His mind wandered back to his cottage days again. Being alone in the woods transported him back to his exploring days and he smiled at his self-determination as a kid. Hearing some rustling off the path he recalled the thrill of trapping and killing small animals. After his first conquest of the rabbit, it became a regular part of his excursions. He always carried his Swiss Army knife, wire, and rope for setting traps plus some rags and water to wash off the blood and guts. And matches to light the fire he used for cooking.

Initially he only killed what he could eat that day. He wasn't particular about what it was; rabbit was good, but he also trapped and ate squirrel, mongoose, and hedgehogs. He took pride in the humane way he quickly killed his catch. He knew other boys got a thrill harming or even torturing animals, but that wasn't his thing. His thrill was in the chase and the conquest.

The oppressive nature of his private school environment didn't provide any room for self-direction during the school year, so these excursions provided a method of exerting control. His father was so overbearing, Jack felt crippled when presented with any decision-making situation.

During his young years, he was angry his mother didn't care about his whereabouts. But this feeling wore off with the realization this gave him freedom to roam freely, alone, and he could fantasize about his adventurous alter ego. He secretly went to the library to learn how to set snares and hunt. He looked for natural funnels or pathways indicating an animal's travel route. Areas near water proved to be fertile hunting grounds. He would make a small noose with wire then secure it to a tree trunk with some rope and set the noose in the pathway. He was careful to mask his scent by rubbing leaves or animal dung on his hands when setting the trap. He got very good at being patient and waiting. More days than not he was happily rewarded with some animal blindly scurrying into his trap. He would pounce on the creature as it struggled, panicking to get free. With his knife at the ready he would deftly put an end to the fight.

Jack was so caught up reminiscing he couldn't believe he was coming to an opening at the end of the trail. He'd finished the whole loop in less than two hours. He was sad to leave the forest and his childhood memories behind. They felt so vivid, his adventures so real. He scoffed at the hyper-protectiveness around kids these days. The idea of kid going into the woods alone for a whole day was unthinkable now for most people.

He crossed over the gravel road and made his way back to their suite. He found Rachel resting peacefully in a terry cloth robe under a duvet. A wood fire crackled. Curling up behind her, he nuzzled his stubble into her neck.

"Who is it?" sang Rachel.

"Who do you want it to be?"

"Let's see now, give me a minute," she replied as she shifted her robe.

"Have you forgotten about the massage you ordered, Ms. Madison?" Jack said in a curt French accent.

"Oh good, my massage. I thought you'd forgotten my appointment, Stephan."

"We Swiss are very punctual, Ms. Madison. We had better get on with it before your husband returns."

They woke from their deep, post-sex slumber at seven, showered, and went down to the bar. Michael and Sarah looked very happy holding hands while going over numerous real estate sheets on the table.

"Hey, you two, how was the afternoon?" Sarah asked.

"Wonderful," said Rachel. "I could get used to this country life." She shook her long damp hair with her fingers.

"Not that she saw the light of day," joked Jack. "At least I got out on the trails for a couple of hours."

He signaled the bartender and ordered a bottle of wine.

"Good for you," said Michael. "God, I just love it up here! We had a great afternoon with Donny and Claire, they showed us some great properties. I can't believe how lucky you were to grow up with this every summer, Jack."

"Did you see anything you'd consider?" asked Rachel, leaning in to look at the glossy pamphlets.

"Not really, not yet. I mean look at these places. Four bedrooms with a dishwasher—only four hundred fifty thousand!" He passed Jack a listing. "There is this one at five twenty-nine—a real bargain. It's crazy! I guess they missed the part where I told them we wanted a cottage, not a compound."

"It was beautiful to see the lakes and get a handle on what's up here," Sarah said. "I'd love to be able to come up here with Paige, I mean the kids," she corrected with a shy smile, looking down at her tummy. "To get out of the city in the summer; I think we'd love everything cottage life has to offer: the swimming and boating, hiking, campfires..."

"The repairs, bugs, traffic, freezing water," Rachel cut in.

Sarah snuck a look at Michael that Jack didn't miss. It was only a second but he caught the *she better not ruin my weekend* look.

"Anyways, we won't be able to buy for a while. With baby number two on the way, we'll need to watch our spending," Sarah added, gaining the upper hand.

"Well, I'm famished!" exclaimed Rachel. "What smells so good?"

After dinner the two couples retreated to the massive bonfire pit in the courtyard. Comfortable low chairs let them settle in with their heads tipped skyward to watch the night sky and the carpet of stars come out. They cradled fine brandy in snifter glasses and Sarah had herbal tea. The cicadas hummed in the background, the water lapped the shore, and the birch logs sent sparks flying. Their waiter appeared with marshmallows and fancy skewers.

Jack laughed as he waved away the skewer, looking at it with disdain.

"That's for city slickers. Real men find their own skewers."

He hopped up and returned after a few minutes with some long thin sticks.

After only a few minutes Sarah yawned loudly, "I'm sorry, but I've had it for the day, my friends."

"Are you sure?" said Rachel.

"Sad but true. Come on, Michael. You'd better come with me to keep me safe from the wild animals up here."

"Here but to serve, my dear," Michael replied in a deep voice and hoisted himself up from his chair. "Maybe we'll see you guys at breakfast. Have a great night."

Jack and Rachel sipped on their drinks. Jack pointed out many constellations and Rachel was only mildly impressed. Astronomy was never her thing.

"So how about it, Rach?" Jack asked. "Wouldn't it be great to have a place of our own up here?"

"This weekend is lovely," Rachel replied, gently squeezing his hand. "But you know it takes a lot of time and energy to keep two places. Not to mention the money."

She went to take a long pull on her drink, but Jack intercepted and pried it from her hands. "Sweetie, I think that's enough for one day."

Rachel's face clouded over at the reference to her lifestyle choices, as Dr. Jordan liked to refer to all his kill-joy advice. She really didn't want to get into any of this tonight.

"I'm pretty tired too; must be the fresh air. I'm going to turn in."

Jack went to follow, but Rachel turned and stopped him, placing an open palm on his chest. "I know how much you love it outdoors so why don't you stay here for a while and enjoy the solitude."

He wasn't sure if he imagined the emphasis she put on the word solitude, but given her brisk departure, he was pretty sure he got it right. Feeling restless at this quick ending to what he thought was going to be a fun night, he paced the grounds. He walked down to the water's edge and stared at the inky darkness that stretched as far as he could see. Across the bay he could make out the jagged edge of the tree line. A dog or perhaps a wolf howled in the distance and a cold wind kicked up. It was only spring, and the nights still dropped near freezing.

Shuddering, he pulled his plaid jacket closed and turned to face the lodge. There weren't many lights on with so few visitors. A couple of rooms were illuminated on the second floor. He knew their suite was the corner unit on the main floor with the TV flickering and the blinds closed. A faint light was coming from the other end of the hall on the main hall. He thought it must be Michael's room as he knew they were on the same floor. Not wanting to go inside yet, he walked up the grassy hill to the exterior of the lodge, closer to Michael's room. The light flickered. Candlelight, he guessed. How romantic. Nice to think married couples with kids still thought of creating a mood.

He took care to crouch while approaching the wall between the candlelit room and the dark room on the other side. Michael's window was ajar and the blinds partially up. He could smell wood burning and remembered their own fireplace. He leaned back and gazed at the sky. He strained to hear something. His senses were on high alert; like being back in the woods, back to being ten years old out for an adventure. He stepped towards the window and squatted low. He heard giggling from inside. He waited. He was good at waiting. The giggles turned into low moans.

"Oh, Michael," he heard through Sarah's shallow breathing. "You do know I love you."

Jack slowly gripped the edge of the windowsill and pulled himself up, just enough to peer inside from the bottom of the window. The orangey/red glow from the fireplace threw a beautiful warm light on Sarah's bare back. The covers were askew and the duvet was tossed to the floor. Her wavy hair spilled down her back. She rocked gently on top of Michael while he gripped her hips. Jack was transfixed. A bead of sweat was trickling down her spine, pooling just at the crevice at the top of her behind. He saw the tempting roundness of the side of her breast.

"Baby, you're so beautiful," Michael said.

"Faster, faster," Sarah panted with desperation. "I'm so close."

Michael's eyes were filled with desire watching his wife.

Suddenly the fire popped with a loud crack, causing Sarah's head to whip around. She screamed and fell low beside Michael. "Oh my God!"

"Sarah—what is it? What's the matter?"

"Oh my God Michael. There's somebody at the window," she cried, burying her head in Michael's chest.

"What are you talking about, darling?" Michael said, gently stroking the damp hair off her face.

After a moment of paralysis, Jack was frantically crawling on all fours to the corner of the building.

"I saw someone staring at us," Sarah squeaked out through clenched teeth. Her eyes were still tightly closed as she clutched the crumpled sheet and held fast onto Michael's body.

"Calm down, darling. If you'll let me go, I'll have a look."

Jack rounded the corner and righted himself. A cold sweat drenched his face, and he madly brushed the wet dirt from his knees. Fuck! What the fuck am I doing? He pressed tight up against the wall.

Michael wrapped a towel around his waist and crossed the room. He pulled on the blind cord and peered into the darkness. Nothing. He shut the window tight, taking care to latch the top, and then dropped the blind fully.

"Honey, I think it was the fire that gave you a scare. That and too many horror movies set in the woods. There's nothing out there," he said, easing himself back to bed and opening his arms for her to cuddle.

"Please just call security. I swear someone was there!"

Michael had never seen or heard his wife so unhinged. "If it makes you feel better, absolutely, honey," Michael agreed, reaching for the phone.

Jack bolted through the empty great room and raced down the hall to his suite. His hands were shaking, and he dropped his card key on the floor trying to retrieve it from his pocket. He heard the deadbolt release on the room down the hall. He snatched up his card and jammed it into the slot in the door. Shit! Red blinking light.

He heard the handle pull down in the other room, 110.

Stealing a split-second glance down the hall he jammed it in again the other way around.

He heard the door of room 110 creak open.

He held his breath, torn between making a run for it out the exit or waiting for his key to respond. The green light mercifully blinked and he rammed down on the handle and slipped inside. He held the door open a crack.

As he heard Michael's door shut, he very quietly did the same.

Facing the door, he exhaled and pressed his sweat-drenched forehead against it, waiting to hear movement. He heard footsteps moving the other way down the hall, towards the main desk.

Straining to swallow, he grimaced, finding his throat parched. He took a quiet breath and turned. Nobody in his room. He heard the trickle of the shower. In his panic, he hadn't thought about what he would say to Rachel. He had caught a break. He slipped off his muddied jeans and rolled them tightly into a ball and shoved them to the bottom of his duffel bag. He tossed his shoes deep into the open closet and stripped off his wet socks. Get a grip, he told himself. Get a grip.

Forcing a smile to steady himself, he tapped on the bathroom door and stepped inside. "Anybody here?" he said trying to sound playful, thankful for the sound of the water covering up his shaky voice.

"Decided to come in from the cold, did you?" Rachel called out. "I couldn't sleep after all so thought a shower might help. Care to join me?"

Jack pulled off his shirt that was drenched in sweat and tossed it to the corner with his underwear. He shuddered as the hot water hit his body.

"Jack, you're trembling," Rachel said as he wrapped his arms around her. "The temperature must have really dropped. Why did you stay out there so long?"

He let the hot water relax him and gulped some water. He held her tight as she nestled into his contours. "I guess I got caught up in the beauty of the surroundings."

CHAPTER 18

The smell of fresh coffee and bacon was heavenly as they entered the sun-filled breakfast lounge. Plaid placemats adorned pine farm tables and there were more people than they expected. It turned out people came from all around for the Lodge's famous hearty brunch on Sunday mornings and often spent the afternoon on the trails. Michael and Sarah looked relaxed perusing the free local tourist tabloids as they approached.

"Hey, good morning!" Jack called out, scraping back the chair for Rachel.

"Good morning to you," Michael replied. "Sleep well?"

"Fantastic," Jack lied as he poured the steaming coffee from their personal carafe into a large mug.

"How about you guys?" Rachel asked. Glancing at the reading options. "No New York Times I'm guessing."

Michael laughed and Sarah looked sheepish. "Sarah gave herself a scare last night at a very inopportune moment," he said, dropping his chin and levelling her with a deep stare.

"What do you mean?" asked Rachel while abstractly looking for a waiter, self-service not her thing.

Jack was busy heaping scrambled eggs, bacon, sausage, and pancakes from the buffet onto his plate but stayed within earshot.

"I swear someone was there," Sarah said, looking back at her husband.

"What are you talking about?" Rachel pressed.

"I heard a loud noise from the fireplace. At least I think that's what I heard. When I turned towards the sound, I saw a man crouched under our window."

"Oh my God, are you serious?" said Rachel.

Jack wasted time toasting a bagel.

"It was dark, of course, but I could make out the outline of a head. It was too dark to get any details," Sarah said.

"That's wild! Did you report it to the front desk?" Rachel asked.

"I did after I tore Sarah's fingernails from my chest," teased

Michael. "Here's proof," he added pretending to unbutton his shirt. He stopped when he saw Sarah looking hurt.

"Did you hear anything down your way?" Michael asked to be supportive.

"No, all seemed very peaceful," replied Rachel. "I think I would have heard something. I got into a good book, *The Art of War*. Have you heard of it?"

"I'm surprised Jack was in the mood for reading on a weekend rendezvous," Michael said.

"Lucky for me, he hung out for a while at the firepit, so I actually got in a few chapters before he came back and pounced," Rachel said.

Jack moved swiftly to his seat while proclaiming how incredible the variety was at the buffet.

"Mmmm, this yogurt is fantastic," Rachel said as she tried the homemade yogurt that was topped off with honey from the Lodge's own bee farm and muesli.

"Sweetheart, you've got to try the sausage here," Michael enthused and held out a piece for Sarah on his fork.

"You won't believe this," Rachel started in, anxious to share Saah's story with Jack.

Jack made sure his mouth was full so he could delay a response.

"Let's not go into it again. One rehash is enough," said Michael. "Let's just say the Lodge didn't find anything suspicious and it didn't dampen our night," he concluded as he stroked the inside of Sarah's bare forearm resting on the table.

"Funny how being terrified can bring a couple together," Sarah said. Switching to a more upbeat tone she continued, "So what do you two have planned for today?"

"Unfortunately, I have a lot of work to get at, so we need to head back right after brunch," Rachel replied, looking only mildly disappointed. "Yesterday was nice but that was enough of a country fix for me."

"But it's going to be a gorgeous day," Sarah persisted. "We're going to drive the dirt roads and stop at every antique store we find. I'm hoping to pick up one of those old-fashioned wooden cradles that cost a mint in the city."

Jack had tuned out, analyzing Rachel's Spartan breakfast. "Rachel, you really should eat something. Everything is delicious. You're not only going to have yogurt topped with birdseed, are you?"

"I'm good with this," Rachel said.

It was driving Jack crazy that Rachel still refused to put on the ten pounds the clinic recommended.

Sensing the tension and not wanting it to affect their precious time alone, Sarah jumped in to change the subject. "Are you going to Brett's party July 1st?"

CHAPTER 19

With Rachel's trip overseas, they didn't get back to the clinic until mid-June. They came armed with two months' worth of ovulation tracking.

"Very nice, very nice indeed," Dr. Jordan said, reviewing their chart. "All looks good here. Mucus behaving?"

Rachel gave him a dead stare and pasted a benign smile on her face.

"Yes sir," beamed Jack, seeking praise over something he had no control over.

"All right," Dr. Jordon went on like a jovial uncle. "We'd like to start tracking your ovulation using a vaginal ultrasound at about day ten of your cycle. This usually doesn't require more than six to seven consecutive visits if you're ovulating mid-month, which appears to be the case based on your charts."

"When you say consecutive, tell me you're not talking about daily visits?" Rachel asked.

"This is the only way we can get a proper read on the build-up of your endometrium lining, the maturation of your eggs, and to ensure you are actually releasing the egg," replied Dr. Jordan. "We can save you another visit if Jack is able to come in as well on your ovulation day and we can conduct the PCT; might as well try conception at the same time."

"So, he gets one visit where he jacks off, and I get seven where I am poked and prodded by a cold hard stick," she said.

"The technical term is a transducer, but we like to call it a wand," Dr. Jordan offered.

Rachel huffed, "Well, you might as well call me Cinderella."

Dr. Jordan was accustomed to volatile tempers in his line of work and expected some drama and hostility over the course of treatment. Rachel was riled up already and they were barely out of the gate. Usually, the woman was more like this at the second or third failed AP or IVF before showing this type of attitude. He was going to have to work at earning this fee and he made a mental note to ensure Cindy padded the bill with a few extra services to make this couple more tolerable.

Jack kept to himself, knowing any reassurances would be swiftly rebuked.

"I'd like to book you to start on July 10th. We can ensure you are out before eight since we open at seven if that helps you manage your work schedule, Rachel."

"It doesn't exactly leave me free and clear since my workday typically starts at seven, but I suppose I can make that happen."

"Very well," Dr. Jordan said as he typed in his computer. "Please see Cindy out front. I've communicated your dates and procedures."

CHAPTER 20

"Jack, can you please join me for a moment?" It was a Monday morning in September when Jeffrey called Jack into his office.

Jeffrey Sanderson was about the same age as Jack. He had come over from their major competitor, Merrill Lynch, and was considered a major coup given the top-level account he brought with him. They paid him a considerable package to lure him over to have access to his prized strategic thinking.

Although they were the same age, Jeffrey was brought in as Senior VP of new business early in the year. Jack was furious when they created this new position for Jeffrey since Jack considered himself well qualified for the job and more deserving of the position. He had paid his dues with almost ten years of loyal service to Boston. But Jack also understood the client cache Jeffrey offered and the importance of acquiring his connections in order to grow the business.

"How are things going, Jack?" Jeffrey asked warmly, clapping him on the back while motioning for him to take a seat at the meeting table in his corner office.

"Great, just great!" Jack grinned. "You know, I've got McMillan this close to signing on that expansion project."

"Fantastic," Jeffrey said. Grabbing a file folder, he joined Jack at the table. "Listen, Jack, I'm going to get right to the point. I've been tracking your closing rate over the past six months and you're well behind projections." He pulled a spreadsheet from the top of his papers and angled it towards him.

"As you can see, we had you set for pulling in four million worth of closures at this point in the fiscal, and to date, you're only delivering at seventy percent. And that's even giving you the Barrick Gold credit even though we're still waiting for the deposit."

Jack leaned back in his chair and draped one arm casually over the back while crossing his ankle over his knee. He was taken aback at Jeffrey's direct accusation. Jack knew Boston followed individual successes, but he hadn't known he was on Jeffrey's radar with this level of scrutiny.

"Well, you know, Jeffrey, things are cyclical, and the summer is always quiet. Now that we are getting into fall, I'll be closing on plenty of business to ratchet those numbers up to projections."

"I sure hope so," Jeffrey said. "With our competition out there offering these new discounted commissions, we're really seeing some challenges from existing clients to match their offers. Our operating margins aren't compatible with this type of price cutting. Boston has always been the industry leader by offering exceptional analytics coupled with stellar service. But, the golf trips, seminars in the Caribbean, and parties aren't seen in the same light as they were even just a few years ago. The ethics bureau is on our ass to cut out any perks, but we've been able to defend ourselves, for now, by saying they are under the guise of client meetings and conferences. I don't think it will last much longer, much to the disappointment of our clients and us." Jeffrey paused for a moment to let this sink in. "Of course, you realize that your annual bonus is looking slim this year."

Jack had a good base salary coupled with an impressive bonus package calculated on his personal performance plus the overall company performance.

"I hadn't really thought about it," lied Jack. "I'm just focused on closing Spartack and Clemments by the end of the month."

"Are they close? Would it help if I stepped in to help with the final push?" offered Jeffrey.

"No, better not to change the dynamics now. It may seem odd or even desperate."

"All right, as long as you've got them under control, I'll leave you to it."

"No problem," Jack assured, standing up and stretching his back with his hands on his hips.

Jeffrey found this posturing far too familiar and boorish. He noticed the strain on Jack's belt buckle and the tacky pull on his expensive dress shirt buttons exposing his stomach. Someone really should tell him that French cuffs are pretentious if you're under fifty and not the CEO.

"Looks like you've been enjoying the beer and the BBQ season."

"HA, I keep meaning to get back into my gym schedule, but you know how it is in the summer with holidays," Jack replied.

Jeffrey didn't support him with a response.

As was Jack's habit when he was nervous, he clawed his hair back off his forehead. Jack felt more self-conscious than usual about his appearance. He still cut a handsome figure at thirty-three. His hair had dulled from his peak golden years in university, but it still had a dark blond sheen. He noticed his hairline receding on his forehead but nothing anyone else would notice. Jack's form-fitted custom-made shirts were far less forgiving than the typical off-the-rack variety. He used a tailor to make all his dress shirts since he liked the idea of exclusivity, and he also liked to show off his normally muscled torso. He only ordered one hundred percent combed Egyptian cotton. The problem was his six-pack was a little padded now. He had eased off his running schedule because of a nagging shin pain that persisted over the summer. He substituted running with biking and some gym workouts, but it didn't give him the same intensity running provided. He made a mental note to hit the gym more regularly and to watch his diet.

"I'd better get back to it. Have a good one," Jack called out over his shoulder as he bumped into the door frame exiting the airy office.

~~

It was a difficult summer for Jack and Rachel. Their seven-day visit to the clinic in July was repeated in August. Rachel was extremely agitated around this time and resented being prodded by some mute stranger in pink scrubs who refused to tell her anything, oblivious to her pain.

"Ow, for Christ's sake! It doesn't go any further," Rachel shouted.

The technician, a different one most days, would mumble a listless apology and go on in the exact same fashion.

After getting undressed Rachel laid back on the table with a flimsy paper cover providing false privacy. The air system whirled in the darkened room and the ultrasound equipment hummed and beeped. The technician always entered the room with a discreet tap and either a monotone or sugary good morning, both of which Rachel found irritating. She instructed Rachel to place her feet in the stirrups. Next, the technician shook a tube-shaped bottle of lubricant and generously squirted it into her rubber- gloved palm. Extracting the transducer from its holster with one hand, she lubricated it with her other hand.

"Here we go," she'd say and using two latex fingers she clinically opened Rachel's vulva.

How many times a day does she does do this? Rachel wondered. Who could possibly choose this for a living? You'd have to be mentally deficient to handle the monotony, or you'd get there in the process. Holding the transducer steady for a moment, like she parked the car in neutral, the technician efficiently keyed in some data. Pressing uncomfortably up against her cervix, the technician held the pressure and stared at the screen for what seemed an eternity. Finding the image she wanted, she worked the keyboard again. After repeating this attempt for a second time, the pressure would ease off for a few moments, and then she'd feel a sharp push into her low right side.

"That really hurts," Rachel complained and moved to shift herself away from the pressure.

"I'm afraid you're going to have to hold still, Ms. Madison. We can't get a good reading on your ovaries if you're moving," the technician commanded. She pushed harder with short strokes and angled the wand sharply until she saw the ovary. Holding it still, she tapped in more entries. More pushing and clicking. "Okay, let's look at the other side now, shall we?"

When the procedure was finished, she handed Rachel some transparently thin tissues and told her she could get dressed.

Rachel's emotions swung wildly. At first, she felt irritated just being at the clinic. She was angry with herself for getting in so deep so quickly. But she felt guilty duping Jack, and was close to making senior partner, so she was somewhat amenable to the idea of pregnancy.

As the days went on, she felt more violated at the repeated prodding. She felt like a vessel. She told herself it was no big deal, but this didn't reconcile with her crying as she cleaned herself up, pulling on her stockings and skirt for the workday ahead. It wasn't lost on her that, in some respects, it wasn't that far off from being raped; a total stranger violated the most private part of her body. The lubricant oozed down her thighs as she was left alone to pull herself together after it was over. Rationally she got it, but emotionally it was brutal. The daily exposure to the stressed-out hormonally unbalanced women at the clinic didn't help. There were always some women crying quietly waiting to be called in and a few couples with hands entwined white knuckled. The odd one would appear calm and be checking her phone; a first timer or a veteran.

Jack offered to come with her to the appointments to be an equal partner, but she flatly told him that was not going to happen.

"I'm perfectly capable of doing this on my own," Rachel said. She wasn't going to be one of those pathetic women whose whole sense of self was wrapped up in making a baby. She had a thriving career, a decent husband, fantastic friends, and all kinds of interests she would love to have more time to pursue. Not having a baby wouldn't be the end of the world.

CHAPTER 21

It was a gorgeous hot morning in August, and they were enjoying breakfast at one of their favorite cafes in the neighborhood. The second round of ovulation tests were behind them, and they were due to go back for a debrief in a couple of weeks. They had a table on the patio under a big umbrella perfect for people watching. Rachel felt content.

"You know, it wouldn't really be so bad not having kids. We could be one of those cool couples that family's envy. The ones with the stylish houses and the latest wardrobes. Bodies not ruined by childbirth. We'd lead interesting non–soccer game, non-minivan lives, filled with trips to Europe, wine tastings, theatre, and dinner parties."

Jack let her ramble, thinking she was being defensive as a coping strategy in case they got bad news from the testing.

"And there's the money thing." Using her toast, she dragged it through the runny eggs and folded it into her mouth. "Do you know how much money it takes to raise a kid? A study I saw last week said the average family will spend a million dollars on a kid up to the age of eighteen! Do you know what kind of fun we could have with that kind of money?"

Rachel searched the patio and called out to the server, "Could I get more coffee here, miss?"

The young waitress hurried by with a tray full of pancakes to a family of five.

Rachel was on a roll, "We could put that money into getting the cottage you want so badly, and I could have my trips," she said with a cheeky smile. She went back to reading the travel section of the newspaper.

"Rachel, you seem to be missing something here," Jack replied with his rage simmering just below the surface. "Having a child or children is deeply engrained in my psyche. It's not like choosing the red shirt over the blue one." He looked at her with disdain. "I swear sometimes I don't know if you really know me. How many times have we had this discussion?" he shouted while throwing down his cutlery down and pushing back his plate.

"I don't know why we can't have a rational debate about the subject," Rachel said, leaning into the table. "It seems to be your way or the highway. Since when did you get to call all the shots?"

"The debate was over once you agreed to see Dr. Jordan last year!" Jack countered, ignoring the stares from nearby tables.

"Oh, so I'm not allowed any say in this now? I'm supposed to keep showing up in that fucking office and letting his minions shove whatever they want into my body and say 'Oh...that's okay...no problem, do whatever you want. My husband wants his Stepford wife to produce a baby.' Well, screw you if I'm not enough for you," she yelled as she loudly scraped back her chair and flew out of the restaurant.

"Damn it," Jack said as he watched her disappear.

Jack walked for a while to cool off before returning home early afternoon. He found his bag packed in the foyer. He tentatively entered the living room to find Rachel tucked in the corner of the couch and a tissue box on her lap. Her eyes were swollen and her nose red and runny. He immediately went to comfort her, but she stood up quickly.

"Don't even think about it," she said. "I need you to go somewhere else for a while. A couple of weeks so I can think things through."

Jack was dumbfounded. "You're kidding, right?"

"Do I look like I'm kidding? I feel very vulnerable right now and I can't handle your pressure. I think it's a good idea to be apart for a few weeks so we can both clear our heads. Maybe after that we can manage a constructive conversation because that obviously isn't something we are capable of at the moment."

Jack dropped deep into the oversized chair. Leaning forward, he took a few deep breaths and let his head drop down between his shoulders holding his forehead in both hands.

Whipping his head up he said, "Where am I supposed to go? This is my house too, you know."

Rachel was exasperated. "It's already back to you! You have family and friends you can stay with. You'd better go peacefully if you really want this to work out."

"Oh, my parents would love it," he said, coming back to life. "I'll just get their concierge to ring them in their perfect empty-nester condo and let them know their grown son's marriage is on the rocks and he needs to crash for a while."

Jack was up and pacing in tight circles. "A roll-away cot will look great in their sunken living room in front of the floating gas fireplace. My father would love to throw this in my face. He was always looking for ways to toughen me up, saying I needed to learn the ropes so I could handle the real world. What do you think he's going to think when I can't even handle my own wife?"

"Okay, forget about your family then. Call a friend, call ... I don't know and I don't care. That's your problem. Stay in a hotel if you need to," she said, pressing a tissue against both eyes.

"Fine. I'll figure something out."

Jack thought about asking Michael, but with Sarah's due date fast approaching, he thought better of it. Luckily Larry and his family were on sabbatical saving a rain forest in Costa Rica. He texted Larry, who was only too happy to help; they could use someone so the place wouldn't be deserted and susceptible to break-ins.

Even though he knew he was lucky to have somewhere to stay, he couldn't stand Larry's hippie vibe. Spider plants hung in macramé plant holders. Baby slings draped over coat hooks. Homemade organic baby food cubes were in the freezer. Children's books included Big Bad Oil and an alphabet book with C for Conspicuous Consumption lined the wooden shelves.

Besides missing Rachel, he missed his house. They looked for a while before settling on the contemporary design they bought two years ago in North Toronto. Most of the houses were traditional brick, center hall homes, but amongst the established dwellings there was a sprinkling of new exciting designs. They both fell in love at first sight seeing the stripped down, sleek, elegant contemporary design of their house; flexible floor space, minimalist decorative elements, and extensive use of industrial mixed materials. He smiled recalling how giddy they were entering the expansive foyer and looking up at the soaring ceiling. They loved the simplicity of open boxy rooms, the concrete flooring, and glass walls. They thought it reflected their modern outlook on life and made them stand out from the pack.

They took a huge leap on their mortgage with the move since they had only had their first home, a modest semi-detached, for two years. But interest rates were low, and they both had high-profile jobs and stellar degrees, so the bank was willing to let them max out on their credit. They weren't concerned; they were fast-tracked to be major players at their respective firms.

Being in this tree-hugger, chemical-free, additive-free space was stifling. He called Rachel every week asking if he could come home.

"I'm so sorry for acting like such an ass," he said after calling her late one evening three weeks after he left. He'd had a few drinks and felt like it was time to let Rachel win the battle. "I know I shouldn't have pushed so much, and I promise to relax about the whole baby thing when we get back together."

"I appreciate you taking responsibility for your actions," Rachel replied in a clipped tone. "I'm glad you're seeing things clearly." She threw on a red silk robe and cinched it at her waist as she left the bedroom and made her way to the kitchen.

He was glad they were talking over the phone so she couldn't see his flushed face given his rising anger. Dr. Jordan's clinic had called to schedule their next session, so he made some work excuses as to why they needed to delay. His hand clenched and unclenched his glass of whisky as he worked to keep his breathing steady.

"I know I was too demanding and I'm sorry if you felt pressured or anxious. Being apart has been very helpful for letting me sort things out. I think maybe the best thing for us is to just forget about the baby thing for at least six months and then maybe reconsider. We are only in our early thirties after all."

"Oh my God, that is music to my ears!" Rachel shouted. "I was so scared we were on separate paths. I thought the only hope for us reuniting was to keep going to that horrible fertility clinic. Do you really mean it? We can get our old lives back and let nature take its course?"

"I'd love that," Jack lied. "It's not worth ruining what we have over what might be. Things happen for a reason so it's probably just not our time yet." He winced and clenched his jaw as the glass sliced into the side of his index finger, the pressure of his grip having shattered the tumbler.

"Jack, are you OK? Did something just break?"

"Yeah. No, I'm fine. No big deal. I just knocked over a glass doing some tidying up."

"Oh, too bad. Be careful not to cut yourself cleaning it up."

"So, are you OK with me coming home?"

Rachel hesitated for a moment. "As long as you're sure you are OK with leaving the baby talk alone. I don't think I can handle even a casual conversation about it right now. I've just started feeling good about myself again these past few weeks. I'm not saying it's all your fault since I agreed to it too. But being on my own has helped me feel strong again. Those visits to the clinic feel like a bad dream involving some other hapless person."

Rachel walked slowly back upstairs towards their palatial bedroom.

"It's late now so let's meet after work tomorrow and have a nice reunion dinner at Misty's," Rachel suggested. "It will make your homecoming special."

Jack was running the cold water over his bleeding finger. "Sounds perfect, I'll see you tomorrow night."

Rachel eased the bedroom door open and looked longingly at the buffed naked body barely covered by the bed sheet draped across his lower half. She smiled to herself thinking he had staged himself. Marcus groaned slightly and shifted as he sensed her coming back. Through half-opened dark eyes peeking through tousled hair he mumbled, "Missed me?" and patted the edge of the bed.

Tempting as it was, she knew it was time for him to leave. "Sorry, Marcus, but your time is up. You've got to leave now."

"Come on, baby. One more for the road?"

"No can do, darling. Hubby is coming back tomorrow. I can't risk a lingering man smell that's not his in our marital bed."

He gathered up his scattered clothes and headed into the bathroom, calling out over his shoulder, "You sure know how to kill a party."

Rachel opened the double French doors off the bedroom facing the backyard and stepped onto the balcony. A couple of black resin wicker chairs with grey cushions made for an inviting place to relax, which never got used by the two people they were intended to serve. Rachel fished a pack of cigarettes out of her pocket. She tapped one free and held it at the edge of her lips as she sourced the lighter she kept tucked in the side of the chair. One click of the lighter produced a flame she expertly cupped as she brought it to the tip of the cigarette and inhaled deeply. She held the smoke deep in her lungs for a couple of seconds and exhaled loudly, staring out into the darkness. Half a cigarette later Marcus emerged and sank down opposite her and took a cigarette from her pack. "May I?'

"Be my guest," Rachel motioned.

He was dressed in his designer jeans, Italian sweater, and expensive black loafers without socks.

"Everything all lovey-dovey again?" Marcus asked, tucking his wavy black hair behind his ears.

"Mind your own business, Marcus. This doesn't have anything to do with you."

"Well, it kind of does."

"Look. You're a big boy."

"I'm glad you've noticed," Marcus teased.

Rachel didn't acknowledge his quip. "We're both married, and you knew from the first time, this was purely a physical thing. A fun distraction."

"Fair enough, but is there anything wrong with wondering when another distraction may be down the road?" Marcus asked. He entwined his hands with hers across the divide of the two chairs.

"I honestly don't know. Jack is coming home tomorrow, and we are both going to give things a fair go."

"Pity for me," he said, exhaling the last of the smoke and stubbing the cigarette out in the tin jar she kept for hiding the butts.

"I think you'll be all right."

Standing above her, he bent over and kissed her gently on the mouth and let his hands travel over the silky mounds of her breasts. She caught his wrists as his hands moved lower.

"I'll walk you downstairs, lover boy."

"As you wish," Marcus said as he let her go first, trailing her to the garage like a hound.

"Please don't let anyone see you leave, this is really important for me," Rachel asked and handed him his thin leather jacket. "It's not exactly something I'm used to doing."

"Not to worry. I parked around the corner as you asked, and I'll go out the side entrance." He pulled her in close for a good-bye hug.

"See you tomorrow," Rachel said, and he slipped out the side garage door and disappeared down the driveway.

All was quiet. Rachel was happy Jack was coming home again, she missed him. What she didn't miss was his obsession about having a baby. It had been a great few weeks of freedom with him not being around. She clocked fantastic runs, enjoyed a couple of fun catch-up nights with old girlfriends out on the town, shopped for new fall clothes, ate what and when she wanted, had the odd cigarette, read late into the night before sleeping. Not to mention Marcus.

Marcus worked with Rachel at Goldman Sachs for the past two years. He was a Senior Executive of Research and Development on the seventeenth floor. The Client Service Group was located on the fifteenth floor, so they didn't cross each other's path often. They did brainstorm together at quarterly meetings when R&D and Client Services met to review product development and client needs. Marcus was fortyish and handsome, sent over from Milan to service a major Italian client who wanted more control over the product development which was all done in the main Toronto office. He was married with two children, and his wife didn't want to uproot their lives by relocating to Toronto, since the placement was only scheduled to last for two years.

Rachel was instantly attracted to him, as was every other woman in the office. While she flirted with him from time to time, she never thought of taking it further. She was married and had no interest in complicating her life. Besides, Jack was usually great in bed.

She went back to the bedroom but felt restless and went to the balcony for another cigarette.

The first time was a shock for both of them. They were working late at the office going over a report. It was right after the initial full week of ultrasounds. Rachel was very irritable, and she and Jack had a couple of big fights. After the report was finished, they sat down for some Thai food. Marcus came into the boardroom with a dashing playboy smile and two cold beers.

"Where did you find the stash?" Rachel asked.

"Secret source. I'd tell you but then I'd have to...you know..."

Marcus purposely grazed her hand while passing her the beer. She guzzled back a third of the bottle. "Mmm, that tastes good."

Marcus slowly sipped his beer without taking his eyes off her.

"I think your client will be most pleased," Rachel said.

"They'd be even more pleased if you came over to help with the presentation."

"I'd love to, but I think I'd have a hard time justifying the trip given the work will be very well delivered in your capable hands," Rachel countered.

"But we make such a good team!" Marcus suggested. He rose and paced the room, passing within a few inches of the back of her chair every time.

"My knowledge of my client needs, your intimate understanding of the product development, my brains and your beauty; you know how we Italians appreciate such things." He paused and placed his hands gently on her shoulders.

She didn't move. He gently massaged the back of her neck. She slowly tilted her head from side to side and then tipped her head back. He didn't pounce as she expected. Instead, he moved his hands to her temples and let his fingers work into her hair with more forceful circles. It felt wonderful and she relaxed into the sensation. The silence only heightened the tension. Her breathing became shallower, and he watched her breasts rise and fall. The massage continued. Her lips parted as she let his hands release her pent-up emotions.

Suddenly she was crying. She felt ridiculous. "Shit, I'm so sorry. I don't know what has come over me," she blurted out. "I never cry. I feel like an idiot."

Marcus spun her chair around and pulled her to her feet, silencing her ramblings with a deep passionate kiss. Pulling apart for a second, he said, "I don't care. All I know is that I must have you."

As she finished off her cigarette, she smiled at the erotic memory of their first tryst. She wondered if the boardroom had ever seen that much action. She was surprised she didn't feel more remorse.

Although she found Marcus attractive and could play along with the flirtation game, she'd never thought about actually having sex with him. It showed her how destructive the fertility path could be that she would want to validate her sexuality with a fling. It was easy enough to rationalize. With everything she was going through at the clinic, it was only natural to become unhinged and to act irrationally. If Jack hadn't pushed so much to get on with the daily temperature tracking, and the testing, this likely never would have happened. The trips to the ultrasound table stripped her of her identity as an individual. Day-by-miserable-day, she felt feel like a walking reproductive system. And if she couldn't conceive, would she be seen as a lesser person, a person of less value to the man she loved?

As if this wasn't degrading enough, Jack's lovemaking had taken on a perfunctory routine since they started with Dr. Jordan. No matter how tired she was, he wouldn't take no for an answer mid-month. They used to enjoy all aspects of lovemaking, but now he only wanted to have intercourse and always forced himself to finish on top. If she tried to get up or even move after having sex, he would *suggest* she stay on her back for at least five minutes. He propped up her legs with a pillow at the knee so his semen wouldn't leak out.

After Jack moved out a few weeks ago, her thoughts drifted to Marcus. It was simply too much fun, sex for the pure enjoyment of sex, with no ulterior motive. Since Marcus was married, he was also very safe since she knew he wouldn't have any serious expectations about a relationship. He was a perfect outlet for her frustrations. And then there were his hands, his intense black eyes, his full mouth, not to mention …. Rachel caught herself giggling out loud and forced her mind into the present.

She went back into the bedroom and stripped off the sheets with one big flourish. She buried her face in the soft cotton and inhaled deeply for one last reminder of Marcus before tossing them into the hamper.

CHAPTER 22

Jack kept to his word and stayed off the baby track. Things went smoothly as they resumed more of their old routine. Rachel was especially impressed when they joined family and friends to celebrate the arrival of Michael and Sarah's second child, a boy they named Connor after Michael's father, Constantine.

It was a glorious day for November, with a bright blue sky and a crisp cool breeze. Everyone went to church for the baptismal mass and back to their house for a celebration. Michael's whole family was there, as were dozens of friends. Michael's mother arrived earlier in the week to prepare the food. There is no love in catered food, she insisted. Sarah loved the smells radiating from her kitchen and she loved Michael's delight even more as she watched him light up as he entered the house after work.

"Mom, you're the best!" he called out as he winked at Sarah and sailed by to give his mother a tender kiss on her cheek. He reached over her shoulder at the same time, trying to pluck some delicious morsel, only to be rapped on the hand with her ever-present wooden spoon.

"You men are all the same," she said while sharing a conspiratorial smile with Sarah. "Now get out of here or you'll have to prepare for Sunday on your own."

With one last attempt Michael snatched what he could and left the master be.

"How was your day, honey?" Michael asked Sarah, gently scooping baby Connor into his arms. "Looks pretty successful," he said gazing down at his new son, who was fast asleep.

"You should have been here between two and five, my friend, not so successful."Mr. Fussy here wouldn't settle down and his crying woke Paige early from her nap. So, she wasn't in the best of spirits either. Luckily your mother was here and nicely offered to take Paige out in the stroller, which got her back to sleep. Our little man here just zonked out about half an hour ago. I'm not too far behind him."

"The excitement of having a young family," Michael said. "You've got to cut the little guy some slack, he's only four weeks old, after all."

"I suppose. Thank goodness for your mother and her love of the kitchen. Otherwise, it would be more take-out or frozen food."

"As much as I love her cooking, I could eat dirt and not complain. We are so blessed to have our two beautiful healthy children. Speaking of children, where is Paige?"

"She is playing in the giant wooden playpen that survived your abuse some thirty years ago. I can't believe your mother kept it all these years. You can't buy playpens like that now; they're all plastic mesh and puny. This one takes up most of our living room but who cares if she's happy."

Michael looked around the corner, careful not to be seen so Paige would continue playing on her own. The solid wooden slats contained a world of wonders: brightly colored stacking cups, plush pastel animals, musical instruments, dolls, a favorite blanket. He watched Paige's gorgeous head of curls bent over the arduous task of getting the doll to sit up.

Re-entering the kitchen, Michael sat down at the casual table and inhaled deeply.

"Mmmmm, that smells amazing, Mom. What have you whipped up today?"

"Zeljanica, vegetable stew, grape leaves, and pilaf, but it's for Sunday. Tomorrow I'll do the Punjena and spice the lamb and beef kebabs to cook Sunday morning."

Sarah crinkled her forehead. "Zeljanica and Punjena? Translation please?"

"Flaky pastry with spinach and cheese, and my favorite, paprika fried peppers stuffed with minced meat," Michael rattled off.

He passed Sarah a beer to help her unwind and it was also good for her milk production. Not that Sarah seemed to need any help in that department. Her milk came in on the second day after giving birth and she looked like she was carrying a ready supply.

Michael was starving. "Do we get anything tonight?"

"You'll have to make do with the beef stew from last night. I've been too busy with Sunday's preparations and Paige to have anything fresh for today."

"Sounds perfect." Michael gently placed Connor in the white bassinet set on the couch and went to get four dishes.

"Just serve yourself and Sarah," his mother instructed. "Paige and I ate earlier. I'll go run her bath so she can get to bed by seven." She sauntered down the hall singing, then heard Paige squeal with delight as her Buba entered the room.

Michael and Sarah clinked their bottles and enjoyed their semi-private dinner.

~~~

Rachel lifted Paige up in her arms. "I can't believe how big she is now!"

At two years of age, she was the picture of healthy. She wore an old- fashioned stitched bodice dress her Buba made for the occasion of her little brother's baptism. Paige was old enough to play strange and squirmed in protest to be released. Rachel gladly passed her back to her mother, who disappeared into the crowd.

Michael and Sarah took the occasion to invite old friends they didn't see too often, so everyone was having fun mingling and playing catch-up. Larry and Alison were still lugging their son in the sling. Rachel thought Alison looked mousy and tired, probably since she still breastfed Sky on demand. They had some interesting stories about their time in Costa Rica, so that made it bearable for Rachel, something other than baby talk.

Brett and Christy were also sporting the latest must-have accessory, an infant girl. They called her Janice, being big fans of Janice Joplin. Brett was as loud and boisterous as ever. Christy was adapting to motherhood while still trying to hold out with her punk hair and funky clothes that cut too tightly across her now thick waistline.

"How are you two finding parenthood?" Rachel asked.

"It's fine for now since she pretty much just sleeps," Christy shared as she rocked back and forth. "I take her on the road, but I only do the backroom logistics as I'd like her to be able to hear the teacher when she goes to school. But I can still manage most of my accounts so that's good."

"Who knew being a father could be so natural for a fat fuck like me," roared Brett.

Christy raised her glass in mock salute to Brett. "Everyone keeps telling me that with girls you get it down the road, that the teen years will be brutal. We might as well enjoy things while we can, right, baby?"

The young people were hanging out in the kitchen creating a party atmosphere. Michael's father, plus his godfather from Sudbury, and another male family friend stood bravely in the backyard, not minding the elements while tending the kebabs sizzling on the BBQ. Baby Connor was napping in his room upstairs giving Michael's mother, godmother, and Michael's old Aunt Tatijana time to bustle about the kitchen and lay out platters of food. Their attempts to shoo the younger adults out of the kitchen were futile.

The love was palpable in the house. The sense of optimism for the next generation of Babics and the other babies infused every conversation—and it was enough to make Jack physically ill. With all the commotion nobody noticed Jack slip downstairs. He made his way to the guest room thinking he might lie down for a few minutes to stop his head from racing. He felt detached from the scene, like he was watching a movie unfold.

"I'll be right back, I'm getting the other tablecloth," Sarah shouted back up the stairs as she went downstairs to the laundry room.

Feeling foolish about hanging out alone downstairs, Jack tucked in behind the guest room door. He felt her breeze by and stop in the laundry room to retrieve something from the dryer. He chanced a peek through the crack and could see her if he shifted to get the right angle. Even getting laundry she was radiant, and only a month postpartum. Her dress, turquoise and accenting her eyes, was beautifully cut around the bodice. It fell just above the knee and was bordered by a rich paisley pattern of deep blues and greens to match the trim on the neckline. Her shapely legs in her kitten heels looked lovely. He barely blinked. She took a moment to lean back against the dryer and close her eyes, steadying herself with her hands. With her back to the machine, eyes still closed, she made slow stretching movements side to side. It was just the two of them and nobody else knew they were down there. His mouth was dry and slightly agape.

Suddenly she lifted her head and opened her eyes. He immediately pulled back from the crack, careful not to shift to avoid making any noise. He heard the dryer door open, the rustle of clothes, then heard the door slam shut. Expecting her to head back upstairs, he was totally unprepared to have the guest room door pushed open, wedging him behind it. He froze. He couldn't see anything. He held his breath. Sarah only opened the door part way before she entered, leaving him enough room to stay concealed. He heard her place a few things on the dresser then turn to the bed. She paused for a moment and Jack struggled with what he could possibly say for an excuse if he was caught. Nothing came to mind. He felt sweat start to drip from his forehead and tickle his temples. He didn't budge.

Sarah crossed the room quickly and Jack felt the door pulling away from him. Panic engulfed him as he expected to be discovered. But he was spared since Sarah had taken hold of the handle on her way out and closed the door behind her.

Jack waited for several minutes to collect himself before he opened the door a crack. All was quiet. He didn't want to risk getting caught coming up from the basement. Turning right, he slipped through the laundry room into the cellar side of the basement, careful to partially close the accordion door behind him, to leave it as he found it. Even in the middle of the day it was quite dark and cold. His eyes adjusted and he found the side window that opened onto the driveway. He gently moved a plastic bin and placed it under the window. He stepped up and undid the latch and cracked it open on rusty hinges. Peeking both ways along the driveway, he found it deserted. He levered himself up onto the sill. With a quarter twist, his upper body was outside, and his seat rested on the ledge with his legs dangling inside. He swung his legs out, hopped to his feet, and pushed the window back flush with the frame. Careful to dust off the dirt from the back of his pants, he walked calmly back to the front of the house and let himself in.

As he rejoined the group, Rachel gave him a puzzled look. "Oh, there you are, I wasn't sure where you went."

"I went to the car since I thought we forgot the champagne."

"You've really got to cut back on work. Don't you remember? I put it in my bag with the gift and handed it to Sarah when we first came in."

"Oh damn, you're right. I'm glad one of us is thinking clearly."

Rachel was looking back at him strangely when the attention suddenly shifted.

"Look who just woke up!" gushed Aunt Tatijana. She had Connor tightly swaddled in her gnarled arthritic hands, holding him close so there was no chance of her dropping him. His embroidered white christening gown peeked out from under the covers.

"The guest of honor!" bellowed Michael's father, coming inside with a heavy platter stacked high with delicious-smelling lamb scented with basil and lemon. "Just in time for the feast!"

Everyone applauded. The women crowded around to see the new arrival and the men drifted over to the dining room table.

Rachel leaned closer to Jack. "Are you okay?"

"Of course," he snapped back. Sensing her hostile reaction to his tone he softened. "I mean sure, I'm fine. I'm starving, that's all." He flashed a wide grin that she knew was a bit forced but she didn't want to get into anything at the party, so she played along. She slipped her arm through his. "Lead the way, darling."

Everything was served in abundance and was delicious. Michael and Jack's friends generally were either too busy to cook or simply not that interested in learning, so today's homemade spread was a treat. After seconds were enjoyed the group quieted down and settled into sofas and chairs. The older men went outside to smoke away from their wives and children. Jack saw one man chuckling and motioning to his buddies as he shuffled out the door with a bottle of port under one arm and a stack of short glasses in the other.

Rachel and Jack were talking about making an excuse to leave before much longer when Michael and Sarah came over to join them at the kitchen counter. The baby was awake and content to be tucked into Sarah's arms. Paige was running around making goofy faces at anyone kind enough to laugh.

"I hope you're having a good time and enough to eat," Sarah said.

"Everything was truly wonderful," Jack said, shifting his gaze between the parents and the new baby. "You've got an amazing family and a fantastic group of friends. You're really lucky."

"That's for sure," said Rachel. "Thanks for including us and we're sorry to be the first to go, but I've got a lot of work to do."

Sarah looked hesitantly at Michael.

"Jack, Sarah and I would really appreciate you being a stand-in godfather for Connor," Michael said. Lowering his voice he went on, "We're obliged to officially pick Sarah's sister and husband since we had my sister and her husband for Paige. But, with them living in Edmonton, they won't have any influence on Connor's life. You're like a brother to me and it would make me very happy to think Connor had a great role model to follow."

Jack was speechless. Rachel kept sipping her Sauvignon Blanc, not knowing what she should or shouldn't be saying anything.

"But you know I'm not religious," Jack stammered.

"We know that and quite frankly, neither are we," Michael laughed. "It's more secular nowadays. Most people pick godparents for the moral direction and support they provide. You're my closest friend and I can't think of another person."

Jack was dumbfounded. "Wow, that's such an honor. Of course I'd be happy to. Do I need to sign anything?"

"We just need to seal the deal with a drink," Michael replied. "Sarah, can you grab that champagne they were nice enough to bring?"

Rachel felt like a third wheel and excused herself. Much to the delight of the older men gathered in a smoky circle near the shed, she joined them for a cigarette.

Sarah passed over the bottle of champagne and a couple of glasses. She wanted to leave them alone and used Paige's antics that were starting to annoy some of their guests as a good reason to pull away.

Michael poured two glasses and toasted, "Here's to the smartest, toughest, bravest, all-around nicest guy I know." They clinked glasses and knocked back enough of their drinks to get the effect they were looking for.

"Oooooh, that's good stuff," Michael winced with the bubblies bringing tears to his eyes. "Remember the way we'd party it up at Queens? We were so young and carefree."

They both got lost for a few moments recalling those heady days. "So much action. We could find a party any night of the week," Michael said.

"But we worked hard too. That program was no picnic," Jack said, going for another swig.

"True, but you seemed to pull off both, effortlessly."

"Things have always come pretty easily to me," said Jack. "It didn't hurt to have wealthy parents that could buy private tutors and coaching. Hell, they even bought my friends by sending me to Stanford with the kids they wanted for my peer group."

"Seems like a lifetime ago rooming with you at university," Michael said. "It's hard to believe almost ten years have passed since we graduated."

"Must be all the changes in such a short time," stated Jack.

"True; the career, marriage, home ownership and now kids ...." Michael cut off abruptly, thinking that the mention of kids might be a sore spot for Jack.

Picking up on Michael's discomfort, Jack said, "It's okay to mention the kid thing. Rachel and I are going to have kids too, it's just not our focus right now. Rachel wants to travel and make partner and that's cool with me."

"Oh, good to hear. I was worried it might be a sensitive topic."

"Loads of time for all that! Once you're in, you're in—am I right?"

"Well put, my friend."

Jack took a last tug on his drink as he found Sarah and followed her with his eyes. "It will give me a good excuse to hang around a bit more too. It seems we're all so busy with life, we forget to make time to get together and shoot the breeze."

Sarah circled back and slipped her hand into Michaels and addressed the two friends. "That Paige is already trying to test my limits. Controlling at two if you can believe it!"

Snapping out of his haze Jack exclaimed, "I was just saying that I am honored you both think so highly of me, that you'd like my guidance in Connor's life."

Sarah smiled, not sure exactly what had been said between the two friends.

Jack reached across and placed a hand over Michael's and Sarah's intertwined hands, "I'd be happy to check in on the little man when Michael is travelling and generally be here whenever you need me. Without my own kids yet, I feel blessed to be part of the inner circle for such a special family."

Sarah she felt Jack's thumb ever so slightly stroke the side of her hand. She pulled it away and crossed her hands in front of her. She gave Jack a quizzical look, but it was met with a beatific blank reply.

"It's flippin' freezing out there," Rachel announced as she slammed the door behind her and stomped her high-heeled stilettos. "We've really got to be going now, thanks for such a lovely party."

"Oh, no problem. Thank you for coming. Let me grab your coats," Sarah offered, since Michael had been pulled away by some relatives. She went to the bottom of the stairs, relieved they were leaving.

"Don't be silly, Sarah, I'll get them," Jack said, nudging past her.

"Are you sure? Do you know where to go?" Sarah asked.

"I'm assuming they're in your bedroom?"

"Yes, the first door on your right after you go past the bathroom," Sarah instructed. She knew as she said this that Jack knew exactly where their room was from his overnight visit.

"I'm sure I'll find it," he said not risking making eye contact and was gone in a flash.

He took the stairs two at a time. He easily found the bedroom with coats piled high on the bed. He fished through the heap and extracted Rachel's form- fitting back wool trench and his camel-colored dress coat. On his way out, he lingered at the dresser. All was quiet upstairs. He gingerly opened the top right drawer and saw Michael's undergarments. He closed it. He tried the top left drawer and saw a jumble of feminine underthings. The bras were in all types and styles; lacy and black, practical white cotton, a sexy demi-cup red satin, a beige nursing bra that exposed the breast by releasing a Velcro flap.

He let his hand skim the materials, felt his heartbeat quicken as he dug deeper and felt the underwear; matching bikini bottoms and thongs for the sexy brassieres along with basic cream and white cotton. He rubbed the satin material between his thumb and fingers. He raised a pair to his face, a fresh mountain scent. Pure, just like Sarah. He was lost imagining Sarah dressed in the red satin set when heavy steps coming up the stairs startled him. He shoved the underwear back in the drawer and shut it quickly and turned back and hunched over the bed.

Michael came through the door. "You've been up here a while. Having trouble digging out?"

Jack made a tugging gesture and spun around, "Here it is!" holding his wife's coat aloft.

"Great, glad things weren't totally lost. Let me walk you out."

Jack chanced a look at the dresser and noticed Sarah's drawer slightly ajar with a bit of black material caught on the side.

"No worries, mate, I can find my way out if you need to get back to the party."

"And let my son's unofficial godfather leave unescorted? It just wouldn't seem right." Michael gently placed a hand on Jack's back and steered him out to the hall.

Driving home, Jack couldn't get the image of Sarah dressed in her lingerie out of his head. Rachel made small talk about the food and the guests, but Jack just mumbled some agreeable monosyllabic replies, not wanting to break the spell.

Coming through the door, Rachel kicked off her shoes and continued to their bedroom to change into some comfy clothes to hunker down to work. Jack followed her down the hall. As Rachel entered the room, Jack threw her down on the bed.

"Wow! Who knew a baby christening party could have that effect," teased Rachel. She kissed him without much passion.

Jack had mentally been tamping down his erection all the way home, but he was now fully engorged and wanting relief. He closed his eyes; envisioning Sarah scantily clad in the red demi-cup bra and matching thong. He hungrily kissed Rachel, letting his hands roam over her body.

"Hey, big fella. I'd love to another time but I'm just not in the mood after all that food," Rachel protested, attempting to push him off to one side.

"Well then, I'll just have to get you in the mood," Jack said in a low voice while biting her lower lip.

"I've really got to ...."

"Shut up, will you, and enjoy yourself."

He shifted lower and pulled her tight sweater over her head, just high enough to expose her mouth but keep her eyes covered. He unhooked her black bra to expose her hard high breasts. Her nipples contracted with the assault of the cold air, and he greedily took them in his mouth. She relaxed a little and he pinned her arms to her side. She squirmed, enjoying the attention, and switched into the submissive role. He continued to make his way lower, covering her stomach with kisses and playful bites on his way down. Her mouth stayed parted; her breathing accelerated. He peeled off her skirt and was pleased to see she was wearing a thong.

Rachel was ready for him, but he enjoyed making her wait. He worked his way up her inner thighs. She was begging him to hurry. He waited; he was good at waiting. She writhed and moaned with pleasure, and he stayed low. He didn't want to face her and ruin his fantasy. He rotated his body to let her take him in her mouth while cupping her bottom in each palm. He pulled her open and let his tongue dart inside her. Wildly aroused, she let him plunge deeply into her mouth and he penetrated her orally and digitally. Afterwards, lay panting beside each other, totally spent.

"Wow, that was amazing," Rachel said as she finished pulling off her sweater and running her fingers through her sweat-soaked hair.

"Not bad for me either."

Rachel folded herself into his arms. "Isn't this more fun, I mean not limiting our sex life to only intercourse?"

"Let's just enjoy the moment in silence," Jack said as he replayed the scene with Sarah in his mind.

CHAPTER 23

Christmas morning Rachel came downstairs to the scent of fresh ground and brewed coffee, a fire blazing in their large fireplace, and the ten-foot Christmas tree lit up with its small white lights setting off the silver ornaments.

"Jack, this is so wonderful! Merry Christmas." She gave him a tender kiss and snuggled beside him resting her head against his chest.

After a couple of minutes, Jack left Rachel tucked under the faux fur blanket and went to the kitchen to get their coffee. Rachel noticed a black velvet box with a satin bow under the tree. Intrigued, she assumed it was jewelry but couldn't guess what he'd purchased. She was content to linger over the options while reflecting on the last few months.

Since they reunited after their separation in September, things had been great. Jack was relaxed and finally parked the baby project on the back burner. Even his firm's mediocre performance for the year hadn't dampened his spirits. The company did some layoffs, but no one from Jack's group. As far as Rachel's career went, she was within months of making senior partner after her stellar direction had landed three major deals over the year with record profits.

Jack took his time whipping the milk. Over the past couple of months, he made a real effort to appear light-hearted and uninterested in pursuing the baby-making topic. It was all an act, but he knew it was necessary to buy some time. He didn't want the stigma of a failed marriage and was aware that pushing Rachel back into fertility treatment, or even talking about the timing of things, was dangerous territory. His father instilled in him the importance of having either a solid marriage or more realistically, the appearance of a solid marriage. A broken marriage or worse, a broken family, was a sign of weakness. Jack discovered as a young adult his father had 'lady friends' that his mother tolerated. Part of the bargain to get him to stay. Those liaisons existed on another plane and never threatened to intersect with their tight family circle.

"Come on, Jack, the suspense is killing me!"

Jack grabbed the two steaming cups and came into the living room.

He made a low mock bow. "Here you are, madame."

"Lovely, just perfect," she said, taking the mug in both hands and letting the aromatic steam engulf her face. She took a small sip and set it down on the coffee table.

"For me?" she asked, lifting and gently shaking the velvet box.

"Of course, for you my love, Merry Christmas, darling."

Rachel slid off the bow and smiled at Jack, wanting to stretch out the anticipation. "A gold matching jewelry set is my best guess."

She was surprised it felt so light, she knew he wouldn't skimp on spending. She pried open the box at the hinges and saw a glossy image of a safari scene. Primed for jewelry, she was taken aback. She dug into the box and saw the familiar red and white of the Air Canada envelope.

"Oh my God!" she cried with her free hand flying to her mouth. She fumbled with the brochure, and something dropped to the floor. She bent over and scooped up two first-class plane tickets.

"Oh, Jack, this is amazing! Oh my God. I can't believe you did this!"

Jack beamed at her with satisfaction.

She poured over the brochure that detailed their itinerary in South Africa: Capetown, a wine region tour, a first-class safari excursion, and an exclusive beach resort with thatched roof bungalows.

"Three weeks! They'll never approve three weeks," she exclaimed, looking concerned.

"I've already taken care of it. Jim said after everything you did this year, especially your hard work and dedication on the Italian job, you deserved it."

Rachel didn't miss a beat and threw herself into his arms.

"This is going to be the trip of a lifetime! Thank you so much. This is so generous of you. I know it isn't really your thing, so it makes it that much more special."

"I just want you to be happy. I know how much you wanted to get away considering this last year. I was being a selfish and not thinking enough about what you wanted."

Jack took her hands in his and looked intently into her eyes. "The time we had apart let me come to terms with how much give and take

116

there needs to be in a marriage. I'm thrilled to make this trip happen." He smiled lovingly at his wife.

She distractedly wiped away tears that had sprung out of nowhere. "Jack, what a lovely thing to say. I think we are heading into a brilliant year."

~~~

Jack bided his time. The trip was a huge success, and they came home with the usual safari mementos: hundreds of animal photos and bragging rights for spotting the big five, the requisite cases of Constantia and Stellenbosch wine, and deep tans.

Jack's firm was reluctant to let him take vacation at this time, but he convinced them it was critical for his marriage, semi-joking that marriage counselling would be much more disruptive for him than this trip. Boston was getting hammered by price cutting from the competition and the aggressive sharks in their industry smelt the blood in the water. Jack promised his boss his team would be totally up to speed to handle any crisis in his absence. He believed he had covered the bases, so three weeks of being unplugged wouldn't rock the boat. The day after returning, he was blind-sided to hear his major account had pulled their business.

Jack paced the room like a caged animal, gesticulating wildly at his team seated at the meeting table.

"Three weeks! I was gone for three weeks and that's all it took for you idiots to lose this account. It was thirty percent of our revenue stream, for Christ's sake! We had them for seven years and they never indicated there was a problem. What the hell happened? Can one of you morons tell me—"

The door flew open, and Jeffrey shouted inside, "Jack, in my office. Now!"

"I'm in the middle of finding out—"

"Now!" Jeffrey belted out, disappearing down the hall.

"You heard him," Jack directed back at his team. "Get back to work and we'll take this up later."

They gratefully filed out and scurried to their desks. Jack took a moment to calm down and collect his thoughts. He tucked in his shirt that came loose at the sides. He couldn't resist the abundant and delicious food that was continually offered on the trip, and the wine and beer. The excess was showing. He patted down his hair. He needed a haircut as well. One last deep breath and he felt more composed as he strode down to the corner. He straightened his posture and jutted out his chin. As superficial as appearances were, he knew that image played a part.

"What the hell do you think you're doing?" Jeffrey challenged before Jack was even fully in the office. "Where do you get the nerve to launch a fit against your team when this was clearly your fault."

"My fault? Jeffrey, you know I've trained Paul and—"

"Don't interrupt me. You are hardly in a position to play defense on this one."

Jack stayed quiet, standing by the door frame until Jeffrey waved him to sit down.

"We went through this last fall when things were falling through the cracks. I warned you to step it up but obviously you either didn't take it seriously enough, or you don't know how."

"Of course, I know how, Jeffrey. I've been at this game for ten years and can do it with my eyes closed."

"Well, maybe it's time you opened your eyes and looked at things differently. A lot has changed in terms of client expectations and things keep accelerating. Everyone wants things faster and better and cheaper. If we're not delivering, they'll find someone who will."

Jack stayed quiet, not sure if he should look contrite or offended. Before he could compose a response Jeffrey started up again. "The accountants finished with Q4 while you were frolicking with the lions. The firm is down eighteen percent. More than thirty percent is from your division."

Jack was stunned. He knew things were slow, but he didn't know the extent of the damage. He was so wrapped up in his personal life, he hadn't been following things closely.

"I suppose this will affect the bonus pool," Jack said.

Jeffrey went ballistic, "You've got some fucking nerve. This is what you come up with when I've just told you your department has tanked? Unbelievable. No wait, not so unbelievable. No big surprise you'd immediately try to push off the blame at a time like this."

Jeffrey slid the folders across the table. "There will be no bonus for you and you're lucky I don't kick your sorry ass to the curb. Get the hell out of my office before I change my mind. Meet me here at seven am tomorrow morning, once I've cooled off and you've got your head out of your ass, and we can figure out what to do with this mess."

Jack slunk out of the office. It was late afternoon and already near dark. He grabbed his laptop, satchel, coat, and keys from his desk and announced to anyone within earshot that he was leaving for the day. After driving too fast along the side streets, he came home to an empty dark house.

He paced the house, going over the chain of events; I thought Paul had a handle on things. The timing of that vacation on the heels of Christmas was brutal. I've never taken three weeks off work. If only I'd been around, maybe I could have seen it coming. The more he turned the situation over in his mind the more frustrated he became. He pulled the bottle of scotch from the liquor cabinet and poured himself a generous portion. He knocked back a big swig. The burn in his chest felt good even though he grimaced.

Fuck, we never should have taken that trip. We never should have needed that trip. If Rachel hadn't been so selfish and stayed the course with the fertility clinic, she probably would have been pregnant by now. We would be focusing on making plans for raising our child and not gallivanting off to some foreign place looking for kicks. We could have been happy and grounded at home and able to put our energy into building a good life for our children. Damn her anyways. No willpower.

He threw back the rest of the golden liquid. It's her fault my pay will be half of last year's. Jack fumed. He imagined the look on her face when he told her. Won't she love having the upper hand when it comes to our earning power, as well as everything else. Her last year was stellar, she pulled down some serious coin. I can already picture how she'll look shocked and sympathetic at first. She'll try hard to hide her pathetic condescending look, but it will be there, barely contained.

He cursed himself for letting her get such a strong upper hand. Another strong drink didn't help. Feeling trapped and more agitated as he continued to process the sequence of events, he put on his down parka, grey toque, and gloves, and went out to walk off some steam. He passed a young couple pushing a stroller. The child was invisible under a thick sheepskin blanket. They smiled at him as they passed, content within their cocoon. He wasn't in the mood to return the courtesy. His phone rang but he ignored Rachel's call. He couldn't trust himself not to lose it on her right now. He ploughed on thinking about the financial hit.

The mortgage was huge since they were anxious to pay off as much as possible quickly. They had some money set aside for fertility treatment. In vitro, if they needed it, would be $15,000 a shot so that could be quickly depleted. Rachel would use his lack of bonus money as another reason to put off treatment. He thought he'd better not share this part of the story.

Maybe I shouldn't tell her anything at all? He lightened up at the thought of keeping this as his secret. No good can come of her knowing so it's best not to tell her. Since I handle the finances, there shouldn't be any reason for her to know about it. If things get really tight, I can dip into the account we're building to fund the next house move or cottage purchase.

The thought of even the possibility of needing to deplete his dream fund exacerbated his foul mood.

He passed the shops and restaurants on Yonge Street and kept heading east. He knew the general direction where he was heading but didn't let himself think about what he was up to since he wasn't sure himself.

Eastbourne Street was quiet as usual. It was past eight and he imagined mothers reading to their children after bath time; a time of night when all the hustle and bustle slowed for a few precious minutes. Calm damp bodies, cozy in flannel and terry cloth PJs, cuddled up against their parents as they read their favorite bedtime stories. The dishes, laundry, TV, and the dog wait. The voicemail and emails wait. All that matters is the love and security radiating from the ritual.

One fish...two fish...red fish...blue fish.... Paige will be giggling and pointing at the funny fish, the little red car. Everything else pales in comparison. At least that's what I think happens. I wouldn't know from my screwed-up childhood.

For the brief periods when Jack was home for holidays or breaks before getting shuffled off to boarding school again, his father was too busy and his mother zombied out from fatigue or alcohol to pay him any attention. The nannies offered a reasonable facsimile, but it was just part of the job for them. Paid service.

Only one car sat in the driveway, the silver minivan, with no sign of Michael's new BMW. No snow tonight. Nobody in the windows. After glancing up and down the deserted street he crept along the driveway. He paused at the basement window and gave it a shove with his boot. It budged a bit. Another shove and it swung freely.

Holding the window up with one hand he braced himself with his other and slid inside. The cellar was dark. He closed the window and crouched down. He could smell the fresh laundry, which calmed him a little. As his eyes grew accustomed to the darkness, he could make out shapes. Nothing had been moved since his last visit here. He guessed they didn't have any reason to check on the window he had left unlocked. Michael and Sarah were trusting people and never felt the need for an alarm given the safe nature of the neighborhood. He paused as he heard light footsteps overhead charging through the kitchen.

"That's enough, young lady, time for bed," Sarah called, sounding more amused than anything else. The high-pitched laughter let him know who had the upper hand. "I'm just checking on your little brother upstairs and I'll be back."

He heard Sarah go upstairs. He was in a far-off place imagining what she might be wearing when he was shocked to hear the door open from the laundry room. He heard the rapid breathing before he saw her. Paige had found her way into the cellar.

She stopped in the darkness, and facing back towards the door called out, "Weddy or not."

She covered her eyes with her little hands. She stood no more than hip height, clad in a pink onesie. He considered slipping out the window, but was afraid Paige might call out. He heard Sarah trying to calm Connor's crying.

Sarah shouted from upstairs, "You better be a good girl down there. I'll be down in a second."

Paige stood stock-still, waiting for the game to continue. She looked so sweet. He just wanted to give her a cuddle and tell her what a good girl she was, what a great mommy she had. He crept a little closer and from two feet away couldn't resist and whispered, "Found you."

Paige pulled back her hands, delighted that Uncle Jack had joined in the game. She threw her arms around his neck, "Unca Ack, you turn," she said.

Shushing her he whispered, "No, I think Mommy is still it and you should find a new hiding spot." He pushed back her damp curls that were pressed to her forehead. So lovely, so like her mother.

Purposeful steps came from overhead.

"Paige, come out this instant." Sarah called.

Jack lifted Paige and placed her back in the laundry room and shut the door. He moved quickly to the window and was about to make an exit when he heard a cry as Paige pushed back through the door and fell against the hard concrete floor.

Right behind her Sarah scolded, "Paige—I've told you that you are not to come into the cellar. It's too dangerous. Your feet are freezing too."

She raised her up and kissed her neck and squeezed both feet in one hand, "Mommy will warm them up in no time."

"Mommy, Unca Ack's turn."

"What a silly girl. Uncle Jack isn't here.".

"He turn," Paige tried again, squirming to get down and point in his direction.

"Somebody is overtired and needs to get to bed."

Sarah stepped down to the laundry room and turned to close the door, hesitating ever so slightly while peering into the room. A second later she was gone.

Jack calmed down while listening to the bedtime ritual. He smelled his hands over and over, taking in the innocent smell of a freshly bathed toddler. He thought about how wonderful it was going to be when it was his turn. All that other bullshit with work and life so inconsequential. He stayed in the dream state of the happy domestic scene playing out overhead for another few minutes before tearing himself away. Leaving as he had arrived; he was careful to make certain the window was closed.

CHAPTER 24

The next few months went smoothly. Jack made an effort at work and landed a modest account, enough to keep Jeffrey off his back.

Rachel was in full gear with frequent trips to Italy with her team. She appreciated Jack keeping up his end of the bargain and not badgering her about getting back to the clinic. It let her concentrate on securing the senior partnership that was tantalizing close. It did make her feel a little guilty about still indulging in the occasion romp with Marcus while in Milan, but she liked living life close to the edge. It felt like a whole different life that she could simply put away like her suitcase when she was back in Toronto.

Jack dropped by Sarah and Michael's place occasionally on the pretense of checking up on Connor. He made a point of going over when Michael was home so nobody would be suspicious. He'd drop off a little hockey stick or stuffed animal, saying he was passing a store and saw something he thought they would like for Connor. They were always so touched by his thoughtfulness and for taking the time to come over.

"I wouldn't miss out on this for the world," Jack said when they expressed their thanks.

That spring Michael mentioned they were making another trip up north to do some more serious cottage hunting. They had rented a place the previous summer for a couple of weeks and fell in love with the idea of owning a place of their own.

"I really want the kids to grow up with those classic Canadian cottage memories," Michael said to Jack over a beer in his backyard.

Michael had redone the backyard to include an elaborate play structure, a new patio complete with the latest outdoor BBQ gear, a pizza oven, and a gas-fed fire pit sunk into the center.

"Who needs a cottage when you've got all this," Jack declared. "It must have cost you a bundle."

"True enough; any work will set you back a fair bit in this city. Sarah told me that Rachel was talking about you guys doing something similar once she saw our place."

"Well, she'll have to wait since we're saving up for more real estate. A bigger house and maybe a cottage as well."

"Hey, that's fantastic! Not that I'm surprised with the dough you two must be hauling in."

"The damn tax man takes most of it," Jack said to shake him off the topic.

Over the last five months without his bonus income, Jack needed to dip into their account to manage the mortgage and all their other payments. The South Africa trip set them back a lot. He knew they would be okay for a while, but he needed to keep the account substantial enough to fund their fertility treatment when it resumed.

"Maybe you guys want to make another weekend of it like we did last year?" Michael asked, passing him another cold Heineken.

"That would be great. We certainly enjoyed the scenery last year. I'll check with the missus."

When Jack tabled the idea with Rachel, she scoffed. "The mosquitoes will be terrible with all the rain we've had this spring. And besides, I really should stay in town to work. But if you want, it would be good for you. This way I can plow through my work and not feel guilty about ignoring my husband."

"I wouldn't mind it if you're sure you're okay with me leaving, I've been thinking I'd like to take a swing by our old family cottage to see if it's still standing. Maybe bring my rifle and spend a night at the old hunting cabin."

"Such a he-man," Rachel cooed playfully, encircling his waist and looking longingly at him while pressing her body up against his.

"You like your men rough and rugged, do you?" Jack said sweeping her off her feet.

"Put me down this instant, Jack McDermott," Rachel struggled, playing along with the game.

"I'll put you down, all right," he said in a low voice as he carried her back to their bedroom.

~~~

The day was overcast but still had some sunny breaks as he left the city behind early Saturday morning. It was the beginning of a three-day holiday weekend and the traffic was fairly heavy with the parade of cottagers making the pilgrimage north to start the season.

Jack drove on his own and Michael and his family went in their minivan. They agreed to meet at the Algonquin Lodge for lunch since Michael and Sarah were staying there again. Jack was going to sleep at the hunting cabin. Although it was extremely basic, he was looking forward to the solitude.

Lunch took on a whole new frenzied nature with the toddler and the baby. Jack tried to play the gracious uncle but still found the scene infuriating. Michael and Sarah were constantly responding to a question here or a demand there. He felt like a fifth wheel. He excused himself right after the main course, saying he wanted to make tracks to drive by his old cottage and then get set up at the hunting cabin for the night.

The drive calmed him down. The sun was shining, peeking in and out of huge cumulous clouds. Deep blue lakes greeted him at various turns on the back roads. Within an hour he was passing through the four-corner town of Boshkung so he knew he was close. Boshkung had the same general store as when he was a kid. It still had the original worn hardwood plank flooring and carried everything a rural guy needed: booze, fresh meats, canned goods, cigarettes, dry goods and paper goods, junk food, pickled eggs, and pepperoni sticks.

He stopped and bought a few supplies. He thought he recognized remnants of the young woman that worked at the store when he was a kid. The years hadn't been kind to her. Her once perky figure was lost behind a sloppy gut barely contained by her polyester blouse. Dimples from her cellulosed lower half gave her cheap stretch pants a pock-marked appearance. Thin grooves extended from her upper lip towards her nose. Her long thick hair was now a bob streaked with grey. It looked like she had given up on making time to see a dentist with the coffee and wine stains on her teeth.

"Have a good day now, eh?" she said..

Back in his luxurious car he shook off the image. He passed the coin- operated laundromat, milk shake hut, and greasy burger joint. He smiled at the memory of coming in for the best milk shakes in the world. After another ten minutes of driving, he turned off on the gravel road that led to his old family cottage. Some of the family signs looked familiar on a tree pointing the way to the lake; The Millers, The Hughes, The Sandersons; land in the family for generations. There were some newer ones he didn't recognize; The Sparts, The Hilders, not to mention the ones who named their cottage like a resort; Acorn Run, Whispering Pines.

Must be new money, he thought.

He parked at the small parking lot at the boat launch and continued on foot. He was wearing a plaid shirt and khakis to look like a fellow cottager out for a walk. He felt an ache at the strongly familiar smells of lake water and pine trees and the sight of tall birch and maple trees. It was like time had stood still. A dog barked in the distance, and he heard a boat come to life. He walked down the dirt lane and passed a few more cottages before he paused before marker #781. The Hilders. Not The McDermotts. The Hilders. It seemed deserted so he walked down the driveway and waited. Nobody was there so he kept going around the side. The white clapboard was unchanged, but they had added an extension off the back. The worn path took him back to the front and down to the water's edge. A fast-looking tricked-out yellow speedboat was securely tied to the dock with a set of four pine Muskoka chairs.

He heard a car door slam then another three in quick succession.

With no way of getting back to the dirt road except by the way he came, he felt foolish lingering on someone else's property.

"Kids, help me in with the groceries before you tear off to the water," called the mother.

"Awwww, come on, Mom. Let us just jump in," pleaded a boy.

"Can we please, Mom," a young teen whined, "Then I *promise* I will help with *everything*."

The Dad saved them. "Go ahead, kids, I'll do the unloading." Turning towards his wife he gave her a squeeze and laughed, "You know they'll be out of there in about five seconds this time of year."

The kids hurdled themselves with abandon off the dock.

"Ahhhhhhh! It's freeeeeeeeeeeezing!!" they shouted and scrambled out as fast as they went in and tore for the cottage ignoring the loaded car.

Jack managed to skim the edge of the property and disappear back down the road unseen by the Hilders.

Pressing hard on the gas pedal, he roared back to the main road and was shocked to feel the tears burning his cheeks. Was it too much to want a simple place with a family? He felt the world was moving ahead as he watched from the sidelines, his feet stuck in the mud.

Another twenty minutes along, he pulled over down a grassy lane with Angus Smith's farmhouse in the distance. He parked at the side of an old barn. Jack's father Jonathon and Angus had been cordial since Jonathon bought a huge parcel of land from Angus to set up his hunting cabin and have the right to roam the large area. Angus was an old-fashioned rural gentleman and wouldn't hear of taking any fee for letting Jack continue to keep the family's Quad Bike that they used to access the hunting cabin at his farm after Jack's family sold the cottage.

Fishing out a set of keys, he unlocked the dark red door. He dusted off the Quad Bike and turned on the ignition. He maneuvered it outside and hopped off and opened the car trunk. He unloaded a few bags from the general store, a sleeping bag, and a duffel bag with some clothes and personal things. After placing the things in the back, he drove down a narrow path and disappeared into the woods.

The woods darkened as he pushed in deeper. He hadn't been up in a couple of years, but he knew the area like the back of his hand. He didn't pass any sign of life on his way.

Five kilometers from the farm, he made a sharp right and travelled another ten minutes before coming to a halt in front of the cabin. He walked around the back to the outhouse. He felt behind the loose board on the side of the outhouse for the key. Back at the cabin, he wiggled it into the rusty padlock and worked it free. The dusty room was just as he left it; the beaten-up olive-green sofa, the old burgundy plaid chair, the wooden table and chairs, a wood-burning stove, a small freezer, and a gun rack on the far wall. A small alcove served as a sleeping area with a double bunk bed. A cabinet in the kitchen housed a few bottles of rye and whisky. A stuffed deer head was the only decorative touch; it had special significance being the first deer he killed with his father.

He hauled in his few supplies and opened a beer from his cooler bag. The dust danced in the air as he sank down. He guzzled half the can in one go and let his head drop back against the chair. He closed his eyes and let the memories wash over him. His father had been so proud to show him how to load a rifle properly. He was only seven at the time.

Now don't tell your mother I let you do this. You're a young man now so I know you can do it.

Jack got up and crossed the room in three strides and lifted the Winchester M70 in both hands from the rack. He held the rifle close to his face and inhaled the distinctive smell of worn varnished wood and metal.

Be sure to pull the bolt right back. That's it.

His father had guided his small hand to assist with getting the action correct. Jack remembered how shiny and new the cartridges looked all stacked up like neat soldiers in the ammunition box. He was so scared when he dropped the first one he took out. He had closed his eyes, afraid it would explode. His father laughed and reassured him that it couldn't do any damage on its own.

The Winchester M70 was his father's favorite. The walnut stock was worn but lovingly maintained with regular polishing and it felt warm in his hands, his right fingers resting in the grip groove. Pulling back the bolt, he smelled the faint scent of burnt gunpowder, the smell of a successful day. It was rare they didn't kill something, usually deer. The hardest part wasn't the tracking, that was exciting, the anticipation of the kill. They'd be rewarded when they found low branches nibbled on trees, deer droppings, faint tracks from regular travel paths, small water holes.

The hard part was waiting once his father established a good spot. The first few trips, Jack was fidgety and talked too much. His father was stern with his warnings to stay calm and quiet. He told him he would leave him at the cottage with the girls to do more arts and crafts if he couldn't handle the mental discipline required with hunting. He got better quickly, and after only a few trips, had trained himself to wait quietly without moving, for long periods of time. He wanted to make his father proud.

Jack stood up, still clutching the rifle in one hand, and went outside. He squinted in the sunlight after the dimness indoors. He sauntered over to the butchering rack. The bloodstained rope hung off the top rail, and the whetstone for keeping the knife sharp, stood sentinel to the side. He remembered how horrified he was when they butchered their first deer. He cried, thinking his father was hurting the animal. He hadn't wanted to get close to the carcass, but his father insisted he make a few cuts to participate in the whole process. Jack was vaguely aware this was a test, so he choked back tears and did as he was instructed. It took a lot of strength to cut through the hide, but he managed. His father didn't let him do much, just wanted to see if he had the stomach for it. Turns out he did.

Moving back inside, he set the gun back on the rack and fixed himself a sandwich with kobasa, pickled eggs, and cheese, and sucked back another beer. It was only early afternoon, so he went out for a walk in the woods. Initially it felt good walking the familiar paths, but as he got deeper into the woods, his mood darkened along with the dense foliage. It reminded him of his long walks alone as a child at the cottage, of how his father came to the cottage more infrequently as he got older. When he was a young kid, seven-eight years old, they had a few hunting trips a year and Jack thought this was the most special time in the world. No mother. No bothersome sisters. He had cherished this time. By the time Jack was ten, his father rarely came north so Jack was left to his own devices most of the time.

He had mixed emotions thinking back to his private excursions into the woods and his dedicated efforts to build himself his own bunker. He had wanted a place away from the drama and fighting at the cottage. He envisioned himself as a rugged adventurer living off the land, not needing or wanting anyone. After the constraints of private school, this was wildly liberating. He had proven he could hunt well enough to stay full. His bunker was originally barley deep enough to shelter him from the elements, clawed out from the sloping side of a hill. He saw himself as the master of his universe and in complete control. He kept a few essentials there—matches, a hunting knife, rope for snares, and a change of clothes. He would have loved to have had a rifle but didn't know how to get one without his father noticing. He even made a basic bed out of tree limbs he tied together with rope to make a frame to stay off the damp ground. He added sticks across the frame to hold up a makeshift mattress he made from a sleeping bag stuffed with leaves. On another trip, he brought a blanket to keep warm.

Jack had never spent the night in his bunker; he was too frightened by the time dusk fell. The sounds in the forest seemed amplified in the darkness: animals scurrying, a distant howl, a hawk screeching overhead. As much as he tried to endure the encroaching sense of danger, he always gave in. With his heart pounding, he frantically swung the flashlight along the path, terrified that something would leap out from the darkness. The red eyes that flashed back at him from the reflection of the flashlight seemed like something out of a horror movie. Once the light from the cottage was in sight, he'd slow down to compose himself and to wipe the sweat from his brow. He entered the cottage with a casual hello, and nobody would seem fussed by the fact that he had been out in the woods for hours. More freedom for me, he'd think as he dug through the fridge for leftovers.

He was an hour into his walk and absorbed in his childhood memories. He hadn't thought about his private hideaway for a long time. He wondered if it was as he left it as a fourteen-year-old boy, the last summer he went out there. The summer he turned fifteen, his attention turned to girls and partying with the new friends he'd made taking sailing lessons at the lake's marina. It turned out that sex and drinking were even better outlets than his boyish adventures to release his rage against his family.

Later that night after a simple dinner of sausage and beans, and a bottle of bourbon in hand, he had lots of time to turn over recent events. His mind kept jumping from scene to scene, including the happy family now occupying his family cottage. What a prick my father was not at letting me buy the place, if not giving it to me outright. It would have been nothing to him financially.

His mind jumped to Sarah and Michael. They had it all; two beautiful children, a lovely home in the city, money, a successful career with a stay-at-home wife/mother. Soon they'd probably buy a cottage to complement their perfect world. It wouldn't be a fixer-up either, thinking about what Michael must be earning with his company doing so well.

Jack's own dream of owning a place up north was dwindling month by month along with their savings since his income was slashed without his usual bonus. Rachel hadn't found out yet. She didn't care about buying property in the country, but she was combing the Toronto real estate listings more regularly and popping into open houses, drawn by the investment opportunity to make money without getting hit with capital gains.

It was almost a year since they'd been at Best Start. He'd kept up his end of the bargain and it cost him dearly. He was certain the delay caused the stress that contributed to his skid at work. That, and their overly extravagant trip to Africa.

The bourbon was going down easily.

Jack felt the shift viscerally; it was time for Rachel to step up and get their life plans back on track. He couldn't take another holiday gathering when people asked them when they planned on starting a family. All their other friends had either one or two children already. His parents' snide remarks on how Rachel shouldn't wait much longer with the dramatic drop in fertility at age thirty-five only a few years away were especially grating. She simply had to get pregnant this year, then everything would be all right.

CHAPTER 25

On Monday morning of the holiday long weekend, the management team at Goldman gathered in the executive dining room. Rachel was called into the meeting on the pretext of needing her advice on the new textile account they were pitching. She waltzed in with a sense of confidence since she had poured a huge amount of time and energy into their strategy.

The group of eleven men stood up and Mitchell cleared his throat and began after a slight pause, "Before we get down to business, could everyone please first say hello to our new senior partner, Ms. Rachel Madison."

The group burst into applause.

Rachel's hand flew to her mouth, "Oh my God!".

She was the youngest person ever to have made senior partner, and the first woman. Although she expected the announcement, it still came as a shock to hear it.

"Do you accept the position?" Mitchell asked, with forced formality and a slight smile already knowing her reply.

"Yes, yes, I accept. Thank you so much for putting your faith in me."

"We are lucky to have you, Rachel. How about we pop the champagne and have a toast".

The lunchroom attendant pulled the chilled bottle of Mumm's from the silver bucket. He retrieved a tray of champagne flutes and paused at each chair to fill their glasses.

Mitchell held his glass aloft. "Please, raise your glass and toast the latest member of our elite team of partners. To Ms. Rachel Madison for your brilliance, hard work, and dedication. We thank you for all your efforts and look forward to your continued contribution as we take this company higher and further than ever."

After clinking glasses and taking a sip, Rachel responded, "It's been my honor to be part of this incredible group of professionals. I look forward to embracing my new responsibilities as senior partner to continue building the success of Goldman."

"Terrific. Now, let's get down to business and nail this pitch!" Mitchell said, and everyone opened dossiers and laptops while a hot lunch was served.

~~~

As Jack crawled along with the other cottage traffic into the core of the city, he was excited to talk to Rachel about renewing their focus on having a baby. He concentrated on not holding a grudge over the past, her selfishness, her ego, her cold-hearted attitude. He gritted his teeth and did some deep breathing.

Rachel was elated to see Jack and gave him a big hug as soon as he stepped through the door. "You'll never guess what happened! I was going to call you, but I wanted to wait and tell you in person. They made me senior partner today!" She jumped back to fully see his reaction.

"Wow, that's terrific, Rach. That's fantastic news! Lord knows you deserve it with all the time you've put into that place."

"I know! I'm so excited! I'm the youngest person ever to make senior partner, not to mention the first woman."

"I'm really proud of you, honey. They're lucky to have you."

"This will give me extra clout when orchestrating the takeover bid of LMN this summer. Shall we go out to celebrate tonight?"

"Whoa, whoa. The takeover bid of LMN? That sounds like a major commitment. I've spent the whole weekend getting excited about getting back to the Best Start clinic and making a baby."

"Oh, Jack, I thought we agreed to let that rest for a while. I mean, I just made senior partner so I can't be slacking off now."

"Rachel, as much as it killed me, I did back off the baby track for the past year. Did I once ask you to track your ovulation?" he asked with his voice starting to rise. "Did I ask you to skip that trip overseas mid-month last November?" Did I say anything to discourage you from running that full marathon in March and dropping to ten percent body fat?"

Rachel reeled from his verbal assault and was shocked he had so closely monitored her cycles.

"God damn it, Rachel. It can't only be about you and your wants." He backed up abruptly and began pacing the room. His hands furiously raked his hair. "I'm really trying to maintain some balance here, but you're making this extremely difficult."

Before Rachel had a chance to retaliate, he pounced again. "Why don't you ask about my weekend? There's a novel concept, asking about me. I spent the weekend watching other normal families doing normal holiday weekend things. Parents and their kids having fun! Couples bonding over simple things like playing with their kids." Grabbing her at arm's length he tightly gripped her arms. "I've sacrificed more than you can imagine this past year and it's time for you to hold up your end of the bargain."

"You're hurting me, Jack. Let go of me!" Rachel struggled, twisting free of his hold, stumbling backwards.

"WE have an appointment with Dr. Jordan next week. Oh wait, you'd better go fetch your precious phone to squeeze this in between board meetings and presentations. I talked to Dr. Jordan last week and he says we should start with Artificial Insemination since we've been trying naturally for over two years now with no success. After three sessions of AI, we can move on to In Vitro Fertilization."

Rachel was too overwhelmed to say anything. Jack took her silence as a sign to continue. His pacing slowed and he said in a robotic tone, "AI involves seven to ten days of shots that will help stimulate your ovaries to produce several eggs. A shot of HCG will force your ovaries to release your mature eggs and voilà, conception."

"I can't believe you've gone so far as to set up this invasive procedure without discussing it with me first!" Rachel blurted out through her tears.

"But we did discuss it, sweetie. Remember what we agreed to when I moved back home in September? I promised to give it a rest until next year. I've been true to my word. Now it's time for you to keep up your end of the agreement."

~~~

The next day Rachel turned up at Marcus's apartment. Before he had a chance to welcome her in, she threw herself at him. Passionately kissing him, she tore at his shirt as they tumbled back into the hallway. Not caring about what prompted this unexpected visit, Marcus was happy to respond and quickly unzipped her skirt and pushed her back against the wall. Their lovemaking was fast and furious and both were satiated within minutes.

Sitting upright and disheveled on the couch, Marcus produced two glasses of red wine and a pack of Marlboros. He lit both cigarettes in his mouth and passed one to Rachel. "Now that you have taken advantage of me, do I get an explanation?"

Rachel inhaled deeply on her cigarette and swilled her wine. "Jack is on my case about going back into fertility treatment. He's even booked the next appointment."

"How thoughtful of him."

"This is serious, Marcus. I've just made senior partner. The timing is terrible. I don't know how I can push this off any longer without losing him completely."

"How long have you been together? Married for five years? You're both in your thirties so it hardly seems hasty. As much as I hate to take the bastard's side, I'm afraid I'm with him."

"Oh, who asked you," Rachel shot back.

"Listen, it's not like your life will change that much. You have money so you can hire a full-time nanny and get back to work right away. Your husband sounds like he'll throw himself into the daddy role, so you won't have to do too much of that parenting crap, like dragging them to lessons and play dates. Let him buy that cottage he craves, then he can take the kid fishing and hunting or whatever you Canadians do, and you'll get them both out of your hair."

Rachel took a last drag and stubbed out her cigarette in the crystal ashtray.

Setting down Rachel's wine glass, Marcus took her hand and pulled her off the couch, "Now come with me and let me make love to you properly, before you get all hormonal and pregnant."

CHAPTER 26

Dr. Jordan looked as tanned and smug as he did the previous year. A new abstract original piece of art had been added to the wall.

"You're looking well, Rachel," he said. "Glad to hear you're ready for the next step."

He went on to explain the series of shots, "I'll be honest with you that they do sting a bit. When you're in for the shots, we'll perform a quick trans-vaginal ultrasound to follow the egg maturation, so we know when to trigger your ovulation with a shot of HCG. You'll be in and out of here within twenty minutes."

"And how much is this round going to cost?" asked Rachel.

"Only twenty-five hundred per cycle, and this includes all the drugs and ultrasounds," Dr. Jordan replied.

Jack squeezed Rachel's hand. "I've got a really good feeling about this, Rach,"

What the doctor neglected to tell them about were the wild mood swings the drugs induced. Within days of the first injections, Rachel found herself hysterical over the smallest things.

"Do I have to do everything around here?" Rachel screamed when she found Jack's clothes on the bathroom floor or dishes on the counter. "Is it not enough that I'm letting that freak inject me with poison? I'm supposed to put up with your crap as well?"

At work Rachel was irritable with her subordinates and bullied them into taking on more work. "It's so frustrating working with these juniors," Rachel lamented to another partner, Simon, who had been with the firm for ten years. "I thought this promotion would elevate me beyond dealing with these lightweights."

"I hired those lightweights as you refer to them, who happen to have MBAs from Schulich and York," Simon said. "They're the ones with the fresh ideas and will be the future of this firm so be careful what you say."

Rachel bolted to the washroom with a wave of tears rising to the surface.

After her tenth day of injections, the clinic told Rachel to have Jack come in the next day as she was ready for the AI procedure. Jack arrived the next morning and provided his semen to be washed, to concentrate the sperm, to maximize effectiveness. He insisted on returning with Rachel for the insemination at 1pm. Rachel laid on her back. The technician guided the catheter through her cervix. She was swollen and sore from the drugs artificially stimulating her ovaries making the procedure painful.

Jack held her hand, "It's going to be all right."

The tech plunged the semen through the tube and it traveled into her uterus; it was over in thirty seconds. After extracting the catheter, they said she was free to leave, or she could stay on the table for as long as she wanted.

"I think it's best to wait a bit. I read how the sperm takes a few minutes to start swimming, so if you stay on your back, we'll have a better chance at conception," Jack said.

Rachel simply shrugged her shoulders and dutifully stayed put. As much as she hated the drugs and the invasiveness of the treatment, she secretly was praying for success to get this all over with.

For the next two weeks Jack gave Rachel a wide berth, except for her running. "I think it would be better to take it easy for the next couple of weeks and see what happens," Jack said.

"For Christ's sake! This whole thing is making me crazy enough already, and running is one of the few things that calms me down. You heard the doctor. He said I can continue with my usual exercise routine so running is non- negotiable."

"If you love me, Rachel, you'll listen to me. Lay off the running and ease up on your workload, just for these couple of weeks."

"You're lucky I'm going along with treatment at all so back off."

Rachel laced up her shoes and flew out the door, shouting back, "It wouldn't hurt for you to lace up too you know. You're looking pretty loose these days."

Jack waited a few seconds after she was out of sight before letting lose a string of obscenities. Grabbing the closest thing he could find he hurled the ceramic fruit bowl to the floor smashing into dozens of pieces.

Two weeks to the day of insemination, Rachel's period started. She was disappointed but Jack was beside himself.

"I told you to ease up on the running, but you didn't listen! Maybe it would have worked if you'd just done what I asked. Fucking selfish as usual!"

Rach stormed upstairs, stopping on the landing, "Screw you Jack. Here's a new flash – you don't get to control what the fuck I want to do. You got that!"

Afraid of thing escalating to a dangerous place, Jack grabbed his keys and drove over to Michael and Sarah's to blow off some steam. Sarah graciously asked him to join them for supper, saying it was no imposition, there was plenty of food. She laid a fourth setting at the table opposite Paige and beside Connor's highchair.

"It smells delicious" Jack said, tucking into their dinner of roast chicken with the mashed potatoes and root vegetables. He couldn't remember the last time Rachel cooked a good comfort meal like this. Paige, who was going on three, was eating like a big girl using a fork while Connor enjoyed spreading the mashed potatoes all over his tray, squealing at his messy work. Sarah hopped up and down with pleasure to fill the vegetable bowl and get more milk for Paige and beer for Michael and Jack.

Jack thought Sarah looked beautiful in her bright coral capris and tight sleeveless T-shirt.

"Why don't you two relax and catch up while I get these two troublemakers in the tub," Sarah suggested.

Paige protested, throwing herself on Jack's lap. "I want to stay with Uncle Jack."

With Connor on her hip, Sarah said sweetly but firmly, "This is not an option Paige. Come and help me with your brother in the tub." Paige was still refusing to go so Sarah sweetened the deal. "You can come back after your bath to say goodnight if you're good."

Paige released her grip on Jacks arm. "See you soon," she smiled brightly and scurried on all fours up the stairs.

Helping himself to seconds Michael asked nonchalantly, "So how's life?"

"A little challenging at the moment."

"What do you mean?"

Jack took a long drink of his beer and pushed back his plate back. "You know Rachel and I go through our ups and downs. Well, we've been—"

"Michael, can you give me a hand for a moment please?" Sarah hollered from upstairs.

"One second, buddy." Michael said to Jack as he excused himself from the table.

Jack heard hysterical laughter coming from Paige and a firm voice from Michael.

A few minutes later Michael came back to the table rolling his eyes, his shirt soaked. "She's been a real handful lately. Look at what the little rascal did to me. She thinks splashing water at anyone within reach is a great game, so Sarah thinks we need a united approach to set her straight. You know, nip those antics in the bud. Now where were we?" Michael asked.

"Nothing of significance. How about you guys Anything come of your cottage hunting last time you were up?"

"Well..." Michael leaned in smiling. "We were going to keep it as a surprise and announce it with a big party at the lake. But since you asked, we've bought a place!"

"Wow, that's fantastic! Which lake?"

"Hawkeye Lake, up in your old neck of the woods. It's about thirty kilometers northeast of your Bruce Lake." Michael's eyes danced with excitement.

"Well, good for you. Never a dull moment with you guys."

"We figured there's no point in waiting. With young kids, we might as well go for it. I think it'll be good for them to get out of the city, enjoy the country, the clean air and swimming. We're super excited!" Michael said, sounding like a little kid himself.

Jack drank the dregs of his bottle. "For sure. Mind if I help myself to another beer?"

"Oh shit—nice host, right?" Michael bounced up and grabbed two beers from the fridge. "We bought it mainly for the lake and the land. It sits on three acres, but the cottage itself needs a ton of work. It's one of those original cottages built in the 1940s so puny bedrooms, small windows, mishmash of flooring, etcetera. But the view is amazing, and we figure we can work on it slowly when we have the time."

Jack was quick to seize on the opportunity to spend more time around Sarah. "Well, I know a thing or two about cottages. I'd be happy to lend you a hand."

"Really? That would be terrific. I could really use the help," Michael said, shifting to the edge of his seat. "Sarah thinks we should just hire someone to fix it up, but I like the idea of putting my own time and effort into it. A summer project type of thing. My dad thinks he can redo the whole thing but at his age, and with his heart problems, I don't want to burden him too much."

"You know Rachel is a bit of a workaholic, so I have time on my hands.".

"Well, great, here's to cottage life!" Michael toasted.

CHAPTER 27

The clinic recommended back-to-back tries with AI and the second attempt yielded no results.

"God damn drugs! I can't fit into any of my clothes" Rachel complained as she tried to get dressed.

"Do you have my charger?" Jack called from the bathroom.

"How the hell should I know. I'm not your mother."

Rachel continued to toss skirts aside as she searched for something more forgiving. The drugs were making Rachel bloated and irritable. Her tense mood extended to their sex life as well. It was virtually non-existent since the treatments started.

Jack, happy for any excuse to get away from Rachel's moods, went with Michael to their new cottage for several weekends to make a dent in the renovations. He was disappointed he had yet to cross over with Sarah since Michael wanted to do some of the messier work without exposing her and the children to hazards. Regardless, Jack loved being up north, away from the pressures of the city. The work of pulling off the old deck was tough, but he enjoyed doing it. He hadn't done much to stay in shape over the past year, so it felt good to do physical labor and get his mind off things. His company hadn't recovered from the previous year's dismal performance. His boss was always on his case to make more happen. Between work and Rachel, it was enough to make him crazy.

The cottage wasn't quite as rough as Michael had made it out to be, the fixups were more cosmetic than structural. They had the new deck on in three weekends, having enlisted the old gang to help once they had the footings and framing in place.

Brett was still a bear of a man and hauled up the new cedar boards like twigs, jokingly cutting up the rest of them in the process. "Hey, Josephine," he called down to Joe, a friend from Michael's work, after delivering a stack of five boards. Joe struggled to balance two or three. "Could you get me some iced tea?" he asked in a high falsetto voice.

"Very funny, Mr. Neanderthal," Joe shot back with his boards tipping as he tried to navigate the stairs.

Michael laughed and came to the rescue, taking the front end.

"I really appreciate you guys doing this. I guess I had to buy a cottage to get all of us together."

"We appreciate the gesture," Joe said, happy to drop his end after reaching the top. "It's true, though; between work, wives, and kids, we hardly hang out other anymore."

"Well, let me fire up the BBQ and show my appreciation with some fine T-bones."

"No argument from me," Brett responded. He rummaged around his overnight bag and extracted a bottle of forty-year-old scotch. "I hope you all don't mind that I invited Glen to the party."

"All I ask is that you stay sober enough to make sure this deck is secure. I don't want my kids crashing through it on the inaugural visit next weekend."

As the following week wore on, Jack became more furious he wasn't invited to join Michael and Sarah for their first weekend at the cottage since the renos.

Jack complained to Rachel, "Can you believe it? What have I put in, three full summer weekends? And no invite."

Rachel looked at him with mock pity. "Do you really think they want a third wheel encroaching on their precious little family, Jack? Wake up! Michael used you and the good old boys to get his work done, but now it's back to family time like before."

"Put a lid on it, Rachel. You wouldn't understand friendship if it smacked you upside the head. All you do is work-work-work. What do you know about giving? When was the last time you spent a night out with your girlfriends? Do they even bother to call you anymore?"

"You're such an asshole. I need to go." Rachel pushed by him on her way out the door.

"That's it. Run away as usual."

Jack went into work in a foul mood from the events of the week. He was brooding over his lack of plans for the weekend when an email from Jeffrey popped up on his screen: Meet me in my office in 10 minutes.

Jack entered Jeffery's office, ready to defend himself.

"Take a seat, Jack." Jack was barely in the chair for more than three seconds when Jeffery began. "Listen, Jack, there is no easy way to say this so I'm just going to come out with it. We need to let you go."

Jack sat dumbfounded, not able to process the comment. He felt a loud ringing in his ears and pressure in his head. He stared mutely at Jeffrey.

"I'm sorry, but we've given you plenty of warnings over the last year and you've still not picked up the pace. We simply can't carry any non- performers with the demands on our business."

Coming out of his stupor Jack replied, "I can't believe I'm hearing what I think I'm hearing. You're kicking me to the curb after giving you ten of the best years of my career?"

"I'll admit you were stellar up until the last year or two. You were a trailblazer when you joined us, when it seemed our growth was unstoppable. We were making piles of money. But you know as well as I do, things tanked a couple of years ago and we had to restructure. You should be thankful you weren't axed in the first round of cuts last year after the Horizon mess. It's because of your history we gave you another chance and we hoped you'd get back on track this year. But look at these numbers. With the exception of a few fits and starts, the trend is clearly downwards. If this is the best you've got, then I'm afraid you've left me no choice."

"This is bullshit!" Jack exploded, poking repeatedly at the graph. "You can't blame me for Magna Enterprise going under. That company was dysfunctional and never accepted my recommendations."

Jeffrey leaned back fixing Jack with an accusatory stare. "And whose fault was that, Jack?"

"Well, what about Zencor? Why the hell are they not on your lousy graph?"

"Zencor's success is a factor of Talia's brilliance at nailing their output problems and offering them a solution that they accepted which shot them back to the top of their game. Talia should have had your support on this, but when she reluctantly came to me in the spring to express her frustration at your lack of direction, I moved her with the account to Stacey's team."

Jack knew he was losing the battle. "What about United …"

Jeffrey looked at his computer screen and cut him off. "You can talk to HR about your package. You'll get good help through Knightsbridge recruiting services. Take this as an opportunity to re-launch yourself with another firm before it's too late. Good luck." Jeffrey stood up, buttoning his suit jacket, and extended his hand over his desk.

Jack stormed out of the office. There was no way he could face going home. After the nasty exchange with Rachel in the morning, and now this blow, he needed to think. It was late morning when he screeched to a halt in front of his house and kept the motor running. He was in and out of the house in ten minutes; just long enough to grab a bag of clothes and leave Rachel a note saying he wasn't coming home tonight.

Traffic was still moving quickly on the highway since the midday exodus of city dwellers had yet to fully get underway. He didn't have a destination. All he knew was that it was away from everything he hated this morning. He let himself follow the familiar twists and turns that led up to the Haliburton Highlands. After two hours he took Highway 12 that led to his old family cottage. Since visiting the hunting cabin, he hadn't stopped thinking about his old bunker in the woods, wondering if it was still there. It had been a long time; almost twenty years. But it was buried, literally, deep on crown land, so there was no reason anyone would have disturbed his hideaway.

He made a sharp turn down the gravel road leading to the Hilders, the family now owning his old cottage. He parked his car beside the pick-up trucks at the boat launch. He reached into the back seat and pulled out his hiking boots, gladly stepping out of his black leather brogues. He kept on his designer jeans but stripped off his dress shirt to pull on a T-shirt and a red padded lumberjack shirt. He had stopped for some sandwiches and water, so he brought these along in case he got lost. He also took the flashlight from the emergency kit in the trunk. Twenty years was a long time, and he thought it would be shocking if he remembered the location.

Taking the path off the boat launch, after 20 minutes of walking, he saw where the other paths from the back of the cottages fed into his old trail. He noticed the signal had dropped from five bars to one. He marched along unperturbed, enjoying pushing himself to expel some of his anger.

Three months. Three months was all they offered for my incredible ten years of service. I'll only be able to fudge things to Rachel for a couple of months with all our savings depleted. The last payment for the third round of AI drained the room on the credit card. Not that I hold out much hope with our history to date, but I want to see it through as Dr. Jordan had recommended. If we need to try invitro fertilization, we'll just have to sink deeper into debt.

He played these scenarios over and over in his head and barely noticed an hour had passed. The path was barely visible, and he thought he was randomly making his way through the trees until he spotted a flat-topped boulder up ahead to the right. He had the sensation of meeting an old friend as he got closer and the boulder came into full view. The craggy edges within the boulder shifted in his mind and he was able to make out a face, a familiar and welcoming face in the rock: two deep depressions made up the eyes, a long vertical crevice running between the eyes made up the nose. A jagged gash lower down finished the face with a menacing silent laugh.

He climbed on top and opened his lunch. He ate slowly, taking in his surroundings. Nothing had changed in twenty years. It was completely silent except for the odd skirmish in the leaves or the cry of a bird or hawk overhead. He thought about navigating his way forward and recalled using his compass as a kid. He pulled out his phone and lined up the sun in the sky with the position of the sun on the phone and it showed him true north.

It came back to him like a flash: NW315. He felt like he was a twelve- year-old boy again, like slipping into an old skin. The excitement of the adventure was tinged with a sense of isolation. The rejection he felt today from losing his job and fighting with Rachel wasn't so different from how he felt roaming the forest as a kid feeling rejected by his family. His adult body was now being propelled by the memories of a sad and lonely kid. Keeping his phone in front of him as his guide, he pulled branches aside to continue his trek. Another rock face offered him a greeting, so he knew he wasn't far away. Trees would have fallen, and new ones sprouted, so the forest itself wouldn't lead him, but the boulders had remained unchanged since the ice age; he relied on their guidance.

He'd been on the move for over an hour when a rise in the ground made his heart jump. He rounded the mound cautiously. He was fragile and couldn't handle more disappointment. He felt like he was treading on sacred ground; like coming across a time capsule of his life.

His heart pounded upon seeing the remnants of the crude trap door. From the larger piece of plywood that made up the roof, he had cut out and hinged the corner to create a small entrance. Part of the board had rotted through, but there was still enough intact to hold it together. He brushed off the leaves and debris to find the rope handle on the small door. He tugged upwards. Nothing budged. A few more attempts and he realized twenty years of immobility made the roof and door sink into the earth.

Getting down on his hand and knees, he clawed away the soil at the edges. He methodically worked his way around the perimeter freeing the two-by-two-foot door. Panting and sweating he resumed his upright position. Again, clasping the rough handle, he gave it a few more hard pulls and the door swung upwards. It caught him off guard. The handle slipped from his grasp as he fell backward, and he heard the loud thud of the door falling back in place.

"Oh, no you don't."

Standing up and brushing off the dirt from his fall, he firmly planted his feet and slowly lifted the awkward door and propped it up with a large stick.

He peered down into the darkness, thrilled to have actually found this place. The familiar mossy odor of damp earth and the timber walls with the smell of vegetation was welcoming. He went back to his canvas satchel and grabbed the flashlight and looped it around his wrist. Kneeling over the edge, he swung his light directly down from the entrance to illuminate the ladder. Perfect, just like he left it. The scouts had trained him well and this ladder was a testament to their fine instruction. Birch limbs were skinny and easy to cut. He had lined up two longer branches and then fastened shorter branches across as rungs, securing each one with nylon rope in an X-pattern and then pounded in a few nails. The top of the ladder was just underneath the lip of the door. As he slid in backwards on his stomach, his foot found purchase on the third rung down. He descended the remaining rungs to the bottom of the pit.

It was much cooler compared to the surface. He was thankful he remembered the flashlight not wanting to count on his phone battery holding. The door opening only let in a shaft of light. The fact that it hadn't caved in was remarkable. The boards he put in place to hold back the earth were, for the most part, still secure. He smiled, tracing his hands over the rough boards, remembering how he embedded the wooden planks into the first wall going from the bottom to the top. He'd layered over the first corner with the boards making up the second wall in the same fashion. He continued with the same technique all around, in essence creating a wooden box.

The digging had been the first part. It took him almost two summers to get it this deep and wide. He had taken a shovel from the cottage shed that nobody missed and kept it at the bunker. He loved the repetitive nature of digging, finding that it calmed him, and he liked the concrete results that came from his actions. His muscles ached from the pitching and lifting of the earth, but he liked the new definition in his arms and the strength he gained. When he started at age twelve, he had only been thinking about digging a bunker large enough to have a safe place to sleep. Not wanting to sleep alone in the open air once it was finished, he continued to enlarge the bunker. He dug through to the end of the second summer when he turned fourteen. He shot up six inches over those two summers and had real biceps from his secret project. He let his parents think it was the swimming and sports. He finished off the walls the following summer, built the roof and trap door, and constructed his makeshift bed. He'd thought about bringing a girl to his bunker but never did. Instead, he brought out some magazines and enjoyed the privacy to act out his fantasies. He didn't trust anyone to keep his secret.

The makeshift bed had disintegrated, the moldy remains of the sleeping bag in tatters. Seeing the size of the bunker as an adult, he was impressed. He paced the room and guessed it to be about 10 x 14 feet. You could fit a double bed down here, a small table, and even a propane cook-top. He laughed at the thought of people he knew paying ridiculous amounts of money to travel companies to be transported to rough and rugged places to gain bragging rights as an extreme adventure traveler.

He shivered against the cold. After taking a last look around, he climbed the ladder back out and carefully closed the door. He gathered leaves and sticks and covered the top, so on the rare chance of anyone happening by, all that would be visible would be the forest floor. He didn't want his special spot sullied by human imprint. He was careful to gather up any trace of his visit—the wrappers from his sandwich and granola bar. He obscured his own footprints.

He got back to his car late afternoon. Famished from the long walk, he stopped at a road-side food truck for a burger and fries. He watched different families come and go in their flip-flops, tank tops, and bathing suits. Children with sunburnt noses and freckles begged for ice cream.

He started thinking about Michael and Sarah along with Paige and Connor. It was their first weekend as a whole family at their new cottage. Michael mentioned they were going up today to beat the weekend traffic. He imagined feisty Paige never wanting to come out of the water, and Connor being carefully lowered off the dock to feel the cold lake for the first time. Michael would be putting that camera into overdrive.

Best friends for fifteen years! The weekends of helping with the renovations. The pseudo-godfather status. I'm practically family. What the hell, I'll just drive over and take a peek from a distance and not disturb them.

Jack GPS'd their cottage address and found there was a road just above their property leading to another part of the lake. He could check things out at a distance and see if they'd be receptive to a drop-in. After driving for about half an hour, he pulled over on the dirt road shoulder and parked. He was careful to close the door with a gentle push. After a few minutes of cutting through the woods, he saw the sleep cabin, affectionately known as the bunkie. It was set back a good 200 feet from the main cottage. It was a classic bunkie with a double bunk bed. An outhouse stood nearby. He paused, picking up voices by the water.

"Come in, Mommy, it's not cold," insisted Paige.

"Maybe not for you and me honey, but Connor doesn't seem to agree," Sarah replied while bounced baby Connor swaddled in a thick towel to warm him up.

Jack heard some hammering and assumed Michael was working. Jack boldly crossed into an area where he had a clear view down to the dock. Sarah was sitting cross-legged with Connor, who was sitting the same way, with his back to her front, watching his sister in the water and squealing in response to her antics. Paige made silly faces and Connor belly laughed. It was a fun game for both kids. Jack saw Paige's torso bobbing on the surface with an orange life jacket keeping her afloat. Sarah was wearing a one-piece fuchsia bathing suit that dropped into deep V stopping just before the swell of her backside.

"Hey, Brett, can you give me a hand over here?" called Michael.

"Yeah, hold your horses," Brett responded. "Let me secure this fence rail and I'll be right over."

Jack was shocked. He took a few more steps and saw Christy sauntering to the dock with a tray of drinks in one hand and a baby in a carrier in the other.

"Now that's what I call multitasking," Sarah said.

"The best kind there is," Christy said. Her little Johnny flying by, a blur of orange, as he threw himself off the end of the dock to join Paige.

"Johnny, don't splash the babies!" Christy admonished. "Such a little hellion, just like his father."

Laughter rose up from below as the guys did big cannonballs and the kids screamed in delight. Sarah jumped up, trying to avoid the splashes, and handed Connor to Christy.

"I'll be back in a minute once I get some dry nachos," she said, giving the guys an eye roll as she headed up to the cottage. Jack dropped down low on the remote chance she came around the back for something. She went in from the side door.

Jack crept lightly down the hill, staying safely out of sight. Peering from behind a large tree, he could see Sarah moving around the kitchen. Her wrap fell from her waist, but she didn't bother with it since her hands were greasy from cutting cheese. Her bathing suit cut high on her hips.

Without any warning, Sarah's head jerked up and her hand flew to her mouth letting out an anguished scream.

Jack pulled back fast to hide completely and stayed perfectly still.

"Sarah, Sarah. Are you okay?" Michael shouted flying up the stairs.

"I'm such as idiot," Sarah cried, accepting Michael's embrace. "I cut my finger while slicing the cheese and made a big mess."

Michael gently took her injured hand and rotated it slowly. "There's a lot of blood but it doesn't look too deep. I'll get some ice. Just sit down, darling, and keep pressure on it."

Sarah glanced distractedly at the dense forest through the kitchen window. "I could have sworn I saw someone."

"What do you mean, saw someone," Michael muttered.

"Ouch, that hurts," Sarah said as Michael applied antiseptic ointment before wrapping her finger with white gauze. "When I cut myself, I yanked my head up and thought I saw a person out back."

"We're on three acres sweetheart. Nobody is going to be walking on our property. Everyone knows this is private land owned by cottagers."

He finished with the bandage and taped the ends down.

"Still," Sarah trailed off, wandering over and peering out the window.

Michael spun her around, gently forcing her chin up to look her straight in the eyes, "I told you it would take a bit of getting used to, being in the country. The wilderness after living in a city can be unsettling. All those scary movies. You'll get used to it," he promised, and lightly kissed her lips. "Let me get the tray. Can you manage the chips?"

"Of course, thank-you. I'll be right down." She reached for the bag of chips from the cupboard and stole one last look. Nothing but trees.

Jack waited until he heard their voices carrying on with the party by the water before crouching low and sprinting to his car.

CHAPTER 28

Jack kept up the pretense of going to work over the summer. Luckily, he and Rachel never called one another on a work line since they lived on their cell phones. Jack hadn't told a soul about losing his job.

During the first couple of weeks after being terminated, he went to Knightsbridge to do some initial prep to find a new job. Part of the support package included a personality assessment.

"Initial testing and your profile review indicates you would benefit from anger management training," offered Carolyn, Jack's assigned case worker.
"The job market for consultants is slow, so we want you to have the best possible opportunity when presenting with prospective companies."

Jack fidgeted in his seat. "How long is that going to take?"

"We offer a four-week course of therapy with twice weekly sessions. If you wish to continue after that, we have extended packages available, for a fee".

He laughed in her face, "Four weeks? You think eight sessions can even scratch the surface given my history with my fucked-up family and control freak wife? Try a couple of years. I'm not into your psychobabble crap anyways, or letting Knightsbridge profit from my so-called issues, so thanks, but no thanks. I'll deal with things on my own and come back when I want to resume looking.

Jack kept up the routine of leaving for work at the usual time. He visited a coffee shop or greasy spoon in the east end of the city where he was certain not to be seen. He returned home late in the morning and parked in their underground garage. He was surprised how fast the days passed without doing much more than scrolling on his phone and napping.

It was late September and Rachel was going through her third AI. She was on a higher dose of HMG than the last two cycles. It was eight days into her cycle when she collapsed at work. The pelvic pain was sudden and severe coupled with nausea. An ambulance was called, and they raced Rachel to Women's College Hospital. Due to rapid swelling of her ovaries, fluid had leaked into her abdominal cavity. She was more upset about throwing up and passing out in her office than about her actual condition, which turned out to be nothing serious.

Dr. Jordan came to see Rachel and Jack and assured them they could still go ahead with the AI this month. Rachel's eggs were mature and ready to be released.

"I don't know. This just doesn't feel right," Rachel said.

Jack looked crushed. "But sweetheart, this will be our last AI attempt."

"*Our* last attempt," Rachel said. "I love how you give yourself equal credit."

Jack held her hand while sitting on the edge of her hospital bed. He fought to contain his rising frustration. "We've come so far, and just think, in two weeks this will all be behind us one way or the other."

"I can assure you it's very safe, now that we have you stabilized," Dr. Jordan counselled. "I'll give you a few minutes to talk it over."

Rachel rolled her eyes at him and looked away.

"It'll get better, Rachel. I promise to do everything I can to get our relationship strong again. I know we've had a rough go of things lately."

A few minutes passed in silence.

Rachel was still looking into the distance avoiding eye contact. "Do you promise not to bully me back into treatment if I go along with this?"

"I promise, Rachel," Jack said.

After a few quiet tears Rachel said, "Okay, I'll do it."

Jack made a point of being extra helpful with household chores over the next two weeks. He had nothing but time. He made sure the clothes and linens were in hampers for the cleaning lady, shopped for lots of fresh fruit and veggies, and made wonderful home-cooked meals most nights.

After a few nights of this treatment, Rachel commented after a delicious beef bourguignon with French green beans and mini roasted potatoes, "This is really great! How are you managing to get away from the office in time to prepare all this?"

"I'm a master delegator," he boasted, looking pleased with himself.

"Well, you're certainly doing something right. I should take a few pointers. Even as a senior partner, they expect me to keep jumping through hoops and burning the midnight oil, the almighty billable hours rule. Nothing is ever enough for that place. God, I could use a drink right about now."

Jack jumped up and pulled back her chair. "How about a nice foot massage instead?"

"Well, I'd rather have the drink, but I'll accept your offer." She smiled and moved to the couch.

Since the AI treatment was completed, Jack treated Rachel as though she was already pregnant.

"You know, a woman's body is armed with a natural defense to protect a fetus during the first few weeks of conception from the harms of drinking and other toxins. Women don't know they're pregnant until two or three weeks after conception, so obviously many are still drinking, therefore, I don't see the harm," Rachel tried.

"Let me fix you a nice mint tea to go along with that foot rub."

~~~

Two weeks to the day after the insemination, Jack had the pregnancy kit waiting. Rachel hadn't noticed anything different since the procedure. If anything, she felt better and less bloated than she had earlier in the month on the meds. The sun was barely up as Jack paced in the kitchen with Rachel in the bathroom.

She tore open the package and slid the plastic stick out of the foil. Removing the cap, she squatted over the toilet and peed onto the absorbent end. Recapping it, she set it on the edge of the tub and brushed her teeth. She was sure it would be negative. She took her time.

While combing her hair, she picked up the stick and looked at the indicator window. The control line was dark red, showing that the test was working. Then a faint second red line appeared. She sat down on the edge of the tub. Goosebumps spread across her body. Holding the stick straight in front of her face, she was shocked. She suppressed a nervous reaction waiting for the second line to darken. It did. She stared at it for the next few seconds letting the results sink in.

"Jack," she called out of a crack in the door. "You better get in here."

Jack charged down the hall, sliding to a stop in his stocking feet while grabbing the door frame to make a quick turn.

"What's wrong? Are you okay?"

"Oh, I'm better than okay. I'm pregnant!" she shouted, breaking into a beautiful smile.

"You better not be joking," Jack said, dead serious.

Rachel passed over the pregnancy test. "Look for yourself."

"Oh, my God! OH MY GOD!" His eyes flew between the test and Rachel. He couldn't believe it had happened. "WE DID IT, Rachel, we did it. You're finally pregnant! Yeaaaaahhhh!" he shouted as he fist-pumped the air.

Rachel started to cry. "I can't believe it. I figured this wasn't meant to be after the last couple of years."

Jack wrapped his arms tightly around her. "We deserve this, Rachel. We've waited a long time. We've been through a lot and now it's our turn to be happy."

"I guess it is," Rachel said with the shock still apparent in her voice.

~~~

Although Jack wanted to shout the news from the rooftop the next day, he reluctantly agreed with Rachel to wait a couple of months.

"Let's just keep this as our special secret," Rachel suggested shortly after having the pregnancy confirmed with a blood test. "Besides, I don't want my work finding out any sooner than necessary. If I'm careful, I should be able to keep it under wraps until my fifth month."

"You can't really expect me to wait five months?"

"Well, maybe family a bit sooner."

"Oh, come on. I'm dying to tell our friends too. They'll be so happy for us."

"Can you just enjoy me being pregnant and shut up?" Rachel teased, after another wonderful dinner.

"You mean us being pregnant," Jack answered.

"Whatever," Rachel said.

Rachel's due date was June. Jack wanted to get into decorating the nursery right away, but Rachel slowed him down.

"It's only October, Jack, we'll have plenty of time for that over the long winter."

Over the next couple of months, Jack managed to continue to hide the fact that he wasn't working without too much trouble. He rationalized it by telling himself he didn't want to burden Rachel in her state. He felt a little sheepish fabricating stories about work, but he usually steered the conversation with Rachel back to her work or the baby, without too much difficulty. He had almost convinced himself he was still battling with his co-workers, so the stories seemed credible.

Without much to occupy his time, Jack obsessed over the pregnancy and having a child; who it would look like, how they would raise them, school options etc. He played over and over the scene when he would tell his parents—his father would be so proud. They'd been asking ever since he'd gotten married when they were going to give them a grandchild. He was so glad they didn't need to be disappointed any longer.

And their friends! He imagined being part of the unofficial but very real 'young family club', soon to be included in the family getaway invitations, Saturday morning park meet-ups, the playdate circuits. He dreamed about saving again for a cottage so he could provide his child with the luxury of summers up north. It gave him extra incentive to get back on the job hunt.

Sometimes he worried about their finances. It had been almost four months since he'd been let go. Their savings were totally depleted. Carrying the mortgage and keeping up on all their usual expenses was tough on one income, even a good one like Rachel's. With her promotion she had been given stock in the company which would be lucrative down the road, but it didn't help boost their current income. He'd managed to extend their line of credit by putting up more of the house for collateral. He was sure he'd get a job in the New Year, if not before, and get back on track financially.

Rachel was lucky in her first trimester not to experience any nausea or fatigue. She was excited about the baby, and happy about how thrilled Jack was and the positive effect on their relationship. He was a changed man.

On the first weekend in December, they invited fifty people, including friends, family, and a few of Rachel's work friends to their house to kick off the holiday season. Jack went crazy decorating their imposing front yard with white lights and fresh garland. They put up a ten-foot tree in the formal living room and another in the family room off the kitchen. The hundreds of little white lights shining against the silver and gold ornaments looked beautiful. A fire roared in the fireplace with cards clipped to a metal wire strung above a simple, clean mantle. Massive white poinsettias lined the foyer. The dining room table was laden with goodies: cheese platters with figs and olives and clementines, chacuterie boards piled high with prosciutto and rosemary ham, gourmet crackers and breads, and delicious sweet treats. Specialty beer was packed on ice in silver beer tubs. Bottles of red and white wine from South Africa and France lined the kitchen counter, like girls in a middle-school gym waiting to be asked to dance. Michael Bublé crooned carols from their sound system. Everything was perfect.

All their friends had busy lives, but everyone made a point of coming to the early Christmas parties. The invitation was addressed to families, so people turned up with their little ones in their finest.

Michael and Sarah arrived early, and Paige gave Jack a lovely greeting. She looked adorable in her full red satin dress with white lace trim on the collar.

"Uncle Jack, Merry Christmas," she shouted raising her arms to be lifted. Connor toddled in holding his mother's hand.

"Wow! When did this happen?" Jack said, crouching down to greet his little godson.

"They have a way of growing up fast. I swear, he can run the length of a football field now," boasted Michael.

Rachel looked down at Sarah's swollen belly. "And how about THAT?"

"I guess it's pretty obvious now," said Sarah, sounding almost embarrassed. "We want a big family, three to four kids, so we figured we might as well keep going while we are deep in the baby years. No point in getting our heads above water only to plunge back in, right?"

Jack leaned in, giving Sarah a very affectionate hug. "Wow, congratulations."

Jack was thrilled he could one-up Michael with their own news

156

soon.

"Thanks for being so happy for us," Michael said, genuinely touched.

Jack pumped Michael's hand. "I'm thrilled,"

Brett and Christy arrived shortly afterwards with two kids decked out in black leather with red shoes.

"Very hip," Rachel nodded in approval, handing out Crantinis, while greeting the guests.

Larry and Alison joined in later with their Sky finally out of the sling. The child was thin and quiet.

"He'll just find a quiet spot and read. Don't let us forget him on the way out," they joked.

"Stopping at just one?" asked Christy after catching up for a while with Alison.

"With all the problems we have with the environment, we feel it's irresponsible to have more than one child," Larry said.

"Well, Brett seems to keep breaking through the condoms, so please, go and talk to him about responsibility," Christy slurred, tossing back her cocktail.

The house was noisy with festive cheer. Jack's and Rachel's parents were present, plus a few other older friends of the family. A dozen children scooted in and out of adult legs. Everyone seemed to be enjoying themselves.

Jack entered the living room carrying a kitchen chair. Setting it down near the mantle, he climbed on top. He tapped his cocktail glass with a knife. *Ding, ding, ding.* The din of the crowd didn't relent. *DING, DING, DING.*

"Can I have your attention for a moment?"

The group quieted and someone turned the music down.

"I have an announcement I'd like to share with this special group of family and friends."

Rachel's look of curiosity changed to alarm. She maneuvered through the crowd to stand beside Jack and looked at him sternly while tugging his arm to get him off his perch. He ignored her while people waited for him to speak.

"I'm so glad we have such a great turnout today and I hope everyone is having an awesome time," he said with a big smile.

A few people called back their thanks and held up drinks to toast.

"As most of you know, Rachel and I have wanted a baby for a long time now."

Rachel looked mortified and slipped out of the room.

Undeterred, he carried on. "It looks like our dream is coming true. We're thrilled to announce we're expecting!"

The crowd erupted in a cheer.

"Way to go, man!" Brett called out.

"Fantastic! Welcome to the club," shouted Christy.

"We couldn't be happier," beamed Jack. "Let's have a toast to baby McDermott!"

The crowd clinked glasses and drank to their happiness.

He searched for his father to gauge his reaction, anxious to catch his look of approval. He jumped off the chair and was surrounded by a crowd of well- wishers. After a few minutes of enjoying the moment, Jack looked for Rachel upstairs and entered their bedroom.

Rachel's face was a mess with tears, her face stained with mascara. "I can't believe you."

"I thought you'd be happy. I figured why wait when we have everybody here and the mood felt so right."

Rachel was on her feet now and frantically pacing the room. "We had agreed to wait until January. We had a plan."

"Well, plans change, and I don't know what the big deal is."

"It's a big deal to me! You knew I didn't want it out there yet. My work had no idea and now they're sure to find out!"

"Calm down, sweetie, this can't be good for the baby."

"Screw the baby! What about me and what I want?" she screamed.

"Keep it down, will you? People will hear you."

"No, I won't keep it down. I don't give a shit about what people think. It's still all about you, and what you want, isn't it? Here I was thinking you'd changed, we were back on course as a couple. What a fool I was. I should have known better. It's always been about you getting what you want, when you want it. You're a selfish bastard, Jack, and you know it."

Jack intercepted her pacing and tried to guide her to the bed. "You better sit down; you seem very upset."

Rachel yanked her arm free. "Get your hands off me. Don't tell me what to do," she spat with fury burning in her eyes.

"It must be the hormones," Jack said. "You are totally overreacting. You should be happy to share such good news."

"You son of a bitch. Don't try to blame me. This situation is your fault. You should have asked me first."

"Well, what's done is done and you should get over it."

"You're unbelievable. You're still trying to control me. Get the hell out."

"Gladly," Jack said, slamming the door behind him when he left. He took a minute to compose himself at the top of the stairs.

Rejoining the party below, he reset his expression to one of triumph and contentment and floated back into the scene. His father greeted him in the living room with a firm handshake and pressed his other hand on his shoulder.

"Congratulations, son, this is wonderful news."

Jack felt like crying but held it together. "Thanks, Dad, we're really thrilled."

"Where's Rachel? I'd like to give the future mother of my grandchild my blessing."

"Oh, you know pregnant women. She's a little emotional right now and needed to lie down."

"Fair enough. Let's pour ourselves a drink and have a proper toast."

Jack glanced up the stairs while heading over to the bar cart, relieved not to see Rachel. He didn't want her spoiling this special moment.

CHAPTER 29

They were still barely speaking a week after the party as they drove to the hospital for the ultrasound. It was a bright cold day as they went south on Avenue Road and pulled into the underground parking lot.

"Thirty dollars a day!" Jack said as he took the parking ticket from the machine. "It's enough to make you sick." He thought his lame word play might get a smile out of Rachel, but he was disappointed. After parking and turning off the engine, Jack turned in his seat towards Rachel.

"I don't know how else to make it up to you. I've said I'm sorry over and over. I never figured telling our close group of family and friends would have been so bad. Obviously, it was and I'm truly sorry for that."

Rachel was silent with her eyes cast downwards with her hands on her lap.

"This is such a big moment for us Rach," Jack pleaded. "I can't imagine seeing the first image of our child and being on the outs with you. I love you, Rachel. Please."

"I would like nothing better, but I still feel this fissure between us. Your announcement without my consent was huge. You broke my trust, and I can't get over it like I normally do when we fight. I'm trying but I can't make the leap, I need more time."

"Maybe seeing our little miracle will do the trick," Jack said.

Rachel gave back a little with a faint smile.

"Come on, we don't want to be late," Jack said. He hopped out of his side and opened the door for her. She didn't resist when he took her hand as they stepped into the elevator.

They didn't wait more than ten minutes before they were called into the ultrasound room. A middle-aged nurse named Wanda greeted them warmly and asked Rachel to put on a gown and left them alone. The room was dim and full of equipment. As Rachel pulled the gown closed with her back to Jack, he hugged her gently from behind and buried his face in her neck. After a moment, she turned to face him and lifted her hands and rested them across his forearms. Tears trickled down her cheeks.

Patting his arms lightly, she said, "Okay. We're okay."

Just then, the radiology technician tapped on the door twice and asked if she could enter.

"Of course," Jack quickly replied but then looking at Rachel, "If that's okay with you?"

"Yes, of course."

"Hello, I'm Teresa and I'll be doing your ultrasound today," the technician said.

Rachel and Jack looked at each other in anticipation.

"All right, Ms. McDermott. If you can get up on the table, and rest back please, we'll have a look at your baby."

Rachel and Jack exchanged smiles. He stood by her side and held her hand while the technician punched in data on the machine from a chart.

"Here we go," Teresa said as she squirted a small circle of cold goop on her belly.

Jack watched Teresa start her slow circling motion, thinking Rachel hadn't shown much for fourteen weeks, assuming this was due to her disciplined fitness routine. Teresa angled the screen a little more her way. She pressed down gently on Rachel's belly and paused while she entered some information. The screen was a grainy black and white blur. She pressed a little more firmly and made more notations. Jack and Rachel waited patiently.

Teresa pulled out the chart. "It says you're fourteen weeks along. Can you tell me when you had your last period?"

Rachel responded easily, having been asked this question a few times now. "September seventh."

"Thank you."

Jack was intensely watching the screen and broke into a huge smile when he thought he saw the outline of the baby. "Oh my God, Rachel. Would you look at that! There he is!"

"Jack, you're crushing my hand." Rachel winced.

"Oh... sorry, honey, but did you see him?"

"It's all pretty grainy to me but maybe."

"Is that the baby?" Jack asked Teresa.

Teresa responded with a weak smile.

Jack and Rachel shared a loving exchange and looked from Teresa back to the screen, awaiting more details. They were surprised when she told them the exam was finished.

"Aren't you going to show us more than that?" asked Jack. "I thought we'd get more of a blow-by-blow on the little fella."

Teresa shut off the machine.

"You can get dressed now, Ms. McDermott, and the doctor will need to speak with both of you. I'll leave you for a few minutes and then Wanda will come back and bring you to his office."

Teresa quickly left the room.

"Huh? That's strange. I hope everything is all right?" Jack said as Rachel stood to get dressed.

Rachel felt time slow down. She heard what Teresa said as though she was speaking in a deep slurred voice. She felt like she was in a movie. She heard the words but didn't want to compute the meaning. For the first time in the last three and a half months she felt sick to her stomach. She knew. The news hung in the room like a foul odor. She felt it all around her. Her knees buckled and Jack grabbed her under the arms to ease her landing as she went down and vomited on the floor.

"Rachel—Rachel! Are you alright?"

"Oh no, please no, please no," she repeated, beginning to rock side to side.

"Help! We need help in here," Jack shouted while holding Rachel upright.

Wanda quickly slipped inside the room and took over. She eased Rachel back on the table and laid her down while she checked her pulse and took her temperature. All was normal.

"She dropped like a stone and was sick." Jack blurted out. "I don't know what happened. She was fine a minute ago."

Wanda gently cleaned Rachel face. "If you're ready, Dr. Peters can see you now and he will explain everything."

The doctor's office was right down the hall, strategically away from the waiting room of happy expectant parents. Dr. Peters introduced himself and asked them in a soothing tone to take a seat. The fact that Rachel's face was a mess of tears and mucus didn't faze him, he dealt with this every day.

"I'm terribly sorry to tell you this, and there is nothing to make it any easier. Your fetus isn't viable. There is no heartbeat."

The sobs Rachel had been struggling to hold back burst forth like a dam giving way. "Nooooooooo," she cried with her chest heaving for air. "There must be a mistake. I'm fourteen weeks pregnant." She looked frantically from the doctor to Jack, trying to find her footing in a world that had caved underneath her.

"I don't understand, Doctor," Jack said. "We had a doctor's appointment a few weeks ago and the heartbeat was strong and regular. They picked it up with a Doppler. Perhaps if we try again with a Doppler that would work better?"

"I'm afraid there is no doubt. The ultrasound always picks up the heartbeat after the seventh week of gestation and you've been fourteen weeks since your period."

"But why would it just stop after twelve weeks?" Jack asked. "I thought once you got to twelve weeks you were virtually past the miscarriage stage."

Dr. Peters thought how typical it was for the man to be information driven at a time like this while the woman would be drowning in despair.

"It's more common than you might think," Dr. Peters informed them, sounding cold and clinical. "An estimated fifteen percent of all conceptions end with miscarriage in the first trimester."

"But it was there two weeks ago!" Jack said, getting louder with each question and comment.

Dr. Peters responded calmly, "Again, I'm very sorry for your loss. This is often nature's way of taking care of things that aren't meant to be. There isn't anything more we can do. You have the choice of letting your body expel the fetus naturally, but this can be a very emotional experience. It can take days or sometimes weeks for this to occur. We recommend a scheduled D&C, a Dilation and Curettage, within the next couple of days; to remove the fetus and other tissue."

Jack's hands were trembling, he was totally at a loss for words.

Dr. Peters slid a brochure with a sad looking couple on the cover that read 'Coping with Pregnancy Loss.'

Through her tears and barely audible Rachel asked, "Was it a boy or a girl?"

~~~

Rachel was devastated and curled up in a small ball on their king-size bed. She was shattered, broken. She cried forty-eight hours straight, only stopping when she fell into short, exhausted sleeps. Jack brought her soup, cheese and crackers that she didn't touch.

Jack's head was spinning, piecing together fragments of his life. He told Rachel he was taking the week off to be there for her. She still didn't know he'd been fired and wasn't working.

The third day after the worst day of her life, she was back in the hospital for the D&C, pale and exhausted. She handled the anesthetic well and couldn't believe it was over so fast. She was home in a matter of hours and relieved to have Jack so attentive.

"Can I get you more Tylenol, darling?" he asked after settling Rachel into bed.

"I'm okay with what they gave me at the hospital."

"Anything else?"

Tears flowed easily and she didn't bother to wipe them away. "No, I'm going to try and sleep for a while. Thanks for everything."

Jack sat by her side, stroking her forehead. "I can't believe this. What we've gone through. After waiting so long to get pregnant, it feels like a cruel joke."

"I can't even go there right now. I keep thinking about the baby, our little boy. What could have been."

"Shhhhh, it's okay. We'll be okay," Jack said. "We'll try again as soon as we get the green light from Doctor Jordan."

He was startled when she pulled back, glaring at him through bloodshot eyes. "We can't just go and replace him, you know," Rachel said with more strength than he expected.

"No, no, of course not. That's not what I meant. I know how much we both looked forward to parenting and having a child. I thought it would help with the healing process if we had another child to look forward to as soon as possible."

"You really don't get it do you. You should get back to work, Jack.

164

I'll be fine. I'm going to go to sleep now." She tossed on her side with her back to him and pulled up the duvet, virtually covering her head. As he was heading for the door she added, "It would be better if you slept in the spare room so I'm sure to get a good night's sleep."

Jack went downstairs and poured himself a large tumbler of scotch. He drank it in two gulps and poured another, then flopped down on the couch. "What a mess," he said.

Rachel's D&C was the previous day, so he was surprised to see her in the kitchen, dressed for work the next day.

"Do you really think this is a good idea?" Jack said.

"I feel fine physically," she responded. "Mentally I'm completely hollow, but that shouldn't interfere with me being good at my job."

"I think you're pushing it," Jack said. "The doctor recommended taking a couple of days off for your physical and mental recuperation. If you feel well enough, you can go back to work on Monday."

Rachel sipped on a strong cup of black coffee.

"The good doctor doles out the same advice to secretaries and shop workers. Is he the one who will handle the pile that's been growing on my desk? I've already lost almost the whole week. I want to at least get a handle on what's been happening before it hits me like a tidal wave Monday morning. I've had hundreds of emails over the last four days." She took a few more sips from her mug and set it down on the counter.

"I'm sorry, dear, but I really insist you take the day at home. I'm worried about you," pleaded Jack.

"Well, that's sweet but don't be," dismissed Rachel. "Oh...and I don't take too well to insisting either." She gave him a peck on the cheek followed by a frozen smile. She grabbed her briefcase and keys and sailed out the door.

He stood shell-shocked and alone at the huge kitchen island. He had to find a way to get her to listen. He wanted her healthy and strong so they could try again right after her first period.

~~~

The stream of consolers from work and friends and family meant well, but it only exacerbated their grief.

You're young, you have plenty of time.

165

At least it was early.

It just wasn't meant to be.

Just relax and it will happen.

Their house looked like a funeral parlor with the number of flowers they received. Rachel swept them into the trash within moments of receiving them. She didn't need any reminders.

Only Rachel's mother knew the right thing to say, which was nothing at all. She came over delivering only hugs and meals. Jack was careful not to broach the subject. Their first weekend after the D&C they did a lot of sleeping and watched movies at home. Rachel spent some time in their home office. It was January and the temperatures stayed well below zero. There was fresh snow daily. The snowbanks along the sidewalks were three feet high. It was like a massive white blanket had been thrown on the city, making everything feel muffled and subdued, a perfect to match their moods.

Rachel lost herself in work. It was a good way to numb the pain and made her feel needed.

Rachel's management team gathered in the executive boardroom for a Monday morning meeting waiting for Rachel to arrive. A server in black and white attire silently moved to each seat filling their cups with steaming hot coffee.

"Can you imagine having to hold her job for a year?" the senior partner stated.

"Ridiculous," replied another. "It's no wonder there aren't more senior female executives with commie government programs like ours."

"That's for sure. You don't build up relationships trusting someone with billions of dollars and then turn it over to a one-year contracted consultant," piled on another.

Rachel entered the room at eight am sharp looking ready for the day. The team awkwardly shuffled some papers and reached for their cups.

"Good day, Rachel," Mitchell said.

"Good morning to all of you," Rachel replied pulling files from her briefcase and motioning to the server for coffee.

"Great to see you looking so well," Mitchell said. "Let's get started, shall we?"

While Rachel seemed to have found a way of compartmentalizing her grief, Jack's spread like red wine on white cotton. His long days at home provided hours for brooding and reflecting. After going through his false routine in the mornings, he came home and changed into sweatpants. He had his lie at the ready in case Rachel came home midday; he was doing some project work from home that required deep thinking. He knew he should at least get to the gym, but didn't have the drive.

Luckily there wasn't much going on socially. Jack couldn't stand the thought of seeing their friends with their babies and young children. They were invited to Brett and Christy's ski chalet a few hours north of the city for a three-day getaway mid-February. They used Rachel's work as an excuse to back out.

It was late afternoon on a Saturday and already dark at five pm. Rachel stretched as she came down the hall, drawn in by the delicious smell of lamb stew. She'd been happily holed up in her home office for the past few hours. She loved her new personal office on the second floor. Of the four large bedrooms, they already had one converted into a home office before the miscarriage. They were planning on converting the larger of the two spare rooms into a nursery. It was her present to herself after the miscarriage to have this room set up as her own personal office. She was tired of sharing a workspace with Jack and worked better in control of her own environment. The modern color scheme she chose of deep browns and neutrals, along with her sleek walnut desk and wall unit, did a good job displacing any nursery cobwebs lurking in the room.

"That smells amazing." Rachel enthused, inhaling deeply over the simmering pot. The apricots and raisins added a delicious, sweet flavor to enhance the lamb stewing in saffron, rosemary, and fresh tomatoes. The gas fireplace made the large space a little cozier.

"I know one thing that will make this better," she said, pulling a Chilean cabernet from their wine rack recessed in the island.

As she reached for the corkscrew in the drawer, Jack covered her hand, halting her movement. "Darling, I don't think it's a good idea."

"Well, I think it's an excellent idea, if you don't mind," she said shaking her hand free and pulling out the corkscrew. "Nobody is putting a gun to your head to make you join me," she added pulling the cork from the bottle.

"I was hoping we could talk about things tonight," Jack said, testing the waters. "Our plans."

Rachel poured herself a generous glass of wine and dropped down on the couch. She extended her stocking feet to rest on the slate coffee table where glossy picture books were arrayed waiting for someone interested in art or architecture.

"Sure, I'd love to," Rachel replied, surprising Jack.

"Oh really? Well, that's fantastic. Are you sure it's not too soon?"

"Not at all. I've been dying to get away with winter dragging on like this. I've been looking at resorts in St. Lucia or a sailing trip off St. Bart's."

She took a long sip of her wine.

Jack was careful to check his response. He joined her on the opposite sofa and poured himself a glass of wine.

"Both sound wonderful," he said. "It would be a great way to rest up and have some fun after these past weeks."

He didn't want to miss the opportunity with Rachel appearing so open and relaxed, so he got up and sat beside her.

"After our holiday, we can get back to Best Start and moving on with our lives." He went to put his arm around her, and she shot up like a bullet.

"I knew it!" she yelled. "I knew you couldn't just live with things the way they are! It's never enough, is it, Jack? You'd drag me kicking and screaming back to that horrible clinic, and have me injected with poison, to get your prized offspring! Oh, and when I miscarry for the second time, it can't be nearly as bad as the first, right?"

Rachel stormed towards the stairs, but Jack was right behind her and yanked her by the arm, spinning her around inches from his face.

"You're talking crazy," Jack said, firmly holding her in place. "I thought you were ready, but I guess it's too soon. You're clearly still on edge from the loss. I can wait a bit longer."

"It is not too soon, my friend. I never bought into your baby making plan, but you refused to listen. I never wanted a baby this way. I think it happened for a good reason. It was never meant to be."

"I'm going to pretend I didn't hear that. I'm going to walk away until you come to your senses. You're obviously still in distress," he said, releasing her arm and turning away.

It was Rachel's turn to halt Jack.

"Don't you walk away from me. And don't patronize me by implying that I'm the one on edge and the one who needs to come to my senses. You're the unhinged one here. You're the one who pushed for this, who virtually gave me no choice in the matter. I did my part and guess what? It didn't work. Well, that's the way life goes sometimes. Like the song says, baby, you don't always get what you want."

"Oh, but I do and I will," Jack said. "We McDermotts have always succeeded."

"Oh really," she said. "That will be a little difficult without my consent."

"You look a little pale, Rachel," Jack said, turning away and walking slowly towards the kitchen. "I think you should go and lie down. I'll bring you dinner in bed in a while."

"Nice try, Jack. But I'm feeling just fine, thank you very much. How sweet of you to be so considerate."

Jack looked at her over his shoulder, mildly amused, and kept walking.

"You realize you're a control freak, don't you?" Rachel layered on. "You really should get some counselling, you know."

Jack slowly stirred the stew, now burnt and stuck to the bottom of the pot. "What a foolish little bitch," he said quietly. "She's gone and ruined everything."

~~~

The icy divide refused to thaw after their heated row. Rachel stayed busy with work and friends and slept in the guest room. They were civil to each other on logistical matters but that's as far as the communication went. It was an unseasonably warm day in late March when Rachel came home early to take advantage of the milder temperatures to get in a longer run. She was training for the Toronto Marathon held early May every year hoping to break her personal record she'd nailed in the Boston Marathon a couple years ago.

Rachel flew in the front door and nearly wiped out sliding on the mail splayed on the floor. "God damn him."

Jack always brought in the mail since he liked to pay the bills and control their finances, and he was usually home first. He was emphatic about wanting to take care of their finances from the time they were married. He said he knew it was old-fashioned, but that's how his father handled things, and he wanted to be able to do the same for his family. Rachel didn't really care, although it seemed a little chauvinistic at the time.

The house was quiet. Rachel scooped up the envelopes and tossed them on the hall table. The red lettering marked URGENT NOTICE halted her stride. She backed up and pulled it from the pile. Normally she would disregard a notice like this, figuring it was a lame attempt at a company enticing you to sign up for something. But this one had an official-looking Scotia Bank address in the top left corner of the envelope. All their banking and investments went through Scotia Bank. Slightly curious, Rachelle sliced it open.

Scotia Bank

March 20, 2007
Dear Mr. McDermott and Ms. Madison, Re: **Petition for Foreclosure**

We regret to inform you that your house at 63 Brettcliffe Ave. Toronto, ON B2V 1X8 will be auctioned as of April 30th, 2008. Our concerted attempts over the past few months to obtain payments as per your mortgage contract #B8491 have yielded no payment. We have obtained an Order Nisi with the Supreme Court Registry.

 Sincerely,
Bob Jones, Senior Default Manager

Rachel read the letter over three times. Petition for Foreclosure? There must be a mistake. She went to phone Jack but held back. She was getting close to putting the fight behind them, but she wasn't quite there yet. She had barely spoken to him for almost five weeks and wasn't ready to engage in any real conversation.

Rachel had never heard of Bob Jones, so she searched her contacts for their usual account manager at Scotia Bank. She found Ingrid Singer, Senior Account Manager, BCom, MBA and dialed the number.

"Ingrid Singer speaking."

"Hello, Ingrid. I don't know if you remember me, I'm Rachel Madison, Jack McDermott's wife?"

"Yes, hello, Ms. Madison. How may I help you?"

"Please, call me Rachel. We received a letter from your bank today saying something about a Petition for Foreclosure. There must be some mistake."

Rachel heard the fast clicking of typing on a keyboard.

"There is no mistake, Ms. Madison. You failed to make your January 15th and February 15th mortgage payments. After numerous phone calls and emails to your husband, with no efforts or payments made to remedy the situation, we sent a letter on March 8th stating our next course of action; the Petition for Foreclose."

Rachel was dumbfounded.

"I'm sorry, Ingrid, but there must be some mix-up. Jack and I have very good incomes so this makes no sense."

"With all due respect, Ms. Madison, I suggest you speak with your husband. I also suggest you get legal advice. You have seven days to file for an Appearance from the Supreme Court Registry."

"A what? Court Registry?"

"Again, I'm sorry, Ms. Madison, but this is out of our hands now. You'll need to go through the proper channels. Good day."

Rachel wandered around the living room playing back the past few minutes. She wasn't overly concerned, certain it was a clerical error, but still, she wanted some answers. She was mainly upset that she was going to miss the last of the sunlight and have her run delayed.

Reluctantly she called Jack. It clicked into voicemail. She stopped at the fridge and poured herself a veggie smoothie and added protein powder. Upstairs in the office she rummaged through the filing cabinet where they kept their bank statements. There were no statements from last year or this year.

Rachelle kept a written record of her banking password for the joint account they used for their auto pay deposits, savings, paying the mortgage, car payments, credit cards etc. It also linked them to their investment accounts Jack managed online. She hadn't had any occasion to look at this account since last summer when they made a new financial plan together to move some money around. They each kept a separate account for regular expenditures with funds automatically transferred from the joint account monthly. She went into a dresser drawer and opened the small notebook where she hid her passwords. Before doing anything else she took the time to get into comfortable running gear, hoping to still cover some distance before it was too dark. With the notebook in hand, she sat in front of her computer screen and pulled up the online banking window. She keyed in her password: NVR356&. *Incorrect password, please try again.* She slowly typed in the seven-digit code. *Incorrect password, please try again. Warning! For your protection, any further incorrect attempts will result in suspension of your account.*

"What the hell!" She tried one last time. *Incorrect Password, Account Suspended. For security reasons please visit your closest branch for assistance in resetting your password. Two pieces of ID will be required.*

"Great! This is just great," Rachel shouted, slamming her hands on the keyboard. She spun her chair around and looked out the big bay window on the brilliant orange setting sun.

"Where the hell is he?" Snatching her phone, she tried his cell again. Voicemail.

Although it was virtually useless to get a live person at Boston, she dialed the number. All employees used their personal cell phones as their direct line, so they had done away with a staffed reception. She figured she was destined for an automated dead-end loop but didn't know what else to do.

When she dialed the main number, an automated response prompted her to enter an extension or a last and first name.

M-C-D-E-R-M-O-T-T J-A-C-K.

We're sorry, we don't recognize the name entered. Please try again.

Rachel took a deep breath and repeated the entry. She received the same response. She automatically hit zero and was shocked to get a live person.

"Boston Consulting, Daniel Turner speaking, how may I help you?"

Rachel was caught off guard and stammered, "Hello there, I was looking to see if Jack McDermott was still at the office."

"Who?"

"Jack McDermott," Rachel said, thinking Daniel was some wet-behind- the-ears new hire that never got close to senior management so didn't know Jack's name.

"I'm sorry, ma'am, but Jack isn't here. May I connect you to Jeffrey Williams?"

"No, I don't want Jeffrey, I want Jack. Do you know what time he left?" she asked with her frustration on full boil now.

There was a slight pause before Daniel answered, "Jack hasn't worked here for six months."

Rachel felt a chill spread over her body.

"Are you sure you are talking about Jack McDermott?" she asked.

"Yes, ma'am."

Without saying goodbye Rachel killed the call. She clutched the phone to her chest as her mind spun, trying to piece together the disjointed information she'd received in the last half hour, blowing her world apart.

Beep, beep, beep. The front door opened. She stayed glued to her chair listening to Jack walk into the kitchen and open the fridge. She wanted answers but was terrified at hearing the response.

After a few minutes she went downstairs and found him wolfing down a sandwich on a bar stool.

"Hello, Jack," she said, startling him.

"Shit, you scared me! I didn't know you were home."

Rachel had the foreclosure letter in her hand. She tossed it on the counter. "Do you know what this is about?" she said, trying to stay neutral although the fear and anger were already obvious.

"No," he responded with a mouthful of ham and cheese.

"It's a foreclosure letter," said Rachel. "It says we haven't paid the mortgage for the last three months."

"Those bastards. I told them it was just a matter of making some funds available."

Rachel was stunned. "Are you telling me you actually haven't been paying the mortgage?"

Jack took another big bite of his sandwich.

"Answer me!" Rachel screamed.

"All right!" Jack barked, throwing down his food. "For Christ's sakes, you're as bad as they are!"

"I can't believe this," Rachel said while turning away, holding the wall for support.

Jack tried to regain his composure to defuse the situation, to buy a little more time. He followed her into the living room.

"It's...it's no big deal. I've been going through a bad patch with our investments. It's just a cash flow thing. I told them we were good for it. The greedy pricks just couldn't wait."

"I can't believe what I'm hearing," she said, shaking her head and looking at him like a stranger trying to place a face.

"Rachel, I'll make it work. Don't worry about it."

Rachel caught sight of his muddy hiking boots in the foyer.

"Where were you today?" she asked, pointing to the boots, still in shock from the information she'd received in the past hour.

"I went hiking. I needed to get some fresh air," Jack replied, watching her closely, slowly chewing the remains of his sandwich.

"Hiking," Rachel said.

"Yeah, I cut out of work early."

"Well, that's the funny thing, Jack. I tried to call you at the office. They told me you don't work there anymore. Daniel Turner said you haven't worked there since Sep-tem-ber."

Jack jerked forward and felt a shortness of breath. His heart was pounding, he was sweating profusely.

Rachel didn't need to hear what he had to say; she already knew the answer. She backed away as Jack moved towards her.

"Get away from me!" she yelled "I don't even know who you are anymore!" She bolted for the front door.

Jack felt severe pain in his chest. He lunged for Rachel, but she was too fast. She darted by him, flung open the door, and ran down the street.

"Rachel!" Jack yelled grabbing the sides of the door frame for support. "Get back here! Don't leave me like this."

He dropped to his knees. His vision blurred and he passed out.

~~~

Jack didn't know how long he'd been out when he came to. A cold wind was blowing in the open front door. It was dark. He shivered and stumbled to his feet. He slammed the door and locked it, hoping Rachel was still out. Feeling tired and weak, he went upstairs and took a hot shower. He felt strangely outside of himself.

For many weeks, he'd been feeling irritable and restless. His mind would go blank, and he couldn't concentrate. He felt constrained in the city with the money pressures building. There were so many reminders at home: the house bills kept coming, invitations to expensive restaurants with friends, Rachel's girls' weekend in New York, new designer clothing purchases, listings for bigger properties that Rachel kept.

He chalked up the headaches and fatigue to the insomnia he'd been experiencing. He was bolder with their investments, taking bigger risks as their savings dwindled. Every month that passed, his anxiety escalated. His few attempts at finding a job went nowhere. Word had spread about his dreadful past year's performance. There was no mercy in the investment business. No safety nets. The hungry new crop of hotshots graduating from the top business schools filled the gap, like water pouring through a crack. He couldn't even get a first interview. It was like he'd been blacklisted.

Jack and Rachel had already used up a good chunk of their savings on fertility treatment, before Jack lost his job. For the first few months he wasn't too worried, thinking he could get more aggressive with his investment choices and make up lost ground. But it was a tough time to make money, and his wild decisions had yielded only losses. In January, he placed the remaining money they had in a real estate fund focused on vacation property development in Europe. Normally they diversified their investments to hedge against any one stock performing poorly. The fund tanked and he was left with a fraction of his purchase. He was out of time.

He tried not to think about everything, but pieces of their conversation crowded his thoughts. He knew Rachel wouldn't be sympathetic about his job loss. Look how wild she was now that she knew! I was right to keep it from her. How she must be enjoying feeling superior. Chalk one up for the female senior partner.

He laughed out loud thinking about how hard she had been working just to have him lose it all. Oh well, good intentions.

Jack stepped out of the shower and paused. All still quiet. He felt hollow and laid down on the bed, naked in the dark. His body was exhausted, but his mind was flying. He tried to think rationally about what was going to happen, but he couldn't. He kept circling back to the fight. He felt relieved she knew.

No more pretending. No job and no money. Hopefully she'll come to her senses and realize all this striving was pointless. For what? All we have is stuff. What really matters is family. We don't need this big house and the city. We can move to a small town and get work as insurance agents or something like that and get started on our family again. It was probably her job stress that killed our baby in the first place. Once we get set up at a slower pace it is sure to happen. Everything will be so much simpler.

He replayed the day, before the fight. It made him feel better. He had driven to Haliburton County where he'd spent his childhood summers. He'd taken one of the many maintained hiking paths. There was still snow on the ground, but signs of spring were there too; promising buds on the trees, bird calls, small animals scurrying about. The earth smelled pungent, so familiar. When he paused for lunch on a rocky outcropping overlooking the water he felt just like he did as a young boy. Detached from the world, adrift from those he loved. It was lonely, but at the same time, comforting. Like pulling on his father's favorite flannel shirt.

He'd been spending a few days a week in the country over the past month to escape the pressures of his situation and to avoid Rachel. Drawing himself back to the present, he thought, she just needs some time to calm down and understand the right thing to do. A new start will be good for both of us. He felt optimistic about the small-town life he envisioned and couldn't wait for Rachel to get home to talk about his plan.

CHAPTER 30

Rachel ran full steam for over an hour before jogging at a moderate pace to methodically reconstruct the last few months of their lives. It was like a bad dream from which she couldn't wake up.

I can't believe he hasn't worked in over six months! And the worst thing about it is that he's kept it from me. Months and months of blatantly lying about his life. Who does that? A freaking psycho. But how couldn't I have known? The pregnancy and the sadness of the miscarriage must have affected my ability to see clearly. He's like one of those desperate people you hear about going to Vegas and gambling the last of their money to make it right again. But all our hard work, MY hard work.

She felt sick to her stomach.

I'm going to lose everything I've struggled so hard to get; ten years with those chauvinist pigs only to have it all swept away by my husband who was supposed to be the good guy. Damn him! And not telling me about losing his job. Not telling me about our life savings going down the drain. Spending all that money on fertility treatment. Obviously having a baby trumped saving our relationship. How many times did I ask, how was your day today? What happened on the Miller account today? Do you have any business trips lined up next week? Incredible! And not a word about financial stress. Not bringing me in on the reality of our situation. For Christ's sake, he is still in denial saying he was going to make it better. I have no clue who this person is. The man I've been sharing my life with, planning my future with, dreaming about growing old with, doesn't exist.

It's like waking up and finding a stranger in your bed. There must have been signs of him losing it! I'm not an idiot. He played this all out so deliberately, so methodically, for me not to have questioned him. I've got to stop thinking about this or my head will explode.

She ran over to her friend Morgan's house and collapsed, sobbing into her arms when she opened the door.

~~~

Jack was quite proud of himself for pulling together the chicken stir-fry. He was sprinkling cilantro garnish on the platter when the phone rang.

"Hello?" Jack answered, without a hint of distress.

"Jack, this is Morgan, Rachel's friend."

"Sorry, Morgan, Rachel's out. I'll have her call you later."

"Rachel's with me and she isn't coming home tonight."

"Put her on the phone."

A few seconds passed before Rachel hissed into the phone, "What can you possibly want?"

"I have dinner ready and was hoping you'd be home soon so we can talk about our plans."

Rachel could hear cutlery and plates shifting in the background. "Dinner and plans? Oh, that's ripe."

"How long will you be?"

"You really are a fucking nutcase, you know? I'm not coming home, you idiot! You've lied to me for six months! How many other things have you lied about? I have no idea who you even are!"

"There you go with the drama again. I'll admit that I should have been more up front. But I know you, sweetheart. It's because I knew you'd go   ballistic, that I kept it from you for your own good. You should be thanking me."

Rachel looked wild-eyed at Morgan, in a state of disbelief.

"Why don't you tell me how badly off we really are since I know how you like to manage our affairs," Rachel said, chugging the cold white wine to steady her nerves as she rocked back and forth on the sofa.

"You really want to do this over the phone?"

"Out with it."

"Okay. Don't forget you asked for it. All our money and investments were gone as of last November. I borrowed on the line of credit for three months after that, but then I couldn't get another extension. Friends helped with contributions this past month to keep us in groceries and gas."

"Groceries and gas donations? That's what we're down to?" Rachel was stunned, the news was even worse than she'd imagined.

"Look, are you coming home or not? The dinner isn't going to keep all night. Come home so we can talk this through. I have a great idea I want to share with you." Jack straightened the place settings and tucked a napkin under each fork.

"Of course you have a great idea," Rachel got out through clenched teeth. "You've done so well with everything else so far. I'm sure you have a brilliant solution! You can tell it to the wall since I'm not coming home tonight or any other night soon."

Silence deadened the call.

"You're really not helping here," he replied. "Why do you insist on being so difficult?"

She heard the clatter of dishes and table wear hitting the floor.

"Me? I'm the one ruining things?" Rachel screamed into the phone. "Get a grip, you asshole."

"I thought we could simplify things," Jack interjected. "For Christ's sake, give me some support for a change. We can move to a small city, maybe even the country, and start over. We don't need all this bullshit; the big house, the fancy cars, demanding jobs."

Rachel cringed hearing glass shattering.

Jack continued, "We could rent something to start and rebuild our savings and then buy a small house with some property. Somewhere we could raise a family. You won't have to work so hard. It will be easier to get pregnant without your stress killing our dreams."

Rachel could barely speak through her tears. Disbelief, anger, and fear all fought for space.

"I've got to go," Rachel cried.

"Don't hang up on me. You've got to come home so we can talk this through."

The line went dead. Luckily for Rachel, she didn't hear the platter smashing against the wall.

He suddenly felt very tired. Hauling himself up from the chair he walked over the food, broken dishes, and glassware littering the floor, taking no notice of the mess. The cut on his foot didn't register. He robotically went up the stairs trailing bits of rice, and blood. Without undressing, he fell back on the bed and stared at the ceiling in the quiet darkness of their room.

"She'll come around," murmured as he drifted off to sleep.

~~~

Jack didn't leave the house for three days. His mind bounced around trying to find a way out of the mess. His moods swung wildly between sadness, rage, disbelief, and hope.

If only she understood I did what any good husband would do, sheltering her from bad news. She should be grateful I kept it from her as long as I did and didn't burden her with money problems. If she really loved me, she'd understand. Has she always been this self-centered? She probably doesn't give a crap about what I'm going through. She'll see it more clearly when we move and things slow down. How much better everything will be.

A few days after their blowout he waited by Rachel's office to catch her as she left work. She didn't notice him until he stepped into her path. Her heart hitched when she saw him only inches from her face. She backed away. He looked like he hadn't slept in days. His hair was disheveled and greasy, dark circles bruised his eyes, and white film caked the corners of his mouth.

"Rachel, I need to see you," he said while suddenly gripping her shoulders. "Why don't you return my calls? Just come home so we can work this out."

Rachel pulled back and said in a steely voice, "Get your hands off me and get out of my way."

"But we can make this right," he insisted, blocking her path. "We've always worked through our problems in the past."

People took no notice hurrying to get home after work.

She looked at him with a cold stare. "Get out of my way or I'll scream."

He was confused and hurt. He shuffled off to the side and she rushed past.

After a couple more attempts to engage her as she exited from work, Rachel secured a restraining order. He couldn't come within a hundred yards of her workplace, residence, or places she routinely frequented.

Rachel stayed at Morgan's for the next two months. She refused to see Jack and blocked him on her phone and emails and alerted her company that he was not to be admitted to the office. She contacted the Court Registry within the seven-day grace period to get a stay on the foreclosure. Her parents lent her four months of mortgage payments to enable her to pay back the bank and put down one additional payment in order to list the house for sale under normal conditions. The house sold in April for less than their purchase price. The new family moving in couldn't believe their good fortune in getting their low-ball offer approved. With the remaining funds from the sale of the house, Rachel paid off the line of credit, a portion of the fertility bills, and negotiated more time for the rest. At thirty-four, Rachel was poor, heartbroken, single, and moving into a one-bedroom rental.

A few months had passed when she agreed to meet him in a public place to go through the shattered remains of their marriage. It was Friday morning at a café downtown.

Jack arrived early to practice his lines. He was excited she agreed to meet, thinking she was ready to talk about reconciling. He was ready to throw off the shackles of big city living. He hashed over their future while waiting for Rachel to arrive.

Jack had already looked at Peterborough, a city of 100,000 people an hour and a half outside of Toronto, for rentals. They could get a nice lower floor in a house for only $750/month. He figured with their big-firm credentials they should easily be able to find work in a professional setting. Insurance sales were usually lucrative enough, or real estate sales.

Rachel spotted him at a table, and seeing he already had coffee for both of them, she sat down. The steady stream of caffeine seekers provided the buffer she needed to get through the conversation. Jack jumped up to embrace her, but she deftly avoided him, pulling off her coat then pulled a sheaf of papers from her purse.

"You look great, Rachel." Jack said. "It so good to see you."

Rachel remained unresponsive, not making eye contact. She told herself she wouldn't get upset and concentrated to steady herself before starting.

"The new owners of the house asked for an earlier closing, so you'll need to move out by the end of the month. We save an extra ten thousand dollars by giving them the earlier closing. My parents have bailed us out with the bank. We will both still be in debt after the sale with the liabilities you built up over the past six months." She took a sip of her coffee. "I want a formal separation agreement and have hired a lawyer. You have broken the most sacred tenant of marriage by shattering my trust with your lies." Slowly turning her head to level him with an icy gaze she continued, "You have destroyed our marriage and I'll never forgive you."

"Sweetheart, I've been trying to see you to tell you I'm so sorry. I thought I could keep it from you; losing my job and re-investing our funds so you'd never need to know. I never meant to hurt you," he said with tears filling his swollen eyes.

"You can cut the 'just trying to protect me' crap," she said, gaining renewed control and strength. "What you are is a desperate control freak that can't stand not getting what he wants. I was never enough for you. The love I thought we had? Never enough."

Jack tried to butt in, but Rachel steamrolled ahead. "You were so fixated on having a baby, your ultimate prize to show what a big man you are, it clouded everything else. It didn't matter that our world was crumbling beneath us, driven by your quest. It didn't matter that our relationship was stressed to the breaking point, my body drugged and prodded, pushed beyond what I could handle. You know all too well how families put up good fronts, don't you, Jack. You wanted so badly to produce a child to make your father proud, finally get his attention and a nod of approval. Gain a glimmer of something like love to make the sting of all those horrible years at boarding school and neglectful summers a little less painful. You'd show him what good fathers really look like. That was enough to drive you to ruin us. And to make things even more sad, in case your messed-up childhood wasn't enough, there was your pathetic jealousy of your friends' lives. They had something you couldn't have, and it made you crazy. Your low esteem couldn't be bolstered by the big job, expensive house, or your successful and loving wife. Counting on a child to be your savior didn't pan out and you couldn't handle it."

Rachel saw people staring and realized she was shouting. She looked at the table to let the moment pass and kept her eyes downcast. She resumed in a quiet tone,"What really hurt most was your inability to let me into your sadness and let me help you heal. If you had truly loved me, you would have let me."

Jack had been following her until she mentioned his father. While he didn't agree with any of her accusations of him, it was the attack on his father that sent him off the rails. Snippets of images flashed through his mind like a movie reel: his father dropping him off at school every September and firmly saying no tears, leaving him at the cottage for two months without a visit, telling him about his affair.

He looked at Rachel with hard eyes and said, "You'd better stop right now. You know nothing about my father. He is a good man who takes care of his family."

"You're right, Jack, I don't know your father. Why would I when all he has ever been is a ghost figure in your life."

"Watch it. You're treading on dangerous territory."

"I don't need to take this bullshit anymore," Rachel said, pushing the papers across the table. "I've done nothing but love you and support you, but you clearly have deeper issues that you need to deal with on your own. And I need to get on with my life."

He looked at the envelope as if it was a foreign object, afraid to touch it.

"You've got till the end of the month to get out of the house," Rachel stated. "Sign the papers and let me move on. It's the least you can do."

Rachel stood up and looked down at Jack with pity. Although she had just ended her marriage, and was in financial ruin, she felt tremendous relief. The pathetic individual who sat in front of her barely resembled the man she had fallen in love with. He had morphed into somebody she didn't know.

"Do yourself a favor and get some help, Jack, you could use it," Rachel said with her hands gripping her purse strap. She turned on her signature stiletto heels, confidently flipped her hair, and never looked back.

Jack stayed seated for a few minutes. Drumming his fingers on the table, he slowly shook his head, letting out a quiet chuckle. Unbelievable.

That Rachel. Still so self-centered, completely unwilling to give, to soften. I knew she was a hard hitter when we met but many women are when they are young and trying to prove themselves. I figured she would have relaxed once we got established. But with her, there was never any easing off. It's always been about her needs. And it always will be.

He sipped on his coffee. It was like a heavy weight had lifted and he felt energized and clear-minded. He felt free to let Rachel fade away to the periphery of his life. It was like he had been holding her in his center against her will and he no longer needed to hang on. He mentally released her, and she became very small, floating away. Insignificant. He felt wonderful. He smiled. He let a whole new feeling surge forth. How could I not have seen she was totally the wrong woman for me? Now I finally have room in my mind to match the fullness I feel in my heart. Room for my true love. The perfect woman.

He was hurrying to leave the shop when someone caught his sleeve and handed him Rachel's envelope.

"Excuse me, sir, you forgot your package," an earnest young woman offered, thinking she was doing him a favor. He took it from her in slow motion and mumbled his thanks and proceeded to slide it into the trash on his way out the door.

CHAPTER 31

Jack's friends were supportive at first, whether it was over beers with the guys or the few dinners and house parties that followed. They considerately shared their disbelief at their breakup.

The guys were sincere enough about setting up future get-togethers, a night out for drinks, northern getaways, golfing. For a while they did have some good times. That summer they enjoyed a successful fishing weekend and a fun long weekend party at Michael and Sarah's cottage.

But people were busy.

Jack figured it was the woman who controlled a couple's social life and women side with women. He could only imagine the job Rachel had done on them. After about a year the invitations stopped coming; about as subtle as a door slamming shut in his face.

He didn't mind; he wanted time to prepare for his new life. He made sure to work his side of things with Michael. He convinced him there are always two sides to a story. He knew he could still count on his best friend to support him. Rachel and Sarah had never been close, so he figured Sarah had only heard the break-up story from secondary sources.

Jack made any excuse to drop over at Michael and Sarah's house. He took full advantage of invitations to come over for dinner or to watch a game. It took some real effort to appear sad and adrift when he felt elated and alive just being around Sarah.

He noticed Sarah appeared only somewhat interested in his company, tuning in for a few minutes at a time, but then became easily distracted. Having three children, with the addition of Amy being born last year, was bound to keep anyone busy. After dinner she was quick to excuse herself. Jack figured she was using the excuse of tending to her young children as a good cover to hide her true feelings.

As he watched her carrying baby Amy while shooing silly Connor upstairs for his bath, he thought Michael had only himself to blame. All that traveling for work. Gone at least half of the time. Nobody would expect their marriage to survive that kind of stress, especially with young children. Jack was willing to bide his time.

~~~

Two years passed since the break-up. After the first year of dwindling invites, he contentedly settled into life as a recluse. During the week he rarely left his dingy, dark, basement apartment. He was lucky to get what he had being badly in debt; a bachelor apartment in an older house divided into five units in Chinatown. The house was wedged between a commercial strip of markets, restaurants, and cheap trinket stores selling things like plastic sandals and cheap clothing.

Jack's sisters secretly took turns sending him five hundred dollars a month from an indirect source to keep him off the streets by covering his rent. They figured the shelters could do the rest to provide meals and clothing. Part of the deal was that there would be no attempt at contact or acknowledgement of the funds. Influenced by their parents, they didn't want anything to do with him given the disgrace he had brought on the family. They also didn't want to risk losing out on their father's good favor, and wealth. His mother followed suit, being a dutiful wife. There had been no direct contact from anyone in the family for over a year.

There were two bachelor apartments in the basement. The main floor had a two-bedroom unit with an extended family of ten. There were two more single-bedroom flats upstairs. It was in a densely populated part of downtown and the smell of cabbage permeated the air. Given the numerous food markets selling everything from pig's feet to fresh produce, the rentals were infested with cockroaches. The occasional rat sighting was a common enough occurrence. He slept most of the day. At night he stumbled outside and drifted along the hectic streets ordering inexpensive noodle dishes he'd slurp at a greasy counter, lost in the cacophony of customers and frying food. In his waking hours he planned out his new life with Sarah.

All his energy was directed towards his future. He made up reasons to stop by Michael and Sarah's house for a visit, to drop off something for the kids. He found talking about fabricated dates and non-existent job searches very easy. He knew he needed to maintain the façade of normalcy until Sarah was ready. His feelings only magnified over time.

It was a blistering summer, one of the hottest on record. Michael and Sarah planned virtually every weekend at their cottage. Jack let Michael know he was happy to help with the ongoing fix-up jobs and Michael found it an easy way of giving him some of his limited time for the odd weekend. Jack slept in the bunkie near the back of their property, so it wasn't like he was always around.

The whole gang arrived for the July long weekend on a glorious Saturday morning; Christy and Brett with their two kids and Larry and Alison with Sky. They played cards to see who would get the sleep bunkie with lots of good-natured hollering about cheating. Larry snagged the prize. Brett couldn't care less, saying he preferred camping anyways. Jack also didn't mind camping out although he did feel somewhat territorial about the bunkie.

It was late in the afternoon and Michael offered one last boat ride around the lake.

"Thanks anyways," Larry replied. "We're going to enjoy some forest bathing and down time in your sweet bunkie before dinner. This fresh air makes all of us a little sleepy."

"No way I'm missing out on strapping on those water skis!" yelled Brett. "My little lady here wants to witness the action firsthand, don't you sweet cheeks". Christy simply rolled her eyes and made sure all the kids had their life jackets secured.

Sarah offered to stay back to get the dinner ready for their return. Jack pretended he wanted to finish securing some loose boards on the shed, so he passed on the ride.

Sarah had the radio tuned to the local station pumping out the hits from the seventies and eighties and didn't hear him come in. She was chopping onions and tomatoes for the burgers and her hair fell around her face, blocking her side view. She stood barefoot wearing a pink and yellow sundress that suggestively hugged her hips and scooped low in the front, exposing the swell of her breasts. He gently put his hand on her shoulder.

"Oh my God, Jack," Sarah blurted out, putting one hand on her chest. "You scared me to death!" She held the knife aloft and it dripped tomato juice on the floor.

"Oh, I'm sorry. I thought you heard me come in."

Sarah went back to chopping. It annoyed her how much Jack had been hanging around their Toronto house and now the cottage. She saw the cottage as sacred family time, wanting only occasional visitors. She loved the big gatherings like the one they were having this weekend, but for the most part, given Michael's busy schedule, she wanted to carve out as much time as possible for their family unit.

"Can I give you a hand? I just finished up with the shed," he said, eagerly taking a step closer.

"No thanks, I'm good here. Not much more to do," she answered, turning away to grab some condiments from the fridge.

He watched her bend over to rummage through bottles, his desire now physical. He strolled to the front of the cottage to hide his embarrassment. He wanted to make sure the timing was just right. Sarah turned back to the counter and continued prepping.

"You do such a great job with the kids," Jack said, taking in the pictures on the wall. There were great black and white shots from their past few summers; Paige planting flowers with Sarah, Connor looking awestruck showing Sarah a massive bullfrog, baby Amy bouncing and laughing on Sarah's lap.

"Thanks. It's a lot of work."

He thought of how great he would be with the kids. Sarah's children were young enough so they would still have plenty of time to grow to love him as a father. He fantasized about how they would have custody and send them to Michael's every other weekend. Children that age need their mother.

He watched as she quickly moved about putting cutlery and the salad on the picnic table on the deck that extended off the front of the cottage. She passed within a couple of feet of him each time. The warm day had caused her dress to cling. He turned and intercepted her on her third trip to the table, placing his hands over hers as he offered to take the plates

"Let me get those for you," he offered as his eyes bored into hers.

His hands felt cold and clammy even though it was a hot July afternoon.

"It's okay but thanks anyways," she said, trying to pull her hands away.

"I insist," he said, and Sarah released her grip on the plates. "I love being here and helping out."

Sarah strained to hear the sound of the boat returning, but all was quiet except for the radio. She glanced out the back window up to the bunkie but there was no sign of movement from Larry's family. Jack moved quickly to place the plates on the table to get back inside to be alone with Sarah. She felt stifled by his overbearing presence and scrambled to grab a stack of fresh towels and hurried out the side door down to the dock. She knew she was probably reading too much into it, but she felt anxious with Jack acting so strange. He wasn't more than three feet behind her.

"I thought I heard the boat," Sarah said, feeling the need to explain her quick departure, staring out to the lake.

"Probably just another boat," he replied.

The silence was brutal. She placed the towels at the end of the dock and would have loved to go for a swim, but she didn't want Jack for company. Just then Alison appeared, ready for a dip before dinner.

"Anyone care to join me?" she asked.

"I'd love to," Sarah said and peeled her dress over her head in one fluid motion. She caught Jack leering. He didn't look at Alison, who was also just clad in her bathing suit.

Sarah dove in as fast as she could with Alison hollering good-naturedly, "Hey! At least give me a bit of warning!"

Sarah didn't stop swimming, using a fast front crawl until she was a good hundred yards from shore. Panting, she turned and faced the cottage treading water, waiting for Alison, who was using a relaxed breaststroke to catch up.

"What's the rush", asked Alison. "It's cottage life after all."

Sarah, still looking back, felt a cold chill shake her as she saw Jack transfixed, watching her.

"Just a little chilled, that's all, trying to warm up," she said, forcing a smile she didn't feel.

The night was a big success with steaks and burgers, fresh salad, and corn on the cob. Plenty of beer and wine kept the party humming. The kids were tired and crashed right after an early campfire with their bellies full of marshmallows. The adults hunkered down in campfire chairs with drinks in hand, gazing up at the stars and into the fire.

"This is the life," Brett said. "If we could ever save any money, I'd love to get a place up here, away from the craziness of the city."

The fire crackled and crickets chirped. A bullfrog released a loud croak.

"Who are you kidding," Christy challenged. "You'd be lost without the bar scene!" They all laughed in agreement.

There was a monitor to hear the kids, who were all nestled and quiet in the main cottage for now.

After lots of drinks and alcohol-induced philosophical debates, the fire died down and everyone drifted back to their sleeping places, leaving Sarah and Michael alone.

"Great day, huh?" Michael said, finishing off the last of his beer.

"It was beautiful," Sarah said, taking his hand across their chairs. After a pause she went on. "Michael, are you finding Jack acting odd lately?"

"How do you mean?"

"Maybe I'm just imagining it, but he is acting very unsettled around me. I get the feeling that he likes me."

"Well, of course he likes you, who doesn't?" Michael said, planting a kiss on the back of her hand.

"I mean more than just likes me. Ever since he and Rachel broke up, it feels different with him around. He's too intense or something."

"I'm sure he's lonely if that's what you mean. Geez, honey, can you imagine how it must be for him? All his dreams smashed to pieces. His job, his house, and his wife all gone. No money, no children. I'd be acting strange too if my life was the train wreck his is right now."

Sarah felt a bit mean voicing her concerns about Jack to Michael.

"Maybe it is just a phase Jack is going through," Sarah said. "Hopefully it will be better when he meets somebody special and gets his life kick-started again. I know how blessed we are with everything we have."

She vowed to herself to try to be more patient. She wanted to be supportive of her husband's best friend.

Jack was careful not to move a muscle behind a large oak tree. Sound carried easily at night, so he caught every word. He hadn't wanted to leave the campfire with the warm glow of the fire illuminating Sarah's face like an angel. But after everyone else left, he thought his emotions may appear too obvious if he stayed. He pretended to go off to his tent but didn't go far. For a long time, he dreamily gazed upon Sarah from a distance while they recounted the sweet moments of the day.

He stayed hidden until Sarah and Michael finished the campfire and moved inside for the night. As Jack moved from this hiding spot he noticed the red light from the baby monitor. They left it behind on the picnic table by the fire pit. He took it and turned the volume down low. He padded lightly around the far side of the cottage to his tent. He was far enough away from the cottage not to be heard. He tucked into his sleeping bag with the monitor and zipped the bag over his head to muffle any sound. He heard them whispering about not waking the kids as they moved them from their bed to the kids' bunk beds. The three of them liked to fall asleep together in their parents' queen-size bed. It was a special treat on campfire nights when they got to stay up in the cottage alone. They usually fell asleep within a few minutes after a full day in the water and playing in the hot sun.

Jack heard Sarah and Michael murmuring and placing quiet kisses. The monitor played back everything.

He listened intently as he heard the sloughing off of clothes and their hushed laughter as they tumbled into their bed.

Now the kisses he heard were quite different. Passionate kisses. Expectant breathing.

"Michael are you sure they won't hear us?" Sarah whispered.

"Who cares," came Michael's urgent response.

Jack heard Sarah sigh with pleasure, and it pained him. He knew Sarah must go on with her charade of being in love with Michael, but it still hurt.

Jack heard her sharp gasp followed by the rhythm of their lovemaking. He kept the monitor pressed close to his ear, not wanting to miss a single sound from Sarah. He slipped his hand into his pajama bottoms and eagerly joined their rhythm.

~~~

A few weekends later, Jack could hardly wait to see the cottage as he and Michael pulled into the car park area late Friday night. He felt the same happiness he felt as a young boy heading up to his family cottage with his parents. They were going to work on the roof that needed repair. Jack was counting the minutes to Sarah's arrival the next morning.

The sun rose over the tree line as they drank their coffee on the deck. They had just grabbed their tool belts when Michael's cell phone rang.

"Hi, honey, have you left yet?" After a minute of silence Michael added, "That's a shame. Do you need me to come home? Are you sure? Okay then, call me in a few hours and let me know how she is."

Jack tried to sound casual. "What's up?"

"Paige has a fever, so Sarah needs to stay home."

"That's too bad. Do you need to go back? Because I totally understand if she needs you. We can do this another weekend."

"She's fine. It's nothing major. She'll let me know if she needs me to come home. Let's get this show on the road!" Michael said, rubbing his hands together, eager to get started on the work

Jack matched his enthusiasm with a convincing phony response, "Bring it on man!"

Secretly he seethed. I can't believe I'm stuck up here doing manual labor for Michael without even a glimpse of Sarah to make it worthwhile. Here's Michael abandoning her again. Doesn't he see it? I'm sure Sarah does. I would never not be there for her.

The summer sped on with Jack hovering at the edge of the real world, watching life swirl around him; people speeding to work, families in the park, office workers enjoying drinks after work.

He had nothing but time on his hands to imagine the future with Sarah. We'll negotiate keeping the cottage for ourselves and give Michael the house, netting us a nice lump sum cash payout. Michael will need to make large support payments since Sarah hasn't worked after having Paige. We won't have any of the pressures and expenses of city living. We'll invite our friends up for summer weekends of swimming and boating, and winter weekends of cross-country skiing and winter cookouts. It is going to be amazing! Sarah will homeschool the kids. And of course, we'll have one or two of our own kids as well. Blond, blue-eyed, and good looking, just like us.

Every now and then he was taken aback at his own rough appearance in the streaked mirror in his moldy bathroom. He had lost a lot of hair over the past two years, his skin was blotchy and pale, his eyes bloodshot. Most of the time he had a patchy stubble, not able to grow a beard. His weight loss accentuated his jaw.

He knew this was only temporary. With the love of his life by his side, he was sure he'd bounce back.

CHAPTER 32

When Michael went to California for a conference at the end of July, Jack decided it was the perfect opportunity. He was in a terrific mood as he rehearsed his speech in the dank shower, being careful to wear his cheap shower sandals to avoid catching a fungal disease. He shaved for the occasion and put on fresh clothes. He bought cheap carnations on the subway platform before heading uptown.

Jack wanted to surprise her. It was nine in the evening when he rang the bell. Sarah was on her laptop at the kitchen table paying bills. She peeked out the bay window and saw Jack standing at her front door. She saw the flowers. She did a quick mental search for occasions but came up blank.

Swinging the heavy door open, she feigned a small smile. "Hey, Jack, how's it going?"

"Fantastic!" He waited a moment. "Can I come in?"

"Actually, Michael isn't home right now. I'll have him call you when he's back," Sarah said, giving him another tight smile and stepping back into her house.

"Sarah, can I come in for a minute?" he asked, putting a bit of pressure on the door with the palm of his hand.

"I'm sort of in the middle of something."

"I won't stay long. I promise."

"All right, come in."

He stepped into the foyer.

"Kids asleep?" he said to buy time to fortify his nerves as he followed her into the living room, knowing full well their bedtime routine.

"Yup. All quiet in the house," she said, crossing her arms and legs, folding herself in a protective gesture in the living room chair to avoid the intimacy of sharing the couch.

He swallowed hard, challenged by his dry throat. "Sarah, as you must already know, I've had feelings for you a long time now. A very long time."

Even though Sarah had suspected this, she was floored to hear him say it out loud and to her face.

"I think it's best for you to leave now," she said, calmly rising.

"No, please. You need to hear me out. I can't leave until you hear what I have to say."

"Jack, I mean it. You've got to—"

"I'm in love with you, Sarah. I'm in love with you and have been for years. I want to spend my life with you." He beamed, approaching her with the flowers extended.

Sarah froze. It seemed like a farce, but she knew he meant every word. She saw it in the desperation in his eyes. She had felt the uncomfortable vibe many times with him before, his longing, barely disguised. She knew she hadn't imagined it despite Michael dismissing it.

"Jack, listen. I'm in love with Michael. My life is with Michael," she said backing away into the hallway.

Jack shook his head slowly. He worked hard to stay on track, ignoring her last comments. "I've loved you for eight years, Sarah. I know now that I never loved Rachel. It's always been me and you. You must feel it too if you'll just let yourself be truthful."

"No, Jack, you're wrong. You're distraught over the turn your life has taken and you're not seeing reality."

"I know exactly how things are. Michael has never been good enough for you. Look how he leaves you all the time! You've got to be a fool not to see it. Who knows who he's with? Leaving you to raise your kids on your own. Poor Paige, Connor, and Amy; they are practically fatherless. I know how that feels. I can make it better for them. For all of you."

Jack cornered Sarah against the wall. She was repulsed by the stink radiating off his body and the sharp odor of damp clothing left to fester too long on the floor.

At the sound of her children's names, a fierceness replaced her fear. "Don't you dare mention my children. What do you know about children and their needs, Jack? Nothing, that's what! You've lost it. You lost your job, your wife, and obviously now your mind."

Sarah pushed him back with a forceful shove. "Get the hell out of my house."

Jack let the carnations fall to the floor. His face crumpled and he dropped to his knees, lunging to clutch her waist. She quickly moved aside, and he fell forward on his hands.

"I know you don't mean it," he muttered, staring down at the floor. "Tell me you don't mean it," he begged with great sobs escaping from deep within him.

Sarah's mind raced, thinking of protecting her kids and herself from this madness. She inched towards the door, ready to call for help if she needed to.

"You don't know what you're saying," Sarah said, hoping to de-escalate the situation. "You need help. You've got to talk to a professional,"

"You can't abandon me too," he cried with tears and snot streaming down his face. "My life will be ruined. I have great plans for us." He pawed the wall, getting back on his feet.

"Go now," she ordered, barely keeping her knees from buckling.

"Please—just let me—"

"NOW!"

"Mamma, Mamma," cried Amy from her bedroom.

Jack swayed to the door and down the steps.

She quickly bolted the door and ran to check the back door as well. Holding the wall for support she ran to the stairs. By the time she raced into Amy's room, the toddler had fallen back to sleep. Checking the other two and finding them peacefully undisturbed, she dropped to the floor in Connor's room. Throwing her head on the duvet, she gathered it to her face to muffle her cries.

~~~

Jack awoke to find himself restrained to a hospital bed with ties on his wrists and a drip in his arm. His head throbbed, taking in the brightness of his surroundings; the white walls and floor, the shiny metallic monitor, the overhead fluorescent lights.

"Hey, can somebody help me?" he called out with his tongue thick, slurring his speech as he pulled against the ties. "What the hell is going on here? God damn it! Somebody help me!"

A nurse appeared and calmly addressed him. "Hi, my name is Erica and you're at St. Patrick's Hospital. You were found wandering in traffic on Yonge Street and appeared to be in a very agitated state, unable or unwilling to give your name to many people that tried to help you."

"What the fuck?"

"If you'll please be patient, I'll call for Dr. Spencer, who will give you a full rundown of what's happening."

"Can you untie me first?"

"I'm afraid I'm not authorized. Dr. Spencer is in charge. She'll be back shortly, so it won't be much longer. It's for your own protection," she added as she left the room.

Jack racked his mind trying to piece together what happened. He could only grasp snippets of negative feelings; shock, hurt, confusion, anger, frustration, despair. He tried to pull the drip out of his arm, thinking it was the medicine that was keeping him foggy, but was unsuccessful. He drifted off again and jumped when a woman gently pressed on his arm and called his name.

"Jack, I'm sorry to have startled you." she said. "I'm Dr. Spencer. How are you feeling?"

Jack blinked hard a few times, trying to get his bearings. "I don't know. I mean why am I here? Did something happen?"

"You were on your own and had some sort of breakdown based on what people told us." She lightly put two fingers on his wrist while monitoring her watch. "Can you tell me happened?" she asked while checking her notes.

July 22, 2010
51st Precinct, Toronto Police Services
At 10:15 pm a white male, late thirties, was seen erratically and dangerously crossing intersection at Yonge and St. Clair. Witnesses claim he was cursing, threatening, and yelling at random people. Caused disruption to traffic. Appeared to be intoxicated, thrashing his arms and legs. A 911 call triggered our response paired with an ambulance.

Jack took a moment to collect his thoughts. He felt it before he remembered it—the rejection and shame. As the feeling and the flashback of the night with Sarah engulfed him, he turned his head to the wall so the doctor couldn't see his face.

"I'm sure it will come to me. You said Dr. Spencer, right?" he asked, delaying his response to gain control.

"Yes, I'm Dr. Spencer," she replied, jotting some notes on his chart as she sat on the edge of the bed: blood pressure high 140/90, palms sweaty, breathing erratic.

The first responders called Rachel, seeing her last name matched Jack's in his cell phone contacts. Jack never liked the fact that Rachel hadn't taken his name when they married, so he always recorded her name as Rachel McDermott when he could. Rachel refused to get involved and gave them Jack's sisters' numbers. She didn't bother providing his parents' number. Jack had deleted his family contacts a long time ago.

"We've tried contacting your sisters, left messages, but have yet to hear back. Perhaps they are away? Your ex-wife Rachel didn't want to get involved."

Rachel had spoken to the doctor and given her a ten-minute spiel on how Jack ruined their marriage and his family history. Dr. Spencer thought about the list of stresses that could cause this type of major nervous breakdown and Jack had them in spades.

Divorce
Dismissal from Work
Financial Troubles
Infertility Treatment
Dysfunctional Family
Boarding School

Rachel also shared information about his severe mood swings, paranoia, isolation, and drinking.

Dr. Spencer called out to Jack more than once to get his attention back.

"Jack, I'd like to undo your restraining ties since you seem calm now. You were very agitated last night; we were worried about self-harm. We have an IV in your arm to get you hydrated since you were disoriented and hallucinogenic, speaking about people who weren't present. The solution has a mild sedative in it as well to let you get some rest."

Jack felt overwhelmed. Feelings of anger, helplessness and frustration, fought to gain the upper hand. But he knew he had to play along and say the right things so they would release him.

"That would be great, Doctor. Thank you."

Dr. Spencer reached across his body and snipped the plastic cords with a pair of small scissors that appeared from her pocket. "Sorry about that, but I hope you know it was for your own good."

Jack slowly rubbed his wrists and tried to appear nonchalant. "You folks know best," he agreed.

"We'd like you to speak with our resident psychiatrist, Dr. Gunther Turner. It's voluntary, but we think it would be good for you and help you with your coping skills."

Jack knew it would be best to appear helpful and serious. Even though he was desperate to get out, he offered a conciliatory tone. "That really would be helpful. I have been dealing with a lot lately."

"Right, then. I can have him come around early this afternoon. If all seems good, we can get you out of here in time for dinner."

"Perfect. Thanks again for everything," Jack grinned, digging deep to find some of his long-dormant charm.

"I'll see you later today. Try to get some rest."

Rest was the last thing on his mind. He kept going over the scene from Sarah's house, struck by her cruelty every time, absorbing it like a physical blow. How could she have thrown me out? I would do anything for her. Michael's taking advantage of her kindness, placing the burden of raising those kids and running the household on her delicate shoulders. It's only a matter of time before she sees things clearly and stops with this facade of marriage she's living.

As he processed his feelings and the circumstances, he felt his anger ebb and compassion build. I guess it wasn't really fair to surprise her. I thought she knew how I felt. I know deep in her heart she loves me too. Her sense of duty is keeping her anchored. She needs to get stronger and leave him so we can start our life together, our future, our family.

CHAPTER 33

Michael was on an overnight flight home from California and didn't get Sarah's frantic messages left six hours earlier until he landed. He immediately tried calling home and got no answer. After three tries he went back to his voicemail to see if there were any other messages from Sarah and heard the following message from Rachel.

"Hi Michael, Rachel here. The hospital called last night, and it seems Jack had some sort of mental breakdown. The police and ambulance people took him to St. Patrick's Hospital. I'm sorry but I simply can't get involved after everything he's put me through. I know his family is useless and you're his closest friend. Anyways, take care."

He went back to dialing. Finally, Michael got an answer.

"Hello, this is the Babic residence."

"Thank God, David. It's Michael. Where's Sarah? Is she all right?"

"Hello Michael," came Sarah's father's clipped response. "Sarah is fine, *now*. She was very upset when we arrived after she called us last night. Her mother and I slept over since she was extremely distressed and to help with the children since you weren't available."

"David, you know I've been on a business trip to California, right?"

"It's hard to keep track of where you are since you're gone so much of the time."

Michael knew nothing good would come of defending himself. "I'm about twenty minutes away from home now, so let's talk when I come in. I want to get the story in person. You have no idea how grateful I am you and Kate are there."

Michael could never convince Sarah's parents of the importance of his business trips. After working for City Hall in human resources for thirty years and living a modest life, David saw business trips as vacations with fancy dinners and hotels; a way of shirking family obligations.

Michael raced into the house looking shaken and immediately called Sarah's name.

"Calm down, Michael. Sarah is resting after a very long night," said Kate.

"Okay. I just want to peek in on her, I'll be right back."

Michael tried not to make a sound as he walked over to Sarah's side of the bed, troubled at the disturbed look on her face. The floorboard creaked and made her jump. He was at her side in an instant.

"Sarah, my love. Oh Sarah, are you alright?"

"Thank God you're back," she cried. She felt small and vulnerable, and sobbed against his chest. He let her cry for a minute before hushing her to let her speak.

"It was Jack," she got out through short breaths. "He barged in here last night saying how much he loved me, that we were meant to be together. Michael, he tried to grab me. I was so scared," she trailed off, consumed by her crying again.

"Shhhh, it's okay. I'm home now."

After a few more minutes she continued, "He said things like he's been in love with me for years, that the kids are virtually fatherless, how our lives will be so much better once we are together." Sarah pushed back her hair and blew her nose.

"Did he hurt you? Did he touch you?"

"No. Nothing physical. He went to grab me at one point, but I got out of the way in time. I told him he had to leave. I had to scream at the top of my lungs before he finally left. He was a mess."

"Unreal," Michael muttered, trying to envision the scene.

"I'm going to speak with your parents and let them go home now that I'm here," he said, easing off the bed.

"Michael don't leave me. I'm really scared," Sarah said, grabbing his hand.

Michael kissed her cheek. "You're fine now. I'm here, and Jack is long gone."

He didn't want to tell her about the call he received about Jack getting taken to the hospital. She didn't need more drama at this point.

It was the weekend, and they went about their usual Saturday routine, skipping Amy's Kinder gym session to enable all five of them to stay together while they ran errands and ferried Paige to soccer practice and Connor to his hockey game.

Michael ignored another call from a Dr. Spencer around noon

202

asking him to call. Later in the day, Sarah seemed back to normal and was getting dinner underway. The kids were watching TV and Michael said he was going to catch up on a few emails and went downstairs with his laptop to the spare guestroom. He got Dr. Spencer on the second ring.

"Hello, Dr. Spencer, this is Michael Babic returning your calls regarding Jack McDermott. I've just come home from a business trip."

"Hello Michael, I appreciate your call. We were given your name and number by Rachel, Jack's ex-wife. She said you may be willing to help."

Michael listened noncommittally.

"Jack was picked up on Yonge Street. He was displaying many of the classic signs of a breakdown; hallucinations, paranoia, threatening behavior, crying and yelling, to name a few. The police went to his apartment to see if there was anything of concern and to check on medication Jack may have needed since he was non-verbal. It was filthy with signs of vermin. It looks like he is really struggling. We tried the phone numbers given to us by Rachel for his sisters, but we've had no response."

"Wow. This is crazy. I'm frankly shocked by what you're telling me. I know he's gone through a bad patch with losing his job and his marriage breaking up, but he never mentioned feeling desperate or depressed."

Michael held back the story Sarah had told him about last night, wanting to digest the situation first, especially if the police were involved.

"Jack seems very willing to cooperate and spoke at length with our resident psychiatrist. Dr. Turner diagnosed Jack as having a major nervous breakdown and says it could take a lot of time and support to get Jack well again."

"What kind of support are you talking about?" Michael asked.

"We prescribed anti-anxiety medication called Duloxetine. It is used to treat depression and anxiety and should improve Jack's mood, sleep, energy level, and decrease his agitation. Assuming Jack seems stable tomorrow morning, which we believe he will, he will be released. We strongly recommend ongoing cognitive therapy so Jack can get to the root of his problems, in addition to staying on the medication for some time. Love and support are going to be critical for his recovery."

"Honey, dinner is on the table," Sarah shouted from upstairs.

Michael heard the clamor of little feet.

Dr. Spencer pulled him back to their conversation. "Would you be able to come and take him home upon his release tomorrow? It should be around noon after Dr. Turner has one more session with him in the morning."

"Uhhhh," Michael stuttered. His mind was reeling with the conflict of supporting his life-long friend versus his alliance with his wife. "Would it be all right if I call in the morning and let you know?"

"That's fine. I do hope you realize mental illness is something as a society we need to be open about. It's no different than physical illness. The idea that people should be shunned or avoided simply because they are experiencing mental health issues is very old thinking, Mr. Babic,"

Michael felt ashamed. "Of course, I understand, and you are completely right. Please let Jack know I'll be happy to come for him at noon tomorrow."

"Jack is fortunate to have such a good friend. Unless you hear from myself or Dr. Turner, please come to the main admitting desk and they will be ready to call Jack down for his release. Have a good evening."

Michael climbed the stairs feeling shell-shocked at the news of the day. The smell of roasted chicken with the comforting sides of mashed potatoes, peas, and applesauce made him feel grounded. The attention from the kids made him feel loved. He knew how blessed and lucky he was. He felt good thinking about helping Jack get his life back together.

After dinner, bath time, and the last of the bedtime stories and tuck-ins, Michael and Sarah were finally alone. They sat deep on the couch with their feet extended on the coffee table enjoying the bliss of silence.

"Do you hear that?" Sarah said, smiling, raising a glass of wine to her lips.

"Nope," Michael replied.

"Exactly. It's perfect," Sarah said, taking a sip.

Michael clinked his glass with hers and did the same.

"Are you feeling, okay? asked Michael. "I mean, after the scene last night?"

"Oh, I'm fine. A little drained still. I was thinking we should invite my parents over for dinner next week as a thank you for hustling over here so fast and staying the night."

"Of course, darling, whenever you like. My schedule is pretty open."

Sarah tucked under Michael's arm, enjoying the weight of his body against hers.

"Honey, I received a call from the hospital, about Jack," Michael said.

The effect was like tossing a hissing grenade in the middle of the room.

Sarah immediately pulled away and looked at him in confusion. "The hospital?"

"It appears after he left here he lost it and was found incoherent on the street. He was wandering dangerously in traffic and shouting. People called 911 for help." Michael purposely left out mention of police. "They kept him overnight at the hospital for observation and will do the same tonight. They've prescribed anti-anxiety and anti-depression medication and have him scheduled to get therapy. I guess the pressures of the past few years got to him."

Michael refilled their glasses to make the evening seem as normal as possible.

"That's incredible. It sort of makes sense given how erratic his behavior was with me. He scared me to death. You should have seen the look on his face, like he was possessed," Sarah shuddered.

"The doctor said it's not uncommon for people experiencing this type of breakdown to exhibit delusional behavior, emotional outbursts, and aggression. They said Jack is co-operating and is grateful for their help."

"Didn't his mother have mental health problems? Like coping issues and depression?"

"Yeah, you're right. I'd almost forgotten about that. Jack never mentions it now."

"Well, as long as he steers clear of us, I wish him well," said Sarah, shutting down the conversation.

"I'm afraid it's not that simple. The doctor asked if I would pick him up tomorrow when he's released."

"Oh, no you don't. I don't want you to have anything to do with that lunatic!"

"Take it easy, you'll wake the kids."

"He-attacked-me-Michael. Maybe I wasn't clear enough?" She looked at him with a mix of exasperation and anger.

"But you said he didn't touch you."

Sarah jumped to her feet. "I can't believe we're even having this conversation. You would actually choose Jack over me?"

"I'm not *choosing,* sweetheart," Michael said quietly, "I'm trying to help my oldest friend of nearly twenty years with a mental health problem. It's not like a hundred years ago when you locked them up in a sanatorium and threw away the key."

"You can't be serious? How am I supposed to act normal around him knowing how he feels? You can't put me in that predicament," Sarah said, getting more agitated.

"I'm not asking you anything. I don't plan on bringing him here for afternoon tea. He may not even remember all that nonsense he spewed last night from the sounds of things. I want to show him he doesn't need to face his problems alone. The doctor said he'll need support. You know how useless his family is and most of his friends have written him off."

"Jeez, I wonder why that it is?"

Michael resumed in earnest, "I was raised to be a compassionate and caring person, and I know you were too. I can't walk away from a dear friend at what may be his darkest hour. I'm sure you will understand once you've had some time to think this through."

~~~

Michael brought Jack back to his apartment after getting him from St. Patrick's Hospital.

"I really appreciate the lift. You can drop me off here at the corner," Jack said, embarrassed about his place and not wanting Michael to snoop around.

"At least let me get you something to eat," Michael offered. "Let's hit up a greasy spoon, just like the old uni days."

Shoveling runny eggs on toast into his mouth with the yolk dripping over his fingers, Jack said, "I can barely remember Friday night. From what I was told, that's probably a good thing."

Michael, relieved to see him looking so relaxed, started in on his omelet.

"Seems like you put on quite a show, my friend. Do you remember shouting and crisscrossing Yonge Street?"

"Nope. Not really. I only remember people coming up to me and getting in my way asking if I needed help. I thought they were just messing with me."

Jack flagged down one of the busy waitresses in her bright yellow apron for more coffee.

"Do you remember anything else from last night?" Michael pushed.

"Oh yeah. I remember trying to fight off the cops that were on me like stink until the hospital guys took over. That shot they gave me in my arm took the fight out of me," Jack said, enjoying the attention.

They continued their breakfast in silence for a few moments.

Michael put down his cutlery and looked Jack straight in the face. "I don't know how else to bring this up, so I'll just say it. Sarah told me you came to the house, before you were found on Yonge Street."

Jack looked confused. Stirring his coffee after adding a packet of sugar, he stared at Michael waiting for more information.

"Just tell me the truth. Do you remember coming over?"

"To your house? No way!"

"Well, it seems you did. And it seems you also went on some rant about being in love with Sarah and wanting her to leave me so you could be together."

"What the hell? Holy shit, I really have gone bonkers if I can't remember that!"

"You'd better be telling me straight," Michael cautioned. "I know you've had a mental breakdown and I'm willing to try to understand as long as you're being completely honest."

"I swear on my life I have no recollection of anything like that. I can't believe I don't remember. That's really scary. Poor Sarah! What a thing to go through. I've got to get over to your house and apologize. I

207

hope I wasn't too much of an asshole." He threw down his napkin and pushed his empty plate away from the table.

"Hold on, Jack," Michael said, placing a firm hand on his forearm. "You can't go over there right now. You shook her up quite badly and she isn't ready to see you yet."

Jack looked at Michael with a pitiful expression. His face crumpled as he sat back down in his chair. He slumped forward and buried his face in his hands. "I can't believe I did this. I'm so ashamed. I must have been so messed up to do something like this." He looked at Michael with despair. "You've got to believe me, Michael. I only see Sarah as a dear friend, and I think you guys have the best marriage I know. I respect you both so much and would never dream of doing anything to come between you."

Jack was weeping openly now, and people were staring. Michael threw down a few bills and put his arm around him. He steered him out of the restaurant and down the street. They walked for a couple of blocks before Jack got a hold of himself.

Michael halted Jack and placed a hand on each of his shoulders, turning him to face him square on. "You listen to me. You are going to get better and we're going to help you. You've had a terrible couple of years. Yes, you've made some mistakes but that doesn't mean you don't deserve our support."

"You have no idea how amazing that sounds," Jack said. "I don't know what I'd do if I didn't have such a great friend like you. It's been terrible and I've been so lonely."

After they said their good-byes, Jack descended the stairwell to his apartment. He collapsed down on his couch and reflected on the conversation. A smile spread across his face. It was one of the toughest performances of his life, and he felt like he carried it off beautifully.

~~~

Jack knew he wouldn't hear from anyone over the following week. He was sure to keep his appointment with Dr. Turner, so no flags were raised. He didn't mind going through the crap about his childhood, it helped him clarify what he really wanted. He had known for many years he wanted his own family, his own children. He was certain once this piece of the puzzle fell into place, the rest of his life would sort itself out. He'd be accepted back into his circle of friends, find work again, be seen as fitting into society.

After the Wednesday morning appointment, he made his way to Home Depot and Costco. He had already packed some blankets in the trunk of his car. He knew if his plan was to work, he needed to be organized and get everything set. He hadn't figured out how or when he would pull the trigger, but that was a minor point. First, he had to deal with logistics.

It was a stunning summer day, and he blasted the radio, singing along to old rock songs. It was quiet when he parked at the old barn and pulled the tarp off the Quad Bike. He carefully balanced the supplies he needed for the minor fix ups and to stay a couple days. He drove through the woods, careful to keep the throttle low. He parked behind a large oak tree and unloaded the goods then carefully camouflaged the vehicle with large leaf-covered branches.

He needed to walk this last part of the trail since the forest was so dense. He also couldn't risk having any signs of life close to his special place. He smiled as he loaded the first of his supplies into his large pack and started along the overgrown path. Familiar smells and sounds greeted him like old friends. The rock faces greeted him kindly along the way: the joker, the giant, the idiot. Each of the boulders with their cracks and protrusions had a distinct personality and he was grateful for their reassuring presence. They hadn't changed over the years, these kindred spirits. They brought back good memories of his youth, stalwarts of his sanctuary in the woods.

He was dripping with sweat upon his arrival and dumped the supplies on the ground. After brushing off the newly fallen debris on the door, it gave way much easier than it did the last time. He took one last look around and dropped to the ground on his hands and knees. He backed up to the edge and dropped to his stomach and let his right foot drop into the opening and find the ladder. Being careful to balance his pack, he made his way down one foot at a time.

CHAPTER 34

It had taken a couple of weeks to win her over, but Michael convinced Sarah that Jack's mental illness required them to be more compassionate than usual. They sat on their dock sipping their beer while the kids played in the water.

"Just think, honey, how lucky we are with our lives," Michael said.

Paige and Connor were good swimmers, making their way easily from the main dock to the swim dock anchored thirty yards offshore. At five and seven years of age, they already had years of swimming lessons. Amy loved the water more than any of them and valiantly tried to keep up, her little arms and legs kicking furiously while trailing behind them. The life jacket she wore was a bit of a hindrance, but they always insisted on it when she was near the water. They weren't ready to let her try to swim without it. She was not yet three, and besides, they would lose their precious alone time if they needed to be with her all the time.

Michael playfully pressed his cold beer against her back.

"Hey, that's freezing!"

"I was thinking you look a little hot and bothered, young lady," he breathed heavily into her neck.

Even though she sneered at his comment, she enjoyed being reminded she wasn't just a cook, maid, and servant to these four people she loved more than anything.

"We'll need to let them swim for a while longer to make sure they go to sleep quickly tonight," she said, leaning in to give him a slow passionate kiss.

"Mommy, Mommy! Watch me!" hollered Paige as she did a cannonball off the swim dock.

"Mommy, Daddy. Watch me!" parroted Connor, landing almost on top of Paige.

"Be careful, you two, and be sure to watch out for your baby sister!" yelled Sarah.

"So, are you okay if I invite him up next weekend?" Michael asked.

Sarah was quiet.

"Dr. Turner says he's making good progress and he's taking his meds. Jack says he honestly doesn't remember coming over that night and I believe him," Michael said, while gently stroking her arm.

"I suppose I can handle it. I'll just be sure to keep busy, which is never a problem with this family."

Michael jumped to his feet before Sarah had time to change her mind and shouted to all of them, "Hey you guys, watch me!" as he did a ridiculous belly flop into the water. All three kids squealed in delight at his performance and shrieked as he plowed through the water to join in the games on the swim dock.

CHAPTER 35

Jack managed to get everything into the bunker after four drives north and many more treks through the woods. He bought a piece of foam to put on the bed frame. The collapsible small table and chairs hardly took up any room at all. The portable stove was a nice new addition, and the twenty-pound tank option could come in handy depending on how long they stayed. He knew she liked to read and bought several books by authors he knew she liked from looking at her book collection on a previous visit to her house. On his last trip, he remembered to bring Earl Gray tea, her favorite. With the glow from the battery-operated lamp in the corner, he thought the place looked positively cozy. A perfect romantic hideaway to start their new life.

~~~

It was one of the last weekends of the summer when Jack arrived at Michael and Sarah's cottage on Saturday afternoon. He cautiously showed up late to not appear too intrusive. He knew he was going to have to work hard to hide his excitement at being around Sarah again. She hadn't seen him since he declared his love for her. He had seen her plenty of times lately; dropping off the kids at play dates, putting out the trash, going about her daily routine. He had her schedule memorized. He was careful to change his appearance during the day by wearing different hair pieces, hats, different clothes, even changing his walk. The sunglasses helped as well. He loved watching her while hiding in the cedar hedge at night when he could see her in the kitchen and family room. He timed these visits with Michael's absences. It was better this way, without the children being around. He fantasized about it being just the two of them. It was like having her in a glass box. He couldn't wait to take her out and place her in his world.

Michael greeted him warmly and thanked him for the expensive steaks and the case of beer.

"You didn't need to bring all this. I know things are tight right now," Michael said.

"It's the least I could do. I really appreciate you having me here,"

Jack said while stealing a glance up to the deck trying to catch a glimpse of Sarah.

The kids came barreling at him at full speed, the three of them piling on and just about knocking him over.

"Uncle Jack, Uncle Jack!" they called as they clung to his legs.

"Hey, guys! Let him at least put his things down," Michael scolded.

Sarah watched from the protection of the glared glass in the sunroom.

"I had it first," declared Paige.

"No, I did," Connor insisted as the two of them fought for control over Jack's overnight bag.

"Why don't you each hold a handle, then you can let Uncle Jack follow you up to the bunkie so he can unpack his things," Michael suggested.

"I'd love that," Jack said. "You are always the best helpers in the world!"

"What about me?" came a pouty voice from behind.

Jack spun around and smiled at Amy, "Wow, just look at what a big girl you are now!" She instantly raised her arms, and he lifted her up high overhead.

"But not too big to get a shoulder ride, I hope?" he asked as he plunked her on his shoulders with her tanned chubby legs dangling over his chest.

"Yeah, a horsey ride! Giddy up, Mr. Horsey!"

Jack did a little gallop and broke into a run up the path to the bunkie.

"Hey, wait for us!" Paige and Connor hollered as they struggled, bumping his overnight bag between them as they ran. Michael watched them disappear inside the bunkie then popped his head into the cottage.

"Hey, sweetie. Are you going to come down to the water?"

"I'll be down in a couple of minutes. Are you sure it's safe to leave him with the kids?"

Michael heard them shrieking with laughter. "They're having a riot. Can't you hear them?"

Sarah looked up the hill towards the bunkie.

"Last one in is a dirty rotten egg!" Jack teased as he emerged from the bunkie and tore down the path in hot pursuit by the three youngsters.

Sarah stepped into the sunroom again to watch them unseen and softened a little. Michael hugged her from behind, watching over her shoulder. Jack let them catch up and tackle him on the dock and they were attempting to roll him off the edge.

"See how fantastic he is with them? They're crazy about him," Michael said.

At the sight of Jack rolling off the dock, landing hard on the water, Sarah couldn't help but smile a little. Michael restocked the drinks cooler, and Sarah followed him down to the water with the snack tray. She was wearing a thin blue cover-up with daisies over her tankini.

Michael finished his beer and jumped in to join in the nonsense on the swim dock. They were playing "name the animal," where one person would call out the name of an animal just as the player would jump. Before hitting the water, the player needed to make the animal sound. It made for hysterical laughter as the caller might say *pig* and the jumper might respond late with a *meow*, or call *bird* and get a *bark* in return. It took all of Jack's focus not to look back to Sarah. When the kids finally tired of the game, they flopped like hooked fish on the dock before jumping up and descending on the snacks.

Jack pulled himself up on the dock. "Hi, Sarah, how have you been?"

"I'm fine. How are you doing?" she said, turning it back on him.

He wasn't sure if she was just being polite or referring to his mental health.

"I'm doing okay. Much better over these past few weeks. These doctors nowadays are terrific. Ever since I started with Dr. Turner, I feel so much better."

"What doctor?" asked Paige.

"Are you sick?" Connor added.

After an awkward silence Sarah chimed in, "No, Uncle Jack isn't sick. Dr. Turner is a different kind of doctor, one that helps people feel better in their head."

"But his head looks fine," Connor said.

Not wanting to get into things with the kids, and also looking to get away from Jack, Sarah piped up, "Yes, Connor, Uncle Jack is fine. It looks like you three could use some time out of the sun. How about I set up a movie and we let Daddy and Uncle Jack get caught up?"

"Awesome! Can we watch Aladdin again? It's the best," asked Paige.

"Sure, darling. Please gather up a few of the cups too."

Jack was quick to get on his feet and offered to help carry things inside.

Sarah immediately took a few steps back. "Oh no, the kids are good helpers. It will be nice for you two to have some time on your own. Come on, kids, let's go!"

Jack watched her turn away towards the cottage with her brood following closely behind. The rebuke cut deep. Jack had so looked forward to being around Sarah. He had fantasized about their future and figured she'd be happy to see him. Of course, he knew she needed to appear cool to keep her hidden desires for him from Michael. But to use a weak excuse to avoid him completely was almost unbearable. Very unsettling.

"Hey, Jack, did you hear me?" Michael said loudly, intruding on his dream state. "I was asking if you've made any headway on the job front. Did you follow up on that lead I gave you with Dave Spelding from Universal Equity?"

Jerking back to the present, Jack lied, "I left him a couple of messages but haven't heard anything yet. I'm sure he's just busy. The fall will be better."

Jack had no intention of calling anyone for work. He wouldn't be in a position to be working for some time.

"I think I'll go change and take a walk down the back road. It's so beautiful in these woods and I could use the exercise," Jack said. "If that's cool with you."

"Go for it," Michael said. He was glad to have him disappear for a bit since he could tell things were tense between the three adults. "Take your time and we'll have dinner ready when you're back."

Jack trudged along the trail, trying to make sense of the situation.

Sarah seemed standoffish and cold. He knew he had come on strong that fateful night.

She must know I was simply trying to tell her how much I love her. She must see how much happier she would be with me. Maybe she is playing a game to ensure Michael isn't on to us until she can break free.

He was half an hour deep on the trail with these thoughts firing through his head when it came to him like a revelation.

The kids! Of course! It's all about the kids. She is too good a person to break up her family. She couldn't live with herself if she left Michael and created a broken home. She is staying for the sake of the children like so many people do. How noble. How admirable. But how unnecessary. She is truly a saint thinking she needs to sacrifice her own happiness for the sake of her children.

He was ecstatic as he bounded back in the direction of the cottage after alighting on the impasse.

The evening was lovely and warm and surprisingly bug free, so they ate dinner at the picnic table by the water. The steaks were grilled to perfection, the salad crispy, garlic bread tangy, and the beer and white wine chilled. The children created a nice buffer between the adults and kept the night lively with light conversation. Jack was happy to forage for wood with the help of Paige and Connor. Amy crashed right after an earlier dinner. With all the swimming and fresh air, she was usually fast asleep by seven.

"How many s'mores can we have?" Paige questioned her mother as Jack fanned the fire.

"I think two will be plenty," Sarah replied. The graham cracker, marshmallow, milk chocolate dessert was always the request for a campfire treat.

The sky was deepening into a beautiful indigo with brilliant red streaks from the fading day. Sparks shot up as the dry wood crackled. A crescent moon began to rise over the inky outline of the trees across the bay and stars started to emerge from the endless sky. It was like he always dreamed it would be—the love of his life, surrounded by children, a beautiful setting, away from all the pressures of the city. Once he made the necessary adjustments, this would all be his.

It wasn't late when everyone turned in for the night. They practically had to carry Paige and Connor up to their bunk beds. Jack thanked Michael and Sarah for such a nice day and made his way up the hill along the narrow path with the help of a flashlight to the bunkie. After tidying up the cottage while Michael checked to make sure the campfire was out, Sarah looked up the hill towards the bunkie. All was dark. She let out a sigh of relief. She lit a candle in their room and slipped into a silky soft pink nightgown. She tucked into Michael and enjoyed snuggling in close after the day. Even after three kids and almost ten years, she still found Michael very sexy. She ran her hands over his smooth bare chest, playfully stroking the area above his pajama bottoms.

Michael lightly scratched her neck. This was the first chance they had to talk about Jack since he arrived.

"See, that wasn't so bad, was it?" Michael asked.

After a few moments Sarah responded, "It was a nice enough day. I still get this creepy feeling from him but maybe it's just because of that bizarre episode before his breakdown."

"It might just take some time, honey. He certainly is trying. Did you see how great he was with the kids?"

"Yes, they are fond of him."

Michael worked his hand from her neck down to her lower back.

"That feels great," Sarah whispered. She turned her face to his and her lips landed softly. They knew they were in sync when they could land a kiss like this in total darkness. One small kiss led to another. They were a bit giggly since they felt like teenagers with parents down the hall with the kids' room being so close.

"Shush," Michael scolded. "If you can't behave, I may have to discipline you."

"Promises, promises," Sarah teased.

Jack was careful to make his way slowly down the path. It was challenging without the flashlight. He had it in his pocket as a back-up.

Michael silently slipped the thin straps off her shoulders and peeled her nightgown to her waist. The total darkness made it seem that much more forbidden. Although she was tired from the day, he always managed to lure her back to him sexually. He quickly yanked off his bottoms.

Jack tested the porch deck for creaks with each step as he lightly made his way along the side of the cottage, stopping just short of the bedroom window.

Michael rolled on top and easily entered her. She arched her back in acceptance. Sarah's moans grew louder with each thrust. He playfully clamped her mouth with one hand to stifle her cries.

Jack approached the side window and slowly leaned in to look through the glass. He saw the candle flickering with its light weakly showing the coupling. He was transfixed. Sarah's shapely legs were wrapped around Michael's waist. Her hands were above her head against the headboard to brace her body. Michael's strong back shielded her face.

Taking a step away from the window, Jack leaned one hand against the cottage. His other hand found his erection. Jack was caught up in the moment, fantasizing about Sarah, and let out a low groan as he came.

Sarah immediately bolted upright. "Did you hear that?"

Jack froze against the wall.

Michael laughed, "Did I ever! Silly of me thinking I could keep you quiet."

"No, seriously, Michael. I'm sure there is something out there. Just outside the cottage. I heard a sound, like a growl," Sarah said while pulling up her shoulder straps.

Michael was slow to respond.

"Please go look!" Sarah insisted, pushing him towards the edge of the bed.

Michael found his bottoms tangled up in the sheets at the foot of the bed. "You're still not use the cottage sounds, are you? There are lots of creatures that come out at night. It doesn't mean they plan on harming you," he said.

"I'd feel better knowing what's out there."

Michael planted a light kiss on her check, "Yes, dear, I'll be back."

As soon as Michael was outside, Sarah moved to the kitchen window and stared hard into the forest. She could barely make out the outline of the bunkie. It was still dark, just like it was when she had gone to bed. She shuddered in her bare feet and flimsy nightgown.

Michael came back inside with his report. "All quiet, my love. If there was anything, I guess it knew enough not to hang around once it heard me coming."

Sarah visibly relaxed. "Sorry, darling. I'm a little more jumpy than usual. I'm going to get a snack then come to bed. Do you want anything?"

"No thanks. You wiped me out. Don't be long."

Sarah opened and closed the fridge door to stall. A few minutes later she killed the kitchen light but waited by the window. She gasped when she saw the flashlight light go on in the bunkie. It stayed on only a few seconds.

Jack needed the light to find the bottle of whisky to dull the pain. He'd been careful to pace his drinking to remain stable and in control of his emotions all day. It was brutal on his nerves. He drank straight from the bottle. A few more gulps and his belly was on fire and his head was spinning.

He had to find a way to move the process along. The more he thought about it, the more certain he was she was staying for the sake of the kids. People do it all the time. She probably doesn't even see it herself. Michael is so smug in his own little world. He doesn't see us suffering. Poor Sarah, so burdened. And me; he figures I'll just bump along and join in the campfire songs. Where was he when I spiraled deeper with every failed attempt at conception? Sure, he traveled overseas a lot, and three kids would keep anyone busy. But he was supposed to have been my best friend. He should have been there for me. He's shunned me like a wet stray ever since he's had his own family. If he'd really cared, he would have seen I needed help. What a fool he's been, a selfish fool.

He reached the bottom of the bottle.

I'll have to find a way to break Sarah's obligation to the kids. Loosen the glue on their cute little family unit.

He paused to let his mind twist around his new tactic and let it take shape. Images of the kid's day flashed across his mind.

For Christ's sake, kids have accidents all the time. It's incredible it isn't more common with the risks kids take. Shit, with three kids, it wouldn't be so shocking if their parents weren't keeping an eye on all of them at all times. Good old Uncle Jack. Doting Uncle Jack. Well, this time, Uncle Jack isn't going to play so nice. Sarah won't understand at first, but eventually she'll see it's all for her own good.

~~~

Sunday was just as glorious as Saturday. Cottage days had a way of passing quickly although not a whole lot happened.

"I'll give you a countdown of a hundred this time," Jack roared, and they screamed with delight scattering to hide again. Hide and Seek was one of their favorite games. Jack had offered to keep the kids occupied while Sarah and Michael tended to a few chores and got dinner ready.

"100...99...98..."

He knocked back his rye and lemonade. He couldn't remember if it was his 5th or 6th drink. After he reached 80 it got very quiet. What good little hiders. He squinted up to the cottage deck and saw the BBQ smoking and smelled the steaks beginning to cook. Michael and Sarah were inside. He knew the older kids couldn't resist wanting to win and would forget all about their little sister in their quest to find the best hiding spot.

"79...78...77..."

He stumbled on the path by the water and caught sight of Amy on the dock next door, clearly not engaged in the game and simply caught up in watching the sunlight sparkle on the water. The trees provided a lot of privacy between neighboring lots.

"66...65...64..."

He kept an eye on Michael and Sarah's upper deck through the trees as he moved in beside her tiny body, now leaning precariously over the edge of the dock to watch the sunfish. Her tiny toes gripped the rough edge of the dock. The fading sunlight danced on her beautiful golden curls that hung about her face as she peered into the water. He slipped off his sandals and sat on the edge beside her. They shared a sweet smile as they watched the water. Amy was fascinated by the shiny, quick-swimming yellow fish darting under the dock. Jack took one last glance up.

"58...57...56..."

He grabbed her soft little wrist and pulled her over the edge in one rapid movement. She was about to produce one of her famous giggles as she looked expectantly into his eyes, delighted with his game. But as she opened her mouth to squeal, he sunk her swiftly and quietly under the water.

"51...51...50..."

Amy instinctively struggled and flailed but it was easy to keep her small body submerged. Still seated on the dock, he watched as his feet pinned her to the sandy bottom. She swallowed more and more water with every desperate but futile attempt to breathe. Her big blue eyes wildly implored him for help. Her hair swayed around her face. Her little hands clawed at his feet with the useless strength of the babe she was.

"45...44...43......"

He slowed his count as she struggled and involuntarily sucked in more water.

"34...33...32"

Her movements slowed and her limbs went limp as she lost the fight to survive.

"25...24...23..."

Her mouth gaped open, and her pupils dilated. He could smell the succulent grilling of the steak now and knew it wouldn't be long until someone came out. He eased one foot slowly off her chest and wedged the other foot underneath her back. He flipped her body over, face down. She floated to the surface but made no further attempt to breathe.

"18...17...16..."

Her arms limply floated, resting at her sides, as he nudged her under the dock.

"10...9...8..."

He slipped his feet back into his sandals and finished his countdown while watching the surface to be sure she wasn't going to pop up. All was calm. He thought of the kid's favorite story:

Red fish
Blue fish
Old fish
New fish
This one has a little star
This one drives a little car
Say, what a lot of fish there are!

"3....2...1.... Ready or not, here I come!"

Five minutes later Jack, Paige, and Connor tumbled inside, laughing and short of breath.

"Sounds like somebody had a lot of fun," Sarah said as she tossed the salad. Michael was on the deck taking the last of the steaks off the grill.

"You almost blew it," Paige scolded Connor.

"Did not!"

"Did so."

"Did not"

Sarah looked bemused with her eyes scanning the room. "Where's Amy?"

With Connor and Paige's banter it took a few moments to get everyone's attention. "Hey, you two. Where is your sister? Wasn't she hiding with you?" Sarah asked. Her rising concern matched her increasing volume with each question.

"No, I thought she was here with you," answered Paige. "I bet she is hiding in here. Amy, Amy. Come out, come out, wherever you are."

"Jack, did you see her?" Sarah asked.

"No. I figured I'd find them all together, but I only came up with these two rascals," he replied while starting to tickle them.

"Amy. If you're in here come out this instant. AMY!" yelled Sarah.

Michael came in off the deck, looking mildly concerned. "What's going on?

Sarah's grave look told him this was serious. "Amy didn't come in with the others. You two, don't move," she ordered the children as she ran to the door.

Michael slid the platter across the counter and followed her out. Jack was right behind them.

"Amy! Amy!" Sarah called from the top of her lungs. Only the sound of Sarah's calls echoed back. Her panic bubbled to the surface. There was no sign of any movement.

Michael was down at the lake in a flash, running along the water's edge, scanning the surface. He darted back and forth searching the lake and the woods. Jack did the same. Sarah tore down to the dock and ran to the edge looking frantically for any sign of her little girl. Her mind raced, trying to remember if she had put on Amy's life jacket but came up blank. She couldn't think.

"AMY!" she screamed, her eyes wide with fear. "Jack, run up to the bunkie and see if she's there. Michael, look in the shed. I'll keep looking down here."

Jack ran up the hill. He waited for a minute before descending with convincing urgency to show his concern. "I'm afraid there no sign of her."

After checking the shed Michael called 911.

"You've reached emergency services for the Haliburton region. Please state the nature of your call."

"My child is missing," choked out Michael.

"How long have they been missing?"

Michael found her voice irritatingly calm. "About ten minutes, but she's only two. We have a cottage."

"The odds are she is just playing a game, sir. Give us a call back if she doesn't show up in another 30 minutes and we can send out a patrol to help."

Michael stood frozen on the dock. He knew he should go into the water but couldn't budge.

Sarah told Jack to stay in the cottage with the older two. She flew by Michael and plunged in. She dove over and over again into the familiar swimming area around their dock. Her breathing was coming in shallow bursts. She swam out further while scanning the murky bottom. She yelled back at Michael to call 911 again for help. She swam to the swim dock praying Amy was hiding on the far side. Nothing. Her heart pounded from exertion and the drag of her clothes. She was standing on the swim dock, combing the shoreline, when she saw the bright pink T-shirt.

"AMY! Oh my God. Oh my God!" "Michael! MICHAEL—she's in the WATER. Under the dock. The WILSON'S dock. Hurry, Michael! GET HER OUT OF THE WATER!"

Sarah cried as her arms pounded the water with frantic strokes.

Michael sprinted to the neighbor's dock and wildly scanned the water. Sarah was thirty feet away.

"Michael! Under the dock. Oh my God. Please no, please no. AMY. God no, please, please, please."

Michael pulled Amy to the surface. She was wearing only her T-shirt and shorts. He swept her inert body into his arms and placed her on the dock. He vaulted up beside her and did mouth-to-mouth resuscitation. He didn't give up until the emergency team took over, twenty minutes later. After further attempts, including trying the paddles from the defibrillator kit, they rushed her to the hospital.

Jack stayed with the other two children when the ambulance whisked Amy and her parents away.

Amy was pronounced dead at 7:12 pm. Sarah felt the knife twist when they asked if she had been wearing a life jacket. They told them they could transport Amy's body home themselves or call a funeral home for the body.

Michael arrived back at the cottage near midnight, leaving Sarah to spend the night at the hospital with Amy's body. Sarah couldn't bear to leave her little girl alone. The funeral home said the car would arrive first thing in the morning. She and Michael didn't want the other two children without a parent since they knew they had left them wondering what happened. They would tell them together, later.

Jack played the grief-stricken uncle. "Is there anything I can do to help?"

"There's nothing now," said Michael. "Thank you for staying with Paige and Connor. Its best if you leave quietly first thing in the morning."

CHAPTER 36

The next week was a blur for Sarah and Michael making funeral arrangements, dealing with well-meaning friends and family, and showing up for the visitation. They chose to have only immediate family at the funeral. Sarah was so sedated she barely remembered any of it. Her mother was a rock and took care of her as well as the children. It was probably best that school started again in a week so Paige and Connor could have some semblance of normalcy in their lives.

Sarah stayed in bed for days, vacillating between crying with rage and despair. She couldn't piece together how they could have let this happen.

"It was all our fault, it's all our fault," she repeated like a mantra.

Michael took a four-week leave of absence to grieve and to try and help Sarah and the children cope. Michael couldn't process his feelings, not yet, not so soon. He managed to get through the days skimming the surface, not daring to let himself feel. Work was a good distraction. He knew he should be at home more, but it was too painful to be around all the reminders. The office provided the artifice of normalcy, a place where the physical ache wasn't quite as acute.

Sarah was inconsolable. She clung to him one moment then pushed him away the next, agonizing on how they could have been so negligent. He didn't have any answers, which only infuriated her more.

Jack stayed low for two weeks before he called Michael to see how things were. "I've been worried sick about you guys. How are you?"

"Barely coping. Sarah is a mess."

The line went quiet, and Jack could hear Michael's quiet crying on the other end.

"Anything I can do to help, anything at all, you'll let me know, right?"

"Sure," Michael squeezed out in a thin voice. "Thanks, Jack. I'm sorry you had to be part of this nightmare. This can't be easy on you either."

"I appreciate that, Michael. I'll be okay."

Setting down the phone Jack surveyed the plans. Amongst the squalor of his apartment, the overturned cardboard box serving as his table held the promise of their future. The map was well worn from his measurements and poring over the best routes. Nearby lay a list of items bought and those still needed, greasy with food smudges. Not much to get now. Mainly just the rest of the medicine, which he planned on getting on his next and final visit to Dr. Turner.

He'd been careful to maintain his regular visits. He wanted to appear cooperative, and Dr. Turner's positive assessment could be useful should suspicion turn to him. More importantly, it was his access via Dr. Turner to the medication he wanted on hand as a safety measure. He was hopeful Sarah would at least be a compliant if not a willing participant right from the start. If this wasn't the case, the diazepam could come in handy.

Dr. Turner's glass cabinet sat directly behind his desk. The rich pharmaceutical companies stocked the doctors with trial meds, and diazepam was especially popular for people suffering from anxiety. It was surprisingly easy to gain access. When Jack excused himself to use the washroom, often Dr. Turner would use the break to check some files at the main nursing station and leave his keys in his top desk drawer. Jack discreetly slipped back into Dr. Turner's office to grab a few of the sample bottles and carefully returned the keys. Needles were available by the handful in the hospital utility closets.

Jack reviewed the timelines for how long their food would hold out. *Their* food. He loved the sound of it. His dream of being a couple was within reach.

CHAPTER 37

On a windy October morning, Sarah sat comatose on the sofa, staring out the front window. The kids were in school, and Michael was at work. Ever since Michael had gone back to work it seemed like he didn't want to come home. He claimed there was so much that had piled up in his absence he didn't have much choice but to stay late most nights to catch up. She knew it was too painful to be home and around their old life that had contained the five of them. But it wasn't fair that he had an out and she didn't. She went through the motions of living; picking the kids up from school, dinner, bath, bedtime.

"You said six o'clock and now you're telling me nine o'clock?" Sarah cried.

"I told you I have to get through the Phase Three testing if we have any hope of making the RFP deadline next week."

"You think I give a crap about a RFP? My baby is dead and you expect me to care about a fucking RFP?"

"I need to get some balance back, Sarah," he said. "Work provides a place where I can do that. It lets me forget about that horrible scene, the worst day of my life, for about one minute a day. If I don't get that minute, I'm afraid I will fall apart and never get up. I can't be any good to you, or to Paige, or Connor, if I can't function."

"Screw you," she said and slammed down the phone.

Sarah muffled her cries in the couch pillow. She curled up in her blue flannel pajamas. She'd lost fifteen pounds since the drowning and looked drawn and exhausted. Her hair was greasy, she rarely bathed. She didn't care. She knew she should pull it together for the sake of her other two children, but she simply didn't have the strength.

~~~

Jack was worried about Sarah but didn't risk contacting her after what Michael told him. He thought it was better to stay out of their lives and let them absorb their perceived negligence. He didn't want to give them any reason to reconsider what they believed to be their terrible lack of judgment, their dreadful parenting. He had done quite a bit of reading about the effects on marriages after the loss of a child and knew it should work in his favor. They believed Amy's death was their fault, which was bound to put a huge strain on the marriage.

Jack observed Michael's late nights over the past few weeks. He cautiously set up his surveillance again at their house and was pleased to see Michael resuming his old ways, pouring himself into his work and ignoring his family obligations.

~~~

Sarah entered Amy's room as quietly as possible. She hadn't opened the door since they returned with her body late August. Sarah was adamant that nobody enter her room. Even now, she felt like she was violating her memory. She caught her scent immediately, all sweetness and innocence. The pink polka-dotted bed covers on Amy's big-girl bed were rumpled since Sarah hadn't time to make the beds before leaving for the cottage. Amy had only used the bed for a couple of weeks, having recently outgrown her crib. The board books were piled on her dresser. A stack of alphabet blocks sat at the end of the bed. Stuffed animals were piled high on the chair. Sarah wanted to fold her clothes, straighten her books, and hold onto the lingering but fading sweet scent of her toddler. But she couldn't bring herself to disturb her baby's last day. To touch anything would be to take away from what was. The pain was physical. Her chest ached. Her throat was constricted. She crumpled to the floor and gulped for air through her tears. She needed to see her, to hold her. She needed to go back to the place she had last been alive. If only to relive Amy's last day, their last day.

She sent Michael a text, not wanting to contact him directly. She was too upset to deal with him. Sarah hastily put on track pants and a sweatshirt and grabbed her purse and coat on her way out the door. It was late morning.

"Hi, Mom. Yes, I'm okay today," she lied, trying to sound normal. "Listen, I was wondering if you could get the kids today from school and keep them for dinner, maybe over-night? Michael needs to work tonight and I have a slew of errands to run. I'd really like to have the day to myself."

"Sure, dear. I'd love to. Are you sure you're all right? You sound a little off."

"Don't worry about me, I'll be fine. Thanks, I appreciate it,"Sarah said and quickly hung up.

~~~

Jack was patiently observing her house from his car parked down the block. He wore his baseball hat low and kept a few packages on his passenger seat to appear as a delivery man to avoid suspicion from anyone passing by. He liked to follow her about town but hadn't had many chances as she didn't often leave the house. He let her pull out of the driveway before following at a safe distance. She stopped at the gas station. She maneuvered through the city and then turned north onto the parkway. His heart quickened as he let himself think maybe this was the break he'd been waiting for, the chance to get her away, so they could start their new life together.

Sarah hit the gas hard. She turned off the parkway onto the main highway that led to their cottage.

"This is it," Jack said as his heart jumped a beat.

He took the next exit and made his way back into the city and was parked near the school by noon. He wore dark blue jeans, hiking boots, a dark grey hoodie, a baseball cap, and a loose brown oilskin coat.

The playground was one big field with a climbing structure at one end and a baseball diamond at the other. Jack walked slowly along the sidewalk, watching the kids pour out of the main red doors exiting to the yard.

Boys swarmed the climber, and their shrieks pierced the air as their game of tag picked up. Connor was a regular monkey, so he was easy to pick out, racing up the highest climber while daring his friends to try and catch him.

Kids were darting every which way. With the cutbacks at the school board, there was only one monitor on the field at lunch minding a couple hundred kids so his lingering at the fence wasn't noticed. Connor hit the ground and was manically surveying his opponent's moves.

Jack called out, "Hey, Connor. Looking good out there!"

It took a second for Connor to figure out who it was.

"Hey, thanks, Uncle Jack," he said while trotting up to the fence, happy to get the compliment.

"I was out for a walk and thought this must be your school from what you've told me," Jack said as his eyes continued to scan the field. The bright orange–vested woman was busy in the far corner of the field separating a few scrappy children. Jack needed to move fast while he still had Connor's attention and proximity to the fence.

"Listen, I think you've got a while before the bell rings, so I thought you might like to go and get a chocolate bar," he suggested. "What's your favorite?"

"Wow, really? That would be great. I love Kit Kat. I'll meet you at the entrance." He turned to run for the gate, but Jack caught his jacket.

"Hey, I can give you a lift. No point to going all the way around," Jack said.

Before Connor could respond Jack pulled him against the fence and hoisted him up and over in one easy move.

"Cool. You sure are strong, Uncle Jack."

"I've already signed you out, so we're good to go," Jack said lifting him onto his back for a piggy-back ride. Both their backs were now to the fence as Jack crossed the street and galloped Connor down the block and around the corner.

"Awesome! This is SO fun. Giddy-up, giddy-up, faster, faster," Connor laughed.

Jack stopped at his car that he parked between the school and the store. "It will be faster if we drive. This way you won't be late for school."

"Okay," Connor shrugged, blindly trusting his Uncle Jack, yet slightly hesitant before getting into the car. Jack was concerned Connor sensed something wasn't right and his opportunity might slip away.

"Don't I need a booster seat?" Connor asked.

Jack paused momentarily then recovered. "You don't need one if we are only going a couple of blocks. In my car kids are even allowed in the front seat." Jack grinned and quickly slid Connor into the front seat and strapped on his seatbelt.

Jack jogged to his side of the car, hopped in, and turned on the ignition.

After driving a few blocks to get out of the neighborhood, on the pretense of tightening Connor's belt, he leaned across and plunged a needle into his upper thigh. Connor screamed and looked at Jack, confused.

"Ouch, that hurt!" he cried with tears immediately pouring down his cheeks as he grabbed his leg.

Jack stared straight ahead, ignoring Connor's pleas for an explanation. Within thirty seconds Connor passed out and slumped against the door of the car.

Jack hated to waste any of his precious stash of medicine, but he knew how pesky and inquisitive kids could be. Jack didn't want to get agitated on his big day. The sky was overcast and there were only a few leaves still clinging to the trees. The roads were quiet now that they were north of the city. He envisioned Sarah wandering on her property, staring into the dark water, walking through the motions of the day. He was surprised it had taken her so long to want to go back. He knew most people were drawn back to the scene of a tragedy as a way of getting closure.

~~~

Sarah turned onto the lane leading to their cottage. It was grey and dark with heavy clouds low in the sky. She passed by the dozen or so other cottages on the road leading to theirs. Not a person in sight. Everyone usually closed their cottages on Labor Day weekend. The bare docks, the absence of motorboats, canoes, colorful umbrellas, and water toys was soothing. She wasn't looking for any reminders of happy family times. It looked lifeless and bare, a good match for her bleak mood.

Jack forked left, before Sarah's cottage, and took the high road. He parked and killed the engine. He lifted Connor's limp body from the passenger seat and placed him on his side in the trunk. He zip-tied his hands behind his back, then did the same to his feet. He duct-taped his mouth.

"Sorry little fella," Jack said to the mute child, "but I need to be sure your mom will cooperate."

The forest was dense enough to keep the car camouflaged from the cottage below. He took a few minutes to collect himself.

Jack saw Sarah walking slowly along the water's edge with her arms wrapped tight around herself, her head bent into the wind. She wore a thick plaid jacket as a buffer against the chill. Jack needed to move quickly before it got too dark to reach their destination. He descended the leaf-strewn path from the high road, down past the bunkie to the driveway.

Sarah knelt back on her haunches on the dock, staring across the inky water, numb to the frigid temperature. Black waves lapped the shore, providing no answers.

Jack smiled, envisioning Sarah's face melting with relief at finding him here for her. He calmly stepped onto the dock.

Sarah felt the motion before she heard anything. The dock movement startled her, and she drew in a sharp breath.

In that split second, Jack placed a gentle hand on her shoulder and whispered, "It's okay, I'm here for you now."

Sarah screamed as her head wiped around. Scrunching up her face bloated from crying, she squinted through bloodshot eyes in disbelief.

"Jack! What are you doing here?" She looked beyond him and searched the road. "Did Michael make you drive up with him? Figures he's too weak to come alone. He better not have brought the kids. They're not ready for this. They'll never be ready." She barely got the words out before her sobs consumed her again.

Jack extended both hands. "Shhhh, it's okay. I'm here now. Let me help you."

Confused, she let him take her hands and get her to her feet. She wiped her runny nose with her sleeve.

"How did Michael know I was here?" she asked in confusion. "Where's the car? Did you have car trouble?"

"We have lots of time to talk things through later," Jack replied, handing her a tissue and steering her towards the driveway.

Getting a grip on herself, Sarah took a step back. "Where's Michael?"

Jack mocked her in a high-pitched voice, "Where is Michael? Where's Michael? Where he always is, working, I'm sure."

Sarah swallowed hard, feeling confused. The hair rose on the back of her neck. Her mind raced.

"Oh. I see. Okay," she said quietly, realizing how alone she was. "It was very nice of you to drive out here to check on me, Jack, but I'm fine. You can stay and use the cottage if you like." She choked up, hoping she didn't sound as scared as she was.

Jack stared at her blankly.

"I'll just go and get my purse. I need to get back to the city," she said, trying to sound casual as she climbed the stairs to the cottage.

Her heart was in her throat as she felt him only inches behind her. He was right on her heels as she walked through the door. She didn't look back as she crossed the kitchen and slid her purse, keys, and phone off the table. She feigned a weak smile as she tried to pass. Jack side-stepped in front of her, blocking her way. He placed his hands on her shoulders. It took all her strength not to scream.

Jack looked deeply into her eyes. "Sarah, you've been through so much. It's time for you to let go and let me take charge," he said as he stroked her hair and tenderly moved it off her tear-stained cheeks.

"That is very sweet. I appreciate you wanting to help but I really need to go now," Sarah said attempting to turn away.

Jack gripped her shoulder with one hand and her chin with the other, tilting her face up to his. "Maybe you didn't hear me? I said, it's time for you to let me take charge."

Feeling her stiffen and seeing her eyes widen, he tried again more softly, "Sarah, you must know that I love you. I've waited for this moment for so long. We were meant to be, but fate kept us apart. Until now. Don't you see! We have both been challenged by circumstances, obstacles, and loss. But that's all in the past now. We finally have each other and there is nothing to stand in our way."

His eyes shone with tears of joy as he waited for her to fall into his waiting arms.

"Jack, you need help. Get the hell out of my way."

Sarah wrenched free and ran for the door. He easily caught her upper arm and spun her around, holding her tightly against him.

"I know you're very upset and this is a lot to process, my love. Don't worry. We have lots of time before we need to deal with the rest of the world."

Sarah rammed her knee up hard against his groin and he dropped to the ground, wheezing for air. She turned and flung open the door, raced down the stairs, and hit the ground running for her car.

Jack stumbled out the door to the top of the stairs and shouted down, "Connor came along for the ride, you know."

Sarah stopped dead in her tracks. "What did you say?"

"That sweet little boy of yours just couldn't resist my offer. The chance of him getting his grubby hands on a Kit Kat was all it took. Proves my theory that all the street-proofing crap is a bunch of bullshit. It's a good thing some creep hasn't come along already and lured him away."

Sarah grabbed her stomach; she was going to be sick. She couldn't move. She knew she should be running for the car instead of watching this man menacingly come down the stairs but instead she stood stock-still. He could be bluffing but she couldn't take the chance.

"Now that's much better," he said in a measured tone. "See, you're already coming around." He grabbed her wrist and dragged her back to the stairs. He pushed her down on the bottom step and cuffed her wrist to the railing rung with one of the zip-ties he brought along for insurance.

He snapped on rubber gloves and took her purse, phone, and keys from her grip.

"Just in case you were thinking of doing something stupid like screaming, remember the fate of your son lies in my hands."

"Don't worry, I won't. You have my word," Sarah said.

"You are such a sweet, honest person, Sarah. Just one of the many things I love about you. Thank you," he said and kissed her cheek.

He walked over to her car and opened the driver's door. He tossed her purse and phone on the front passenger seat. He backed the car out of the driveway and onto the lane that ran parallel with the lake. He parked a few cottages down where the properties front lawns slopped more steeply down to the water. After cranking the steering wheel towards the water, he braked then he opened the driver's window. With the engine still running, he got out and closed the door. He leaned into the car, and using the handle of a shovel, he pressed lightly down on the accelerator while steering the wheel towards lake. The car immediately lurched forward, and Jack ran beside it, continuing to depress the gas pedal as it travelled down the adjacent property's front lawn until it plunged five feet off the edge of the embankment. It didn't go in far, but it was enough for the choppy current to slowly float it out into deeper waters.

Jack knew he needed to buy a few days to keep them off their trail. He imagined the headlines,

DOUBLE TRAGEDY. Suicide suspected by mother at the site of her daughter's drowning two months earlier.

He chuckled as he heard Sarah's phone ringing as the car was pulled further into the lake.

"Maybe that's the diligent husband now?" Jack laughed. "A little late, I'm afraid," he added as he walked towards the love of his life.

"Where is Connor? Is he safe?" Sarah begged.

After cutting the zip-tie, he rubbed her wrist which was sore from her efforts to break the hold. "Of course he's safe. What kind of monster do you think I am? I love that little boy like he's my own."

"I need to see him. Can you take me to him?"

He motioned for her to take the path to the upper road, "Ladies first."

A few minutes later when they reached the deserted road, Sarah peered into his car. Looking madly at Jack she blurted out, "I don't see him. You said he was here. You lied to me!"

"I would never lie to you unless it was for your own good, Sarah."

He walked to the trunk and popped the latch. The door arced upwards, revealing her son. Connor looked frantically from his mother and back to Jack, struggling to speak behind the duct tape. He squirmed against the ties on his feet and hands.

"Connor! Jack, what have you done?" Sarah snapped. She reached down to pull off the tape off his mouth but was stopped roughly by Jack.

"It's no big deal. He was probably sleeping until just a few minutes ago. I gave him a little sedative to keep him quiet. I was hoping I wouldn't need to bring Connor into this, but from your pathetic resistance down there, it seems like Connor will need to come along with us a little further."

"Oh no, please. Please let him go. I beg you. We can drop him off in the village and you and I can keep going wherever you want," Sarah pleaded through glassy eyes. "If you truly love me then do this for me."

"I wish I could. Really, I do. But a five-year-old without parents is bound to draw attention. Also, I can see you need a little longer to adjust to our new life together, so Connor needs to stick with us, for now."

Looking down at Connor bent on his side, he pulled the chocolate bar slowly from his pocket said sweetly, "Don't worry, little buddy, I'm good for my word. You can have this as soon as we get to where we're going."

He slammed the trunk shut.

"Connor! No, no, no," Sarah cried as she pounded on the trunk.

Jack forced Sarah into the front seat. "You really shouldn't worry so much. Boys generally love a good adventure!"

After Jack got into the driver's seat he cuffed Sarah's left hand to his right. "This is only for Connor's safety in case you try to do something silly like jump from the car. If you stay calm and give me a chance to explain, we'll all be just fine."

Sarah held back her panic and stared straight ahead. "Of course, Jack. I'm sure it will all make sense soon. How long before we get to where we're going?"

"Not too long. It will go faster once you put this hood over your head and lie down." He handed her a rough black burlap hood he extracted from the middle compartment.

Sarah looked horror-stricken at the hood but forced herself to only to think of cooperating for Connor's sake. Slumping back and closing her eyes she said dreamily, "Don't worry. I'll just close my eyes, and you can tell me when we arrive."

Jack yanked hard on the cuff, causing Sarah to wince from the pain as he pulled her close. "Put it on."

The back roads Jack had memorized were dead this time of year. Only the occasional pickup truck came from the other direction. Sarah stayed still under the hood with her head in his lap as commanded. She concentrated on her breathing, which was challenging given her fear and the heat of being hooded.

Jack affectionately rubbed his hand over hers. He played country songs. He smiled thinking of the two of them taking this road trip with no one to intrude on their intimacy. He couldn't believe his dream of having Sarah all to himself was unfolding. He was so happy; he felt like his heart could burst.

All was quiet at Angus Smith's country property as Jack expected. Angus had become a snowbird over the past few years, going south with the start of the cold weather. Jack had received a letter from Angus three years back saying he'd had enough of Canadian winters and would be gone October through March. He was happy to leave Jack and his family free access to the old barn with the family's old Quad Bike for trail riding and hunting.

He sat Sarah upright and addressed her through her hood after cuffing her hands together in front of her. "Sarah, sweetheart. I'm sorry to do this but I need to tape your mouth shut to be certain you won't scream. I know this seems crazy, but it's not what it seems. It's for your own good, yours and Connor's."

"Jack, please, I need to see him and tell him we're going to be okay." Sarah started to cry, fumbling with the hood. "He must be so scared. He is just a little boy," she choked out, fear constricting her throat.

"You can hold his hand, since he'll be sitting beside you, but you can't see him until we reach our destination."

Relief washed over her at the thought of having Connor beside her.

"Thank you, Jack. That's very kind of you."

Jack tore a piece of tape from the roll and reaching under the hood, he placed it firmly across her mouth, then wrapped another piece around the outside of the hood around her neck. Jack pulled a second hood from the middle compartment. He kept an eye on Sarah sitting immobile in the front seat of the car as he went around the back. He took another glance around the deserted property. He released the trunk and Connor began to struggle.

"Hey, Connor, great hiding place!" he exclaimed. "You're doing so well on the adventure so far. Keep it up and the Kit Kat is all yours."

Jack quickly slipped the hood over his head and under his chin as Connor struggled like a small animal in a trap.

"Easy, my friend," Jack cajoled, lifting him to his feet. Connor nearly fell over, losing his balance with his zip-ties still secure. Jack caught him before he struck the ground.

"I'm going to do you a favor and undo your ankle ties, if you promise not to run. Deal?" Connor nodded in agreement.

"Of course, Connor, this adventure wouldn't be any fun without your mother," he said. "Let's go get her, shall we?"

Pulling Sarah from the front seat and holding each of them tightly by the upper arm, he led them over to the Quad Bike and got them seated and belted. Sarah fiercely pulled Connor to her side.

Jack quickly drove his car into the barn and locked the barn doors.

The sun was low in the sky and dusk was already upon them. After 20 minutes he stopped the Quad Bike off the path and covered it with the tarp. Jack marched Sarah and Connor down the rough path, with one on either side of him. There was a lot of debris from the storms and high winds over the past couple of months; large branches, slippery stones, and tree roots made the walking treacherous. Sarah and Connor fell several times. When their pace slackened, all he had to do was threaten to hurt the other one to keep them moving at a good clip.

Jack's excitement grew as they got closer to the bunker. "I can't wait to get you inside to have a look at our new place!"

All the months of preparation and dreaming of their new life together was feeding his anticipation of his big reveal.

"All right, you two, take a seat," he ordered, after they arrived. They dropped to the ground cross legged in the damp leaves. They trembled from cold and fear.

Getting down on his hands and knees, he brushed off the brown leaves and dragged his fingers around the edge of the trap door to push away the moist earth. He felt for the small rope handle that was buried under the loose soil. Standing off to the side, he gave the handle a couple of sharp pulls, and the trap door creaked as it fell open on the rusty hinges. Extracting a small flashlight from his pocket he crouched low, peering down into the bunker, sweeping the space with the faint beam of light.

"Perfect," Jack smiled. "Just like I left it."

Chapter 38

It was almost nine o'clock and Paige and her grandma Kate had played Guess Who three times and Go Fish four times. Paige had done her required reading. They ate homemade beef stew for dinner and baked a batch of world-famous (in Paige's world anyway) chocolate chip cookies.

"When is my mom coming back?" whined Paige while looking out her grandma's front window.

"Don't you worry about your mother," replied Kate with a gentle hug. "Sometimes she needs to take a bit of time away to let herself be sad without upsetting the whole family. It's very considerate of her."

"I miss her too, you know," Paige said, her tears coming easily.

"Oh, my dear, of course you do. You are the best big sister anyone could hope for. Amy knew that."

"No, I'm not! If I was so great, why did this happen? Does she hate me? Is that why Mom went away? Because I didn't take good enough care of Amy?"

"Heavens, child. It was an accident. Everyone knows it was a very, very, terrible accident. It's nobody's fault."

Thankfully Kate heard the car coming up the driveway and the car door slam.

"Look, it's your dad now, sweetheart. Now dry those tears as you don't want to worry your father. Here, have an extra cookie. We'll keep that as our little secret." She winked as she moved to the front door.

"Hello, Kate. How are you?" Michael said, still in work mode.

"I'm doing as best I can under the circumstances," she answered, not able to suppress her sadness.

"I'm sorry, Kate. I know this is an unbearable loss for all of us."

"Come in, Michael, and I'll get Paige," she said, wiping her greasy hands on her apron trying to sound a little more upbeat. "Is Connor waiting in the car?"

"In the car?" replied Michael looking back. "He's not with you?"

"No," Kate said slowly. "I received a call from your office saying you were picking Connor up early. I thought they said something about a tryout?"

"Hi, Daddy!" Paige shouted, charging into his arms.

"Hey, darling. How was your day?"

As Paige rambled on Michael reread Sarah's text.

My mother will get the kids after school and keep them at her house for dinner. Pick them up when you're done with your precious trials. I'm off for the day and will be home late tonight.

Michael looked down at Paige, "Okay, honey, gather up your gear. We had better get you home and into bed. It's a school day tomorrow."

"Is Mommy home yet?"

"Not yet. I'm sure she'll be home any minute."

Michael tried Sarah's cell, but it went immediately to voicemail.

With Paige out of earshot Michael pulled Kate aside. "Tell me again about the phone call you received."

"It was about one o'clock and a very friendly gentleman called on your behalf saying you were in a meeting. He told me that I only needed to get Paige after school since you were picking up Connor early for a tryout."

Michael racked his brain for who could have possibly called from his office. He did have a heavy day of meetings, but he certainly never instructed anyone to call Kate. Connor must be with Sarah. It was the only thing that made sense.

"Okay, Daddy. I'm all ready."

Back home, after making some excuse to Paige about Sarah and Connor being out late, and getting her reluctantly to bed, he started calling again.

Hi, you've reached Sarah. Please leave a message at the tone and I'll get back to you as soon as possible. Beeeeeep.

Michael called some associates and his administrative support person, but no one knew anything about a call to Kate.

He looked at her text again, No *Dear* or *Hello*. No *Love, Sarah*. She was obviously upset sending such a terse text. She hated it when the kids broke their routine on a school night so she must have been really upset to leave like this.

Maybe this was her way of getting back at me? He knew she was all over the map on blame for what happened to Amy. One day it was her fault, the next his. He thought of how much she hated the fact that he worked late but it was his only means of coping. It was his lifeline on sanity. He felt himself break into hundreds of tiny sharp pieces when he thought of Amy being gone; Amy drowning with no one to hear her cry or come to her aid. He had to work as a way of buying enough time, so he could hope that one day, he might function as a father and a husband again. He owed this much to Paige and Connor and Sarah. But he wasn't capable. Not yet.

He called his folks up north on the pretext of getting some home repair advice, not wanting to alarm them. After doling out instructions on how to fix the phantom leak, they both asked how Sarah and the children were doing. Clearly Sarah hadn't said anything to them. He tried Sarah's close friends, but none had heard from her today. Most hadn't heard much from her since the accident. He waited until 10 pm to call the police. He didn't know what else to do.

"54th Precinct, Constable Larry Maudry here. How can I help you?"

Chapter 39

Sarah watched her little boy sleeping fitfully on a mat in the corner. It was warm enough as he had a sleeping bag. Sarah tried to think methodically so she could find a way out of this nightmare.

Jack stood at the cook stove keeping an eye on Sarah sitting close by as he stirred a pot of canned stew and vegetables on the camper stove. He had removed their hoods, tape, and cuffs once he got back from returning the Quad Bike to the barn and moving his car to an abandoned property a few kilometers from Angus's place. He ran back to the bunker in the dark being careful to take a convoluted path, deviating many times in different directions in case people came looking. He wore Scent-Lok camouflage gear and sprayed himself with a red fox urine product to further thwart any efforts potentially made by tracker dogs. He knew the anticipated snowfall and high winds would be helpful as well.

Sarah was terrified to ask questions but she needed to try to understand.

"Jack, what is going on here?" she said.

"Do you like our new space? I've fixed it up especially for us. It has everything we need to make a new start."

Sarah took her time looking around the dirt floor and plank walled room, equipped with bare necessities for an indefinite stay. Battery-powered lanterns threw dim light on the space. A rough platform held a double mattress in one corner, a small mat with Connor in another, a camper toilet and another bucket were set up for toileting, and a small food prep area with a camper stove table and chairs finished off the room. Food and water supplies lined the walls and there appeared to be one small black pipe covered in steel mesh in the roof for ventilation.

"We are underground," Sarah replied, her voice cracking. She breathed slowly to control her fear.

"I realize it will take some getting used to. Once you give this —I mean us—a chance, I know you'll be happy. This is just a temporary setup before we move on."

"But there is no us," Sarah said. "This is craziness! You can't keep

242

Connor and me against our will. Michael will contact the police, and they'll find us."

At the mention of Michael's name, Jack tensed and set down the spoon. His expression turned from contentment to fury and he loomed over her in a flash.

"You're hurting me!" Sarah cried out as he gripped both of her wrists.

"Shut up!" he commanded, yanking her to her feet. "Now you listen to me," he parceled out with great effort to stay calm. "There will be no more mention of Michael. Do you understand? He existed in your previous life. That life is over. I don't want to hear you mention him ever again. Do you understand?"

"Let me go! You can't do this!" she said while trying to break his grip.

"Oh, is that so?" he laughed, releasing her and letting her fall back on the ground. "I don't think you've thought this through. Have a look around. You have no idea where we are. I have taken great care to make sure our place is secure and virtually untraceable. I have soundproof insulation on the ceiling. I will gag you for days if you so much as try to call for help, which would be pointless anyways as there is no one around. There will be consequences for not trying to give our relationship a chance."

"Our relationship?" Sarah spat out, her eyes flaring in defiance.

"Yes, *our* relationship," he replied. "Our relationship," he repeated with tears filling his eyes. "Do you know how long I've waited to hear those words coming from your beautiful mouth?" he said as he moved in closer.

"Get away from me! Don't come any closer!"

"Oh, Sarah. Settle down. I'm not going to do anything against your will," he said and returned to the stove. "I've already told you I know this may take an adjustment period. I'm a very patient man. I've waited for you a long time. If it takes you a bit to get on board that's okay. We have our whole lives ahead of us."

As he spooned out their dinner on tin plates, she looked around for something to use to attack him.

Seeing her sizing up the materials he said, "That's more like it. Have a good look. I've spent months getting this ready. We have all the comforts we'll need. No need for distractions from the outside world. We have food and water, medicine and vitamins, reading material, a kitchen, and a bed."

She noticed a strongbox mounted high up on the wall.

Jack poured two glasses of red wine into tin cups. "To mark this very special first night together darling, let's propose a toast."

As she moved to avoid his touch, he grabbed her roughly and angled her harshly into a chair.

"Sweetheart let's be civil. You don't want to wake up Connor, do you?"

"No, I don't," she said, feeling stunned and overwhelmed. She clamped her mouth to contain her sobs as she looked at her sleeping son.

"Now there," he consoled. "He'll be fine." He handed her a cup and she took it. "I'd like you to focus on us now." Raising his cup he proclaimed, "To new beginnings," and clinked his cup to hers.

CHAPTER 40

"Sir, has anything happened in the past couple of days that might have upset your wife enough to leave in this manner?" Constable Larry probed after listening to Michael chronicle the events of the day.

Michael kept the phone to his ear, not knowing where to start.

"Did you two have a major argument?"

"Things have been very difficult these last few months. I believe you know about our daughter downing this past summer."

"Yes, I'm very sorry. Usually in cases like these, the wife is staying at a girlfriend's place. Probably getting things off her chest. My guess is she'll be in touch any time now."

"Our daughter died in August."

"I'm terribly sorry, sir."

"She was only two years old. A terrible accident by the water," Michael said almost as much to himself as to the police officer.

"Do you have another property your wife may be at? You mentioned water so perhaps a cottage?"

"We do have a place up north, but I can't imagine her going there without telling me."

"We can dispatch a patrol to check and see if there is any sign of your wife at your cottage, sir. What is the address please?"

"5792 Eagle Lake Rd., Algonquin County."

"We've got a station about twenty minutes away so we'll send an officer over right away and they can call you from there. Is the number you're calling on the best way to reach you?"

"Yes, it is. Thank you. That would certainly help." Michael thought it was a long shot, but he was grateful to have something to hang on to.

"I hope you don't take this the wrong way, but I need to ask, are there any custody issues with your son?"

"No."

"All right then, our Algonquin officer will patch me in when he calls you from your cottage so we can determine next steps if your wife and son aren't there."

~~~

It was all Sarah could do to choke back a few bites of food. Jack ate with gusto, filling up on seconds and refilling his wine. All the physical exertion of the day had left him famished.

"I know you've gone through a terrible time lately," Jack said while ploughing in large mouthfuls of stew.

"Don't speak to me about that," Sarah flared.

Jack slammed his fists down on the table, "If you'll just give me a chance to finish!"

Connor stirred a bit, then settled back to sleep.

Jack swallowed hard and spoke slowly, "I was going to say, that I'm here for you now." He reached across the table to hold her hand. She pulled back before he had a chance.

"You don't have to shoulder your burdens alone any longer. I'm someone you can count on to be there for you, to help you through things, Sarah. I've always thought you deserved more than you've received. Couples should be there for one another, not racing off on business trips, spending time away from home, long nights at the office. I know what that's like. I can relate. We have a lot in common. Don't you see? People have taken advantage of our generous ways and that's simply not acceptable. We don't need that in our lives. Things will be so much better this way, my dear."

Sarah felt an incredible wave of fatigue. The trauma of the day was taking its toll. "I'm exhausted. I need to lie down and sleep. I'd like to lie beside Connor," Sarah said, looking over to her son.

"I guess that will be okay for tonight, you'll need to share Connor's mat," Jack responded. "I'll need to cuff you to the ring, until I can trust you completely."

"I understand," Sarah conceded. She didn't care about being cuffed. She was simply grateful she could be close to her son and stay as far away from Jack as possible.

Jack motioned to the camper toilet and bucket in the far corner of the room. He handed her dry toothpaste and a toothbrush.

"I bought you new night clothes," Jack said. He handed over a pair of red flannel pajamas. "I know you wear a size six." He was saving the black satin nightgown for their first special night.

Sarah took them silently.

"Go ahead and put them on. I won't look if that's what you're worried about."

"I'm fine sleeping in my clothes."

"Don't be silly. You'll be much more comfortable in the pajamas," Jack coaxed.

Sarah tossed them down and Jack pounced. "Actually, I insist. I want you to feel like this is your home. You wouldn't sleep in your regular clothes at home, would you?" He pressed the clothes firmly against her chest.

"All right then," Sarah agreed.

Jack partially turned around but still kept an eye on her. Sarah turned her back to him and pulled her grimy sweatshirt over her head. His heartbeat quickened at the sight of her bare back and her black bra straps. She slipped the top on and buttoned up the front. She slid off her track pants as fast as possible and yanked on the bottoms. She went to get down on the floor with Connor, but Jack held her back.

"No goodnight kiss?"

"Jack, please," Sarah replied.

"Okay. I know you're tired. We've had a big day. A peck will do for tonight." He kissed her cheek.

She suppressed the desire to vomit.

"Oh, I almost forgot," Jack said as though referencing the milk he had forgotten at the corner store. He produced a handcuff from his pocket and attached it to her wrist. Once she was settled on the floor beside Connor, he took the other end and closed it around the same ring that he used for Connor, the one embedded in the cement block he had placed near the mat.

"Sweet dreams, my sweetheart," he whispered.

Sarah wrapped her free arm around Connor's tiny waist and pulled him tight to her body. She buried her face in his hair to hide her tears. She felt like she was trapped in a horror movie. She needed to find a way out. She wanted to stay alert to think through the options for escape, but her fatigue was too demanding, she was asleep within minutes.

CHAPTER 41

"Randy here, do you copy, Larry?"

"Yeah, I'm here, Randy. Michael?"

"Yes, please go ahead."

"Hello, Michael. I'm Officer Randy Steller and I'm with Officer Hal Mann from the Algonquin police force. We are at your property at 5792 Eagle Lake Road."

A cold wet snow lashed their faces, and their dark blue down-filled coats protected them from the harsh winds. The cruiser's headlights beamed at the dark cottage. The two men stood outside the vehicle as Hal used a strong search beam to sweep the cottage and the surrounding area.

"There's no sign of anyone present," Officer Randy explained. "No vehicle. Doesn't seem to be anyone staying at any of the other cottages along the road in either direction."

"Can you check inside?" asked Michael. "There is a spare key under our family sign beside the side door."

"Sure thing," answered Officer Randy.

The two officers mounted the slippery steps and found the key easily behind the classic wooden plaque; all five names burnt in a curlicue script with pinecones decorating the edges. They entered and looked around, no sign of a struggle.

"Nothing seems amiss," Officer Randy reported.

"We appreciate you checking things out," Constable Larry said. He cut the connection with the Algonquin team.

"What do we do now?" asked Michael, still in action mode.

"I think you should get some sleep and see what comes of things in the morning. Like I said, usually this sort of domestic disappearance sorts itself out within a day or so. If they don't turn up tomorrow morning, then you can file a missing person's report."

Michael wanted to believe it was going to be that simple, so he agreed to let the situation rest for the night. He had Paige upstairs to think about and he also didn't want to overreact and alarm Sarah's parents unnecessarily.

After a fitful night's sleep Michael awoke with a sense of dread as the events of the previous night came into focus. He walked through the house that seemed unbearably empty. Michael made some excuse to Paige about Sarah and Connor sleeping over at a friend's and dropped her off at school.

He approached the school office desk. "I need to speak with the principal, please,"

"May I ask what this is about?" asked a chipper Ms. Sampson.

"It's about my son, Connor Babic. He will be away from school today and I have some questions regarding his absence yesterday."

Ms. Sampson motioned for Michael to go into the principal's office. After conferring with the office staff and Connor's teachers, it was determined that nobody at the school had placed the call to Sarah's mother Kate about an early pick-up for Connor.

Michael strode quickly to the car with his mind racing. He punched Larry Maudry's direct number into his cell. The five rings seemed to go on forever.

Hello, this is Constable Larry Maudry. I'm in but away from my phone so please leave a message and I'll call back as soon as possible.

"Larry, this is Michael from last night. My wife and son are still missing, and I have new information. I am on my way in and need to see you right away."

He called his office next. "Hi, Amanda. I need to take care of some things today so cancel all my meetings."

"Of course, Michael. Shall I rebook them?"

"You better wait until I know more about my schedule."

Michael purposely stayed in autopilot mode, knowing once he let his emotions take hold, he'd be useless.

Michael screeched to a halt in front of the precinct. He ran into the foyer and leaned heavily over the reception desk.

"Constable Larry Maudry, please. I'm Michael Babic and he is expecting me."

Five minutes after bringing Constable Larry up to speed all hell broke loose with the issuance of the Amber Alert. They scanned the photograph he carried in his wallet. A helpful female officer quickly filled in the required fields.

AMBER ALERT

Boy: Connor Babic

Age: 5

Hair: Light brown, short

Eyes: Light blue

Complexion: Fair

Height: 3 1/2 feet tall Visible Marks/Scars: None

Last seen at Randolph Public School, located in the Heatherton neighborhood in Toronto, around noon wearing blue jeans, dark blue jacket, Transformers running shoes, and a grey toque.

ANY INFORMATION OR SIGHTINGS SHOULD BE REPORTED IMMEDIATELY TO 911.

Within minutes he saw his sweet boy's goofy kindergarten picture, which they just received last week, across CITY-TV news channel with his description scrolling across the bottom. The same happened on a talk show broadcasting on CBC TV. Over the next few minutes, all the TVs in the station mounted high on the wall were running the alert. Radio stations were interrupted with the announcement. All traffic signs on major highways with pixel messaging capabilities flashed the same information. It streamed across the Internet. Connor was now one of those poor kids you might think about for thirty seconds then go back to your normal life. Except now this 'poor kid' was his own.

CHAPTER 42

The coffee with powdered milk, a cinnamon bagel, and an apple sat barely touched.

"Why aren't you eating? Isn't this your usual breakfast?" asked Jack.

"Yes." Her stomach was in knots realizing the extent of his obsession.

"Here you go, buddy," Jack said as he passed Connor an iPad. "A gift for you. I've loaded it with some awesome offline games."

Before Sarah could intercept, Connor grabbed it and gushed, "Wow, thanks, Uncle Jack! Is it really mine?"

"Of course, Connor, I want you to be happy. We might be staying here a little while. I have power bank to recharge it."

"You're the best uncle ever!" Connor threw himself at Jack for a hug.

"I'm glad you like it," Jack said as he returned his embrace and planted a light kiss on the top of his head.

Sarah's eyes flashed her anger at Jack's low attempt to win Connor over. Connor retreated to his mat in the corner and was thoroughly absorbed in trying the new games.

"I brought some books for you. Help yourself," Jack said to Sarah, motioning to the stack of paperbacks.

Along with some of Sarah's favorite authors, he'd bought others based on various Book Club websites that listed popular reads; he knew how women liked redemption stories. Jack thought them quite fitting given her errant choice in marrying Michael and now this chance at a new beginning.

"I'm fine," Sarah replied.

"Suit yourself," Jack said, wolfishly eating the breakfast she had refused.

He was prepared for an adjustment period. After clearing off the table he picked up a book himself and lay down on the bed. The stove gave off a nice amount of heat making the room comfortable. The light threw a warm glow on the walls. He surveyed his handiwork.

"What do you think?" he said, sweeping an arm motioning to the space. Getting no response, he continued a little louder, "A labor of love and I think it shows, don't you?"

He found her silence grating.

"I asked you a question," he said, pulling up to a sitting position and not able to contain the anger in his tone.

Sarah stood and walked over to the bed, trying to keep Connor out of earshot. Glaring down at him she whispered, "I've had enough of your little game. You can't keep us here like caged animals. You must realize the police and my family and Michael will be searching and I—"

Jack was on his feet in a second at the mention of Michael's name. He slapped her viciously across the face and she staggered backwards into the table. Her hand flew to her face, tears and shock filled her eyes. Jack pulled her back on her feet and held her tight.

"Mommy!"

"Tsk, tsk, tsk. What a short memory you seem to have. I remember very specifically telling you last night there was to be no more mention of that name in our home." Jack cupped the side of her face that he struck. "I'm sorry if I hurt you but I can't tolerate any dissention."

"Mommy, are you okay?" Connor asked.

"She's fine, Connor, she just tripped. Isn't that right, Sarah?" Jack said as his fingers dug into her arms.

"Silly me, so clumsy, sweetie. I'm fine, go back to your game."

Still holding her tight, he pulled a book from the shelf and forced her to bed.

"You look tired. You really should lie down," Jack said, pushing her down on the bed. He dropped the book on her chest. He moved in beside her until their bodies were touching. He picked up his own book and started reading. "Now isn't this nice?"

Chapter 43

The fresh snow didn't help with the second sweep of the cottage. The Algonquin police force was back the day after the Amber Alert to look again for anything suspicious. Steady snowfall overnight blanketed the ground with a couple of inches of white powder. Snow clung to the boughs of the pines and the undisturbed carpet of white across the property made the whole scene look deceptively beautiful and tranquil.

A more thorough search through the cottage turned up nothing of interest. From the lack of any garbage or waste, and the stripped-down beds, it seemed as though nobody had been up for weeks. If there were any tire marks to indicate unusual activity, they were now buried under the snow. They walked onto the dock to survey the lake.

"I love it in the winter up here," Randy commented to Hal. "All the city folks long gone. It's like nature needs this time to recuperate and rebuild its strength for the inevitable onslaught of tourists every summer."

They took a moment to listen to the silence.

"Damn shame what happened to that little girl," said Hal quietly, shuffling his boots.

"Yeah, I remember that day like it was yesterday," recounted Randy. "Coming out here on the heels of the ambulance and seeing that perfect little girl being pumped for air on the dock. I can't believe the parents weren't charged. Likely drunk like most cottagers."

"Yeah, maybe," Hal said.

A strong wind hit them hard, and they were pounded with snow as they turned to walk back to their vehicle. A flash of red caught Randy's eye along the shoreline. Something caught on the rocks at the water's edge. Finding a long stick, he fished out a red baseball cap with the Raptors logo. It looked child sized.

"Probably nothing but I suppose we should call it in. At least they'll know we've done our due diligence," Randy suggested.

They stepped off the dock with their heads bent low to avoid the sting of snow on their faces.

"First things first," said Hal as Randy reached for the radio to report back to Toronto. "How about breakfast at Danny's Diner at the four corners to kill a little time? They make the best all-day breakfast in the county."

"True enough," agreed Randy. "Might as well make it look like we really put our backs into it."

An hour and a half later, Toronto police were on the phone with Michael, who was pacing at home while calling everyone Sarah might have been in touch with yesterday, with no success.

"Hello, Michael, Constable Larry here. The Algonquin guys have been to your cottage and had another look and still nothing of interest has turned up. It seems like nobody's been up there for weeks."

Michael was exasperated. "She can't just have disappeared into thin air!"

"It probably nothing, but they did find a kid's Raptors hat along the shoreline in front of your place. It could be anybody's, but we thought we'd better check."

"Connor has a Raptors hat! Red with a black logo?" Michael asked, desperate for a lead.

"Yes, that's what they found. How old was your son's hat?"

Michael searched his memory. "Basically new, from this past September. Connor went to an exhibition game late September as part of a school outing and bought it as a souvenir."

"Hard to tell from the water but it appears pretty new from what we know about the design releases. Do you know when he might have worn it last?" Larry asked.

Michael realized they hadn't been up north since the game. He felt the adrenaline rush he experienced at the idea of a lead viscerally leave his body.

"I... I don't know. I remember him wearing it in Sarah's car a few times last week. He liked to think people were looking at him as though he had a special job with the team. We told him people would think he was a junior trainer since only the trainers had those hats." Michael smiled, thinking of the gullibility of a five-year-old boy. "He'd wave at people from his car seat in the back with a big smile on his face feeling like such a big- shot." Michael had a hard time stifling a cry.

"But you haven't been north since Labor Day, is that correct?"

Michael paused, "Yes, that's right. I haven't, but that doesn't mean Sarah hasn't been up. Maybe she went there with Connor?" he said with new enthusiasm.

"It's possible, but even if she did, there's no sign of her now," Larry cautioned. "We can have them send the hat down in case you can identify it. I'm not sure if this will help in any way but it can't hurt."

The image of his son's hat floating in the water sent Michael reeling. He imagined Amy floating lifeless. He didn't want to let himself go there but he had to be certain. "Did the police go in the water?"

"Uh, no, not that they reported."

"Ask them. Ask them to check the lake," he said, barely audible.

Larry knew of the sad recent family history, so he understood Michael's line of thinking. Larry still figured the mother had taken the kid somewhere to shake up the husband for a few days after a fight, so he didn't put much effort behind this request.

"I'm afraid the police boats have been dry-docked for the winter. Without knowing for certain that it's your son's hat, they won't be able to commission a boat out of storage this late in the season."

"Well then get certain, get it DNA tested," blasted Michael.

Larry thought about the process before responding, "We can do this. It will take three to five days, assuming we can get a hair or skin sample. Depending on how long it's been in the water they may or may not be able to get anything. We'll send over someone from forensics to your house to retrieve an item of Connor's clothing for a match sample."

CHAPTER 44

The snow kept coming all week. Warmer temperatures during the day caused some of it to melt, but fresh snow added to the depth each day. The runoff carried the threesome's scent far away. Every day as the snow piled up, less and less evidence of their trek deep into the forest to the bunker vanished. Jack stockpiled enough food and water to last the first couple months when the search would be most intense.

"Who wants to play another game of crazy eights?" Connor asked.

It was the end of their fourth day underground.

"I'm afraid it's your bedtime, little man," Jack replied, looking at his watch. "Yup, it's almost seven. Go brush your teeth and then I'll read you a bedtime story."

"Okay," Connor replied. "Do you promise to play again tomorrow?"

"Absolutely, scouts honor," Jack replied, placing his hand across his heart.

Jack uncorked a bottle of scotch and poured himself a strong dose.

"Sarah, will you join me?" he asked.

Sarah stared off, unresponsive. He came and sat beside her, handing her a tin cup filled with golden liquid. "Drink up," he said, putting his cup to his mouth.

Sarah sat mutely staring at the drink.

After taking a stiff drink, he turned towards Connor and asked, "Buddy, what shall it be tonight?"

"*Cat in the Hat?*" Connor asked.

"Why not!" Jack replied.

Jack let Connor tuck into the crook of his arm and enjoyed the limp trusting body. The even breathing of the tired boy warmed Jack's heart. Connor's left arm fell across his chest as he began reading,

Today was good, today was fun. Tomorrow is another one.

Sarah sat at the table. It was all she could do to keep from screaming. The confinement, no sense of time, no sunlight or fresh air, no communication, being underground. She forced herself to remain calm to try and dispel the fear she saw creeping into Connor's eyes from time to time. She needed to wait until the time was right to escape. It was exhausting.

Jack hadn't made physical advances yet, letting her sleep beside Connor, but she knew he wasn't going to be put off much longer. She needed to do something soon.

Sarah lied beside Connor saying goodnight, held him tight and whispered in his ear, "Sweet dreams, my love. We'll be home soon," she added as quietly as she could.

It wasn't quiet enough. Once she released Connor, Jack promptly unfolded the divider that provided a half-wall to separate the two sleeping areas. Patting the bed after grabbing their drinks, he motioned for her to sit. Sarah reluctantly perched on the far end of the bed.

"Sarah, Sarah. What's it going to take for you to get it? This is our home now. Not forever, of course. I have plans for us to get a place far away from here once I know you're with me."

Jack slid down and sat beside her and spoke quietly as he stroked her forearm, "I think it will help to move things along, don't you? You know, making love. It will make things seem more normal."

"Normal? Give your head a shake, Jack!" Sarah jumped up and sprinted around the divider to rejoin Connor.

Jack leaned forward and swiped his hair a couple of times making guttural noises. He pulled something small from his pocket. He took two strides across the room and hauled Sarah off the mat and pitched her back onto their bed. With one hand he yanked her hair back and with the other hand he shoved his dirty fingers into her mouth. Sarah gagged and a bitter taste followed but Jack was quick to grab the glass and force the scotch down her throat before she could get free.

"Don't worry. I think your shyness is very endearing. I know what a loyal person you are and I'm lucky to have you. Once you see how amazing this will all be, I know you'll be a wonderful partner."

After the coughing fit that ensued after the burn of the scotch, Sarah felt foggy, lightheaded, and dizzy. She tried to stand but was too weak. "What did you give me?"

"Just a little something to relax you. It's for your own good. I'd

257

hate for our first time together to be a struggle, and I can't wait any longer for this exciting phase to begin. I'm going to freshen up."

Within minutes Sarah was virtually paralyzed, terrified at her helplessness. Jack lit a couple of candles and checked to make sure Connor was asleep.

"Now then, my love," Jack murmured, planting light kisses along her collar bone.

Sarah stared wide-eyed at the ceiling.

Her limbs were heavy and inert.

Tears streamed down the sides of her face.

She felt his hand slide under her shirt.

She could do nothing but feel the terror consume her.

"Try not to be too loud enjoying yourself," Jack whispered. "I'd hate to wake up little Connor over there."

CHAPTER 45

The police in Toronto and Algonquin did their due diligence gathering information on Sarah and Connor by contacting family and friends to make sure Michael hadn't missed anything. Nobody had anything to report since they had been asked to give the family time and space to grieve after Amy's death.

Family was a little different. Michael's mother had offered to stay in Toronto after the funeral to help, but after a week or so, Sarah found her to be more of a hindrance than a help. Sarah wanted to spend the day crying in bed if she felt like it and didn't want anyone trying to cheer her up with useless pep talks. Sarah's mother Kate understood and kept her distance, only helping when asked with the odd meal or picking up the children from time to time.

The only person they dead ended on was Jack. They tried his cell phone but only received a message that it was not in service. The cops had gone to visit Jack a few times but never found him to be at home. He had no place of employment and virtually no contact with his family.

On the fourth day after Sarah's disappearance, Michael drove to Chinatown. After squeezing into a tight parking space, Michael battled the crowd of shoppers to find Jack's place. Shiny, orange, whole roasted pigs hung from large metal hooks adorning the restaurant window above the basement stairwell. Michael descended the broken concrete steps that led to the peeling brown door. Plastic bags and paper swirled in the corner. Given the lack of a doorbell, Michael knocked, then pounded on the door. No response. He blew warm air on his hands and stamped his feet. He knew it was ridiculous to wait, but he was running out of people that may have heard from Sarah or seen her over these last few days. It was a stretch, but it was better than going home defeated.

"Hey, mister!" shouted a Chinese middle-aged man from above. "You know Mr. Jack?"

"Yes, he's a friend of mine. Do you know where he is and when he'll be back?"

"You tell me, friend. Mr. Jack gone missing for long time now. He owes me money. No rent for two months. I ask cops but they say I not allowed to throw out person in the winter, rent or no rent. How that for fair? He very slippery. I no see him come and go."

Michael climbed the stairs and pressed his card into the landlord's thinly gloved hand with the fingertips cut out exposing long dirty fingernails.

"You cop too?" the landlord asked with suspicion.

"No, I told you, just a friend." Michael peeled off two twenty-dollar bills and passed them over. "Please call me if you see Jack. It's very urgent."

"I give you my card too, ha ha. I need more than forty bucks," he laughed as he pocketed the money and turned away.

~~~

Michael took another leave of absence from work to deal with the police and search for his family. Paige was sent to stay with Sarah's mother. Her phone had been rigged to record any calls in case Sarah tried to get in touch with her or Paige.

Back home, Michael despondently poured over the makeshift bulletin board of clues he laid out on the dining room table.

Michael's family in Sudbury: No clues or contact.

Sarah's family in Toronto: Kate called by Sarah at eleven am to pick up Paige and Connor the day Sarah and Connor went missing. A male posing as a person from Michael's company calls Kate the same day around 1 pm to let her know Connor doesn't need to get picked up as he will have left early with his father.

Brett and Christy: No contact since the funeral.

Larry and Alison: No contact since the funeral. Away in Nicaragua since mid-October on NGO assignment.

Claire, Tess, Mandy, Heather, Jennifer (book club friends): Some drop overs for a few weeks with food after the funeral but no contact since end of September.

Rachel: Contacted in Italy: on assignment there since August. No contact with anyone after calling Michael re Jack's breakdown in July.

Connor's School: Last saw Connor the morning he disappeared. No calls received by the school to report Connor's absence. School only does attendance in the am for kids that stay for lunch. Sarah too depressed since Amy's death to get the kids so they had been staying at school for lunch most days.

Jack: Last contact was two weeks after the funeral offering to help.

The shrillness of the phone ringing shattered Michael's concentration.

"Hello," he said.

"Hi Michael. Constable Larry. We just got the results back from forensics. They got a positive match between the hat and your son's DNA."

Michael had gone over this scenario numerous times while waiting for the results. "Well, that's good, right?"

"Not sure," Larry replied. "What it tells us is that somehow Connor's hat got from Toronto to your cottage. Based on the lack of decay, it doesn't appear it was in the water too long. It's tough to nail down, they say anywhere from a couple of weeks to a couple of days."

"She must have gone without telling me," Michael said with a new sense of urgency. "She went up then drove off somewhere...but where did she go?"

Larry cut him off. "If you're available now we can come over and review next steps."

"Of course, please do."

Larry looked at his partner, Constable Scott. "I feel for this guy. I really do. His youngest kid drowns and now his wife leaves with his son. She's got to turn up soon. Not too many mothers can go without seeing their kids for too long. She is bound to reach out and try and contact her older daughter. You better put some extra surveillance on the grandmother's house in case she tries to do a dash and grab with Paige too."

"You got it, Larry," Scott replied as he called in the order.

"Damn shame," Larry sighed. He knew the scenario: the wife blames the husband for the child's death to rationalize her innocence in the affair. Losing a kid can rip a family to shreds.

CHAPTER 46

It had been two weeks. Not a rustle, not a sound, came from overhead. The days passed in a surreal rhythm; three meals a day together broken up with games and reading. And the nights.

The nightly administration of drugs physically dulled the assaults to a certain degree as they made her almost catatonic. But she was lucid enough to feel the weight of him violating her and the stifling heat of his heavy breathing. She could smell his sour breath and hear his groaning as he did what he wanted to her defenseless body. It made her sick to think of his sperm coursing inside her body. When he finished, he'd ask her with a self-satisfied smirk if she thought it was good. Too drugged to speak, her tears told her thoughts. Drool leaked from her mouth. It was pure torture.

Jack tried to reason with her, "I know it's a big change and you need to get used to me. I want to please you and can't wait to ease off the drugs to have you as an equal partner. I think it's better this way for now. Once you accept my intentions for what they are, to simply love you and take care of you, I think you'll be able to enjoy it too."

He pulled her ragdoll-like body close to his and pulled her onto her side so she nestled into his armpit with her head resting on his chest. He reached with his left hand and pulled her right leg across his, so their legs were entwined. He gently stroked her low bare back, enjoying the sensual rise of her hip. She was grateful for the drugs and forced herself to only think of escape, of saving Connor and herself, and seeing the rest of her family again.

Sarah knew after the first week when he drugged and raped her nightly, she needed to play along. She had to gain his trust so he would let down his guard and ease off the drugs. She started to initiate conversation in an effort to seem more pleasant and accommodating. She had to get him thinking they could leave this hellhole if she was to have any hope of survival.

Jack did some calisthenics most days and Connor had fun mimicking him doing jumping jacks and push-ups. Jack told Connor they had been specially selected for army training, and this whole thing, right from the 'pretend' kidnapping to this underground experiment, was a test to see how well they did.

After dinner, Jack said to Connor, "If we do a good job, we'll be heroes when we leave, but you must be patient and stay strong. No crying for your dad or your sister, or wanting to go back to your old house, like you did the other night. I hope you know you were disciplined like any good soldier would be."

Connor was quiet while remembering Jack yelling at him the night before and holding back food and water all day until dinner. He didn't like staying on his mat all day either and being cut off from them. He was scared hearing his mother begging Jack to give him water.

"Soldiers need to be able to handle adversity, tough times. You'll come out of this stronger and better. Trust me," Jack said. "I know."

"I do, Uncle Jack. I'll try not to let it happen again," Connor promised.

"That's my boy. Now drop and give me ten more."

"Yes sir!" answered Connor, getting down in a push-up position and struggling with spindly arms to get his chest off the dirt floor.

"That's good, Connor. Uncle Jack knows what he's doing," Sarah said. She was heating their dinner of vacuum-packed chicken and canned vegetables. Jack liked watching her prepare their meals.

Jack was proud of his survival plan that could keep them set for many more weeks. He hadn't opened the door once, let alone left them alone.

"You boys must be hungry," Sarah said. "It'll be ready in a few minutes."

"You bet we are! Right, Connor?" asked Jack.

"Starving!"

Jack crossed the room and leaned over Sarah's shoulder from behind while discreetly squeezing her waist. "I think we'll all enjoy dinner and then an early night to bed."

"Sounds perfect", Sarah replied.

CHAPTER 47

Michael followed the Toronto police car dispatched to join the Algonquin police orchestrating the lake search. He was surprised to see the accumulation of snow, another climate zone compared to the city. As they approached the cottage, he saw the Ontario Provincial Police boat anchored in front of his property. The boat had two officers and plus two divers. Michael blanched at the sight and the thought that they might find something. He fought his emotions as he emerged from his car. The cold air caught his breath and provided the jolt he needed to keep it together.

"Good morning, Michael, we spoke last week. I'm Officer Hal."

Hal warmly extended a calloused hand extracted from a large black mitten while holding a steaming cup of coffee in the other. "Officer Randy is the other officer involved on the case. He's on the boat now."

Michael squinted, watching them check their gear. They looked like aliens, covered head to toe in black rubber dry suits to fend off the frigid waters.

"Hey, Randy, this is Hal, do you copy?" Hal said into the walkie.

Randy gave a wave to the men on shore. "Copy that. We are just about ready to go," the voice crackled through the speaker.

The boat made a slow turn and stopped. The divers stepped straight off the dive platform at the rear of the boat and disappeared like two black pins into the dark water. A few minutes passed. The bottom was twenty to thirty feet deep.

Michael felt anxious standing around, nervous about what they might find. He went into the cottage. The lifeless space made him feel even more hollow than he already was. The place they imagined to be their sanctuary had turned into his worst nightmare. First Amy, now perhaps Sarah and Connor. He wandered from room to room, hoping to see something the police wouldn't have noticed. He looked down to the lake from the front room and saw the boat slowly trolling. Leaving the cottage, he tromped through the snow up to the bunkie and peered in the windows. Nothing amiss. He turned to make his way back to the water when he heard shouting.

"Michael. You better get down here," Hal called up the hill.

Michael ran down as fast as he could, trying not to slip. He wanted answers, but now that they were coming, part of him wanted time to stand still. A minute ago, he was desperate but had hope. Now, he might be losing this too.

Seeing the devastated look on Michael's face as he approached, Hal raised his hands to slow him down. "We found your van. They've sighted a silver Honda Odyssey with plates. WG4T 162."

Michael crumpled to the ground, landing on his knees. An animalistic cry echoed across the water, as he pressed his forehead into the snow.

"Michael, let me finish," Hal added urgently, placing a reassuring hand on his shoulder. "They looked inside the van with their flashlights and didn't see anything. Nobody was inside the vehicle." Hal pulled Michael to his feet and continued, "The doors were all closed, one window was open."

Michael searched Hal's face for more information.

"We've got to tow it out, and have a thorough search," Hal cautioned.

Blubbering like a child, Michael muttered, "Thank God, thank God. They're not in the van. They can't be in the van."

The divers spent the remainder of the day combing the shoreline and the bottom of the lake in the area where the van was found. Nothing else was found linked back to Michael's family.

The sky was a fiery orange, and the sun was setting fast when they slowly pulled the van up to the boat launch and hoisted it onto a special flatbed truck fitted with a winch. The police were careful not to touch the vehicle but peered inside now that the water had mostly drained. It appeared to be empty.

As the truck pulled away destined for a special crime lab for investigation, Hal checked his watch and suggested they all get some dinner, both to warm up and to review which way the investigation would turn.

Michael sat in the booth with the officers, torn between the initial feeling of elation knowing Sarah and Connor hadn't perished in the freezing cold water and the horrible feeling of helplessness still not knowing where they were.

Black coffee was poured.

"It will likely take a couple of days to go over the van for any clues before we get new marching orders," Randy said while inhaling his corn beef sandwich, his appetite unaffected by the events of the days.

Michael left his food untouched. "Now that there seems to be foul play involved, won't that escalate the search?"

"It should," confirmed Hal. "I think they'll allocate at least a chopper and maybe even tracking dogs to search the surrounding area.

Randy chimed in, "You'll definitely get more manpower on this. People don't just walk away from their vehicles in November with their kid and start walking."

"Do you think someone took them? Kidnapped them?" Michael asked.

The men chewed in silence and sipped their coffee to buy time.

"It's possible," Randy replied. "But if that was the case, it's strange there's no sign of a struggle."

"But what if they had leverage?" Michael added. "Something to make them compliant…. like harming a five-year-old boy."

~~~

The canine unit was dispatched the next day. The handler showed up early that morning, meeting Randy at the boat launch with his three-year-old German shepherd. Randy handed over a couple of plastic bags with clothing worn by Sarah and Connor.

"Hi, Pete, how are things?" Randy asked.

"Pretty quiet, but that's a good thing, right?" Pete responded with squinty eyes framed by deep lines; a testament to his profession that kept him outdoors most of the time.

Pete had been training Shepherds and Labradors for over twenty years and was considered one of the best in the province. Randy had worked with Pete and one of his dogs on a case of a missing child four years ago. He was thoroughly impressed at the dog's calmness and perseverance in tracking the scent over a two-day period. Pete was still in the same top condition now as he was then. It was critical to be able to keep up with the dog, which could entail navigating tough terrain and rough trails for hours. Randy prayed they would have the same good outcome this time.

"All right then, what've we got?" asked Pete, anxious to get started.

"Mom and her little boy are presumed to have been here in the last two weeks. It was their van we pulled from the lake a couple of days ago. They've been missing for three weeks, last seen at home and school in Toronto on the morning of October 29th."

The search and rescue police team had gone to Michael's house to retrieve unwashed clothing after the van was pulled from the water. Pete pulled one of Sarah's sweatshirts from the pouch.

Pete crouched down and held the article under Max's nose. "'At a boy, Max, we'll find them, eh? Where are they, Max? Go get 'em," he encouraged steadily but without much excitement.

Handlers knew not to hyper-stimulate tracker dogs so they would concentrate on their task. After a minute of sniffing the shirt Max pulled away. With his nose to the ground, he quickly led Pete to Michael's property. Max pulled along the road then turned sharply towards the dock. He trotted to the end of the dock and sat down looking imploringly at Pete for approval.

"Looks like we have a good start," Pete called back to Randy.

"Would Max be able to pick up Sarah's scent if it was ten weeks old?" Randy asked, worried that perhaps the dog was simply picking scents left over from the summer.

"Not likely with all the rain and snow we've had. My guess is that it isn't more than a month old."

"Well, that would fit with the timing of her disappearance," Randy said.

Pete rewarded Max with a small treat as a way of praising him and also to tell him he needed to move on to pick up where the trail led next. Max was quickly on the move, crossing the front lawn. He trotted towards the steps leading up to the door and abruptly stopped on the first step. He sniffed the lower spindles and whimpered.

Pete leaned in close and after peering at the spindles he said to Randy, "There could be a bit of blood here. You should get it tested, see how old it is, and see if you can get a match to one of the family members."

Pete and Max climbed the stairs and Max paused at the door. Before Pete could let Max in, the dog turned his massive shoulders and pulled towards the rear of the cottage. Pete expertly let out enough slack to let Max feel he was in control. Max quickly followed the path to the high road. He tracked the scent another 100 meters down the high road, and after circling a few times in the same small area, then sat down. Pete fisted him a treat and surveyed the spot. Randy scrambled up a few minutes later.

"Did he find anything?" he huffed.

"Looks like we've hit a fast dead-end," conceded Pete.

The two men surveyed the forest. The woods looked peaceful yet guarded. If there were any secrets to be discovered out there, they weren't about to show themselves easily.

Randy carried up the other plastic pouch with Connor's things. After going through a similar routine of letting Max get a good scent, Pete started walking the area. Max sniffed intensely at the ground in various places but was unable to pick up on anything worth following. Pete coaxed the dog in the direction of the path they had just ascended but Max showed no interest in following. Pete lured him with treats until they got back down near the water and tried to start again. But after a few attempts Max wouldn't cooperate; there was nothing new for him to track.

"Seems like the mom was here but I'm not sure about the kid," Pete announced.

"Maybe the mom came up here to ditch the car to throw everyone off her plan. Maybe she planned to meet someone here and then they took off together," deduced Randy.

"But then what happened to Connor? Why would she or anyone else have taken him from his school? If she was looking to meet a boyfriend to make a run from the family, she would have left Connor at school just like she did with Paige," Larry said.

Stumped, the scent was as cold for them as it was for Max.

CHAPTER 48

The four weeks underground felt like an eternity to Sarah. The bizarre passing of the days while being buried underground, punctuated with normal activities like reading and games and cooking was suffocating. It shredded her nerves to appear okay for Connor's sake. The slow grind after dinner that preceded Jack's nightly physical attacks made her hyperventilate and physically ill. She struggled with chronic headaches, terrified of what the drugs were doing to her body. Her weight loss was accelerating and her gums bled easily. Waking each morning to stare at the mud and timber packed walls and ceiling brought on waves of claustrophobia.

As time passed, she realized it was possible nobody was going to find them. She was making slow but steady progress pretending to like Jack. After a couple weeks, he eased off forcing her to take the meds before his nightly attacks. Hiding her mounting anxiety and fear as the days slowly ground on was torture.

She pushed down feelings of guilt when she saw Connor watching her, looking confused, but she felt there was no other choice if they were to have a chance at surviving.

The key to the lockbox holding his gun and the knife was kept high up on a shelf on the wall. She couldn't reach it without using the ladder and he was careful to keep it flat on the ground. He tied bells to it so he would know if it moved. She shuddered at the thought of using the weapons.

Sarah lightly touched Jack's arm while clearing the lunch plates. "Jack, can I get you another helping of spaghetti" Sarah asked.

"No, I'm good but thanks for asking, honey."

"Anything else I can get for you? How about a top up on your drink?"

Jack drank steadily throughout most days, but today she topped up his drink whenever it was low to get the effect she needed.

"I won't say no to that. Thank you. You're just as considerate as I knew you would be now that you're getting used to us."

"Of course, Jack." Looking around the bunker Sarah added, "This isn't exactly what I had in mind to start our relationship, but I guess it's for the best for now."

Her perseverance paid off. It happened after Jack ordered Connor to his corner that afternoon, tossing him the tablet. He secured him to the heavy ring on the floor so he couldn't move before pulling the divider out to block the mat from view.

"Jack, please not now. Can't we wait until later tonight? When Connor is asleep?"

"Are you telling me what I should and shouldn't do?" asked Jack, swaying with the effects of his afternoon drinking.

"No, of course not. I just don't want Connor overhearing our lovemaking."

"Lovemaking! Now I like the sound of that," laughed Jack as he pushed her back hard on the bed.

"Mom, are you okay?" asked Connor.

Jack didn't take his leering eyes off Sarah as he stood beside the bed slowly undoing his belt buckle.

"Oh, I'm fine sweetie. Just having a little nap. I'll see you soon, darling."

After he finished his assault, he dozed off. The smell of alcohol radiated off his body. His filthy pants lay crumpled beside the bed. Slowly she eased away from him.

"Where are you going?" Jack mumbled through slurred speech.

"I need to pee. I'll be right back."

He smacked his gums a few times and drifted off again.

Sarah silently pulled on her pants and shirt. She slid on her boots. After going to the toilet, she gingerly took the small paring knife and went over to the ladder lying horizontal against the wall. She severed the string holding the bells Jack had attached as an alarm. She had gone over the possible scenarios hundreds of times. She was terrified of plunging a knife into Jack, doubting her strength and nerve to slit his throat or stab him. She thought about smashing his head with the portable stove but worried her first blow wouldn't be enough to knock him out. Shooting him was the only option where Sarah thought she stood a chance.

Crouching down, she gently slid her hand into Jack's pant pocket and found the keys. As she rounded the divider, she immediately held her forefinger to her lips making a silencing gesture. Connor looked up wide-eyed and didn't budge. Holding her breath, she slid the key in the shackle and released the lock holding Connor's wrist. It made a small clicking sound. No sound came from the other side. She quickly pulled on his boots and slipped on his coat. Keeping her finger on her lips, she motioned with her other hand to the trap door in the ceiling. Connor nodded his head up and down and stayed mute. With one last tender look at Connor, Sarah turned away and went over to the ladder.

The ladder wasn't heavy, and she placed it against the wall under the trap door. The strongbox was mounted on a ledge about eight feet off the floor and two feet from the ceiling.

Sarah lightly climbed the first four steps on the ladder. She saw the dark green metal box over the edge of the ledge. There was a padlock on the closure. Stealing a glance over her shoulder and finding everything quiet she slowly pulled the box closer to the ladder so she could place the key into the lock. Her hands were sweaty and shook as she tried to insert the key in the cylinder.

"What the hell?" Jack bellowed, hearing the metal on metal. He stumbled off the bed and around the divider and flung himself at the ladder. With flailing arms, he went for her legs. Pumped up on adrenaline, Sarah dealt him a violent kick to the temple. It was enough to throw him off balance and he hit the floor hard on his side.

"What the fuck? Jesus Christ," he slurred.

"CONNOR, NOW!" she yelled. Connor scrambled to his feet and ran over to the ladder and started to climb. She reached down and yanked him up in front of her and shoved him upwards towards the ceiling.

"Go, Connor, go."

Jack was on all fours, getting to his feet. "You lying little bitch."

With no time to try the lock again, she grabbed the handle of the box and swung it as hard as she could at his head, as he went for the ladder. The metal corner hit his eye, tearing a deep gouge. Blood poured down his face and he stumbled backwards.

"Aahh, fucking hell!" He swiped at the blood blurring his vision.

Sarah pushed Connor tight up at the ceiling door. She pushed hard with one hand, and it barely moved. She tried again, not daring to look down, too terrified at what she would see.

"Come ON, PLEASE," she cried.

She heard Jack grunting. Sarah gave the door one last heave with her shoulder and was shocked to feel the cold rush of air and the icy snow hit her face before it slammed closed again. With renewed hope and using all the strength she could muster, she pushed and held the trap door open a crack with her shoulder and shoved Connor through.

"GO, Connor, RUN! Run and don't stop until you find somebody."

Connor froze in the woods, waiting for her to follow. Sarah's body was halfway out of the opening with her elbows securely on the ground when the ladder fell away. She scrambled to gain a foothold on the lockbox shelf while hanging onto the edge of the opening. With one last attempt to push herself free off the shelf, she felt a crushing blow to her leg. She screamed as her grip gave way and she fell back into the bunker crashing to the floor. She passed out on contact.

Jack dragged her inert body to the ring and secured her roughly in place. Wiping the blood that continued to ooze from his gash with the back of his hand, he replaced the ladder against the wall. He grabbed the keys and lockbox on the floor and hurried to the surface. Jack hungrily drank in the fresh air as he crawled out of the bunker. With the snow a good foot deep and a full moon, it was easy to see where Connor had gone. Jack laughed sarcastically at the pitiful attempt of the boy trying to outmaneuver him. Connor's tiny body made a narrow path about forty feet long that disappeared behind a large spruce tree.

"Haven't you had enough of the hide and seek game, Connor?" Jack called, as he tromped along the path, swinging the strongbox as he went. "It didn't end so well for your little sister, now, did it?"

Jack looked behind the tree and saw Connor with his face buried in his hands pressed against the trunk. He was shaking.

"Well, well, look what your mother has done."

Connor stayed rooted in place.

"You were sort of getting in the way anyways. Not to mention you look a little too much like your father for my liking."

Jack glanced around—barely a breeze, all was still.

"How could I have expected her to move on with you hanging around as a constant reminder? Keeping you as long as we did was pretty stupid now that I think about it. You were handy at first, though, but now...tsk, tsk, a bothersome reminder."

Connor peeked out from behind his fingers and asked in a shaky voice, "Is the testing over now? Did we pass? Are you going to take us home, Uncle Jack?"

CHAPTER 49

Michael tried to work but found he was unable to think. Sarah's mother had moved in to take care of Paige. She prepared fresh meals, managed the house, and walked Paige to school and back every day. Michael put up a brave front with Paige about how the police were getting closer to finding her mother and brother. But as soon as she was asleep, he broke down with sobs raking his body before pulling himself together to pore over his notes. By studying his own analysis, he felt some control over things. To do nothing but wait was impossible.

The police claimed they continued to treat Sarah and Connor's disappearance as a missing person's case. Michael was doubtful; there were too many interviews with different cops and psychologists asking him questions about the possibility of Sarah kidnapping Connor and running away.

It's not uncommon for a parent to do something irrational after the loss of a child.
She could be taking time away from everything familiar to get a grip on things.
She may return any day now.

He listened to them politely and repeatedly answered their questions while steaming just below the surface. He thought they were trying to get him to admit it was a possibility so they could list the case as a domestic dispute to take the heat off of them for not finding any leads. Michael found even more ludicrous and infuriating the comments implicating him.

Can we get the names of the people you dealt with on the day of your wife's disappearance?
Did you have a falling out that morning?"
Did you say or do anything that may have caused her to flee?

After the initial days of the investigation and finding the van empty, they hadn't turned up anything substantial.

He converted the dining room table into a crime scene with timelines and names linked to places and events. He was careful to cover things up when Paige was home. He reviewed his notes over and over from people he had talked to since Sarah's disappearance. Given how much Sarah had retreated from her normal life since Amy's death, there wasn't much to work with.

The one person he still hadn't reached was Jack. Michael's few attempts at finding him at his apartment failed. It was the same for the police visits.

Michael blocked out his racing thoughts to focus on Jack these last couple of years, when he became so messed up after his split with Rachel. He seemed better after getting some help this year; more energetic and optimistic. If it wasn't for the good work of the meds and that shrink Dr. Turner, Jack may never have had a chance. This past summer, it finally seemed like he was looking forward to the future. A lot more like his usual self. But that breakdown that landed him in the hospital certainly indicated how fragile he was. It was that same night he had come here over here and made some ridiculous declaration about his feelings for Sarah. What had she said? He closed his eyes and forced himself to try to remember. God, she had been such a wreck. He remembered her clutching his arm and not wanting him to leave her.

Michael started pacing back and forth more hurriedly now that the memory was coming back to him. Could there be a connection? No, I'm losing it. I've known him forever.

CHAPTER 50

Jack trudged along the snow-covered path with Connor was slung over his shoulders like a freshly killed deer. Jack thought about leaving the lifeless body for the wolves and the coyotes, but he couldn't risk the chance of leaving a trace behind. He had come this far already and was too close to his dream to take a chance. He was weak from being underground and needed to rest every half hour to find the strength to continue. Ignoring the biting cold and sounds that closed in on him during the night, he plodded along ten kilometers to reach his family's old hunting cabin. He crashed through the door and flung Connor's stiff body to the floor.

"Jesus Christ, I'm starving!"

He found a couple of cans of frozen beans and pried them open with a can opener. He crunched through them, enjoying the sweetness as they melted in his mouth while resting his spent muscles in the beaten-down chair. His foul breath hung in small puffs in the still air. Three cans later he surveyed his problem. The freezer they kept for animal kills was perfect. Using a rag, he opened the lid and leaned it against the wall, then placed Connor's stiff body on the bottom. After covering the body with an old tarp, Jack took the padlock from the wall hook and locked the lid in place, adding the key to his collection. Since it was well below zero, Connor would remain well preserved for the next few months until he could think of a way to and properly dispose of the body. With the break he had given Connor's weak neck when he found him behind the tree, there was no blood trail to worry about giving him away.

Jack wiped down the surfaces and bagged the empty cans and spoon before he started his way back to his beloved. The thought of the two of them being truly alone for the first time quickened his heartbeat and his pace.

On Jack's trip back to the bunker, he was careful to crisscross the streams that were not yet frozen to create a confusing pattern in case tracker dogs were being used. He climbed trees to cover some ground, traversing across large branches to throw them off. He laughed at the thought of some hound dog sniffing at the base of a tree but not knowing where he may have gone. Pleased with himself at his efforts, he arrived back exhausted but content he had done everything required not to be found.

Muffled cries and groans greeted him as he closed the door above his head and descended the ladder.

"I'm coming, I'm coming. I know I was gone a long time but there is no need to worry. I'm home now and we don't ever need to be separated again."

Jack rushed to her side and loosened the cloth that had gagged her for the past twenty-four hours.

"What have you done with him!" she sobbed, pulling uselessly against the iron restraint that held her to the ring. "Where is he? Where is my Connor?"

"Enough with the drama, everything is taken care of," he said as he poured them both a glass of water. As he went to hold up her head to give her a drink, Sarah thrashed as violently as she could, knocking the cup from his hand with her head and spitting at his face.

"I said, where is he? Answer me! What have you done? You're fucking crazy. You're a monster!"

"You really should have something to drink. You sound positively delusional," he replied, wiping the spit from his eyes with the back of his hand and sipping his own drink.

Sarah looked wild. Her eyes were puffy and bloodshot, her hair matted and filthy, her skin pale and blotchy. The nightshirt he left her in was hiked up to the top of her thighs and she was shivering.

"Is this any way to greet me?" Jack asked. "Don't I at least get a kiss hello?"

He grabbed a clump of her hair at the back of her head and yanked her head up to his as he bent over and kissed her deeply on the mouth.

Sarah gagged and vomited. Her fury was undeterred, "Where is Connor? Connor! Are you up there? Connor!"

The crack to her head stunned her into silence. He wiped her chin.

"That will do. Another sound out of you and I'll shove that lovely vomit-soaked rag right down your throat."

He poured himself a strong whisky. Sarah tasted the metallic singe of her own blood. Her vision was blurry and the scene in front of her pulsed in and out of focus.

Before she could start up again Jack cut in, sounding bored, "Connor is fine. I took him somewhere safe since I didn't think this was a good place for him. We can get him later and bring him to live with us once we've settled in."

"Where did you take him? Who has him? When can I see him?" Sarah cried.

"What is your problem, Sarah? Don't you trust me? I told you he is safe, didn't I? What's with you women always wanting to be in charge. I know you're different, Sarah, so please, stop acting like a control freak like my ex-wife."

Sarah felt the panic in her chest, the tightness was physical. Without Connor, she was unmoored, totally at his mercy.

"Look, I think you'll feel better once you freshen up," Jack said.

Jack dug the keys out of his pocket, then lingered for a moment taking in her bare legs, stroking them tenderly as he moved down to her ankles. The rancid smell of stale urine from the mattress did nothing to deter his desire. Jack unlocked her wrist and saw she had given herself a nasty abrasion.

"I'll need to clean it up and apply some antibacterial ointment on it. I'll take care of it."

He motioned to the clean bucket of water he had poured in the corner. She slowly hobbled over. Looking perfectly at peace, Jack tilted back in his chair, and thoroughly enjoyed the show and the build-up to the night ahead.

Sarah gave herself a rudimentary sponge bath, ignoring him, thinking of nothing but Connor and where he might be. Jack never took his eyes off her.

"Hey? What do you say about getting a little dinner started? I'm famished!" Jack said, rubbing his hands together. He sounded as normal as if they were sitting at home after a long day at the office. Too weak and shaken to answer, Sarah simply nodded and took a few cans off the shelf. After dinner he went to take her hand to lead her to the mattress he had flipped over to freshen it up.

"You must admit this will be better without worrying about the little fellow hearing his mommy having a good time," Jack laughed.

Sarah instinctively resisted trying to twist out of his rough grasp.

"I like a bit of a fight too, you know, up to a point," Jack said and pushed her on the bed.

"Please, Jack, tell me where Connor is and I'll do anything you want," Sarah pleaded.

Jack sneered as he crawled on top of her, forcing her legs apart. "Anything? Well, aren't you sweet. I've got news for you. You'll do anything I want anyways because I'm the one in charge here if you haven't noticed."

Sarah thrashed at him wildly, releasing the fury of her frustration. "Get away from me, you pig!"

"Enough with the foreplay," he said as he forced her loose pants off with one hand while pinning her down with his forearm.

Even though Sarah knew it was useless, she fought with the little strength she had left. She bit hard on his shoulder as he tried to force himself into her.

"Ow, you little bitch!" Jack cried, pulling away. Blood oozed from the bite.

Slowing shaking his head he said, "Why do you have to make this so difficult?"

He left her to find his supply. He unwrapped a fresh needle and plunged it into the bottle of Rohypnol. He came back with the needle held aloft.

"I really don't like it when we fight like this. Your uncooperativeness leaves me no choice for the time being."

The sedative stung as he jabbed it into her shoulder. Her flailing subdued within a minute. Her pupils dilated and glazed over. Her limbs went slack.

"There now, isn't this much nicer?" Lying beside her, propped up on his elbow, he stroked her bruised cheek. "You really are beautiful. I know you are upset now but soon you'll see how right we are together."

He knew the medicine would give him plenty of time. He opened her shirt and covered her breasts with tender kisses.

"I've dreamt about us being alone for so long. I've been watching and waiting for years. All those times I had to creep around—in your yard, your basement, your cottage, your bedroom—just to catch a glimpse of what should have been mine all along."

He felt her tense up with his stalking disclosure.

"I've never meant to hurt you. I love you, Sarah."

He moved slowly inside her, savoring the moment. "I'll always love you. I'll never abandon you."

After his orgasm, he stayed on top of her. Sarah could barely breathe. Before pulling away he took a pillow and tucked it under her backside. He stroked her hair as he lay on his side.

"We don't want any of those future little McDermotts to run away, now, do we," he whispered into her ear.

Her vacant, drug-induced gaze was her only response.

Chapter 51

Michael booked off work for the day mid-December and maneuvered his car through Chinatown. The cold weather kept the smell of cabbage and salted fish down to a bearable level. Christmas carols crackled through bad sound systems, and gaudy gold and silver garland outlined store windows. Dirty slush made walking slippery. He found Jack's apartment and descended the stairs and banged on the door. Nothing.

Michael tried the other apartment doors in Jack's building, hoping to talk to the landlord, but nobody answered.

Hitting the street again, he wandered in and out of vegetable stores and overheated restaurants. The unrelenting crowds added to his frustration as he tried to work his way along the street presenting the card the landlord had passed him on his previous visit.

"*Qing wen?*" Michael asked the shopkeepers, which would usually at least get them to look up while showing them the card. It wasn't until he was on the verge of abandoning his idea after nearly an hour of trying that an old lady responded.

"*Yao, shang lou,*" she said, nodding her head up and down and pointing upstairs.

"*Xie, xie,*" Michael thanked her and wound his way up from the lower shop to a set of doors on the second floor. He went from door to door relentlessly knocking on all of them, desperate for a break. One door opened a crack, and a young boy looked out suspiciously through a chain lock. The shrill command from an adult in another room caused the boy to slam the door shut. Michael was sweating despite the frigid temperatures. 2D was his lucky break.

The door opened a few inches.

"Mr. Lee? I'm Michael. We met when I was looking for my friend Jack last month. Have you seen him lately?"

"No. No money and no Mr. Jack."

"I think I can help you," Michael said while pulling out a large roll of fifty dollar bills. "He called me a couple of days ago and asked me to stop by and catch up on his rent payments. He's out of town. I can't remember what he told me he owes you?"

Mr. Lee let a hint of a smile play on his face. "Five hundred dollars a month so one thousand dollars, and if he not back soon, another five hundred for January too."

"Right. Let's see what I've got here. May I step in?"

"Sure," Mr. Lee replied and stepped back to let Michael inside his modest dwelling smelling of stale smoke.

Michael counted out twenty bills to make it $1,000. He made the motion of handing over the money, then hesitated, leaving Mr. Lee's yellow fingers hanging midair.

"Oh, one other thing. Jack asked that I pick up some medication he left at his place. He needs me to send it to him. He's on a business trip."

"You say Mr. Jack to call me, to say it's okay. Then no problem."

"Well, that is a problem, I'm afraid. He's travelling in a remote area and cell coverage is not reliable. I can try and come back another day if you want," and went to tuck the money back in his pocket.

As Michael turned for the door, Mr. Lee quickly spoke up. "Okay. This time I make it okay."

"That is very considerate of you, Mr. Lee. After you."

Mr. Lee grabbed a large ring of keys from his tiny kitchen and pulled on a thick black jacket. A few minutes later the landlord fumbled with the keys and went to open Jack's door but paused long enough to put his hand out for the cash. Michael had no choice but to hand over the money.

"You take time and get what you need. I come back soon and lock door. *Xie, xie,* Mr. Jack's friend," grinned Mr. Lee, adding a shallow bow as he disappeared out the door.

Michael covered his mouth with his scarf to stifle the stench of rotten food. He moved cautiously, not wanting to miss anything. The place was worse than anything he'd ever encountered. A nubby-worn couch with a few overturned cardboard boxes was all that filled the small windowless living room. The low ceiling contributed to Michael's sense of entrapment. Newspapers and food wrappings littered the cracked linoleum floor and bugs scurried away as Jack moved through the room. He stepped into the alcove serving as a bedroom, noting the single dirty foam mattress in the corner with a pile of blankets. A nice suitcase was a remnant from his former life. A crumpled pile of jeans and T-shirts took up another corner.

He moved to the kitchen. From the black mold growing on fruit partially liquefied on the kitchen counter, to the bread that resembled a green brick, it was obvious nobody had been around for a long time. His eyes were drawn to a large empty bulletin board mounted on the wall. It seemed like a strange item to have in an apartment that hardly had the bare essentials. Push pins were scattered across the table. Opening the fridge, he looked at the milk for an expiry date: Nov. 4th a week after the disappearance.

He riffled through the kitchen drawers and stopped to pull out a map. It was a map of southern Ontario and looked fairly new. He laid it flat on the cleanest spot he could find on the counter and took in the red circles. The first one was around Bruce Lake, which he remembered from the hunting trips they used to take around Jack's old family cottage area. A happy memory of when the guys would take time to hang out was obliterated by a chill running down his spine when he noticed a second circle around Hawkeye Lake. His lake.

Leaving the map on the counter, he went back to rummaging through the drawers. Some flyers and not much else. A time jotted on one of them in black ink; 11:45 am Nothing else of interest. Moving on to the bathroom he found it to be the worst room yet with filth festering on every surface. He opened the medicine cabinet and saw row after row of prescriptions: antidepressants, anti- anxiety pills, sleeping pills, etc.

Back in the living room he bent over to sort through the debris. A box caught his eye, visible under the couch, a new looking portable Coleman stove package, strange in this decrepit environment. Sifting through papers on the floor, he saw some receipts: Walmart for food and paper products and an iPad, an extravagant purchase for a person living in squalor. Other receipts were for take-out food and booze.

He paused to process things while surveying the room. He was running out of ideas but wasn't ready to walk away just yet.

As he wandered back into the kitchen, the bulletin board nagged at him radiating a silent scream. He took one last look in the bedroom. When he kicked around the pile of clothes, some loose change dropped from a jean pocket. Lifting the pants, he dug into the pockets. A bit of change, a pizza receipt, and a thick piece of paper. Unfolding the paper, he was jolted by a familiar picture of his wife in her bathing suit on the dock. She looked carefree and happy, peering out at the water ready to laugh. Michael knew it well as he had taken the shot and tucked it into a hall mirror at his cottage.

Michael was still shaking when he called Larry on his cell phone.

"Larry, it's Michael Babic. Listen, I think Sarah's disappearance is linked to Jack McDermott. You've got to search his apartment."

"Slow down, Michael. What makes you say that?"

"I'm in his apartment. I found a picture of Sarah in his jean pocket. It looks like he hasn't been here for a long time based on the rotten food and what his landlord told me."

"How did you get in if he isn't there?" asked Larry

"Why does that matter? I didn't force entry if that's what you're thinking."

Larry took a gulp of cold coffee. "Did you come across anything else to link Jack to the disappearance? To get a search warrant, we'll need to establish probable cause with a judge."

Michael's mind raced as he stammered out his reply, "Jack told Sarah he was in love with her. Last summer. I didn't think much of it at the time because Jack was going through a tough time. He ended up having a nervous breakdown, so I figured he simply wasn't thinking straight when he told her. He was hospitalized for a couple of nights."

"Any prior convictions or charges on him?"

"None that I know of."

"Best friend in love with his buddy's wife," Larry mused. "You'd better hope we get a lenient judge. Leave it with me and I'll get in touch with you in a couple of hours."

~~~

A search team arrived the next morning, barely causing a stir amongst the throngs of shoppers focused on finding the best catfish and herbal remedies. The team mostly took photos since there was little there; a sad-looking dump left by someone who had gone off the rails.

Constable Arlene was looking through the medicine cabinet. "This guy is a walking pharmacy. He's on every kind of upper and downer going."

Larry was going through the drawers when he found a pair of black lacy underwear. He picked them up with a gloved hand and bagged and labelled them. There were magazines scattered on the floor beside the bed. As Larry flipped through them, several photos floated to the floor. All were shots of Sarah; at a lodge, at her cottage, kissing her baby, getting her kids from school, her wedding day. He let out a slow whistle.

"You got something, Larry?" Arlene shouted from the bathroom.

"Based on my fifteen years with the force, I'd say we've got ourselves an affair," he responded flatly while sliding the photos into another plastic sleeve.

Arlene noted the name of the physician on the prescription drug bottles and they left.

Michael couldn't believe what he was hearing as he sat opposite Larry and Arlene later that same day back at the precinct. He was furious looking at his wife's underwear on display, laid out on the desk beside the photos.

"An affair? This is the best you hot-shots can come up with—an affair?" Michael shouted.

"We simply need to eliminate this as an option," Larry reasoned. "With all due respect, it happens. The husband is busy busting his ass at his job. The wife feels neglected and lonely managing the house and kids. A friend offers some support and bam. The next thing you know."

"This is bullshit!" Michael exploded flying out of his chair. "Whose side are you on?"

"We are not on anybody's side. We're trying to discover the truth and find your wife. Do you have any idea how your wife's underthings could have ended up at Jack's apartment?"

Michael silently shook his head while pacing the small room, trying to regain control.

"Please try and think," Larry instructed. "Did your wife say or do anything at all that may have indicated an intimate relationship with Jack?"

"You people are bloody useless. Looking for an easy out because you can't do your job and find her, or my kid. Call me when you decide to take your job seriously." Michael stormed out of the office.

"Geez, Larry, was that really necessary?" Arlene asked.

Larry was staring at the map with the red circles he pulled out of another file. "Yes, it was necessary. I needed to push his buttons to see if he was holding anything back. Seems to me we're good to go ahead and order an aerial infrared and ground search of Algonquin county number fifty-two. Tell them I'll send up coordinates for the morning."

CHAPTER 52

Two months had passed since the kidnapping. Five weeks without Connor. Sarah had lost a lot of weight. Her limbs were atrophied, and her bones were weak from lack of vitamin D. She was jaundiced. Even with the beatings and sexual abuse, she refused to give up. Without the need to keep the peace for Connor's sake, she wouldn't play along with Jack's dream of their life together. The thought of seeing her family again gave her the strength to resist him in any way she possibly could.

"Sarah, just give me a chance to prove what a sweet and dutiful husband I'll be."

"I will never have anything but hate and loathing for you," Sarah said with a swollen lip and bruised eyes.

Jack moved over to the burner and poured in some enriched porridge and added carnation milk and brown sugar.

"Just to show you I'm not really upset, I'll make us a late-night snack of porridge. Okay, dear?"

Silence.

He walked over with the lighter in hand and flicked it on and held it near her face so she could feel the heat of the flame. "I'm sorry, darling, I didn't hear you."

"Yes, that would be nice."

"I missed that last bit."

Jack let the flame singe the bottom of her hair. She heard the crackle, and the sulfurous smell assailed her nostrils.

"Yes, that would be nice, dear," Sarah said.

"As you wish," he said as he snuffed out the smoldering ends of her hair with his fingers.

Jack placed the pot on the stove to heat the porridge. With a forced smile while breathing heavily, he leaned over her wasted body on the stained mattress. "You mustn't worry. I'm a very patient man, Sarah. I waited patiently for my father to come for me at school. I waited patiently for my mother to notice me. I waited patiently for Rachel to conceive. You see, I've had a lot of practice waiting. I can wait as long as it takes for you to accept things as they are truly meant to be."

An hour later he switched tactics and berated her. "Don't think you can control this situation, Sarah, because you can't. You women are all the same thinking you can call the shots. Jesus Christ, you're even getting skinny and bony like Rachel. We can't have that if we want to start our family. You know what doctors say about the mother needing to maintain a healthy body weight."

The days were slow and monotonous. Jack paced the small space, raked what was left of his stringy thinning hair, and tossed back his daily dose of alcohol. As he approached her, she recoiled as much as her restraints would allow. He hated using the gag since he wanted her mouth free for kissing and other sexual acts. When he loosened the tie at the back of her head, she started screaming. Shaking his head, he retrieved a syringe and extracted a good strong dose. He felt particularly amorous this evening and wanted a willing partner. Although she knew it would be useless, she continued to scream at the top of her weak lungs, knowing her time was limited as she felt drugs sapping her strength.

CHAPTER 53

The OPP dispatched different units to cover three key areas: Jack's old family cottage, the family hunting cabin, and Michael's cottage. Jack's old family cottage, now owned by the Hilders, was quiet. The three-foot-deep drifts engulfing the path to the door indicated nobody had been up since winter set in. Everything was locked up tight. Tracking dogs had nothing to work with given the conditions.

The OPP contacted farmer Angus Smith at his Florida residence.

"Hi, Angus, this is Randy here from Haliburton police force. How are things going for you and the missus?"

"Oh, you know, Randy, mighty slow. Not that I mind, given my advanced years. I use the time to rest and enjoy the weather. Hazel stays busy with her cooking and bridge club but I'm happy to simply take it easy. We might just stay for good one of these days. Is there something I can do for you fellas?"

"We were wondering if you've heard or seen anything from the McDermott folks. We understand you used to let them keep their Quad Bike in your barn. The one they used to reach their hunting cabin. We're following up on some suspicious activity that may involve their son, Jack."

"Mr. Johnathan McDermott has always been very kind since they bought that parcel of land nearly twenty-five years ago now," he said, reminiscing, letting out a long whistle. "Don't know much about their kids. Not sure if the Quad Bike is still there. I don't use that barn at the south end of the property much except for storing old equipment since I had the new one built closer to the house."

"Mind if we come out and have a look, Angus?"

"Of course not, be my guest."

A couple hours later the team dropped the ramp off the back of the pickup truck and revved the snowmobiles. Randy and Hal loved being able to find an excuse to get out on company time and rip through the trails with snow flying behind their tracks. They purposely parked a little further away than was necessary to get in a good ride. The double door barn lock was easy to pick. Sunlight filtered through the decaying slatted walls and dust floated in the air.

The Quad Bike was sitting inside to the right. Hal went over and examined the machine. He exchanged glances with Randy, looking pleased. Based on the layer of dust on the seat versus some of the other things in the barn, it looked like somebody had ridden it in the past couple of months. It was possible one of the other McDermotts had used it but not likely. They'd contacted Jack's family after going through his apartment and found that his parents were sailing in the Caribbean all winter and the sisters had never even been to the barn.

After taking a thorough look around inside and around the outside area, they were back on their machines. Referring to the GPS coordinates, the hunting cabin wouldn't be too hard to find. After a ten-minute ride they spotted the cabin and parked. They tromped through the knee-high snow and produced the bolt cutters to get through the lock. Once inside it looked peaceful and quiet.

"Just like every other hunting cabin," Hal said.

"I'd love a place like this," Randy said. "Somewhere to get away from Suzy and the kids. It's so beautiful out here."

Randy examined the few things in the pantry and Hal went through the cupboards. Nothing but a few tin plates, cups, and cutlery. The mounted deer head wasn't giving up any secrets. Their breath came out in small clouds with the temperature well below zero.

After turning over the cushions on the plaid couch, Randy sat down. Hal leaned back against the small freezer then pushed himself back on the lid to sit. The generator sat in the corner. Hunting cabins often ran freezers like this off a generator to keep a carcass cold enough in the spring or summer. Common stuff.

"Constable Larry isn't going to like our report," Randy said, sweeping the room again hoping for something to report. "They hate it when they think they're wasting their precious resources up here."

Hal blew into his mitted hands to feel the warmth of his breath against his face. The cold was starting to penetrate his snow gear. When he slid off the freezer his pant leg caught on the locked latch. He gave the padlock a couple of strong pulls.

"Randy, where did you put those cutters?"

"Right here," Randy said, motioning to the floor. "Why?"

"Suppose we could have a look inside?"

"You've seen too many *Criminal Minds*, my friend," laughed Randy, getting up and heading for the door. "Our warrant is only for entry into the building. We aren't authorized to be forcing entry into personal items. We need a T61 for that. It's a good excuse to come back, though. A good way to enjoy the next sunny day out of the office."

"I like the way you think," Hal agreed and followed him out.

It was a cold, clear night after the hunting cabin search when the OPP chopper took off from the headquarters in Orillia, not far from the Haliburton area, just after 7 pm. It touched down at the Haliburton helipad to pick up Randy. The temperatures were hovering around minus ten Celsius so it would be easy to pick up someone with thermal imaging. Constable Rick Morety commanded the aircraft while Randy, who also had his pilot's license, sat beside him mapping their coordinates. Their orders were to cover the area that included Jack's old family cottage, the hunting cabin, and Michael's new cottage, about a fifty-kilometer radius.

They were almost finished for the night when a reddish-orange image appeared on the screen in a heavily forested part of the region. Randy felt the hair rise on his neck. They had picked up some animals earlier in the night, but this was different. It was clearly a person.

"Rick, have a look at this," Randy said, urgently pointing to the screen.

"Well, well. Sure is worth a look," Rick said. "Radio in the location to 52 division and have them send out a team."

The four officers they called didn't mind reporting for duty. Not a whole lot happened in the area, especially in the winter. They loved the idea of being part of the team to find this bastard. With high-powered rifles slung across their backs, they plowed through the trails on their snowmobiles, easily finding their way to Lat. 45.37000/Long. 78.91789 within the hour. The chopper stayed within the site location to keep the subject on their radar. The subject had taken shelter under something but there was enough heat radiating through the enclosure to keep a read on him. The team fanned out and circled the target to make it harder to escape. The high beams from the sleds illuminated a small ratty tent. The chopper descended and was now hovering one hundred feet up with the blades creating a high wind and deafening roar.

Hal was the lead on the ground team. He held the bullhorn to his mouth. "OPP. Come out with your hands up!"

All four rifles were trained on the tent. No movement. They crept forward a few more feet, being careful to shield themselves with the trees.

"OPP, come out with your hands up NOW or we're coming in."

Another minute passed. Speaking into the microphone embedded in his helmet, Hal directed his unit, "On my count, Dave and I will move in; Art and Simon to provide cover. Over."

"Roger, copy that," replied all three men.

"Three, two, one, GO, GO, GO."

The officers closed within ten feet of the tent, then dropped to their stomachs with their guns braced against their shoulders, fingers on the triggers, ready to shoot.

Hal took three long strides and ripped open the tent flap and shoved the nozzle of his rifle inside. His headlamp lit up the tent. "Hands up!"

"Don't shoot. Please, don't shoot," stuttered the old hermit, known to locals, visibly shaken, balled up in the corner. "I don't want any trouble."

"Stand down, everybody," Hal said. "Damn it. Stand down. False alarm. I repeat, false alarm.

Chapter 54

With their usual hangovers on January 1st, the three best friends piled into Jimmy's truck and drove to Mark's cottage on Bruce Lake for their annual getaway. It wasn't winterized but it had a good wood-burning stove and lots of booze. One of them usually caught a deer. They always split the prized venison three ways, so their families were happy to have fresh game to look forward to upon their return. It wasn't easy getting away from family obligations over New Year's.

They were in their late twenties and friends since primary school. They loved living in Haliburton and chose to build their futures apprenticing in the lucrative trades of carpentry, plumbing, and electrical. Their grand vision was taking root in their newly minted company, JM&F Contracting. They could barely keep up with the demands from people building summer homes and cottages.

They were happy to be out in the woods away from the demands of work and their young kids. The government added a holiday deer hunting week running January 1st – 7th a few years ago for the sake of boosting tourism. It was their fourth and last day into their getaway and none of them had any success so far.

Rising early, a clear-headed Mark prepared a big breakfast.

"Mmmm, this is fantastic, man," Frank muttered through the mouthfuls of sausages and eggs he heaped into his mouth, practically obscured by his bushy red beard.

"We don't want any lame excuses for needing to come back early, like being hungry," Mark said, needling Frank.

"Today is the day, boys! We need to make this a good one if for no other reason than getting our reprieve for next year," Jimmy said. "If we come back empty-handed, Nancy isn't going to relent too easily next time. Those little monkeys of mine aren't making things any easier."

"Well, if you'd stop turning them out every year, Jimmy, maybe Nancy wouldn't be so demanding," teased Frank.

"What can I say, she's a tiger," Jimmy said with wink and a satisfied look spreading across his handsome, rugged face.

"Have her give Shona some pointers anytime," Frank said.

"Here's a tip Frank, lose the Unabomber look," joked Mark.

Frank sprang to his feet and wrestled him to the ground in a good-natured bear hug. "We can't all be pretty boys like you, Mark."

"Okay, okay, come on, you guys, Jimmy said breaking them up. "Let's get out of here and come back with something to show."

~~~

Despite their focused efforts, their third and last day was proving to be non-eventful.

"Come on, guys. Let's face it. It's just not meant to be this time," Frank said. "Besides, I'm starving, and we still need to hoof it all the way back to the sleds, not to mention getting back to the cottage."

"I agree, it's getting late," Jimmy added, hoping to tip the vote for going back. He rubbed his hands together and wrapped his arms around himself. "It's freezing out here too."

"You're both big babies. Here's the deal," Mark said. "How about we try for another half an hour. If we see nothing, we hightail it out of here. Jeez, it's only three o'clock! Come on – tell me you're with me."

After grumbling their consent, they stopped complaining and walked deeper into the forest, light-footed, single file, widely spaced apart. It was an overcast day, and the sun would set before five. Dusk would fall soon. They had taken their sleds to the edge of the primary growth forest and ditched them to begin serious hunting. Frank figured even moving at the slow pace that was needed when stalking deer, they'd already covered five kilometers.

CHAPTER 55

Even Jack noticed how overpowering the stench was becoming. Ten weeks of garbage and body waste were making their home toxic. While he had planned for a long stay, if necessary, he hadn't calculated how much waste they would accumulate. He'd built a small ventilation pipe, but it wasn't properly circulating the air out. They had two separate buckets: one for urine and one for excrement. Jack boiled down the urine, but the rest wasn't easy to compost without electricity. He knew the animals would eat anything left over from their food, which was minimal. He planned on bagging the plastic and cans and burying them in the spring.

Sarah had been ill for a week and Jack was getting concerned. Her complexion was greyish white, and her hair was thinning. When she ate, she vomited it back up within minutes. At first, he accused her of faking it and rained down punishment, sometimes denying her food and water for an entire day. The next day he begged for forgiveness. Now that it had gone on for over a week, he was getting scared. While he didn't want to disturb the camouflage the snow was providing over the door, he needed to do something.

"Sweetheart, you've got to get better. You need to be stronger for our sake, for our future," Jack said.

"Please, Jack, I beg you. If you care for me like you say you do, then get me help. I'm really frightened," Sarah cried through cracked lips. "Please, open the door for a few minutes. I need fresh air. This place is killing me."

Sarah needed to know the outside world still existed. The world that held Michael, Paige, Connor, and her parents. To catch a glimpse of something unaffected by the nightmare he created, to give her hope. It had been almost six weeks since she had felt fresh air, the day she pushed Connor free and lost him. Sobs wracked her body, and she fell into a fitful sleep. She dreamt her familiar dream, the one where she was buried alive.

After sitting quietly apart from her, thinking of his options, he relented. Sarah startled awake as he forced the filthy rag across her mouth, yanking it tight behind her head. Her eyes looked wild as he secured her wrist to the ring.

"I'll open the door, just long enough to clear the place out."

Jack moved around the bunker collecting large green garbage bags, reviewing his plan. He hauled bags of human waste to the bottom of the ladder. With the ground too frozen to bury anything, he planned on tying the bags to high branches in an evergreen tree where they would be nearly impossible to see.

He ascended the homemade ladder with the first load of waste. It groaned under his weight but held. He paused with his head bent to fish out the key for the lock that latched the door from the inside, installed after Sarah's attempted escape. The door was heavy from the accumulation of snow, so Jack needed to put his shoulder into it several times before it gave way. It finally opened a crack. He looked back down at Sarah on the bed and gave her a menacing cautionary look. She stayed silent.

Jack held the door open a couple of inches and waited. All quiet. Looking back to Sarah, he saw she was overcome with emotion as the cold fresh air flooded the bunker. Muffled sobs were barely audible, and tears ran down her temples.

After listening and scanning the area for several more minutes, Jack fully opened the door and hauled the bags to the surface. It was mid-afternoon and overcast. Little light filtered down into the bunker. Jack got to work.

Sarah strained her head back to inhale as much air as possible. Her eyes were fixed on a pine branch laden with snow. She couldn't make out the sky but the mere sight of something living outside her prison, the simple pleasure of breathing fresh air made her weep. It held the possibility of her future, her family living out there, looking for her.

Jack made eight trips in and out of the bunker before climbing back down to make his last. He hauled the last two green garbage bags full of crushed cans to the surface and paused to catch his breath. He spotted a few good climbing trees about 100 feet away.

After clearing the bags away from the bunker opening, he threw the first bag up to the lowest branch and waited to make sure it would stay balanced. He did the same with the second. With extended arms he held a low branch and threw his legs up to straddle the limb. Once he was upright on the branch, he grabbed the bags and continued climbing. He dragged the bags with him until he was a good twenty feet up, high enough so on the rare chance of a person happening by, they wouldn't see anything. He paused to tie off the bags and looked down. He could see the light from the bunker since he didn't shut the door since the place needed a good airing out. He could hear her mewing but wasn't concerned, he knew she wasn't going anywhere.

"This is the thanks I get for clearing the place out and getting her some fresh air. Never fucking satisfied," he fumed under his breath.

CHAPTER 56

"Go ahead. I'll even pass on my share of the kill if you like," Frank said. "I'm man enough to admit this ain't gonna happen today. I'm done dragging my ass any further. You've got another ten minutes until 3:30 like we said."

Mark and Jimmy moved deeper into the forest as agreed, leaving Frank to wait on a large boulder. Five minutes later Frank could still make out their silhouettes in the fading light as they crouched low, weaving around the trees. Mark was leading when he paused and raised his hand. Jimmy could sense Mark's tension. Coming up beside him hoping to spot a deer, he saw it as well; a weird glow coming from the ground maybe 150 feet away. They exchanged puzzled glances and moved closer. They pulled up short as they heard a distressed muffled sound.

"Maybe a lame animal, but that doesn't explain the light," whispered Mark.

Only forty feet away now, Mark and Jimmy saw the door, and they heard the sound growing louder, clearly coming from the opening.

"It's got to be some sort of nasty trap," whispered Jimmy.

"Maybe some guy is preparing the kill out here, so he doesn't get caught using unauthorized hunting techniques?" Jimmy said.

Jack caught sight of the two men from his high vantage point. Cursing himself for leaving the door open, he silently climbed down, practically holding his breath. He moved when they moved, using their paces of creeping up towards the bunker to work his way down the tree. He landed on the ground fifty feet away as they peered over the edge.

Mark barely had time to register the shocking scene below ground when a single shot blew open the back of his head. Sarah's momentary excitement at seeing a chance for rescue turned to horror as blood and flesh rained down on her body.

Jimmy tried to run for cover, but the second shot came too fast, catching him in his lower back. With an agonizing cry he fell forward. Jack took his time approaching his prey, satisfied he hadn't lost any of his fine marksmanship. He casually walked by what was left of Mark.

Nearby, Jimmy flopped like a fish, contorted with pain, on his back. He gasped for breath as the bright red blood pooled around his body. Jack stood over him, holding the rifle inches away from Jimmy's chest.

"My father taught me a good hunter doesn't let his prey suffer. Lucky for you, I was a good student."

The shot shattered the quiet forest for the third time as Jack put Jimmy out of his misery with a bullet through the heart. Jack was pleased to see how quickly Jimmy quieted down.

Frank's heart was in his mouth. Upon hearing the first shot, he ran towards it, excited they had finally got a deer. When the second shot rang out seconds later, followed by an agonizing scream, he froze and dropped to the ground. He crept forward towards the chaos. He cautiously lifted his head and stifled a scream at seeing his two friends on the ground. When the third shot put an end to Jimmy's agony he was momentarily stunned. He reached behind his back and pulled his gun into a firing position when he heard someone speak.

"Well, isn't this just great! Look what you've done now, *sweetie,*" Jack yelled down the opening. "This is the thanks I get for cleaning up! What a fucking mess."

Jack disappeared quickly underground and yanked the door behind him.

Frank was terrified. In a flash he realized this must be the woman they'd been looking for these past few months, the one from Toronto with the cottage. The kid had gone missing too. Maybe the kid was down there as well. He hurried over to check on Mark and Jimmy but didn't need to get too close to know they were gone. It was eerily quiet. He realized he hadn't been seen. He thought about trying to open the door and save whoever was down there but knew his chances were slim and it was likely locked. Even if he got it open, what chance would he have with the killer ready to greet him with his gun.

After quietly moving away from the bloody scene, he ran as fast as he could towards the sleds. Terror and adrenaline coursed through his body as he stumbled erratically across debris in his path. He chanced a quick look back—nothing.

Reaching the snowmobiles, his hands shook violently as he pulled the keys from his jacket. The keys slipped through his hands into the snow. Falling on all fours, he strained to see them. Tearing off his gloves, he plunged his hands into the snow. Sweat dripped off his face and stung his eyes. He imagined the maniac plunging through the woods coming for him, on him, any second. He felt a warm sensation spread through his snow pants.

"Oh my God, please help me," Frank called out in desperation madly searching for the keys. "The kids and Shona need me. I swear I'll do anything. Please, please."

He felt the cold metal and sobbed in relief. He clutched the keys and threw himself on the sled. Opening it full throttle, he raced towards the cabin.

~~~

Jack berated Sarah while throwing her ominous looks, "I hope you're happy with what you've done."

Sarah continued cleaning up Mark's remains as ordered. She moved slowly, feeling weak. Chills racked her body; her skin was cold and moist, her hands and feet blue. Even without the gag, she found it hard to breathe.

"That's enough of the dramatics. You better snap out of this, or I will do it for you."

Sarah collapsed for the third time. Jack dragged her roughly through the blood congealing on the floor and tossed her on the bed. He needed to think. He knew they couldn't stay here any longer. He figured it would be a matter of hours or at most, a couple days before the families of the dead men reported them missing.

He brightened at the thought of heading south towards their new town of Peterborough. A change of scenery. She'll be so happy to be living a normal life again, everything will be fine. We can claim self-defense; we were minding our own business, camping out, getting rid of garbage, when two male intruders tried to break into our camp. They had guns and were going to shoot us. We would have been at their mercy if we hadn't protected ourselves.

Pain shot through his head. Slamming his forehead with the heel of his palm, he tried to slow down the ideas that ricocheted inside his head.

He wanted to wake Sarah to share the good news about his new plan, but he knew she needed her rest for the long walk ahead. He tucked in close beside her and stroked her blood-encrusted hair.

"Sleep well, my love, sleep well. We'll leave first thing in the morning."

CHAPTER 57

The Algonquin police mobilized immediately after getting the call from the frantic hunter.

"All units, copy. All units. Prepare to move out," Randy dispatched to the ground and air crews.

The helicopter prepared for takeoff and would arrive at the coordinates Frank provided within the hour. Back-up units moved to block all roads that crossed the area. Four teams of two on snowmobiles sped through the dark woods towards the crime scene, their headlights bouncing wildly off trees.

Jack drifted off and awoke to the faint sound of engines. The whirl of a helicopter overhead came next. He felt a tremor in the ground. He had lost track of time.

Bolting upright, he grabbed his rifle and roughly shook Sarah. "God damn it! How did they find us already? Come on. Get up. Move it! We've got to get out of here."

He pulled her to her feet, and she tried to twist away.

"When are you going to realize it's useless to fight me, Sarah?" he said, tightening his hold and applying pressure to the palm of her hand. He snapped her wrist back, breaking it easily. Sarah let out a high-pitched scream. She buckled with pain as her legs gave out. Her emaciated body was easy to toss over his shoulder and he quickly climbed to the top of the ladder.

The commotion was getting louder. He jammed the key in the lock and threw back the trap door. He was momentarily blinded by the floodlights from the helicopter hovering overhead. The sound was deafening. He saw the sled lights getting stronger as they cut through the woods. He pulled Sarah to her feet and held her in front of him and backed up against a tree. He checked his ammunition. The police dismounted quickly and pulled their weapons. Eight officers had their weapons trained on Jack and Sarah.

"OPP. Put down your weapon!" Randy commanded through the bullhorn over the roar.

With his finger on the trigger, Jack shoved the barrel under Sarah's chin. The lights were blinding.

"OPP. Put down your weapon. It's over, Jack. It's over."

"Come any closer and I'll shoot her," Jack yelled.

"Jack, you need help. We can help you. Let Sarah go. If you do what we ask, everything will be all right."

"Bullshit! Nobody wants to help me." His eyes darted across the officers. "Get rid of that fucking chopper. I can't think."

"Okay, Jack. We'll get rid of it. Chopper One, do you read me. Stand down Chopper One, do you copy?"

The chopper pulled up and veered south.

"Okay, Jack, we did what you asked."

Nobody took their aim off Jack. As Jack glanced up to check on the helicopter, a pair of snipers saw the opportunity. They moved back from the group and circled around the side. The four headlights made it difficult for Jack to see.

"Jack, we know you've been through a breakdown. Your medication can cause psychosis and delusion. Dr. Turner knows about the situation and wants to see you. Come with us and we can help you. Let Dr. Turner get you better."

"Oh, that's sweet! Very touching! Look at everyone wanting to help. If I knew it was as simple as putting a gun to someone's head, I should have done this years ago. Maybe my family would have been more attentive with a bit of steel pressed into their temples."

"We know it's been tough," Randy said. "You've been through a lot. We know—"

"You know, oh you know, do you?" Jack cut in. "When did you all get so knowledgeable about me? You don't know me."

Jack pulled Sarah tighter as she squirmed from the crippling pain shooting up her legs standing barefoot in the snow. Her wrist throbbed and she cried out with every movement.

"Here is what you need to know. You need to back off and leave us alone. Sarah and I have plans, don't we, Sarah."

Sarah coughed from the pressure of the muzzle under her chin. The officers shuffled forward.

303

"Stop right there and do as I say or I swear I'll kill her."

"No, he won't," Sarah said, standing stock still.

"What a pity. After all this time together, you still don't seem to understand me either, sweetheart."

"He won't because I'm pregnant."

Jack felt like someone had kicked him in the gut. "You're lying," he hissed into her ear.

"I swear on Paige's life, I'm pregnant." She turned her head to face him. "We've been together for three months. I've only had one period. Remember how furious you were when I got my period? We'd been together a couple of weeks."

Jack's grip loosened a little.

Sarah continued, "We made love every day. You'd know if I was lying. I was waiting to tell you once we settled into our new home."

Jack was confused, trying to do a mental check on the timeline. He was so overcome with emotion he couldn't think straight.

"Jack, you're going to be a father." Sarah said through cracked lips. "We're going to have a family."

Jack further lessened his hold and Sarah slowly turned to face him while inching back. "Jack, we did it. We made our baby."

He cupped her cheek with his free hand.

"A father. I'm going to be a father," Jack said as if in a dream. His face slackened with his grip and tears sprang to his eyes. "Oh, Sarah. I knew it would all work if we just gave it some time. A baby. We're going to have a baby. Sarah, I love you so much."

As he bent over to kiss her, she felt the blow of the first bullet as it entered his shoulder and the second as it ripped open his upper thigh. As the bullets struck, he dropped the rifle and lurched forward, collapsing on top of Sarah. His expression shifted from elation to confusion as the police pounced and hauled him away.

CHAPTER 58

"Come on, Sarah, stay with me. You're almost there," the obstetrician coached.

Dr. Anderson exchanged a worried glance with Michael, who was crouching over Sarah holding her hand.

"Sarah. It's not too late to go to an emergency C-section," Michael said.

Sarah was crying from the exertion, her eyes bruised from pushing, her complexion blotchy red.

"I can do this!" she insisted.

She delivered her other three children naturally and hadn't found it difficult. This time was very different.

"Sarah, we can only let you try for another few minutes. Otherwise, we risk losing the baby and you as well," Dr. Anderson said.

He ordered one of the assistant obstetrical nurses to call for staff to the operating room that was prepped and ready. With everything Sarah endured these last nine months, the medical team strongly advised against a natural birth, but she insisted on trying. She wanted to treat this baby like her other children, starting with childbirth.

After another minute of labored breathing, the pain tore through her again. The four hours of active labor had nearly sapped all her strength. Searing back pain and debilitating cramps ripped through her lower body. Tapping into the last of her reserve, Sarah tucked her jaw into her chest, squeezed her eyes shut, clenched her teeth, and bored down with a primal cry.

"That's it, Sarah. Push! Push!" Dr. Anderson coached.

They saw the head crown then disappear again.

"Sarah, you've nearly done it. Just a little bit more. Please, Sarah, this is it. Your last push," Michael said.

"So help me God, I will not let that bastard win," Sarah cried with her effort followed by an agonizing scream heard clear down the corridor.

The head was clear. Sarah fell back on the bed in a pool of sweat. Dr. Anderson quickly suctioned the baby's mouth and nose.

"You've done it, darling. You've done it!" exclaimed Michael with tears streaming down his face.

"Just the shoulders now," Dr. Anderson said.

Sarah knew this last part was easy compared to the feat she had just accomplished. Without letting herself fall into her exhaustion, she did what was needed to get the baby out completely. Dr. Anderson guided Michael's hands. Michael lifted the baby and placed it tenderly on Sarah's chest. Michael came around beside Sarah and lifted her shoulders. He kissed her and they both gazed down. Michael had secretly asked the doctors about the baby's sex, Sarah didn't want to know. He expected a boy, but held out hope they were wrong. Anything to distance the baby from any possible resemblance.

"What is it?" asked Sarah through a foggy voice.

"It's a boy, darling. A new baby boy," Michael said.

"A boy," Sarah said dreamily and faded into sleep.

The baby was virtually bald with a smudge of light blond hair. He struggled to open his eyes as his tiny fingers opened and closed. The baby opened his eyes in the harsh new light of the birthing room. Dark blue. Michael knew this didn't mean much as virtually all babies were born with blue eyes. The true color wouldn't be determined until six to nine months of age. Michael hoped it would've been obvious at birth but there was nothing conclusive.

Immediately after Sarah's rescue, they air-lifted her to Western Hospital in Toronto and tended her injuries. They did an ultrasound and determined she was pregnant, and the baby was between ten and fourteen weeks. With the drug abuse and the physical and mental abuse Sarah endured in captivity, they were reluctant to be more specific on the gestation. Any one of these factors could have caused a delay in the fetus's development. They couldn't be certain of the parentage based on the ultrasound and timing. Sarah was firmly against any kind of paternity testing in utero. She knew clinically the risks were small for her unborn baby, but she didn't want to take any chances.

Sarah was emphatic that it had to be Michael's baby. The period she had the first couple weeks after her capture was lighter than usual, practically spotting. She thought she must have been pregnant just before she was kidnapped. Sarah spotted early in her other pregnancies, so she held fast to this possibility, although she knew it was heavier than before. With the loss of their two other children, she wasn't going to risk Michael not accepting this new baby. It was part of her and that was enough.

The nurses bundled the newborn and ran through the standard Apgar tests.

"He's a perfect ten," beamed the nurse. "Would you like to hold him?"

She passed the bundle to Michael, who accepted him in the crook of his arm. The baby began to cry the high-pitched cry of a newborn and squirmed. Michael seemed unmoved and stared. He thought he saw a resemblance across the eyes, but it wasn't a clear impression.

The nurse, who knew their history, saw how uncomfortable Michael looked staring without warmth at the child.

"It looks like the baby could use a bit of nourishment," the nurse said, smoothly taking the baby away from Michael. "We'll give him a bit of sugar water to buy a bit of time until mom has a chance to come around."

"Sure, of course," Michael said, clearing his throat and head.

Sarah stirred a bit. She had an IV to hydrate her. "Connor? Where have they taken Connor?"

"Shhhh, my love. Everything is fine." Michael said. "The took the baby to get cleaned up."

Sarah looked panicked. "No, no. Don't let them take him. Where are they going? Bring him back. He needs me. Don't let him go! Connor, I'm coming!"

Sarah struggled, trying to swing her legs off the bed.

Michael held her back as she thrashed.

"Doctor, come quickly!" Michael shouted, alarmed at the strength of her exertion.

Dr. Anderson appeared, and seeing her hysteria, injected a mild sedative into the IV bag. Her efforts subsided quickly, and she fell back asleep.

"This may be a long ordeal yet," Dr. Anderson said, looking sympathetically at Michael.

After the doctor left, the room was quiet with just the sound of the machines beeping. Sarah slept soundly. Sarah's mother was on her way to the hospital with Paige. They were being transported in an unmarked car. The media hounds had stayed abreast of the timing of the birth and were on high alert. News of the pregnancy had been leaked by an unscrupulous staffer at the hospital.

After twenty minutes the nurse wheeled the baby back into the room in the glass basinet.

"He's all set for a while," she said. "May I leave him with you?"

"Of course," Michael replied.

The baby was swaddled tight and fast asleep. Sarah was still sleeping. Michael quietly crossed the room and peeked up and down the hallway. Coming back into the room, he stopped at his jacket hooked on the back of the door. Reaching into the inside pocket, he removed a plastic bag. Puncturing the bag, he extracted the plastic gloves and slid them on. With protected fingers, he pulled the swab from the bag. He calmed his shaky hands as he approached the basinet. With his thumb and forefinger, he squeezed open the infant's mouth and swiped the inside of his cheek with the swab. The baby immediately gagged and started crying. Michael was so startled he almost dropped the gauze. He shoved it back into the bag, hoping he had enough buccal cells to do the testing. He glanced over at Sarah, expecting to see her sleeping, and was shocked to find her looking straight at him.

"Jesus, Sarah, you scared the crap out of me," Michael said, calculating what she might have seen while shoving the bag into his back pocket.

"The baby is crying. Why aren't you holding him?" she asked, still groggy from the drugs.

"He just started up this second. Must be hungry." He scooped up the baby and passed him into Sarah's open arms. She loosened her gown and placed the baby to her breast. He took it easily.

"Can you get me a glass of water please? Breastfeeding makes me so thirsty."

"Of course, sweetheart."

Gazing down at the child, Sarah looked blissfully happy.

"Oh Michael, he's the spitting image of you."

"Really? Funny, I don't see it." Michael replied, handing her a glass of cold water.

Sarah and Michael exchanged a tense look, but the moment was broken when Paige burst into the room.

"Mommy, Mommy! Do I have a new baby sister?"

Sarah pulled Paige in close by her side to give her a look. "A boy, sweetie, you have a new baby brother."

"Can I hold him please?"

"In a minute, honey, he just needs to finish feeding."

With Sarah's mother now joining them as well, the room felt crowded.

"Well, darling. With all my hard work I've got quite the appetite!" Michael joked.

Everyone gave a good-natured laugh.

"Do you mind if I pop out and grab a bite? I won't be long. As long as you're, okay?"

"Of course, I'm fine. I've got lots of fresh help here. Why don't you go home and grab a shower and come back in a bit."

"You sure?"

"Yes, go on. I love you."

He kissed her forehead. "I love you too."

As soon as Michael got into the car, he popped the box out of the glove compartment. He quickly swabbed his cheek and sealed his sample. Placing both his and the baby's sample into the padded envelope provided, he sealed it and drove down the street. He dropped the paternity-testing envelope in the nearest mailbox and the kit box in the trash.

Back in his driveway, he turned off the engine. He closed his eyes. The instructions said it would take two days to get the results once the lab received the package. With the sample delivery time, not more than five days in total. The new email account where he directed the test results to be sent ensured Sarah wouldn't stumble across his deceit. He hadn't processed how he would react if the results were what he feared. He could only focus on the relief of confirming the baby was his. It had to be his. It was the only hope he had of piecing their lives back together.

EPILOUGE

Michael sat motionless at the Superior Court of Justice, consciously controlling his breathing to stay calm. The stale, cool air in Courtroom #12 was in stark contrast to the glorious fall day unfolding this late September morning. The steel barred cage set up for the defendant was only steps away. Michael still had difficulty processing the reality of the situation. The media crush was phenomenal, and it was only day one of what was talked about as being a disturbing and morbidly fascinating trial. The fact that children were involved only seemed to heighten their quest for sordid details. He was acutely alert and anxious for the proceedings to begin, while at the same time, trapped in a state of suspended belief.

My God—how did this happen? Jack was my best friend for nearly twenty years. How could I have been so blind not to have seen his dark side? Had it always been there? Hiding below his charming veneer, waiting for the right circumstances to allow it to manifest? Or maybe his twisted state developed from his failures, losses, pressures, and dysfunctional family life.

The same agonizing loop racked Michael's guilt-ridden mind. With the trial not scheduled to begin for another hour, Michael sat alone with his anguish. He needed time to think. As much as his wife Sarah wanted to be here, her doctors strongly objected. She was still too weak physically and mentally. Her medication and psychological therapy had enabled her to stabilize and begin the long path to recovery. The relapses made it too risky for her to come today. It had only been ten months since her program began after giving birth and the doctors worried that the shock of being anywhere near her assailant could send her back to a hysterical, or worse, catatonic state. She and the children were safe at a location undisclosed to the media where they were being nurtured back to health by trauma specialists and Sarah's parents.

As much as Michael hated Jack and wished him dead for all the cruelty and sadness he inflicted on his family, Michael needed to move beyond the demented images projected by the media to try to understand what happened. Michael struggled with the photos taken of Jack when they finally caught him and a few more recent ones shown repeatedly in the media. Jack's sculptured face transformed into a skeletal husk with his weight loss. The once bright curious eyes coldly piercing, hollow of all emotion; the blue intensity dulled to a flat grey matte, like the lake after a winter storm, an eerie calm just beneath the surface. The old mischievous grin had become a permanent sneer. Bitterness and anger hung at the corners of his mouth. His accelerated hair loss aged him well beyond his years. His once-ruddy complexion was replaced with a pale and sallow hue.

The time passed quickly, and Michael was startled when his lawyer slipped in beside him. Michael looked behind him and found a packed courthouse. A minute later, there was an audible gasp in the courtroom when the side door opened. Two police officers brought in the shackled prisoner, placed him inside the cage, then locked the door.

Michael continued to stare straight ahead, unable to look at the animal that ruined his life.

"All rise," ordered the court clerk.